THE
AGE
of
SHIVA

MANIL SURI

BLOOMSBURY

LONDON · BERLIN · NEW YORK

First published in Great Britain 2008
This paperback edition published 2009

Bloomsbury Publishing Plc
36 Soho Square
London W1D 3QY

www.bloomsbury.com

A CIP catalogue record for this book
is available from the British Library

Paperback ISBN 978 0 7475 9639 4
10 9 8 7 6 5 4 3 2 1

Export Paperback ISBN 978 0 7475 9893 0
10 9 8 7 6 5 4 3 2 1

Printed in Great Britain by Clays Ltd, St Ives plc

Bloomsbury Publishing, London, New York and Berlin

FSC
Mixed Sources
Product group from well-managed
forests and other controlled sources

Cert no. SGS-COC-2061
www.fsc.org
© 1996 Forest Stewardship Council

The paper this book is printed on is certified independently in accordance with the rules of the FSC.
It is ancient-forest friendly. The printer holds chain of custody.

To Prem and the rest of the Bindra tigresses,
for their ferocity of spirit, their fierceness of love

THE

AGE *of*

SHIVA

PART ONE

chapter
one

Every time I touch you, every time I kiss you, every time I offer you my body. Ashvin. Do you know how tightly you shut your eyes as with your lips you search my skin? Do you know how you thrust your feet towards me, how you reach out your arms, how the sides of your chest strain against my palms? Are you aware of your fingers brushing against my breast, their tips trying to curl around something to hold on to, but slipping instead against my smooth flesh?

Ashvin. Do you notice the wetness emerge from my nipples and spill down the slopes of my chest? Is that your tongue that I feel, are you able to steal a taste or two?

Ashvin. Your eyes still closed, drops of moisture dappling your nose. Do you know how innocent you look, how helpless, as I guide the nipple towards your mouth? For an instant, I feel like teasing you. Drawing my nipple across your lips, but only for a touch, and swinging it away. Watching your tongue dart out in confusion, the fingers still opening and closing and curling, worry beginning to crinkle your face. And that helplessness—that exquisite helplessness in your expression, that need for my body, for the nipple that is yours, for the breast I have so cruelly taken away. Yes, love can be capricious, can it not, my sweet?

But of course I relent before I even begin: your look suffuses me with guilt. I let your mouth close around me, I feel the pressure of your gums, your lips. The power in your jaws surprises me—a little more strength, and I can see there will be pain.

Your tongue pulls against my nipple. So practiced, so persuasive, so determined, how does it know what to do? I feel myself responding. Each tug brings liquid flooding up, engorging my breast, pushing out into your insistent mouth. Your feet twist and turn against my belly as you feed, your hands finally find purchase on my breast. Fingers splaying out around tiny palms, your orb, your world, held in your hands.

I lose myself in the rhythm of your intake. Am I imagining it, or is there a parallel rhythm that echoes inside me? A longing that rises through my body and trembles under my skin. I feel myself flush, I feel the color spread through my chest.

Then I see your face. Your forehead losing its worry, your eyelids no longer wrinkled tight. I watch the smile trying to train the corners of your mouth, and the heat inside me turns into warmth. There is nothing, I think to myself, as you let go of my nipple and turn to me, filled. Nothing that can be as satisfying as this.

Afterwards, I lie next to you. You fit so well into my body. Before closing my eyes, I take one last look. Your eyes, your ears, your hands, your feet, all these I check to make sure they are still there, still intact. Even the tiny curl of your manhood, nestling so innocently between the fleshy fold of your thighs. All this I have created. All this has come from me.

As I drift off to sleep, I wonder if you will ever know these thoughts that flow through my mind. These soliloquies I address to you, this conversation I keep up in my brain. Perhaps one day I will tell you about the yearning from which you were born. The lives with which you can play, the planets over which you hold sway. Ashvin, the sign in the sky, Ashvin, the constellation of twins. Ashvin, the one who went before you, the one with whom you share your name. You are the hope and the fire, the absolution, the purifier. You will deliver me, will you not, from this life I find myself in?

―

IT IS MIDNIGHT WHEN my eyes open. The room is dark, someone has switched off the lights. The car horns have stopped blaring, Bombay's buses stopped running for the night. I hear the solitary tinkle of a bicycle bell from the street below. Sprigs of light grow and fade around the room as the curtains sigh in gusts of outside air.

A shadow plucks itself from the walls and moves through the room. It is the figure of a man, he bends over my bed. The blur of the ceiling fan forms a halo behind his head. Rays from a distant streetlamp highlight his nose, his chin. *Your* eyes, I think in fascination through my sleepy haze, *your* chin. I reach out to caress your lips, they feel warm and moist on my fingertips.

I am in a dream, of course. One in which you have dropped by from another time in your life, to show me what you will be when you are grown. I look at your arms and legs, so adult and properly proportioned, the baby fat gone, replaced by muscle. Do you have a mustache, I want to know, does your hair still curl? How do they all fit together, those lips, that nose, that chin?

I shift away from the edge of the bed and you seat yourself next to me. You stroke my head, your fingers run over my hair. My son, my Ashvin, I think, as sleep again begins to mist around. All those years ahead of us for me to watch you grow.

Your hand touches my cheek, the side of my neck. It lingers at my shoulder, then traces the line of my clavicle to the hollow of my throat. I am almost asleep again when a tug at my bosom opens my eyes. Fingers are unfastening the clasps of my blouse, palms are sliding under cloth to ease my breasts out. A swath of chest hair glides playfully over my skin; a stomach, a waist, a navel, rubs against my thigh. I look up at the face I know cannot be yours. The fan makes whirring sounds as it agitates the night behind.

Hands begin stroking me in practiced ways. Lips descend down my chin, down my neck. I feel the pressure ascend rapidly in my chest. Before I can do anything, my front is damp.

"Dev," I say. I know, of course, how could I not have always known?

"You're wet again," Dev says. He holds his palm up incriminatingly and through the darkness I see the glisten of moisture against your father's skin.

LATER THAT NIGHT I am in the kitchen, rolling out chappatis. Your father likes them cooked fresh—reheated ones, he says, are harder to digest. I have dabbed off the moisture as best as I can, but my nipples still darken the material of my blouse.

From the living room, I hear the sound of soda water escaping from a bottle, and then a glass being filled. "Mother's milk for baby and grain's milk for daddy," Dev says. I can tell he has had quite a bit already before coming home—I have smelled the sour sharpness in his breath.

I slap a chappati onto the griddle and press it against the hot metal with a wad of cloth. The smell of browning flour rises to my nostrils. After a minute, I peel the chappati off and throw it on the open fire. Slowly the chappati puffs up and fills the kitchen with its aroma.

When the chappatis are done, I heat the meat, slice the onions, and put the mango pickle on a plate. Then I bring everything out to the living room and set them out next to his glass before Dev.

"Aren't you going to join me?" he says, his voice slurred. His pupils are dilated, his mouth spread in an unfocused smile. Still, he manages to be handsome. I look at his evenly spaced teeth, the clean way his lips frame his mouth. This is what your smile will look like, I think, once you have learned how to smile. This is the way your eyes will project innocence by being just a smidgen too close. This is the way your chin will ground your face, your ears will emerge discreetly from your hair. How closely your features resemble your father's, not mine, even now. I am struck by the unfairness of it.

"At least have some meat," Dev says, thrusting a mutton chop towards my face. The mutton drips gravy on the floor as he waves it in the air.

"I ate hours ago," I say, taking the chop out of his hand and placing it back on his plate.

"The wetness," he says as I'm bending down next to him, wiping gravy off the floor. "It felt so sticky when it dried last time. All over my skin." His voice becomes soft, conspiratorial. "Can't you feed Munna first?" He tries to caress my hair with his mutton and gravy hand, but I bob my head out of the way.

"There's custard in the fridge," I say. "Don't forget to put the plates back in the kitchen. Last night there were cockroaches everywhere."

"Cockroaches," he says, staring at his food, as if he will see a convoy walking across his plate. A smear of pickle dangles from the corner of his mouth. As I walk back into the bedroom, I hear him noisily empty his glass, then fill it again.

I SIT ON THE BED in the dark and look at you. A sliver of light anoints your forehead in gold, then glances off and catches your nose. You look so tranquil, so restful, you could be advertising sleep itself.

I wonder if you would mind being woken. It has been hours since your last feeding. There is a neediness in my chest. I long for the comfort of your mouth at my breast.

But I remain there instead and look at you. The light has somehow shifted, or perhaps your head has moved. Gold outlines your mouth now, and dabs at the small of your throat.

Your father starts singing. He only does this on nights when he is extremely drunk. *"Will you light the fire of your heart,"* he croons, *"to dispel the darkness of my life. . . ."*

He sings softly, so that his voice does not carry to the other flats, but loud enough so that I hear it. Even with the slurring of the lyrics, the fineness of his voice comes through. I hold my breath so as not to miss any of his words.

You open your eyes. With your mouth and throat highlighted, it looks like the song is coming from you. *"Draw closer and take my hand,"* you say, *"lead me to a life with less heartbreak. . . ."*

Abruptly, the lyrics stop. I can see from your eyes that you are about to cry. I pick you up eagerly and offer you a breast. As you start to suckle, the song starts up again.

"For only love can bring back the light. . . ."

I sit there in the dark, listening to your father's voice. Your fingers press against the base of my breast, your lips encircle my nipple again. As the milk flows from my body into yours, satiation spreads in its wake.

"*Only love . . .*" your father sings.

THE VOICE RISES from the stage. It swirls around the darkened auditorium and reaches me in the first row of the balcony above.

"*Only love can bring back the light. . . .*" The words are heavy with longing, so heavy that I wonder how they manage to soar to where I am seated. It is the 25th of January, 1955—the eve of India's fifth anniversary as a republic. We are at Ramjas College in Delhi. I am seventeen.

"*Will you light the fire of your heart?*" the voice continues, and now someone standing at the back of the balcony switches on a spotlight. It sweeps along the floor restlessly, searching the empty stage, and stops on a lone figure dressed in black, his back towards the audience.

"*To dispel the darkness of my life.*" The figure turns around. I see a face painted so white that it seems to float free in the brilliance of the spotlight. The lips are red, almost crimson; the eyes clearly outlined; each lash seems to stand out black and distinct against the whiteness around. Perhaps it is the excitement of the crowd, or just my teenage headiness, but when I look into your father's eyes, I think I discover an emotion that only I can see. A longing distilled from the anguish of the lyrics, a pain, a hunger that calls only to me.

Roopa's fingers press against my forearm—my sister is barely aware of this as she leans forward in her seat. I tear my gaze away from the stage—away from the dark, perfect eyes, the unnaturally red mouth, the cheeks that tremble and burn. Instead I look at Roopa, her face shiny in the light reflected off the stage. In her raptness, her dupatta has fallen immodestly to her elbows, exposing a half circle of skin that gleams beneath her throat. On her lips is the gloss of forbidden lipstick. From her earlobes dangle Biji's earrings, like bunches of tiny golden grapes.

A few stanzas into the song, Roopa starts rummaging around in her purse. She pulls out a silver lighter, which even in the dark, I recognize as Paji's prized possession, the one Teji uncle gave him last year. The earrings from our mother, the lighter from our father—she has purloined from them *both*. I am impressed.

The spotlight goes out. The song continues, rising now from even darker depths. I have read about such tortured souls in novels, seen their stories in films; souls who suffer so that the rest of us can savor the offering of their pain. *"Light the fire of your heart,"* your father sings, and I close my eyes to concentrate on the torment mounting in his voice. Roopa begins to fumble with the stolen lighter, and I open my eyes to see it come alive with a blue and yellow flame. She raises it above her head and all around I notice people holding up matches and candles and even tiny oil lamps. I look over the balcony ledge at the points of illumination dotting the rows below, stretching out like the lights of a city viewed from a mountaintop. Just as the song climaxes, every bulb in the auditorium is switched on simultaneously. Your father throws open his arms to welcome the applause, the illumination, then steps to the edge of the stage and takes a bow.

Later, after all the contestants have sung, the curtains part one final time to reveal the judges sitting behind a garland-decked table, a huge flag of India pinned to the white cloth background behind them. The winner of the 1955 Republic Day intercollegiate singing competition is announced, and it is Dev Arora, from Ramjas College, Delhi.

"Dev, Dev!" Roopa screams beside me, then puts her forefingers in her mouth to whistle. All that emerges is a short spraying sound, and she tries to hide her lipstick-smeared fingers. This is one thing I can do better than my sister, so I emit a long, perfectly pitched whistle, modulating the intensity up and down to show off. Roopa ignores it. "Let's go backstage," she says.

She leads me down a green-walled passage to a door with a DO NOT ENTER sign. "The men's dressing room," Roopa announces carelessly. "Are you brave enough to enter?" I can tell she is hoping to shock me, but I eagerly nod my head. Roopa fluffs up her curls one last time, the curls she has spent all morning coaxing into her hair. Then we are in. Through the smoke, I see several of the singers from the competition. Nobody challenges us.

Dev is standing slender and shirtless in front of a washbasin. His face in the mirror is half white, half flesh-toned—I realize he is washing off a layer of makeup which spreads down to his neck. One eye remains outlined in dark black liner, the other has been wiped clean. He has not yet started on his lips, they are still an impossibly deep red.

I notice the stained towel in his hand, the streaks that swirl around darkly in the basin, and feel a pang of disappointment. Is that all it takes, I wonder, to wipe anguish away?

"My sister Meera," Roopa announces, and Dev turns around. There is a line of hair starting at his navel and curving up to the base of his throat. It is like a snake, a naag, with two heads—one poised with its eye over the left nipple, the other arcing towards his right shoulder. I stare at his naked chest, transfixed by the eye, the nipple, the heads.

Roopa is looking at me, and I realize Dev has greeted me but I have not responded. "Hello," I murmur, and then add, "Congratulations."

"Your sister is almost as pretty as you are," Dev says to Roopa, or to me, I am not sure. Then, to my amazement, your father leans forward and kisses my sister with his red, red lips.

YOUR FATHER STILL has the hair snaking up his chest. He rubs it against me whenever he wants to let me know he has the need. Sometimes, when he lies on top of me, I can hear it rustling against my skin. Perhaps you heard it as well from inside me, with your ear pressed to the wall of my belly.

Soon your father will stop singing in the living room. He will forget the custard and leave the dishes where they are. He will stretch back in his chair and stare at the ceiling, his mouth open. His eyes will close— he will snore, and think he is still awake.

I will smooth out the sheets on his bed next to mine. I will spread out your blanket and lay you on his empty bed. With my cheek on my pillow, I will watch you sleep beside me. My eyes will close following the rise and fall of your chest.

Sometime before dawn your father will be awakened by the heat. He will pull off his shirt and clear the magazines off the sofa. He will stretch himself out and fold up his shirt for a pillow. He will sleep with the naag hugged to his body.

You will wake, too, and cry to be fed. My eyes will open, and I will put you to my breast. Afterwards, I will lay you down again on your father's bed. I will try to get some more sleep before the night ends.

In the morning, I will boil the milk delivered by the ganga. I will throw away the pickle and put the dishes in the basin. I will make no noise, and your father will not awaken.

I will look at your father and think of you. I will wonder if you will have his voice, sing as well. I will imagine your body growing, your muscles firming. The naag beginning to sprout upon your chest too.

chapter
two

SOMEHOW, I ALWAYS RETURN TO THAT 1955 REPUBLIC DAY EVE IN DELHI when I first saw your father. I wonder what my life would have been if I hadn't gone to the concert with Roopa. If I had not allowed her to drag me backstage. If I had not heard your father say those words. "Your sister is almost as pretty as you are." Every time I asked him afterwards, he said he couldn't remember which one of us he meant.

When did the idea first start germinating in my brain? Was it when I saw Roopa whistle at him during the show? When I saw the look that came on her face backstage? "Your sister is almost as pretty as you are." I had never heard anyone say that before to me. Neither had Roopa, to her.

Or was it after the contest, when we all went to the market at Chandni Chowk to stand on the street and eat fruit mix from one of the century-old shops? When Roopa kept insisting on feeding Dev herself, picking up the chunks of spice-doused banana and sweet potato with her toothpick and ostentatiously transporting them to his mouth? All around us, eyes widened at her brazenness, foreheads rumpled in disapproval, voices chittered at the shamelessness of youth. "Should I sprinkle on more chili powder?" Roopa asked Dev, and I could see the flush on her face from the looks she pretended not to notice.

"Meera doesn't like pineapple," Dev said, nodding at the leaf spread out on my palm, which was bare except for the small yellow pyramid of pineapple I had arranged on the side with my toothpick. He was smiling at me, and as I watched, his mouth opened in expectation of the next morsel from Roopa. What would happen if I speared a piece from my pyramid and raised it to his lips? Would I also be able to bask in the heat of the scandalized stares?

"She's always been the fussy one in the family," Roopa declared, annoyed that Dev's attention had strayed. She rummaged around in her fruit for a pineapple chunk to pop into his mouth and glared at me when she couldn't find one. "If you weren't going to eat it, why didn't you tell the man no pineapple, instead of erecting the Taj Mahal on your leaf with everyone's share?"

"I was saving it for the end," I said, picking up a piece and chewing it with relish for Roopa's benefit. "It's very sweet," I told her, then added cheekily, "Should I give you some? For Dev?"

Roopa's eyes flashed, but her words were lost in a blast of January wind that swept through the lane. It had rained the night before, and the cold had a penetrating dampness to it that made us tighten the grip of our fingertips around our toothpicks. I watched the stripes billow on Dev's thin sweater, the kind with the sky blue V-neck which was being touted by street vendors all over Delhi as this year's fashion imported directly from London. Dev stood facing the gusts, his shirt open casually up to the second button, as if he were a tennis player at Wimbledon positioning himself in a breeze on a hot summer day. "Are you cold?" he asked, as Roopa and I pulled at our shawls, trying to eke out enough material to cover our heads. "I could give someone my sweater."

I was almost taken in. But then as he spoke about moving to Bombay to become a playback singer for films, I noticed how his jaw tensed to keep his teeth from chattering. "Roopa says she couldn't possibly leave Delhi, but I dream about it all the time. Imagine living down there next to the warmth of the sea, imagine never needing a shawl or sweater again." He dug his arms in tightly against his lean frame to maintain the nonchalance of his pose as he said this. How endearing it was, I thought, that underneath his bravado, he too was freezing.

Roopa wanted to buy cosmetics, so we walked down towards the fort, looking for the side street with the perfume shops. Everywhere was the smell of charcoal fires, mingling with the aroma of food being fried on giant iron griddles. The air was so heavy with smoke that it looked grainy, lights from the shops swirled and bled as though through a fog. Tiny paper flags sprouted from the ends of wooden sticks everywhere, like early spring blossoms heralding the arrival of Republic Day. Decorations for the celebration had been becoming more elaborate since the original one in 1950, and this year there were strings of bulbs festooned between the lampposts along the street. Just this morning, the newspapers had talked about how the wounds of partitioning the country into India and Pakistan were finally healing after eight years, how Hindus and Muslims all over the Indian side were ready to put the riots and the killings of the past aside and greet a united future.

"Look at the fort," Dev said, pointing at the arches that rose from the twilight ahead. "They say that Shah Jehan employed a hundred musicians, to play in the drum house five times a day. That's the time I should have lived, in the days of the Mughals. When people like me were hired in the royal courts, when the soul of a singer was something even kings could appreciate."

I imagined Shah Jehan and his empress Mumtaz reclining at dusk in the fort on the cushioned interior of the Sheesh Mahal. Dev's lyrics ushering in the evening candles one by one, each flame igniting a thousand images in the mirrors embedded in the ceiling and walls.

"All these centuries later, and everything still stands, just like the Mughals built it," Dev said. "They've come and gone, the British, and these buildings will outlast us all."

The first time I saw the Red Fort was just before the Partition, when I was nine. My family had left behind the ancestral mansion in Rawalpindi, once it became clear the city would fall to Pakistan, and fled to Delhi. Paji took us to a different neighborhood every day to familiarize us with our new home. Darya Ganj, the part of Old Delhi in which we resettled, was filled with narrow streets and crowded bazaars. In comparison, New Delhi, with its wide boulevards and enormous edifices, was so different, it might as well have been London or New York. The immaculate white pillars and polished arcades of Connaught Circus had projected a symmetry, an order, that was unsettling. Biji in particular was so intimidated that she rarely ventured out of Old Delhi after that.

What I remembered most vividly about the Red Fort from back then was the Union Jack flapping atop a pole, its stern geometry of triangles and crosses clashing with the delicate intricacy of the minarets and arches. In its stead now flew the Indian flag, the centuries-old Ashoka wheel at its center forming a bridge between the Hindu strand of saffron and the Muslim strand of green. A new united India, we had been taught, with a unified identity for the future.

"We should come again tomorrow, to see the fireworks," Roopa said, as we watched workers hoist large cloth portraits of Gandhiji and Nehru on either side of the Lahore Gate for a special celebration the next evening. "A full lakh of rupees they're supposed to be spending, to celebrate the five-year mark."

Floodlights started coming on all round the fort, bathing the sandstone in patriotic cascades of white and green and orange. "Testing, testing," someone said over a loudspeaker. Then Nehru's voice crackled through the air, reprising his 1947 Independence Day speech. *"The achievement we celebrate today is but a step, an opening of opportunity, to the greater triumphs and achievements that await us. Are we brave enough and wise enough to grasp this opportunity and accept the challenge of the future?"* I noticed Roopa rub her wrist across the stripes of Dev's sweater, then slide her hand under his.

It seems bizarre to blame Nehru for my life, but I think it was his words that helped egg me on towards my fate. Listening to him made me start wondering what my own future would hold for me, whom would I be spending it with. What were *my* opportunities, dangling ripe and heavy within reach, waiting to be plucked? I stood there, absorbing the bustle and tinsel of the street, as men with scarves wound around their faces bicycled by. Looming ahead was the imposing façade of the fort with its neat rows of windows and doorways and the flag undulating lazily from a pole. Beyond stretched the vast rising expanse of the sky, as smooth and unmarked as a sheet of parchment dipped in ink. *". . . The past is over and it is the future that beckons to us now,"* Nehru declared.

What story did I plan to inscribe across the blank expanse of my own future? Already, my parents had started inviting the families of prospective bridegrooms to come over and inspect Roopa. Even though I was two years younger, Biji, savvy to every marketing possibility, found some pretext to trot me out as well at every such occasion. "My second daughter, Meera. A bit more time, and you'll see her blossom into another Roopa, just you wait." It was quite possible that she might have us both married off within the year, before I even had a chance to get to college, before I could experience any of the adventures I had dreamt about or seen on the screen. I felt something clutch at my heart. Roopa never tired of boasting about her college flirtations, the boys she had met even before the poetry evening where she was introduced to Dev. When would it be my turn for romance?

A small sigh escaped Roopa's throat and I turned around to see Dev brush his lips against her fingers. My sister's eyes were closed, and her head slightly tilted back, as if she had just surrendered herself to the comfort of a particularly soft and luxurious pillow. I looked at Dev's mouth, at the incipient shadow of his mustache, at the half smile playing at his lips. (From the fleeting contact with my sister's fingers, perhaps?) Under the crest of his chin, a streak of makeup still gleamed unwashed on his neck, like a luminous brushstroke of silver painted across the darkness of his skin. *"A new star arises, the star of freedom in the East, a new hope comes into being, a vision long cherished materializes,"* Nehru said, and I suddenly realized that Dev's eyes were open, that his gaze was focused on my face, that he had been observing me while I examined him.

Then the electricity failed, Nehru's voice was squelched mid-sentence, and the great architectural works of the Mughals around us were plunged into darkness.

"DOES PAJI KNOW ABOUT DEV?" It was later that night, and we were alone at home. Paji was on an overnight trip, and Biji had seized the opportunity to drag our younger sister Sharmila to be blessed by a holy man in Dhaula Kuan to make her teeth grow out straight. Roopa sat in front of the mirror in Biji's room, rummaging through the cosmetics she had picked up (in the light of a hurricane lamp) from Chandni Chowk.

"Have some sense," she said, looking at me scornfully. "Would I be sitting here alive if he did?"

"You'll have to tell if you marry Dev."

"Who said anything about marriage?" Roopa scoffed. "His father is some sort of railway employee at Nizamuddin station. Can you imagine us on the platform waving flags at the Frontier Mail?"

She found the bottle she was looking for and held it up. "See this? It's proper rouge. Imported. Not that horrible red paste from Ajmer that the Christian ayahs smear on their cheeks."

"Oh please, could we try it on my face?" Rouge was the cosmetic Biji abhorred the most, denouncing it as something only fit for the faces of whores and English housewives. Biji considered all makeup immoral, and only owned a single stick of red lipstick herself. She used this not to color her lips, but to form perfectly round bindis on her forehead for special occasions.

"I don't know," Roopa said, examining my features with a professional air. "Your cheeks are too coarse—and besides, it's much too expensive to waste against your dark skin."

I had heard things like this so many times from her that it did not bother me. Everyone agreed that Roopa was the one with the film-star looks, the fairer, more radiant skin. Despite the compliments, my sister could still not resist an opportunity to cut me down a notch, to bolster this claim.

"What if I promise not to tell Paji about Dev if you make me up?"

Roopa gasped. "Why you little witch. I'm the one who took you there and now you're threatening me? What are you, so jealous, just because you can't get a boyfriend?"

"I can, too, if I want. I'm just too young."

"You're seventeen. Two years less than I am. That's not young. No, it's because you're too ugly, that's why. So ugly that your own mother sent you back to the village after you were born so she wouldn't have to look at you."

It had happened after they brought me home from my grandmother's. Roopa had taken one look at me and run away, terrified. She dropped to the floor unconscious the next morning when she saw my mouth at Biji's breast. Two days after I arrived, Roopa curled her body into a ball and refused to allow herself to be fed.

Biji became alarmed at the looming prospect—losing her first-born in exchange for her second. Roopa had good teeth, sturdy limbs, and filled the house with joy. I, on the other hand, was still mottled from the delivery and only opened my mouth to cry. The choice was clear—it was not as if I was a boy.

So the next morning, Biji packed me with my clothes back into my cradle and had the servant summoned to return me to the village where I had been delivered. There I was to stay for several months, becoming less ugly as I grew, until it was determined I would no longer traumatize poor Roopa.

By the time Sharmila was born, Roopa had become more used to babies. Or perhaps Sharmila looked prettier than I. In any case, Roopa did not cry, and Sharmila was not sent back to become less ugly. Instead, it was I who did the howling, every time I saw Sharmila's face. But Biji was unmoved by my tears. Sharmila stayed.

It wasn't just Biji who doted on Roopa. Paji called her his "English daughter," so fair that the midwife must have lifted her from a pram in the British cantonment nearby. "You'll light up your father's name, be a doctor or scientist someday." He insisted on feeding her every night with his own hand. Roopa would sit at his right and accept offerings of food and fruit with the self-satisfied benevolence of an idol at a temple.

So entrenched was the rule in our household that Roopa be favored in everything that the question of opposing it didn't arise. It would have made as much sense as rebelling against a law of nature—against gravity or the course of the monsoon. Sharmila and I wore Roopa's old clothes and played with her discarded toys without complaint, we called her "Bhenji" since using her name would show disrespect, and we obeyed (or disobeyed) her decrees as we would those of a parent.

Today, though, I was not going to let Bhenji get away with calling me ugly. "Your Dev thinks I'm pretty," I said, and was rewarded by the annoyance that flared up in her face.

In the end, Roopa relented and made me up, though she purposely put on too much rouge, making my cheeks as bright as candy. I looked at my face, squinting to compensate not only for the rouge, but also the eyebrow pencil, with which Roopa had outlined my eyes so vehemently that they stared back as if out of a cartoon drawn by a child. But it didn't really matter. I had finally blossomed, as Biji had predicted, and someone else had been able to see it. I, too, was beautiful now—Roopa was no longer the only one.

So beautiful, that the idea, at last fully articulated, at last fully engorged with possibility and churning with ambition, engulfed me like a wave. I could win Dev. I could steal him from Roopa, making up for all the years of favoritism my parents had showered her with. I could reach out and pluck my very own apple, bite through its russet gold skin, taste its sweet sensual flesh, before it was too late. All his smiles and glances suggested Dev was someone attainable—besides, who else was there in my circle to target as a possible candidate? Hadn't the prime minister of India, Nehru himself, nudged me in the direction I was planning to take?

I imagine the electricity going out again in Chandni Chowk, but this time there is no commotion as the lights fade. This time, the darkness magically swallows Roopa before she can use its cover to thrust herself against Dev. He stands behind me now, his chest pressing against my shoulder, his fingers stroking mine. His lips hover over the nape of my neck, trying to decide the exact spot on which to alight. I feel them skim along the material of my blouse, making sorties across the edge of the cloth to play against bare skin. It is my throat now from which a sigh escapes, but Roopa is not there to hear it.

The moon hangs high and round above us like a sole surviving streetlight. "Look at the chand, beaming down its chandni," Dev says, turning up his face to the sky. He closes his eyes and opens his mouth as if he can catch the moonlight like rain. Down the curve of his neck, over the throb of his Adam's apple, is the forgotten sliver of makeup shimmering again.

"Sing for me," I tell him. "Sing the song that will bring back the light." I want to watch the crescent of white rise and fall on his throat.

Dev looks at me, and I lift his hands and press against his fingertips in encouragement. *"Will you light the fire of your heart?"* he begins, so softly at first that only I can hear him. *"To dispel the darkness of my life."* I watch the mark on his throat begin to pulse up his neck, spill up over his chin. A circle forms around us, as people stop to listen. *"For only love can bring back the light. . . ."*

In reply comes the sound of a soft explosion from somewhere behind the fort. A single rocket rises silently into the sky, its plume leaving a white trail against the blue-black night. An instant later a galaxy of sparks lights up the sky. More rockets begin to climb lazily, like flower stalks scaling the night and blossoming in bursts of orange, green, and white. *"Will you light the fire of your heart, to dispel the darkness of my life?"*

Flashes illuminate the arches of the fort as if from cannons being fired in salute from behind the walls. The flag emerges from its seclusion of night, its stripes rippling under the national colors unfurling above. Gandhi and Nehru look benevolently on as upturned faces from the crowd around us join in the song. *"Only love can bring back the light,"* Dev sings, his words encompassing every voice, every aspiration on the street.

Then the nautch girls come swinging in. *"Only love, only love, only love,"* they croon, wriggling through the crowd and spinning the tassels on their breasts. Extras dressed as British officers bounce out with their guns, pivoting them smartly, saluting in sync. Shah Jehan sashays past slowly with his Mumtaz, feeding her grapes, followed by his musical entourage. Nehru comes to life and descends singing from his poster, Gandhiji twirls his staff and comes dancing right after.

And here we are, from the Mughals and the British to Gandhi and Nehru, all lined up for the finale. The scene bursts into Eastman Color, the sky stretches to CinemaScope. The volleys rise into the night, the bricks in the street light up like day. Gandhiji taps his cane to the tune of the music, first at his feet, then at me, then at Dev, then at the explosions above the Red Fort, above India. Is this my future that he is pointing to, the path to my happiness that is being lit up? *"Only love . . ."* Dev sings, and I bury my face in his sweater and let his song drown out the world.

I fall asleep with the lyrics still swirling in my ears, the candy glow of my cheeks even redder with the thoughts of my future with Dev. Perhaps it is the rouge, perhaps it is an intoxicant, perhaps Biji is right about how dangerous it is. She returns at midnight, slaps me out of bed, and drags me by the ear to the bathroom to scour it off my face.

chapter
three

THE DAY ROOPA TOLD DEV ABOUT THE NAVY OFFICER TO WHOM SHE WAS
to be engaged, I was standing in the shadows, spying on them. I had followed Roopa to Nizamuddin station, and then down the narrow station
road with the rickshaws all lined up for passengers, through the large
bare plot of land that had been cleared for more whitewashed railway
quarters like the one in which Dev's family lived. There was nothing to
hide behind on this stretch, but I had been stalking them for so long
(once even to the Rivoli cinema in Connaught Place, where I sat in the
row behind them, waiting in vain for them to kiss) that by now I was an
expert at using only air to conceal myself.

In fairness, this bad habit of spying I had fallen into was hardly my
fault. All through the spring, Roopa had been using me as her alibi to
spend evenings with Dev. She would drag me out of the house to show
Paji it was just the two of us leaving together, then expect me to make
myself scarce the instant Dev arrived. Could I really be blamed for
wanting to linger behind a tree somewhere so that I could observe what
transpired?

Sometimes I wondered if Roopa had realized I was a rival, the way
she kept flaunting Dev. "Every great romance depends on a go-
between," she would say to me, "and that is the part life has deemed you

fit to play." I was recruited to carry notes to Dev, messages of (as Roopa made it sound) life-and-death importance that for some unclear reason could not be personally conveyed but had to be hand-delivered by me in sealed envelopes. "I've signed across the back, so don't even think of looking inside," she warned, to make certain I was sufficiently tantalized.

Was this a game Roopa had devised for her amusement, after guessing the mischief kindled in my brain? Could she have plotted my errands with the precise expectation of my hand brushing against Dev's? Accidental contact soon led to something more deliberate, with quick squeezes and stolen caresses coming into play. I kept waiting for the fireworks to bloom once more, for the electricity to arc between our fingertips, but Dev's skin remained cool and uncharged against mine.

"Just how many years younger than your sister are you?" he asked one day.

"Two. But if you see us standing together, you'll notice I'm taller by almost half an inch."

"Perhaps you're even taller than I am, let's see." He moved close to me and ran his hand from the top of his head to my brow. "Yes, amazing, exactly half an inch again."

For an instant, I looked up towards the fingers touching my forehead, astonished at this pronouncement. Then I realized he was making fun of me and swiped his hand off.

"Why don't you come over to the Sangam Café some afternoon?" Dev called after me, as, with flushed cheeks and tingling forehead, I bounded away.

I did venture to the café a few times—it was right across the street from Ramjas College, where Dev and Roopa studied. I even stole some cosmetics from her bag, using the college ladies' room to imitate her makeup techniques as best as I could remember. "What have you done to your eyes?" Dev asked, the first time I unleashed the eyebrow pencil on myself. "This makeup doesn't suit you, like it does your sister—it covers up the freshness of your face."

I was never able to summon up the nerve to sit down at Dev's table with all his friends. "The Sawhney girls are getting prettier and prettier every day," someone would say, and I would quickly blurt out where Dev was supposed to meet Roopa that evening and scamper away. "And what about you, my darling, where will you meet us?" a voice would call after me. The boys would whistle and laugh and I would hear the sound of glasses being thumped down in appreciation on the tabletop.

The specter of my sister's wrath always hovered over me through these expeditions. Roopa could metamorphose from sweet to ferocious in an instant, like an irked goddess suddenly sprouting a phalanx of weapon-laden arms. My parents seemed to encourage this—our grand-mother even fondly called Roopa her "Little Durga." Perhaps that's what made the spying so addictive—the thrill that I could be caught at any time by my demon sister.

That final day in Nizamuddin, though, was different. It wasn't the danger that had pulled me in this time but the need to witness the climax of a story tracked so long. The navy boy had appeared at our house with his parents more than a fortnight ago. His name was Ravinder, he had skin even fairer than Roopa's, and he exuded a sense of control quite opposite to the carefree nature Dev projected. He had been dressed in impeccable white—from the round white hat on his head to the polished white shoes that he carefully unlaced and left just outside our doorstep. Perhaps it was his looks, perhaps his uniform, but I could tell Roopa was taken from the start. She blushed, something I had not known she was capable of.

"Did you see?" she exclaimed as soon as they left. "So young, and already an officer."

With Dev, though, she carried on as if nothing had changed, as if the flurry of matrimonial negotiations that began to swirl around her in the ensuing days did not exist. "It's best not to jinx things by acting in haste," she said, as she handed me another perfumed envelope to deliver to Dev.

"How is she, my sweet and salty one?" Dev had asked this morning, when I had informed him about the rendezvous with Roopa at Nizamud-din. I had nodded, unable to speak, and run away.

I crept behind them now, as they headed towards the abandoned tomb of Salim Fazl. Was that the tinkle of Roopa's laughter—could she really be that cold-blooded as she prepared to dispatch Dev? It was April already, and the bougainvillea that swept wild through the ruins was teeming with flowers. Some said that Fazl was a Sufi mystic before the time of the Mughals, though others claimed he was simply a favorite minister. In any case, the competing shrine of Hazrat Nizamuddin (after whom the area was named) had diverted all the pilgrims long ago, leaving Fazl's tomb to decay in quiet solitude to the ground.

I watched from behind the bushes as Dev led Roopa through a gap in the wire fence towards the shrine with the tiled walls. They didn't stop to kiss or embrace in the outer courtyard as they usually did. The last glimpse I had before they disappeared into the chamber was of Roopa looking back nervously, as if worried about someone watching her.

A few minutes later, she came running out, the end of her sari pressed into her mouth, as if to keep her emotion contained. I waited for Dev to follow, but he didn't. The minutes went by but the entrance to the shrine remained empty. Thoughts about what Roopa might have done began to overwhelm me—how cruel had she been, what condition had she left Dev in? When the wait became too much to bear, I crept in.

It was cool and dark in the chamber, so dark that the floral designs on the tiles appeared as different shades of gray. Sections of wall stood crumbling where mosaics had been ripped out as souvenirs decades ago. The shrine itself was missing, a large cemented depression in the center marking where it had once stood. The rumor was that the British had dug it up and carried it off for one of their museums in London.

I half expected to see Dev in this rectangle, hands crossed neatly over his chest like the Sufi saint laid out in his grave. But Dev was not there. I found him through the small doorway at the far end, in the courtyard on the other side. He was reclining on the grass with his face turned towards the sunset, arms extended above his head as if stretching them after a nap.

"Dev," I whispered, but he did not move. I drew closer and noticed his eyes were closed. The sun had dipped behind the wall he faced, and the light through the arches streaked his face orange and red. Pieces of broken bottle glinted around him from the grass, like jewels surrounding a temple carving, inlaid in a wall. A ray of sunlight just missed his forehead, glancing across his eyelashes, brushing the tips in gold.

I was about to touch him, when he spoke. "I knew you would come." He kept his eyes closed. "You came the last time too, didn't you? I saw you hiding behind the bougainvillea."

He held out his hand and I took it, wrapping my fingers around his. His eyelids quivered but did not open. The sun had settled lower behind the wall, and his lashes were no longer golden. A crow cawed, and I heard the horns of scooters making their way home.

"She's not coming back, is she?" he said, finally.

"She's getting married."

Dev let out a short laugh. "I should have expected it. I'm not rich enough for your family. Not good enough for the Sawhneys. All those promises from her that we'd run away."

When I think back to that instant, I sometimes manipulate my memory to play tricks. I come up with a scene, with dialogue, depicting me as the passive one, the one led on by Dev. But whatever recollection I weave, the words I spoke next always unravel it. "Roopa is not the only one," I hear myself say. "There are others who more strongly feel your pain."

A tear is trembling at the corner of his eye, but Dev doesn't seem to notice. Is he even aware of what I have confessed to him? I feel a fury towards Roopa for the hold she has on Dev. I want to avenge her years of arrogance, the misery she must have wreaked on all the suitors she has boasted about, not just him.

The tear trickles down the side of Dev's nose, then fades into his skin. I notice his lips—they are parted just enough to make me wonder how his mouth would feel against mine. I suddenly inhale Sharmila's milky baby breath, the only person I've kissed, in the games of "house" we played. What would Dev's breath be like—redolent of cigarette smoke, adult, masculine?

And if we were to kiss, would he press his chest against me, as I have seen heroes do in films? Would a sudden shower drench our bodies, so that our clothes stick to our skin? I imagine the two of us running through a downpour, across slopes rolling with thunder, under lightning-lit skies. We come to an abandoned hut and Dev breaks open the door with a kick. Inside, the room is bare, except for a fireplace which Dev quickly gets going. He takes off his shirt and I unwind my sari, which has become transparent in the rain. We find a rope and string it across the room to hang up our clothes to dry. We stand on opposite sides of this curtain, Dev in his trousers, me in my blouse and petticoat, feeling the fire on our bodies, watching the flames dance on each other's faces. Two actors frozen in a movie still, waiting for the next scene in the script.

Except it is April, so there is no rain. But we are racing together anyway, as if being indeed chased by a thunderstorm—through the courtyard, past the wall, into the entrance through which we came. Our fingers are still locked, and Dev runs ahead, but it is unclear whether he is leading me or I am prompting him.

Inside, we are unsure what to do, the darkness makes us shy. There is no fire to stoke, no rope to string, no clothes to hang up to dry. Again, my recollection wavers. Is Dev the one who draws closer or is it I?

I feel Dev's thumb skim across my lower lip as if to brush off a speck he has just noticed. He cups his hand around the back of my neck and guides my fumbling mouth to his. His lips part mine, and I taste not smoke but a freshness, like fennel, on his breath. His tongue eases in and tests the inside of my mouth in an inquiring caress—frightened, I pull away. I stand there willing the rush to subside from my body, grateful that the dark hides my expression. I am filled with apprehension, but also exultation, at joining the ranks of the kissed.

And now here is the rectangle cut out of the ground for us, where the Sufi saint Salim Fazl once lay. Here I am, reclining back on this bed, the fabric of my blouse separating cement from skin. My hand closes around a fragment of tile that has broken off from somewhere. I feel the outline of an imprinted flower and rub it like a good-luck charm. The darkness trembles around me, then parts, to magically reveal the mosaics on the walls. Whorls of blue petals surrounding anthers yellow with pollen, pistils red and feathery, their ends swollen.

Dev hesitates, then bends over me. He has removed his shirt, even though there has been no rain. Light flitters across his chest, as if a fire has sprung up in a corner somewhere. The illumination is too fleeting to make out the naag I know is hiding there. I imagine it come to life, leaving blue petals crushed in its wake. Its body smeared yellow with pollen, the stickiness of stigmas clinging to its scales.

Dev props himself on one arm, his legs between mine, and struggles to undo his belt. His frame looks even more spare from this angle, the muscles still developing, like someone not quite adult. A faint fragrance of perspiration rises off his skin. I notice a growing sensitivity call to me from the part of my body for which I have no name. A warm and liquid awareness that advances unseen under my clothes and flushes my skin. I feel my stomach become hot, then my chest, my neck and face.

Dev pulls himself free of his pants. A clutch of panic seizes my throat. Must I take something off as well—does etiquette demand that I reciprocate? The movies never go this far. There are no songs explaining how the scene progresses, no singers in the background giving hints. The panic begins to dance around, igniting other questions like a runaway flame. Why am I here alone with Dev? How have I ended up in this position with him? Hasn't Biji spent a lifetime warning me precisely of situations like this? What will Paji think, what will Biji do, what will everyone say?

Then Roopa appears. I think that her face will be clotted with anger, but instead she is sporting a smirk. "You couldn't do it, could you?" she seems to say. "You couldn't go further, you couldn't be more daring than I."

All I need to do is blink to make Roopa disappear. Wave my hand at her as if shooing away a fly, to end this silliness, to end this game. But instead, I rise to her challenge. I decide to go past the point where the songs run out on the soundtrack. I decide to forge my own destiny, as Nehru might say. I shut my eyes and guide Dev's hand to the drawstring around my waist.

It is Dev who loses his nerve. He loosens my salwar, then stops and looks down strangely at my face. The naag has crept back onto his chest, its body a line of hair again. "I just—" he says. "I don't know what I was—" His voice is so strangled that the words barely escape. "I'm sorry," he manages to force out. He wilts into the space beside me and crosses an arm over his face.

For a while we just lie there. I can feel the grit of cement along the strip of bare skin around my waist. The tile has slipped out of my fingers, the flowers subsided back into their wall. I hear Dev pull up his pants beside me and turn to look at him. A lingering pocket of heat flares in my brain.

"There's nothing to be sorry about," I say finally, and bring his fingers to my lips. "We didn't do anything—there's no reason to be afraid."

Except that there is. What I don't realize then is that it makes no difference that we stopped when we did. My fate was sealed the moment Dev's body pushed me down into the grave. Perhaps the eyes watching us blended in with the tiles in the mosaic. Perhaps if I had heard the retreating footsteps I would have urged Dev to give chase. But by now the courtyard has already been left behind, the bougainvillea squeezed past, the tract of empty land raced across. The door has been thrown open, the door to the railway quarter next to Dev's.

Here, then, is the stationmaster's son, Rahim, who likes to pretend he is the keeper of Salim Fazl's grave. For the past few days, he too has been spying on Dev. "Not one girl but two," he breathlessly recounts about the encroachers on his domain. "And the second one, he got naked with." He weaves an account so embellished, so provocative, that his mother turns off the stove and hurries out to investigate.

Meanwhile, I am thinking that perhaps it's for the best Dev stopped when he did. He is handsome, it's true, and I know my body still has a craving for him. But do I really feel what the songs promise, am I ready to be in love with him? What if I, too, am destined to marry a navy boy with white shoes and a hat to match? I squeeze my fingers over Dev's, in a gesture I hope will convey nothing more than friendship. It is some minutes before the wife of the stationmaster bursts upon us holding hands in the grave.

chapter
four

"I was married to your mother when I was thirteen," my father said. "My family needed paper in their printing business and her family owned lumber forests and a mill, so it was a logical match. Your mother was ten—she cried when the priest told her she couldn't keep her doll with her during the ceremony. I remember how she clung on to that doll, so tight that the arm ripped right off when her father tried to pull it away. It was nothing more than a threadbare piece of cloth, and the cotton stuffing burst out into the air. I remember thinking what a silly girl this was, and so obstinate as well—perhaps village girls were brought up that way. When we sat in front of the fire, I knew what was happening, I knew I was being married to this girl, who was sobbing even now over the cotton fluff floating in the air. What I didn't know was what marriage meant. What it meant for me to have this girl as my wife, this girl who would come to live in our house four years later, still clinging to the same filthy doll, with the arm sewn back on. Even if I had, it wouldn't have occurred to me to question my parents. They had arranged the match before I was born, and they knew what was best."

Paji's eyes twinkled. Someone might have looked into them and mistaken it for merriment, but I knew it to be the glitter of rage.

"We had almost nothing in common. Not only had Rohini not

been brought up in the city, but being a girl from a family of zamin-dars—perhaps the ones with the most land in the state—her parents had not bothered to school her. The only thing they taught her was to use her right thumbprint, and not her left, to sign her name. Still I did not complain."

I was standing before Paji in the library. The walls were lined with the books his company had published. Roopa and Sharmila and I (per-haps even Biji) were all terrified of this room, since we were only sum-moned there if we had done something terribly wrong. Paji would break into long accounts of his life on such occasions, carefully watching our every tic and movement to appraise the escalating sense of dread he was creating. He would stop only when he was satisfied we had been pun-ished enough, that it was time to unleash the full verbal force of his anger. Unlike Biji, Paji never hit us.

Today, I felt more anxious than usual. I knew, of course, why I had been summoned. The rumors had sprouted almost immediately, like tiny malodorous drupes, whose poisonous scent had quickly covered the five miles our neighborhood lay north of Nizamuddin. Roopa had been furi-ous. "Don't you have any self-respect? Don't you know there are lines one never crosses? Could you really have been that jealous?" She had stopped talking to me before I could explain. The servants were all whis-pering and even the paanwalla around the corner seemed to leer insinu-atingly when I walked past his stall.

Yesterday, after another sleepless night, I had decided that my best strategy would be to declare to Paji that I wanted to marry Dev. I knew Paji would be aghast, and forbid the match—but then the onus of deal-ing with the rumors would rest with him. I didn't worry too much about the unlikely chance that he would agree. Since I didn't have the nerve to make my outrageous proposition to Paji's face, I had written out a letter and slipped it in with his evening mail.

But Paji was not ready to bring up the letter as yet. "My father wanted me to become a doctor," he said. "He wanted to send me to Eng-land for my studies." I stared obediently at the floor as Paji recounted how Biji became pregnant just as they were booking the passage. How the trip got cancelled, only to have the baby, a girl, be stillborn. Biji got very sick herself, and everyone expected her to die—so much so that Paji's uncles started making inquiries about someone to replace her. "For some strange reason she managed to recover. The doctor said that having another baby would kill her. My family insisted I try again anyway, so I did." Six years later, Roopa was born.

Paji never made it to England to become a doctor. Instead, he found himself shunted into his father Harilal's printing business. Their main product was religious calendars—garish pictures of Lakshmi and Ganesh (Guru Nanak for the Sikhs), at the bottom of which were stapled a year's worth of tear-off dates. "Imagine my horror—I, who had always fancied myself an atheist—suddenly surrounded by these divine elephants and goddesses and their dozens of arms all day. I was so depressed I could barely drag myself to the factory. I got my clothes caught in the machinery. I developed allergies to the smell of ink. Fortunately for me, the Partition came."

At this point, Paji always reminded us that we were one of the lucky families, escaping Rawalpindi unscathed, even if someone did shoot our dog the day before we left. Harilal, though, had to leave everything behind. A Muslim employee took over, stapling the 1948 dates (which had already been printed up) to stylized quotations from the Koran instead.

It was relatively easy to set things up again in India. Harilal was assigned a press in Karol Bagh abandoned by the British. "I knew I had to dissuade him from returning to the calendars—I couldn't go back to dealing with the multi-armed Ganesh." Paji spoke desperately to his father about Nehru's secular vision for the new country—how what was needed were publications to soothe the rancor of Partition, to bring Hindus and Muslims together. He managed to sell Harilal on a set of pamphlets he had seen in a foreign magazine: selections from the world's most famous philosophers, everyone from Plato to Nietzsche. Harilal agreed to an initial printing of two thousand sets, each consisting of sixteen small volumes, with embossed covers and gold-edged pages.

"Unfortunately, the Hindus and Muslims were still not quite done with the business of killing each other. My Nietzsche initiative languished unread in the warehouse. Eventually, the covers were ripped off and the pages sold to the scrap collector. To add insult to injury, the collector claimed that the gold coloring was an impurity, and paid us two paise less per kilogram than ordinary newsprint."

I braced myself as Paji embarked on the last part of his tale. The decision by Harilal to start publishing government documents instead. The second press they had to buy within months to keep up with the demands of the rapacious new bureaucracy. A year after Gandhi's assassination in 1948, Paji was allowed to publish a book about the freedom struggle, which sold respectably and brought good reviews from the press. By the time Harilal died in 1952, Paji had reconciled himself to the idea that he would remain a publisher all his life.

"It wasn't something I would have willingly chosen. I still loathed the smell of ink. My wife still had nothing in common with me. Do you know what it feels like to be a publisher and be married to someone who can't even read?

"I suppose my unhappiness must have shown from the beginning. Perhaps that's why my mother started beating Rohini every Friday after Roopa came. Or perhaps it was because your mother only gave me girls. In any case, I didn't interfere. I made it a point to leave early on Fridays, knowing what would happen. When I returned, Rohini would be resting in the dark like a patient recovering from some weekly treatment. She would move slowly as she went to the kitchen to have my dinner prepared. Perhaps some Fridays she was only pretending, perhaps my mother didn't really beat her every week. Looking back, it's not something I'm proud of. I should have put a stop to it. It didn't do me any good to have my wife beaten. Her misery didn't lessen my own.

"There was another girl the year after you came. But she was born with a breathing obstruction and survived only two days. Then came Sharmila. Counting the two that didn't live, this was the fifth girl to emerge from your mother's womb. Seeing your younger sister killed my mother's spirit. She stopped beating Rohini. She died within the year. Sometimes I wonder if Rohini produced girls on purpose, just to drive my mother to her death.

"In any case, I decided to make my peace with your mother. I started coming back on Fridays with gifts. But this made your mother very suspicious. She thought I had kept another woman. When I tried to teach her to write, she refused, saying I should go teach my tart instead. She threw all my presents away. The only thing she kept was the lipstick, and even this she insisted on using, like a rustic might, for the bindi on her forehead, not her lips. A lifetime of ignorance is hard to wipe away.

"Do you know what a struggle it was for me to have you all educated? Your mother fought me every step of the way. 'They're the granddaughters of a zamindar,' she would declare, even after her family had lost every scrap of land they owned to Pakistan. 'They need to learn the supervision of servants, nothing else.' But for all the things I did wrong in my life, I knew one mistake I was not going to make. I wasn't going to send my daughters into the world unprepared. I wasn't going to let them suffer their mother's fate. Or mine, for that matter. I promised myself I would find them good matches. Husbands who were compatible, who were solid, who came from the right background. Who were worthy of marrying the daughter of a Sawhney."

Paji's eyes had turned opaque. On his face was a smile, the edges so curled with bitterness that I had to look away.

"This Dev of yours has not a thing going for him. His father blows whistles after trains. He wants to go to Bombay and become a singer, you say. This is a husband you're talking about—your life, you understand. Even a dog looks around more before he finds a place to relieve himself. What potion did he drug you with to make you disgrace yourself with him this way?"

Paji paused, as if waiting for me to answer, though he knew I wouldn't.

"That's right, be silent now. You've done your damage, what more could you have to add? Roopa says that even her in-laws have heard— what if they were to call off her marriage? Did you ever stop to think what effect your stupidity would have on *her* future? There's only one way to put an end to these rumors. To give in to your foolishness. To have you marry him. This Dev, who doesn't even have the courage to come show his face. Tell his family in Nizamuddin to call on me. They're not fit to eat off our plates, but what choice have you left me with?"

For a moment, I simply stared at Paji, trying to digest his decision. Was he pretending, trying to scare me, trying to teach me a lesson? It seemed unthinkable that he could agree to my far-fetched proposal. Why had I imagined that imposing my will in this way would leave me elated?

I stumbled towards the door. "Meera," Paji called out behind me. "You may not realize this now, but you've just ruined your life."

NOBODY WANTED IT TO BE a double wedding, but it turned out to be too costly to have two separate ones. In a fit of pique, Roopa had her henna ceremony shifted by a day so it wouldn't coincide with mine. She was quick to appropriate the best saris and the most expensive sets of jewelry from the dowries Biji had set aside for us. As the day of the wedding drew closer, she found fault with a thousand niggling details, even complaining at one point that the Brahmin assigned to perform her ceremony wasn't as priestly-looking as mine (they were exchanged). She made sure that Ravinder's family didn't have to mingle with Dev's, arranging the seating so that the bridal guests formed a wall of separation between the two sides.

The shehnai players had just started coaxing out their mournful wedding music from their instruments when the inevitable happened—Roopa came face to face with Dev. He was unable to say anything, looking at my sister with the wide-eyed longing of an abandoned child, cutting such a pitiful figure that I almost felt sorry for him. But Roopa played her part perfectly, congratulating him with just the right touch of modesty, even remembering the correct form of "Jijaji" to address him as her brother-in-law. Then Dev's fifteen-year-old sister Hema sidled up to them. "Isn't this the one you really wanted to marry?" she asked her brother. My only satisfaction in overhearing the comment was that it wiped the demureness off Roopa's face.

For the ceremony, the priests consecrated two identical fires facing each other under the canopy. Paji seated himself exactly in the middle, a role model of impartiality. Hema seemed more interested in what was happening with Roopa's fire—she kept craning her neck to track the offerings made, perhaps to make sure our side wasn't being shortchanged. The separate streams of Sanskrit incantations merged into one and rose with the smoke into the air.

I had expected Biji to cry during the ceremony, but to my surprise, Paji's face turned ashen as well. He seemed mesmerized by the holy thread glistening across the priests' chests—every so often, he pulled out his handkerchief to dab at his lips. As soon as the seven circles were complete, he excused himself to go lie down, saying the smoke from the fire had gone into his eyes. I realized then that the chanting and the oblations had been more religion than Paji could take.

When it came time to throw the rice, Roopa cast it over her shoulder with such aplomb that I wondered if she had been practicing. The women behind her all closed their eyes and let it shower over them like an auspicious rain. Even her tears were perfect, stopping as if on cue midway down her cheeks, from where they could scintillate with maximum effect. "My eldest, my light, my life," Biji wailed, running with raised arms to hug her a second time before she got into the waiting flower-decked Fiat.

Then it was my turn, and the tears clung so thickly that I could barely make out the grains of rice on the platter to gather up in my fist. I let the rice run out behind my shoulder in farewell. The last time I cry, I said to myself, silently repeating the words my grandmother had taught me. I would shed no more tears for what I was leaving behind.

By now Biji had worked herself into a hysterical state, and was going around with her sari outstretched like a beggar. "Two," she kept repeating, like someone trying to explain the enormity of a tragedy, "two of them I'm losing tonight." She embraced me violently, and held me plugged into her chest, as if finally transferring a cache of affection she had been hoarding through the years. As my aunts pulled us apart, I noticed something unusual about her lips. They were the same shade as the bindi smudged across her forehead—my mother had broken down and applied lipstick to them.

Instead of a Fiat, what stood on the road awaiting me was a doli. Dev's family had owned it for generations. "Which century are these people from that they haven't chopped that thing up for firewood?" Paji had thundered, when I told him their custom of carrying their brides home in the wooden palanquin. "Haven't they heard of an invention called a car? Don't they know my daughter isn't some village illiterate they can parade around in a cage?"

What was decided, finally, was that I would be carried in the doli only to and from the truck transporting the women back to Nizamuddin. I could come out if I wanted and walk around on the truck bed, but between the time I relinquished my father's house and the instant I entered Dev's, my feet were not to touch the ground.

I looked at the faded animals and trees painted on the sides, at the worn handle carvings at the ends of the two poles, at the gold-bordered red cloth covering the doli's flat top. It seemed tiny, like something built for a doll. "You'll be comfortable once you're inside, don't worry," Dev's mother said as she helped me in. "Twelve miles they carried me in it when I was married, and not on a truck either, but on their shoulders." She undid the strings at the top of the opening. "Just remember to crouch a little like that—it's a good position for a bride to learn." I had one final glimpse of my mother being held back by her sisters at the gate before the flap came tumbling down.

It was not completely dark inside—light filtered in through a small grilled window in the front. I sat as Dev's mother had instructed, with my hands around my legs and my chin resting on my knees. The air was heavy with the odor of wood, wood that I imagined was perfumed with the hopes and fears of all the brides it had held over the years. I tried to feel the flutter in their hearts, see the anticipation on their faces, taste the salt in their tears. What must it have been like to leave their villages for the first time in this box, to be carried through valleys and jungles, over mountains and streams? To be delivered to an unknown destiny, revolving around a husband whose face one might never have seen?

Doli scenes from movies began to run through my head—scenes where the heroine cries, or sings a song, or even takes poison. Then, abruptly, the screen in my mind went white. It was as if a sudden, terrifying realization had burned right through the film in the projector. The realization that I wasn't in a movie, that I was no longer playacting. That I was an adult now, and this was my life.

Usually when one awakes from a dream, it is difficult to reconstruct the exact flow of events, since only a few vivid scenes might remain in one's memory. When the spell of the last several months finally broke that evening, I was not so fortunate. Every impulse I'd had, every game I'd played, every maneuver and juvenile ploy, unspooled with excruciating clarity through my head. Logically, step by unflinching step, I was guided through the exact sequence of actions that had led me to my crouch in that darkened interior.

Before I could fully absorb this new state of consciousness, the doli shuddered to life. I felt myself jostled forward, then back, as the poles on either end were lifted not quite simultaneously. There was an up-and-down bob, and a side-to-side jounce as well, and I pressed my palms flat against the walls to steady myself. Outside, as if to mock my awakening from the movies, the wedding band struck up a triumphant film tune. I imagined the uniformed musicians sweating as they walked along, blowing into their tubas, pumping their trombones. *"Every treasure in the sky,"* the song went, and I wished I could peel the top off to watch the stars drift over my head. Down below on earth, was my mother still there, had she broken free of my aunts to run tearfully behind? And my father—had he come out to watch, regret blooming inside, his stoniness crumbling as I was borne out of his sight?

But there was no direction to look except forward, through the window with the grille whose shadows left cross marks on my face. All that was visible was the pole extending over the shoulder of the short and sturdy bearer, a tassel swinging from its end as he strode away from my parents' house.

And then I was being loaded onto the platform of the truck. Eager eyes were peering through the window, trying to see the fabulous creature behind the grille. Children's fingers poked in to try and touch my face. I listed against the sides as the doli was pushed and rocked into place. The clinking of bracelets and the chatter of female voices surrounded me as the rest of the party climbed in. I heard the drop-down back of the truck being raised and slammed into place. Then, with the stars above still shining down invisibly on me, the truck began the journey to Nizamuddin.

chapter
five

THE ELECTRICITY WAS OUT ON DEV'S STREET. "IT'S GONE FOR THE NIGHT," Hema announced cheerfully. "We're one of the first ones they cut when the city runs out of power." She held a lit match under a candle to soften its base, then stuck it upright on the arm of a chair. "We're just a government colony, after all, not like the wealthy area where your father has his house."

I sat perched on a charpoy in the only bedroom in the flat, the long gunghat of my sari draped over my face like a veil. It was difficult to maintain the pose Dev's mother had taught me—the sagging of the charpoy ropes kept threatening to topple me. But the position felt as centering as a yoga asana—by concentrating on keeping steady on the bed, I was able to take my mind off the despair closing in on me.

"You can speak now, you know, even take your gunghat off. All the guests have gone. Though you'll have to show your face sooner or later—all those people who've been saying it's your sister who's the prettier one." Hema held up a candle near my head, filling the inside of my gunghat with light and trying to peer through. "Besides, you must be dying under there—not being used to having the fans all off. Tell me, is it true—Dev bhaiyya said you had an air conditioner at your house?"

We had two, one in the drawing room, and one in Paji's library, but I remained silent.

"Well, you at least had lots of servants, didn't you? Dev bhaiyya said your father made a lot of money as a publisher. Not that we don't have servants, mind you. Well, maybe not a servant exactly, but we do have a ganga—she comes in to clean the pots. No cook, though. Don't worry, we won't make you work. Not while you're a new bahu, anyway. When Sandhya didi was a new bahu, just married to Arya bhaiyya, she didn't have to step into our kitchen even once for the first month. Now Mataji makes her do all the cooking, of course—though between you and me, her rice clumps so much the ganga could do it better. I suppose we shouldn't expect you to be good either, being a rich man's girl and everything. I've already told my parents. When I get married, it's going to be to the wealthiest man they can find. Marry for comfort, that's what I want, not for love like you. Tell me though, is it true what you two did in the tomb? They were quite outraged, the Muslims, they're saying you defiled the grave. Even the stationmaster, Mr. Ahmed, said it was an insult to one of their Muslim saints."

I kept my gaze focused at my feet, willing my body to be absolutely still. Sweat trickled down my face and neck under the gunghat, but I didn't draw it back or take it off.

"You can tell me, I promise not to repeat it to anyone. Pushpa down the street says that you both were naked." Hema giggled. "Were you really? Babuji was called into Mr. Ahmed's office, you know. Given quite a firing."

"Hema, stop bothering the bahu," Dev's mother called out from the other room. "You've lit the candles, now come out here."

Hema dropped her voice to a whisper. "Even Arya bhaiyya was upset. He said Babuji should never have agreed to the marriage. He called you"—again, Hema giggled—"a tramp. He said your sister was trying to mesmerize his brother, was doing magic on him, and casting tantric spells. And when that didn't work, the family set you instead upon poor Dev bhaiyya." Hema's eyes widened. "Do you really know magic? Will you teach me your tricks?"

"Hema," my mother-in-law called again. "Stop that Dehradun Express tongue of yours and come right out."

"Coming, Mataji. But it was Dev bhaiyya who stood up for you. He was so kind, so brave. He said he felt pity for you—that it was his duty to marry you—if he didn't, your reputation was so ruined that nobody else would. He's always been the softhearted one—lets everyone take advantage of him. Anyway, we'll talk more tomorrow. Tonight this room is yours. Arya bhaiyya and Sandhya didi are sleeping with us in the other room, even though he's the elder brother. It's going to be tight. Plus all that rich wedding food must have given Didi gas again, and on top of that, she snores."

Hema fluffed up a pillow and laid it at my feet. "You have such pretty toes. But I guess that's what new brides are supposed to have, at least in the beginning. I'm sure my bhaiyya will be very impressed." She skipped to the door. "Enjoy this *special* night of yours."

I kept waiting on the bed after Hema left. At some point, I took the gunghat off, but the claustrophobia from the doli was not dispelled. Beyond the glow of the candle, the walls strained and tilted against the darkness, as if raring to come up and immure me. Pieces of furniture rose ponderously from the corners, their silhouettes radiating unspoken hostility. The moon seemed to have fallen victim to the blackout as well—only darkness filtered in through the bars of the window.

Perhaps I actually dozed off in my asana. The blast of a locomotive whistle jolted me awake. A train was thundering by on the tracks outside, so close that I expected a bogey to come crashing through the wall. Rectangles of light blazed through the room from its windows, like a series of camera flashes, lighting up a cupboard, a dressing table, picture frames, and, standing in his wedding garments just inside the doorway, Dev.

"Sorry it took so long," he said, as he tried closing the door. Strings of marigolds hung up for the wedding kept getting in the way. "They wouldn't let me leave." He scrunched the door shut over the marigolds, launching a flurry of petals into the air. "I hope Hema didn't fill your head with too many of her tales. Don't listen to anything she says."

I lowered my eyes and remained silent. Wasn't that the way a new bahu was supposed to behave? What choice did I have now anyway, except to try and ignore what Hema said? Perhaps I should slip the gunghat back over my head to look more bride-like, to be more traditional by covering the parting of my hair.

"What a long day," Dev said, and began unwinding the silk band tied in a turban around his head. More petals, pink and red this time from the wedding ceremony, fell to the floor from its brocaded folds. He unbuttoned his tunic and pulled it off as well. "Are you as exhausted as I am?"

I nodded my head without looking up. How strange that as a bride I was expected not to meet eyes with Dev. To not call him by name. Wasn't it just yesterday that we had eaten pineapple at Chandni Chowk, that I had been making jokes to his face? How little time I had spent with him since then. And now he was my husband, the man to whom I had been wed. My link to this house, this family, the trains clattering outside, the reason I sat perched on this bed. My head swam. How could my games have led to such enormous change?

"Aren't you going to take off your sari?" Dev asked, sitting beside me and running his fingers down its hem. He picked up a corner of the sari and playfully uncovered my blouse.

There was something cheering about his proximity, surprisingly, something reassuring about being finally alone with him. I allowed my gaze to rise to the level of his chin. His neck was the color of honey in the candlelight, there were no forgotten streaks of makeup tonight. The cotton of his undershirt cut swaths of white over his shoulders. I felt an urge to run my hand under the material, feel my fingertips separate cloth from skin. For a moment, we were back in the tomb of Salim Fazl. Anthers nodding provocatively in the dark corners of the room, corollas unfurling to form giant flowers.

Then Dev kissed me. It took me a few seconds to recognize the sugary odor of alcohol in his mouth. When I was seven, there had been a period when Paji staggered home late every night, when he always seemed to have that same odor on his breath. I stiffened and shifted towards the lower edge of the bed.

"Vijay uncle brought along a bottle of whiskey. It was only a sip—

I had to, for politeness' sake." I sat in silence, remembering Biji's anger towards Paji, her recriminations and threats. Dev tried to touch my shoulder, but I eased it out of the way.

"Tell me, have you ever slept on a charpoy before?" he asked after a moment of silence. I shook my head sullenly. They were only good enough for servants where I came from, I felt like retorting. "Let me show you something then." I looked in bewilderment out of the corner of my eye as Dev started bobbing up and down on the bed.

"Arya bhaiyya and I used to do this in the charpoy we shared when we were small. Sometimes we'd set Hema in the center and try to launch her into the air." He began bouncing more vigorously, and I wondered how drunk he was. "It's better without the mattress, though—here, let me take it out."

Dev pulled out the mattress from under us and threw it on the floor. The wooden frame creaked in protest as he pitched himself against the bare ropes. "We'd sometimes stand up and use it as a trampoline, but that never worked. I don't know how many beatings we got from Babuji for breaking the ropes."

It was such an incongruous sight that despite myself, I began to laugh. My husband, the bouncing groom. Could I have married a boy at heart? Surely life shouldn't be too awful with someone as playful as that. Dev started laughing as well. "You can do it too, you know, from the other end."

He cheered in encouragement as I joined in. Was this what marriage was about, bouncing together on the bed? "Press down each time I go up," he instructed, and I felt our rebounds increase in strength. With each surge, something else got dislodged and fell away from my thoughts—Hema, the doli, the whiskey, the marriage ceremony. I started feeling buoyant and carefree, as if I was back with Sharmila on the seesaws we used to ride in Rawalpindi at the midsummer fair.

Then I missed my cue and descended when I should have risen. The motion sent me toppling into Dev's arms. I was still laughing when I realized he had pulled me free of my blouse. My breasts spilled out against his chest, and he raised me up to take the left one in his mouth.

It was a shock to look down and see my flesh encircled by his lips. My body had never been handled with such a casual sense of ownership before. I tried to lean backwards to pull myself out, but Dev was holding me too tight. I felt him suck my nipple, felt his tongue lap clumsily over my skin. Then he let go to grab the other breast and taste that as well.

"Meera," Dev said, and I was careful not to let the dismay rise to my face. "How long I've wanted . . ."

He began pulling out the sari from around my waist, throwing it to the ground in great handfuls, like wrapping paper torn off a wedding present. He lay me flat on the charpoy and worked my petticoat off. His hardness pressed against me in several spots, like a finger testing the ripeness of a fruit. Then he entered me.

That day in the tomb, the day the warmth had sprung up and risen from between my legs, I had become aware of another sensation. A deep-rooted craving, a hidden emptiness, that had opened up in the same part of my body. Now, the thought that first flashed through my mind was that this emptiness was going to be filled. That this nameless yearning would be appeased, that waves of satiation would radiate everywhere else.

What spread through me, however, the instant I felt Dev inside, was not satiation but pain. Pain so unexpected, pain so vivid, that I squeezed his shoulders and arched my pelvis away to be free of it.

Perhaps Dev mistook this reaction for pleasure, because he licked his tongue across my neck. "Meera," he whispered, and rose until he was almost out, then plunged back deeper in. I tried once again to shrink away, but the ropes beneath me prevented my escape. "Meera," Dev gasped, as he thrashed over me again and again. The charpoy began bucking to a new rhythm as its ropes cut into my skin.

Afterwards, he flopped onto the charpoy next to mine. "You're so wonderful," he said. "I can hardly believe you're mine. You look like your sister in so many ways, and yet you seem so much simpler inside." He kissed me on the forehead and blew the candle out.

I stared at the night hanging outside the window. There was still no moon in sight. I felt the sting of rope burns on my back and remembered my mattress still lay on the floor somewhere. Did I have the energy to drag it back myself or should I ask Dev for help?

He lay quite still next to me, his face turned towards the ceiling. "Don't you wonder what she's doing right now?" he murmured. "Roopa. Whether she'll be happy with the life she's chosen or think she's made a mistake?" He remained on his back for some moments, then turned over on his side.

I AWOKE BATHED IN LIGHT, and thought for an instant it was day, that I had survived the night. But then I saw the naked bulb in the ceiling shining in my face—the electricity had come back on at some point. Dev lay sprawled out on his stomach next to me, his mouth resting open on his hand, as though preparing to bite a knuckle in his sleep. A table fan whirred from a stool in the corner, twisting its head methodically from side to side like someone performing a neck exercise. Through the window, a railway station had materialized in the distance, its empty platforms glowing with a ghostly fluorescence.

There was a dark spot of blood on the petticoat I had put back on. My cheeks burned with embarrassment when I saw it. What if Dev had noticed it as well? I remembered the first time it had happened. "Pay attention, because I'll only show you once," I heard Biji say as she tore off a piece from an old pajama and led me to the toilet. Why tonight, when it wasn't the right time of the month?

I got up to clean myself. Wrapping the sheet like a shawl over my blouse, I crept through the darkened room next to ours. Hema was snoring on a mattress near the outer door, but I was able to open it enough to just squeeze by. There was still no moon, but enough illumination from the street now for the dirt ground within the courtyard walls to gleam a peculiar yellow. An extra charpoy rested stacked against a wall, next to a hand-cranked pump, and the wooden post where Hema said they had once kept a cow tethered.

The toilet was built in one corner, a short cement stall raised three steps above the ground. An old cockroach, its wings bedraggled, shuffled into a crack next to the footrests when I turned on the light. Under a tap in the wall stood an empty tin of cooking oil, its top cut open so it could serve as a mug. A faint smell of phenol hovered in the air, trying vainly to conceal the underlying reek of waste.

I squatted and washed myself, then my petticoat, as best I could. There was less blood than I thought—could it have been an injury received during the sexual act? I opened the door and stepped into the fresh air. Was this something recurrent one had to endure?

Standing at the bottom of the steps, his undershirt gleaming in the night, was Dev. I looked at him in surprise. "I just went to . . ." I began to say, then stopped. The shadows on his face were thicker, the pattern of muscle more pronounced. The shoulders sprouted tufts of hair.

Arya stared at the sheet that barely covered my blouse, at the wetness that blossomed down my petticoat. He took a step towards me, his jaw set in a line, his eyes devoid of expression. For an instant, as I squeezed past with my sheet gathered tightly around, I thought he was going to reach out and grab my arm. But he stayed where he was, not stepping aside to make my passage easier, but not making a move to impede me, either.

My heart beating, I returned to the bedroom and turned off the light. I thought I heard the sound of the gate to the street being opened and closed. I kept listening for Arya's footsteps in the adjoining room, but he didn't return. I arranged my petticoat loosely over my legs so that the fan could blow on it. When I awoke again, to the receding call of a train, the dampness was gone.

FOR THE NEXT FEW DAYS both my dowry and I were on display.

Early the first morning, Hema burst into the room, saying that the handcart pushers from the factory had arrived with the refrigerator Paji had sent. After several absurd attempts to push it through the tiny kitchen opening, Arya had the men set it down in the living room instead. Mataji lit incense to welcome it, as she would a new member of the household, Babuji broke a coconut at its feet, and Arya marked a red holy mark with vermilion on its forehead.

Dev's family had asked for a Kelvinator fridge, but Paji had refused to pay for a foreign brand, saying it would be an Indian-made Godrej and nothing else. Ardeshir Godrej had become famous by finding a way to make soap out of vegetable oil instead of the animal tallow so offensive to many Hindus. His brother had expanded the company rapidly after Independence, branching to talcums and toiletries, large steel cupboards, and very recently, appliances. The fridge Paji had managed to procure was a prototype, not even available for general sale as yet. "I hope they had the sense to get at least the important parts from England," Babuji remarked, as he peered skeptically into the freezer.

Hema went up and down the block, announcing to everyone that the fridge (the first one in the colony) had finally been delivered. Somewhat spitefully, she even told the stationmaster's family next door that henceforth, they would be able to ask for ice at any time they wanted. At one point, fifteen neighbors (mostly children) were milling around in the living room, gawking at Hema playing with the compartments and trays and knobs. The crowd lost interest somewhat when they found out that the ice cubes Hema had promised might not be ready for several hours. One of them tried to climb the shelves to get at the freezer, at which point Babuji used an umbrella to swat them away.

By teatime, the radiogram had been delivered as well. The enormous cabinet housing the components was made of a fine-grained wood stained so dark it was almost black. Mataji declared the color inauspicious, and suggested painting it something more cheery, like red. Hema wanted to alert the neighbors again, but wasn't able to tear herself from the gramophone, on which she kept playing the same film record over and over again. She hadn't listened to it for two years, ever since the family gramophone had broken, she explained. Babuji seemed taken at first by the multiple shortwave channels of the radio and the glow of the tubes inside. Later, however, he complained to Arya that they could have repaired the gramophone, that the old radio had been just fine. "It's mostly wood, this radiogram—why didn't we ask for more money instead?"

Me, they exhibited mostly in the bedroom. Each morning, Mataji selected the sari and jewelry set I was to wear that day, from the dowry chest I had brought with me. She was the one who orchestrated the viewings, making sure my gunghat was in position before the visitors entered, smiling proudly when they commented on the beauty of my ornaments (and, just as often, me). "Truly, Dev has brought Lakshmi to your house," the women said, and a few reached out to appraise the heft of the gold in my bracelet or the size of the jewels in my necklace (one of them even pretending to brush back my hair in place so she could get a better look at my earrings). "Such full cheeks. Such nice eyes. And not too dark-complexioned, just right." The questions they asked me were like those one might put to a child—what was my name, where did I come from, how I liked it in Nizamuddin. Afterwards, Mataji led them on a tour of the refrigerator and the radiogram and the kitchen utensils, tantalizing them with the myriad feats of magic reputedly possible with the pressure cooker (another first for the colony, this time imported in its entirety from England). "All we really wanted was Meera, but look how they insisted, look how they've given us so much," she said.

It was good that there was so much activity those first days in my in-laws' house, since it prevented me from steeping in regret every waking moment. Mataji must have understood what I was going through, because she quickly started introducing chores into my day. She would notice me staring balefully at Dev as he sat down to his evening liquor with Babuji and Arya, and quickly pull out a soda water bottle from the fridge. "Tell them to roll it over their foreheads before they open it. The way Babuji keeps grumbling about the fridge—it will remind him how warm his drinks were before you came."

Every time I entered the toilet and braced myself for a cockroach to scramble over my feet or whir into my face ("The old one's Shyamu," Hema informed me. "You can kill the ones that fly, but not him"), I thought back fondly to the clean white tiles of bathrooms past. I smelled rich curries and Basmati biryanis each evening as I tried to plow through the clods of Sandhya's rice on my plate. The sound of children playing outside transported me to the park in Darya Ganj where Sharmila and I played badminton every summer and flew kites in the spring. I even pictured myself back in Paji's dreaded library, standing in the cold rush of the air-conditioning vents, each time the electricity failed in Nizamuddin.

Most agonizing of all was not knowing when I would see my parents again. Mataji had made no mention of it, although it was clear from her supervision that I was not to venture out by myself. I was too timid to ask her directly, though Hema somehow zeroed in on what was on my mind. "Everyone knows the bride isn't supposed to return to her father's house for three months," she declared. "Didn't you see that movie? Suraiya goes back after only five weeks and her husband gets bitten by a snake and drops dead.

"Don't think your mother can just come by whenever she wants to see you either. She's from the girl's side, so she needs a proper invitation from us before she can show her face here. And who knows how many months it will be before Mataji and I both agree it's time?"

ON MY THIRD EVENING in Nizamuddin, I decided to escape. The idea materialized on the spur of the moment—Mataji was with Hema in the kitchen, berating Sandhya for not browning the onions enough, and the men were all in the living room, their voices already a little unsteady, and punctuated by the pops of soda bottles. Why not sneak out to Darya Ganj while nobody was looking? Perhaps never to come back? My heart began racing at the prospect. I could be sitting on our terrace in less than an hour, enjoying guavas plucked freshly from the tree downstairs. My incarnation as a bride left behind like a spent nightmare—from which I could cull the more harrowing tidbits anytime I wanted to frighten Sharmila.

Then I felt a pang of regret. How to retrieve my dowry? For an instant, I wondered if I could gather up all the jewelry and saris and sling them over my shoulder in a bundle when I left. But there was no way to access the trunk in the bedroom unseen. Besides, it wasn't as if I could tote along the radiogram or fridge. The only choice was to leave everything behind.

The actual getaway turned out to be smooth and quick. I walked along the courtyard perimeter to the gate, pretending to examine the dung fuel cakes stuck to the walls, left over from the time the family had owned a cow. The doors opened at a nudge, the chain clinking noisily, the wood groaning like something alive. But nobody seemed to notice, no voice called out to challenge me even when I stepped across the threshold and closed the doors behind.

It was dark already, but I blinked, as if emerging into bright sunlight. The air was thick with the pungency of chilies being fried in rancid oil—this, I told myself, was the scent of freedom, of liberty. I allowed myself to be swept towards the station in a surge of elation, gliding over the muddy street in my red and gold bridal regalia, the folds of my sari held raised so that the embroidered border didn't get dirty. The vegetable hawkers beamed at me from behind their baskets, their tomatoes shiny and ruddy-cheeked in approval, their eggplants glistening vibrantly in encouragement. I passed the shops selling metal parts, the shanty huts made of gunnysack, the line of rickshaws by the station—all sights familiar from my days of stalking Roopa and Dev. How long ago had that been—years maybe, centuries even? Would this be the last time I set eyes on them? Rummaging through the garbage heap behind the station was the same brown and white cow I had petted so many times for good luck. It interrupted its activity to look up and nod as if in recognition, a wedge of watermelon rind in its mouth forming an enormous green grin.

I stood outside the station steps, contemplating the best way to proceed. I still had the rupee coin Sharmila had pressed into my palm for good luck at the wedding. Was that enough for a rickshaw to Darya Ganj? Or should I take a bus—one of the brightly painted vehicles spewing exhaust fumes opposite the station, the conductors shouting out routes through the windows to cram in as many passengers as they could? There was also a local train that ran during the day, but I didn't know if it went close to where we lived.

Then a more alarming question occurred to me. Even if I made it to Darya Ganj, what was to say that Biji would take me in? Hadn't she always impressed upon us that a woman's place was by her husband, that he was her god, her Shiva, her pati-parameshwar? "Good or bad, she must accept him as her fate," I heard her intone. I remembered all the times she had related to us the tale of Sati, who threw herself in a fire when her husband Shiva was insulted. A strange intensity would light up in Biji's eyes each time she got to the part where the pyre was being prepared, as if this was a test to which she herself aspired, just to prove her mettle. I thought of all the bitterly unhappy years of Biji's own marriage through which she had stuck by my father's side. What if I appeared at her doorstep and she turned me away?

But there was always Paji, who didn't believe in such things. Paji, who had tried to change Biji's views so tirelessly. Paji, who quoted Jung and John Stuart Mill, who read out entire chapters from volumes written by Nehru to his daughter, to teach us we were equal to men. Except could it be possible that he wielded these texts so zealously to convince not us but himself? Hadn't he been the one, after all, with the final say in my marriage, the one who had ultimately said yes? The one who had contracted to hand me over to Dev's family even as he told me exactly what I could expect? "One hundred and ten rupees for the pressure cooker, two thousand for the refrigerator, eighteen hundred for the radiogram," I heard him recite, each figure enunciated with a chilling preciseness. "And that doesn't even include the jewelry or the twenty thousand in cash." If he had spent so much to give me away, why would he now want me back?

I had nowhere left to go, I realized. The only house that remained open to me was the one I had just left behind. All around me people flagged down rickshaws, boarded buses, scurried over tracks to catch trains. Was I the only one without a destination? No matter to whom I turned—relatives or friends or neighbors, what was to prevent my parents from finding out and returning me to Nizamuddin?

"New bride?" It was an old woman on the station steps, squatting with a group of other villagers while the men crowded around the ticket window. Thick silver rings adorned her fingers and her nose, and her gold earrings were so heavy that elongated holes had opened up in her lobes. "So pretty," she said, in a rural dialect of Hindi. "Such a pretty dress. But what are you doing here alone? Where's your husband? Did he go to get tickets too?"

I looked at her, unable to speak. Could this be it? The single point that my existence had been reduced to? Where my husband was, and why wasn't I with him? Was this the essence, the distillation, of all those years of Biji's intonations? Why I wasn't next to my god, my pati, my parameshwar? I started to suffocate at the unfairness of it, my necklace tightening around my throat, my sari weighing on me like a shroud. The woman on the steps looked up in concern, then rose and caught my arm in case I should fall.

"It'll be fine," she said, pressing a palm soothingly against my cheek. Her skin smelled of old tea leaves. "He'll be here before you know it. He's probably around somewhere, watching over you even when you think he isn't. Just tell him not to leave you alone next time, such a pretty bride."

I gazed at the wrinkles rippling her face, like tidemarks on sand. Tiny blue tattoos ran along her forehead below her hairline. In her eyes was the gift of empathy, a solidarity that I could not bear to accept. "May God always keep you with husband," she said, and began to run her hand over my head in blessing.

I didn't wait for her to finish. I tore away and ran back up the street, not caring where I stepped, not worrying whether my sari got soiled. The stallkeepers gaped at me as I stumbled by in my bridal finery—their laughter lingering behind in the air. I had been gone for twenty minutes, maybe twenty-five, but Dev's entire family was pacing outside on the street. "There she is!" Mataji cried, and rushed me inside, as if I was diseased or naked or raving and had to be whisked away from the neighbors' eyes.

EVERYONE GATHERED IN the courtyard to witness my court-martial. Babuji even dragged his chair and drink table out of the living room for a better view. Dev stood next to his mother, looking at the ground so he wouldn't accidentally catch my eye.

"As it is, all of Nizamuddin has heard rumors about your exploits at the tomb," Mataji began. "And now the wedding fire hasn't even cooled and you decide to further distinguish yourself? What were you thinking?"

"Yes, what?" Hema chimed in, as from behind her, Sandhya glared at me silently as if incensed over a personal affront. Babuji muttered that of course the bahu thought she could act as she wanted—after all, hadn't her father bought them a fridge?

"Running off without your husband, roaming God knows where. What must people have imagined—a young woman decking herself up and parading up and down the street like that?" Mataji stepped forward, to hit me, I thought, but instead grabbed my wrist and squeezed it hard. "Aren't there enough tongues you've sent wagging already, enough insinuations we've had to hear? Did you even stop to think what new scandal the Ahmeds next door will make up out of this?"

"The Ahmeds," Babuji nodded, taking another gulp of his whiskey. "Tell the bahu how good these Muslims are at cooking up gossip."

"I just wanted to take a walk, to look around," I said, knowing even as I spoke the words that the guilt on my face would give me away.

"What do you think, this is Connaught Place, that you can—" Mataji began to say, then stopped. Visible under my fingers, which had opened up under the tightness of her grip, was the gleaming edge of the coin from Sharmila. Before anyone could react, Hema had pried it out of my hand.

"Look," Hema cried, holding it triumphantly in the air. "A whole rupee she was running away with."

Mataji let go of my hand. "I suppose you're now going to tell us you went to buy samosas? That you had a sudden hankering for fruit mix?" She shook her head in disappointment. "Tell me, have we been mistreating you here that you have to hide things like that? Have we been feeding you on potato peelings or forcing you to haul bricks on your head? What have we required of you anyway but to sit on the bed all day and look pretty while Hema and Sandhya and I slave away?" She took the coin from Hema's hand. "In this house, we don't hide things. We don't keep pockets of money stashed around secretly. I'll hold this for you for safekeeping. I hope you can at least trust me with this."

"I'm sure Meera didn't mean anything—" Dev finally said, but Mataji raised a hand to cut him off.

"Look, Bahu. We're not the kind of family that believes in mistreating our daughters-in-law. Locking them up or starving them or beating them into submission. We're modern people. You're free to do what you want, go where you feel. Leave if you wish. All we ask is that you remember one thing. How you conduct yourself, what you do, reflects not only on you but on all of us. The reputation of the entire family sits balanced on your head."

"Yes," said Hema. "Remember that. Always."

"I'm sure she will," Dev said, taking my arm. He hustled me past Mataji and Babuji, past Hema with her gloating smirk, past the inscrutable expression on Arya's face and Sandhya's continuing glare.

THAT FRIDAY, HEMA PUT "Light the Fire of Your Heart" on the radiogram. The family had been gathering after dinner each evening to hear Dev sing duets with K. L. Saigal. It was uncanny how close Dev's voice was to Saigal's, how precise was his reproduction of every intonation, every pitch. Dev stood next to the gramophone at the beginning of the record, so that it sounded like twins singing together, then slowly circled around to the opposite point in the room. If I kept my eyes closed, it was only the orchestra that gave the recorded side away.

My failed attempt at running away had driven home an inescapable truth: there were no alternatives left to me, my only hope was with Dev. He was the one with the key to my happiness, my existence was now cuffed to his. He had asked me no questions that evening, just sat me on the bed and brought ice water from the fridge. "Don't ever think of leaving me—I love you too much," he'd said. As the sips had slipped down to cool my throat, I had looked at his head in my lap. He was handsome and not unkind, I had told myself, he had his boyishness, his charm. He too was coping with the newness of marriage—couldn't I be the one adjusting my needs to his? How much easier everything would be if I could believe Dev loved me and I was truly in love with him. I had clung to him that night as he satisfied himself, and tried to rise above the pain. One day, I promised myself, I would find the words to give voice to what I wanted. To take him back to the tomb that day, to the furtiveness we had shared. To proceed from there in slow, unhurried advances, and see if we reached somewhere else.

I resolved to look for the positive in Dev. To search for seedlings that

I could nurture over time so that they bloomed eventually into fondness, into attachment. Every evening I waited for Hema to play "Light the Fire." What better way to recharge myself than to relive the moment of first hearing Dev? I imagined the music swelling up under and around me, the lyrics weightless as clouds carrying me aloft. I would float on them to the same heights as before, and feel a resurgence in my affection for Dev.

But the clouds never arrived. Instead of soaring, what I felt when I finally heard Dev sing that Friday was a stoniness that weighed me down. Could this really be the song that had changed my life, was this the voice that had mesmerized me that January day? Would this be all I had to work with, the magic remedy that was supposed to revive and rejuvenate? *"Light the fire of your heart,"* Dev sang, and the words now had an oppressive edge to them—their import no longer an invitation but a command, an imperative. I knew I had to succeed for my happiness, for my very survival. The realization that I might not plunged me into despair.

I closed my eyes as I had for every song and waited for Dev to begin to circle around. This time, he stopped somewhere midway through his arc. *"Draw closer and take my hand,"* he sang, and I felt an overwhelming urge to flee the room. To cower outside and cover my ears with my palms so that I could keep his lyrics out. *"Lead me to a life with less heartbreak,"* he urged, loudly and more insistently, and I realized he had not moved. As I opened my eyes, I knew what I would see—Dev standing in front, singing directly to me.

Through all my time in Nizamuddin, through the nights with Dev and the days of being a new bride, one thing I had been proud of was keeping the promise I had made before getting into the doli. I had not cried. No matter how suffocated I felt, no matter how homesick or miserable, I had not allowed myself to shed any tears. But perhaps it wasn't true, perhaps I had been weeping all along, because now when I saw Dev, the tears came surging from some hidden reservoir behind my eyes. *"Only love can bring back the light,"* he sang, and I felt huge wracking sobs begin to shudder and break away from deep inside. I looked about in panic, trying to squelch them before they rose, trying to thwart them from reaching my lungs or exploding in my throat. All around the room, Dev's family stood motionless in place, like an audience waiting patiently for the promised spectacle to unfold. Where were the nautch girls to distract them now, Nehru to turn off the electricity, Gandhiji to point out the way for my escape?

But Gandhiji did not appear, the lights stayed on, the spate was not deterred. I cried, savoring the voluptuous joy of each sob, letting the rivulets run unimpeded down my cheeks, allowing all my bottled-up regret to break free. *"Only love,"* Dev concluded, flourishing dramatically towards my tears, like a circus ringmaster flaunting the success of a particularly difficult and exotic trick.

"I almost cried myself," Hema said to me later. "I had no idea you loved him so much."

Hema wasn't the only one impressed by my crying that evening. What happened, paradoxically, was that my tears (of happiness, they all nodded) suddenly endeared me to everyone. Mataji forgave, and seemed to forget, my escapade of running away. She started bringing me presents (a tin of talcum powder, a jar of Pond's cold cream) which I was to keep hidden in my dowry trunk and not let Sandhya see. One sunny day, she even set me up on a charpoy in the courtyard and massaged coconut oil into my hair.

Babuji began saying nice things about the refrigerator, as if afraid that he had hurt my feelings. "Such perfect ice cubes," he proclaimed, even when they were squat and misshapen because Hema had been too lazy to fill the trays all the way. "Such a pleasing color, white. Mark my words, it will have a long life. Tell your Mr. Godrej that with people like him, the country will be on its way."

Hema announced that from now on we would be inseparable, and took me around to introduce me to all her friends. "I could see, the very first time I laid eyes on Meera didi, that she was going to be the elder sister I never had." Even Arya stopped scrutinizing me as he had done that first night in the dark. Before our eyes could meet now, he moved aside politely to let me pass.

The only person who was not moved by my tears (or, for that matter, my dowry) was Sandhya. "What to do?" Hema said, as she chewed on a cube of ice, a habit she had developed, much to everyone's irritation, soon after the fridge arrived. "Her father wasn't rich like yours—lost even what little they had in the Partition. Arya found them in the refugee camp. Her mother had managed to hold on to some earrings—so they wrapped them up, calling it her dowry, and sent her off. Couldn't even afford to buy me a proper sari, let alone get me a necklace or bracelet. Now it's been eight years and it looks like her womb is constipated as well. She's lucky we're not a low-class family, or we'd have thrown her out on the street long ago."

At first, Sandhya refused to touch food put in the refrigerator, but when that became impractical, it was only the ice she boycotted. Once, when Mataji asked her why she wasn't using the new pressure cooker to prepare the chickpeas, she ran out of the kitchen, crying. She was careful not to show any outward hostility, only a lingering sullenness, that slipped into her voice and expression every time she had to converse with me.

Each morning after her bath, I would see Sandhya in the courtyard, performing her pooja of Arya. She would swirl an earthenware lamp resting on a round metal thali in a circle before Arya's face, as one might in front of a picture at a shrine. She would mark his forehead with ash from the platter, and sometimes dab on some vermilion and a moistened grain of rice. She would bend her head and wait for him to color the parting in her hair with a line of the vermilion. Then she would bend even lower to touch his feet—first the right, then the left. She would run the same hand over her head to bless herself as she began to rise.

The first time I saw this pooja, I stood in the kitchen transfixed. The touching of feet was a ritual strictly forbidden by Paji in our house. "All this scraping, all this servility—hasn't anyone in this country heard of human dignity? Aren't there enough gods in the temples already to satisfy this national hunger for groveling? We spent two centuries licking the boots of the British—did you ever see *them* go around prostrating themselves at anyone's feet?"

Our cousins, of course, had all been taught to perform the ritual at the beginning and end of every visit to show respect to their elders. Paji would yank their heads back up the instant they started to bend. "Did you drop something?" he would demand. "Are you preparing to do push-ups? You can look around on the floor all you want, but I'll slap you if you touch my feet."

For a while when we were young, Biji tried to force us to go through the ritual when Paji was not around. "You insolent daughter of an owl, I don't care what your father says, I'll break every bone in your body if you don't touch your grandmother's feet." At other times, she would try to cajole us. "It's a mark of respect, nothing else. What's the harm in bowing before wisdom, before age?" She would tell us stories from the Mahabharata and the Ramayana to further her argument, such as the one where Bharat kept his brother's sandals on the throne when Ram was exiled into the forest. "It's part of our culture, something that's come down to us from the ages," she would say. "It's a dignified custom—you should perform it proudly, not be ashamed."

Once Paji found out, he quickly put an end to Biji's efforts. "What can one expect—the children in her village had to wash their parents' feet and drink the water afterwards in respect. Is that what she's going to teach you to do next?" During the first years, Paji told us, there was a time when Biji wouldn't eat anything in the morning until she had touched his feet. "She would tell me I was her lord, her protector, her provider, and she couldn't start the day without my blessing. When I stopped her, she would pull my shoes out from under the bed and perform her ceremony over them. When I hid those, she started waiting until I was in the bath, to touch my house slippers instead. It was years before I could break her of the habit, before I could keep footwear lying around unlocked again."

One morning, while I was watching Sandhya, Mataji walked up behind me. "She comes from a very uncomplicated family. She's a very obedient girl. She hasn't been able to conceive, the poor thing—you should see all the fasts she keeps for that. I suppose it could be worse, though, she could have given us a series of girls."

Mataji sighed. "It's horrible what we women have to go through. How discouraging it is to know one can't change the world. But perhaps such things arise from a wisdom deeper than ours. Perhaps they're necessary to keep the world running smoothly. One day soon I hope for her sake that God will hear her prayers. Do you know, we used to do the pooja together every morning before our husbands left for work? I'd come out and the ingredients would be waiting for me, all decorated on a thali—sometimes with hibiscus plucked fresh from the bush outside, sometimes with jasmine—I never knew which it would be. Now, of course, my back's gone and I can't even bend."

Mataji sighed again. "But you're still young." She turned me around to examine me, then pulled up the edge of my sari from my shoulders to drape it more modestly over my head. "Dev is your husband now. It's such a beautiful ritual—why don't you think about performing it for him as well?"

THE SLEEPING ARRANGEMENTS SOON CHANGED. It seemed indecent to keep monopolizing the bedroom Arya had lent us, especially since with the new fridge and radiogram, the front room had become too small for five people to squeeze in. So Dev and I moved out after the first week and spent a few days sleeping under the stars. But it was September, and there were showers lingering around, which sent us running indoors for shelter one night. We ended up sharing the bedroom after that, with Arya and Sandhya on the charpoys, and Dev and I on talais on the floor.

Although the talais were thin enough to be mats rather than mattresses, I decided they were still preferable to the charpoys. For one thing, they didn't sag; for another, they put an end to the nightly bouncing, which was no longer playful but had become Dev's way of signaling it was time for sex. The loss of privacy meant that it was too difficult to initiate anything now, a development in which I pretended to share Dev's disappointment. Once, he did begin to take my clothes off when he thought the other two had gone to sleep. Every rustle seemed to get unbearably magnified in the confines of the room, however, and he had to stop when Sandhya suddenly sat up in bed.

Each night, Arya and Sandhya preceded us into the bedroom, while Dev and I pretended to be occupied outside. We chatted with his parents or listened to the radio, stealing glances at the light visible under the door. As soon as it went out, we sneaked in to our talais in the dark, trying our best to maintain the illusion of privacy. I stopped drinking water after nine and made sure my bladder was completely empty, since it was such an onerous journey to the toilet at night. No matter what the temperature, even when the electricity was out and there was no fan, Sandhya was always swaddled in a sheet, every part of her body meticulously concealed. Although Arya was often awake, sitting up in his undershirt and smoking a cigarette, there were never any good nights exchanged.

About once a week, the light under the door did not go out so readily. Mataji ushered us all into the courtyard on such occasions, and smacked Hema when she wondered aloud if this was the night she would finally become an aunt. We were also led outside when Arya and Sandhya were engaged in a fight. Once, Arya came storming through the courtyard where we sat and strode out of the house, returning only the next afternoon. Sandhya was cocooned as usual when we crept inside, but the next morning I saw her left eye was swollen shut. I was about to say something, but Mataji restrained me, whispering that it was about the lack of a child. She had me get some ice from the refrigerator which she wordlessly handed to Sandhya after wrapping it in a handkerchief.

I was always uncomfortable around my brother-in-law. At night, despite every precaution, our eyes sometimes met in the dark. He would capture my gaze and I would feel steadily drawn in, as if I was at the end of a line he was reeling in. What made me so uneasy was that I could never determine what he was thinking. He seemed to be biding his time before revealing his intentions, his cultivated elusiveness wicking all emotion away from his face. Some mornings, I would hear him rouse himself at 4 a.m. and put on his shirt in the dark. He would be away for about two hours, and go back to sleep when he returned. Dev had never been very specific in his answers to my queries about what Arya did, and I had ceased to ask.

I expected there to be reciprocation with the bedroom arrangement —that we would be the ones invited to go in first some night, giving Hema a chance to extend her innuendos to us as well. But Arya never offered, and Dev never asked—perhaps he was too shy, or too proud, or too deferential. Instead, he started drawing his talai next to mine every night so that we could snuggle together in the dark. I would feel him ease under my sheet and nuzzle his face against the nape of my neck, one arm wrapping around my chest, the other forming a cradle between the pillow and my head.

Sometimes, we would fall asleep in this position. One night, it started to rain, and drops from the windowsill spattered us awake. "Leave it open," Dev whispered, as I began to get up to close the window. "We've endured much worse sleeping outside." He turned me around so that my face was next to his. Beads of water streaked by to disappear into the pillow between us—I could feel them landing in our hair, on our skin.

Dev kissed me, and I could taste the rain on his lips. He started to peel back the sheet from my body, but stiffened and let go as Arya snorted in his sleep behind him.

"One day we'll have a place of our own. Soon, I promise." An engine whistled in the distance as if to endorse his words. "We'll move to Bombay, that's what we'll do. I've always dreamt of going there. We'll ask Babuji to get us a ticket from his railway quota for the Frontier Mail."

I imagined reclining on one of the green cushioned first-class seats, the kind that turned into sleepers at night. Waving goodbye to Hema and Arya and everyone else on the platform, as the train eased smoothly out of Nizamuddin. "We could go see the monsoon," I said. "I've heard that the rain falls in sheets there." From somewhere came the rumble of bogies picking up speed, or perhaps it was just the sound of quickening rain.

"And I could meet all the movie music directors in their studios—perhaps even the same ones Saigal must have auditioned for, years ago. If only I could get them to hear me just once, I know our future would be made."

Dev began caressing my hair, gathering the beads of water between his fingers and sliding them down towards my shoulders. He smoothed out the strands sticking to my forehead, pushing them away from my eyes. "Of course it's just a dream. It's such an expensive city, there'd be no way to live."

"We could manage somehow," I said carelessly, turning my head upside down to face the window. Through the cascade of raindrops bouncing off the sill, I could see the Frontier Mail on its freedom run. Its whistle sounding joyously, its engine barreling through fields and villages, its long black plume of smoke unwinding against the sky like calligraphy.

"Perhaps if we could get a flat there, it wouldn't be so bad," Dev said, as he squeezed my tresses dry between his palms. He arranged them in a sunburst around my head and looked down at me lovingly. A flash passed over his face, as if an idea had just struck him, as if inspiration had just bubbled up to the surface. "You could ask your father for help."

THE FIRST TIME MATAJI let me speak to my parents was the morning after I cried over Dev's song. "You're very lucky," she said to me. "How many people in the whole of Delhi must have a telephone at home? When I was married, it wasn't until I went back three months later that I heard my mother's voice." She pulled out an anna coin from a pouch under her sari and gave it to Hema. "It's three paise for a call from what I can remember. Be sure to bring me back one paisa worth of salt."

The telephone was in the ration shop, in the other direction from the station. Hema scampered ahead to a jewelry stall. "Look, red bangles, twelve for an anna—we could get four each if you decided to forgo your call." She lost interest in them when I told her she could dial the number, something she had not done before.

Biji answered the phone. She had never quite managed to get the hang of the receiver, and her voice rose and faded as she tried speaking into each end. Hema crowded in close to me—having dialed the number, she now felt entitled to listen in on the call.

"My daughter, my Meera," Biji cried, bursting into tears once she recognized who was on the phone. I felt a weight in my chest as I heard her weep, but also a detachment, as if the physical distance between us had opened up an emotional separation as well. "The house is so empty now. All of a sudden I feel so old." It was true, I realized with a twinge—Biji did sound strangely aged over the phone.

Paji was composed and formal. He wanted to know if the refrigerator had arrived, and how the radiogram played. The pressure cooker, he cautioned me, could be dangerous if the lid was not locked securely in place. He hoped Dev and his parents were in good health and asked me to convey his regards to them. In turn, I asked him to give my love to Sharmila. I was about to hang up when I remembered Hema standing next to me, all ears. "And don't worry about me," I added. "They treat me really well—everyone's so caring here."

By now, Mataji had confirmed what Hema had claimed—it was considered too inauspicious for me to visit my parents so soon after the marriage. "Settle in first, make this home your own, and then you can even go stay a few nights," she said. When I broached the subject of having Biji come over instead, Mataji explained that in their family, the first such visit was only permitted on special festival days. "We'll have them come on Karva Chauth next month. Such a big day for you—the first time you'll be keeping a fast for Dev. Don't worry, it'll be here before you know it."

She let me telephone them every four days. (How long would it take, I wondered, to use up the twenty thousand rupees from Paji and one rupee from Sharmila at this rate?) Hema always accompanied me, and told me how jealous her friends were getting about all the calls she'd been dialing. "In addition to a fridge and a radiogram and a pressure cooker, I'm going to ask Babuji to include a telephone in my dowry."

A few times, when she insisted, I let Hema say hello to my parents. "I'm not sure exactly who that was, but she chatters a lot," Paji commented.

One morning, Biji didn't come to the phone. Paji told me she'd been crying since morning over Roopa's move to the east coast. "Ravinder's posting came through to the naval base in Visakhapatnam. They're leaving this Sunday. I'll tell them you said goodbye."

"Visakhapatnam!" Dev exclaimed when I told him. "But that's on the other side of the country." He looked so crestfallen that I had to suppress the shiver of exhilaration I felt. "Poor Roopa," he said, and slowly shook his head. "Look what you've done to yourself."

I was never able to bring up Dev's Bombay suggestion to Paji on the phone. Initially, I dismissed the idea of asking for help as preposterous. Surely after everything he had spent for my dowry, Paji would simply laugh at the request. Not with warmth, either, I told Dev, but with rage. "What about the twenty thousand in cash Paji gave?" I asked. "That's supposed to be for us—surely it should be enough for a flat, even in Bombay?"

Dev evaded my queries about the money as long as he could. He finally disclosed that the family had asked to borrow it to keep aside for Hema's wedding. "You've seen yourself how these dowry matters work. Just think of it—Sandhya didn't even bring in anything. Could someone like Babuji ever afford a daughter's marriage on his salary alone?"

"You mean it's not just his own three daughters, but Hema as well, whom my father has to worry about marrying off?"

"It's not like that. Try to understand. It's not as if anyone's keeping the money for themselves. It's all one big cycle of give-and-take, that's all."

"Yes, my father keeps giving and your family keeps taking."

"Why don't you shut your mouth. This isn't your father's house, that you can go around spewing out whatever comes into your head."

I went to bed that night alternately incredulous and appalled. Dev lay on the talai with his back to me, the odor of whiskey so strong in the air that I knew he had purposely got drunk. This was his way of sulking, but I did not care. How could he have let them take the money? I had a lot more reason to be angry with him.

But as I glared at his back, I started realizing his family was to blame. Given the choice, Dev would have surely preferred to use the money to move to a flat in Bombay. As long as we lived with them, it was unlikely he would be able to go against his family's wishes. Which made it even more imperative that we leave this house. An image of a train engine, majestically emerging through billows of steam, came to my mind.

The cash from my dowry was gone, of course—even Dev couldn't possibly believe it was a loan. Would we ever be able to afford our own place? It wasn't as if Dev was going to be making a lot of money anytime soon. Businesses and industry were growing so rapidly these days that for the first time since Independence, jobs were relatively easy to get. But they were mostly entry-level positions, without good prospects for advancement. The best Dev had been able to do with the B.A. in social studies he had received in July was a clerking job with Hindustan Petroleum. "If the country is supposed to be doing so well, how come they're paying you so little?" Babuji had complained.

The whistle blew, the guard raised the green flag, the Frontier Mail was preparing to slip away. There was only one way left to catch the train—follow Dev's suggestion and ask Paji for help. Since I couldn't telephone freely and wasn't allowed to visit in person, it would have to be through a letter. I would explain everything, be honest about where the money went, and tell Paji that although not entitled, I was still coming to him with my apron spread. He could let me know during his visit on Karva Chauth if he had found it in his heart to drop in more.

The sky opened up, the horizon came to focus once more, and along it, there was the Frontier Mail, whistling its way to Bombay again. Had I known the price I would have to pay for that train ride, I would have banished every trace of the letter I was already composing in my head.

chapter
seven

THE FOLLOWING WEDNESDAY, WHEN HEMA AND I GOT TO THE RATION shop to make my allotted call, we found it closed. I was actually quite relieved to see this—ever since sending my letter to Paji, I had been dreading his response on the phone. "It's only seven," Hema said, looking at the shutters drawn across the entire line of stalls. "I wonder what could be going on?"

As we were walking back, the silence rang in our ears—for the first time we noticed how deserted the street was. Nearing the bend that turned towards the colony, both of us instinctively broke into a run. As we approached our house, we began to hear muffled cries and smelled the acridity of smoke.

Mataji was standing outside the gate, waving frantically to us to hurry. "Where were you, roaming around like you were on a stroll? Don't you know there's a riot going on?" She slammed and bolted the door. "Half of Nizamuddin is up in flames around us and you pick this time to go out to use the phone."

We stayed awake until late at night, listening to the sirens in the distance. Mrs. Ahmed relayed from across the wall between us that twenty-three people had died and the railway station had been destroyed, but Arya could find nothing on the radio. I had heard about riots occurring in poor, crowded localities far away from Darya Ganj, but never somewhere I was staying before.

The newspaper report the next day was disappointingly low-key. It stated that there had been an argument at a meat shop in the morning over mutton gone bad. By afternoon, a rumor had spread that the problem wasn't spoiled mutton, but beef disguised as mutton. People started saying that the butcher (a Muslim, like most others in the trade) had lured the brown and white cow that fed at the station garbage heap into the back of his shop and slaughtered it, then palmed off the meat as mutton to unsuspecting Hindu customers. He had fled for his life after being stabbed in the shoulder with his own boning knife, and his shop was torched along with four others (three of them Muslim, and one Hindu, by accident). The cow, however, was unharmed, the paper reassured its readers, and the rioters had dispersed peacefully once it had been sighted ambling near the post office dump later that evening. An editorial inside predicted that such communal incidents may soon become isolated anomalies. It pointed out that the tally of Delhi riots had steadily decreased every year since the Partition, ascribing this trend to an increase in jobs created by the government's five-year economic growth plans. The piece ended with a quotation from Nehru, an ideal, it said, which the nation would always hold indisputable: *"Let us be clear about it without a shadow of doubt . . . we stand till death for a secular state."*

"What's this country coming to?" Babuji asked aloud, as I finished reading him the article. I thought he was upset over the riot, but it turned out he was complaining instead that there weren't *enough* of them. "How can people have forgotten the Partition so easily, forgiven the Muslims so soon?"

Babuji took a puff from his hookah and started working on another knot in the charpoy turned upside down before him. Every morning, he came back for an hour, after checking on the signal token for the Punjab Mail. He liked me to read the newspaper aloud to him during this break, as he tightened the ropes of the charpoys. "You have to retie the knots every few days," he would say as he pulled the ropes against the frame, "otherwise by morning, you'll be scraping the ground with your back." In the beginning, I sat veiled in the gunghat of my sari like Sandhya did in his presence, and he was careful not to turn to me directly. But now I kept my face uncovered, and he spoke as unself-consciously to me as he would to a daughter.

Except Babuji was not my father, he couldn't possibly be more different from Paji. Although I had learnt to look past his gruffness, even developed an appreciation for his directness, there were times when his views left me appalled.

For instance, there was the day he solved the mystery of where Arya went at dawn. "It's a shakha, in that building behind the post office—it's one of the clubs run by the Hindu Rashtriya Manch. Arya works for them, you know—he's their Nizamuddin branch treasurer. He's been volunteering to lead the early morning exercises on the field for the new boys this year."

I was startled by the matter-of-fact way Babuji mentioned this association. "Communalists, thugs, murderers," was how my father usually described the HRM, in his frequent rants against the organization. Although Paji's choicest invective was reserved for the Muslim League, for spearheading the campaign to create a separate Pakistan, he had more than enough ire left to direct towards the other militaristic organizations that had joined in the Partition bloodbath. "They say they've reformed themselves, they've given up violence, they're only interested in promoting a sense of worth among young Hindu men. But you don't have to scratch very deep to expose the HRM's unquenchable thirst for Muslim blood."

I felt myself echoing my father in my response to Babuji. "Weren't they one of the groups banned by the government for killing Gandhiji?" I asked.

"All lies," Babuji barked, his head snapping up as if I had questioned his personal integrity. "Politics and lies, that's what. Nehru had to show the world he was doing something, to save face after such an embarrassing assassination. But the murder plot had nothing to do with the groups he accused—that's why he was forced to lift his ban the very next year."

Babuji fixed me with a look so keen that I wished I still had the filter of my gunghat between us. "Let me ask you something, Bahu—since your family came to this country as refugees just like us. They keep trumpeting Gandhiji this and Gandhiji that, erecting statues of him everywhere, putting his face on stamps. But what did he do for the country anyway? This man whom we call the father of the nation. He got rid of the British, it's true, but at what cost? A million people dead, so many millions like us turned into refugees. Why? So that we could have Pakistan carved out of our own flesh and sitting on our head? What kind of father is this, who hacks off the arms of his nation and gives them away?"

I was stunned. This was such a vicious distortion of every fact I had ever been taught, that I felt tears spring up as if I had just been slapped. I wanted to scream at Babuji that Gandhiji was the last person who had wanted Partition, that he had resisted it to the very end. That he had even offered the prime ministership to Jinnah, the father of the Muslim nation, to keep the country intact. It was the British who could have prevented the carnage, but decided not to, and left the country to fend for itself. Pulling their troops out a full ten months earlier than announced, so that they wouldn't have to expend their own resources in stopping the bloodshed.

Somehow, that day, I managed to hold my tongue. I let Babuji rant on, reminding myself that as the bahu, it was not my place to correct, to be defiant. Now, I repeated the same mantra to myself, as Babuji complained that chasing just one Muslim butcher away wasn't sufficient. "They can say what they want about having enough jobs for everyone, but outrage doesn't die so easily. It just bides its time, lying in wait. Mark my words, there are rivers of blood to come—the day all these buried feelings emerge, ten times as strong."

Babuji tightened the last of his ropes. "You probably think I'm very bigoted, don't you? That Muslims aren't doing anything to me, so why do I hate them?" He took a long inhalation from his hookah, and broke into a paroxysm of coughs. "See? There is a reason. This tobacco that the Mughals brought. The Muslims are going to kill me yet."

He drew in another breath through the hose, then pushed aside the hookah. "Come sit with me then." He turned the charpoy right side up and indicated I was to join him on it. "I'll tell you a story to change your mind.

"Have you ever been to Kasur, Bahu? Dev must have talked about it—it's where he was born after all. A cultured city, the size of a pome-granate, to the south of the giant watermelon that is Lahore. It's where the poet Bulleh Shah lived, where the best leather comes from. For thir-teen years I worked there as a signalman, then an assistant stationmaster, until finally, in December of 1945, they made me stationmaster. It was not a very big station, but we got a fair number of trains from both Lahore and Firozpur. Once I was promoted, I thought this was it—a job, a family, a flat, good friends—I assumed I would spend the rest of my life quite happily there.

"Then the freedom movement started gaining force. All of a sudden, the Muslims, even friends and neighbors I'd known for years, started parroting what their leader Jinnah was claiming—that they couldn't live next to Hindus anymore. They demonstrated in the streets, sometimes rioted, to get attention for this new demand of a separate country. 'We'll be slaves if we're a minority among Hindus,' they claimed, 'we'll be dis-criminated against, we'll be killed.' It was as if an infection had raged through their community and eaten into all their brains.

"For a few days Kasur was calm, even while horrible things were happening in the rest of Punjab. We knew we wouldn't escape—we were much too close to the juicy watermelon that had already been hacked open above. Still, it was a shock when the gouged-out innards of Lahore finally rained down to splatter us. Arya had just brought my lunch to the station, I remember, when Hussein, the ticket seller rushed in and said it had started. We watched from behind the tiny ticket-room windows as the mob came down the road, burning all the Hindu busi-nesses and stores."

I was about to interject, but Babuji held up his hand. "I know what you'll say, Bahu—that Hindus targeted Muslims as well, that as many Muslims died as Hindus did. I can only tell you what I saw myself. They were quite methodical, these Muslims I witnessed in action that day—checking every address, leaving some stores intact, pouring kerosene through the windows of others. After they were done, they didn't seem quite satisfied with their accomplishments. They stood around in the street, gazing at the fires, like children loitering about wondering what to do next in their play hour. Then someone said, 'Soraaj, the moneylender, where is he? He's always squeezing money out of Muslims, let's teach him a lesson.' They looked around, but Soraaj had fled long before they had lit his stall, so instead they caught Bajrang Singh, his watch boy, and set his shirt on fire.

"Somehow, Bajrang was able to rip his shirt off, so then, laughing, they prodded him with their torches until his pajama was lit. He managed to get that off as well, and stood there naked, so they set aflame his turban, because there was nothing else left to burn. You would think that a turban would be the easiest garment to remove, but for some reason—shock, perhaps, or maybe devoutness—Bajrang didn't. Instead, his body uncovered, his head streaking smoke and flame, he ran towards the station."

Babuji locked his gaze with mine. "I'll never forget his face as he banged at the doors we had shuttered, never forget the smell of his burning hair. Had we pulled Bajrang in, perhaps we could have saved him. Stations, we knew, were always spared—they would be too useful after Partition to be needlessly destroyed. But even the Muslims in our group were terrified of the mob. Only Arya, who had played with Bajrang when they were both children, struggled to go outside—it was all we could do to restrain him. We watched together as two of the men sauntered up to Bajrang and, his head still smoldering, dragged him away."

Babuji stopped, to reach for the hookah and take a deep draw through the hose. The smoke made a gurgling sound as it bubbled through the water bulb.

"The day Gandhi capitulated to the demands of the Muslims and agreed to a partition, there were fires all over the city again. Nobody knew whether Kasur would end up in India or Pakistan—the British wouldn't announce that until the very end. People said that it didn't really matter—why not wait and see how things worked out after the violence—understandable, they claimed—died down? After all, Hindus had been reasonably prosperous under Muslim rule during the time of the Mughals, and surely this would be the same. 'Why leave your job behind, why not stay at least to sell your flat?' But by now, I had seen too many throats slit, too many bodies set aflame. That evening, I used my stationmaster's quota to book tickets for my family and myself. We took the train to Delhi the very next day. Which was just as well—within a week, most of the Hindus and Sikhs foolish enough to remain were floating in the canal, their heads separated from their necks. The city founded eons ago in the bosom of Hindustan by Loh, the son of Ram, was gone. Pakistan was the country to which both Lahore and its pomegranate fell.

"Even though we lost everything, we were so much luckier than most. We escaped before the death trains started, before the compartments stuffed with massacred refugees started rolling in. And look at Sandhya's family—they were able to make it out only by joining the throngs who made the crossing on foot. It cost them one of their children—dead on the third day—just one of the hundreds of bodies people cremated along the way or buried in unmarked graves."

Babuji took another inhalation from the hookah. "Do you know who came to our rescue in Delhi, Bahu? Not your Gandhiji or the Congress Party—it was the HRM. I had heard of them back in Kasur—one of the groups the Hindus had formed for self-protection, and yes, retaliation. They were known for their nightly raids against Muslim targets— revenge, you understand, for the attacks against Hindus by day. Arya had wanted to join in the days the trouble first started brewing, but I hadn't allowed him. In the refugee camps, however, the HRM made it clear that their goals were peaceful, that they were there just to assist as fellow Hindus. There must have been a dozen volunteers in our section alone—helping people get settled, distributing chappatis and bedding, making sure we had water and medicine. Once we left, Arya wanted to go back and help new refugees by becoming a volunteer himself. This time, I was only too happy to give him my blessing to sign up with the HRM.

"It took a few months before I was able to get the job at Nizamuddin. Even though I had so many years of service, I was informed the old railway system was dissolved, and I had to start all over as a signalman again. What was much more humiliating, however, was that the station-master was a man named Ahmed. After all I had endured, leaving my job and house and possessions in Kasur to be plundered by Pakistanis, I was now assigned to take orders from a Muslim. Someone who had the gall to call me into his office one day and lecture me about the sanctity of Salim Fazl's grave." I blushed as Babuji bore into me with his gaze.

"See that house next door? It's where Ahmed—*Ahmed sahib*—lives. Take a good look at it—it's the only one in the colony which has two extra rooms and an indoor toilet, built above the main floor. So while they throw all the Hindus out of Pakistan, this is how we treat our Muslims here in India. We erect buildings for them, buildings with two stories, while sleeping four to a room next door. All Ahmed has is that one delinquent son, and here, I can only offer my new bahu the floor.

"Tell me just one thing before you blame me for my views, Bahu. When they have their own country, which they've made clear is only for Muslims, why are they still lingering around? Shouldn't the Ahmeds be packed up and sent to Pakistan and we be the ones in that house?"

WHILE WE WERE GROWING UP in Rawalpindi, Paji often invited Muslim guests over for dinner. He did this partly to provoke his father Harilal, in one wing of whose house we lived. Although Harilal employed Muslims in his publishing business, he did not approve of such fraternization, especially in matters of food and drink. Still, he was careful to maintain a cordiality around his son's guests, never allowing himself to rise to the bait.

Biji, on the other hand, cloistered herself on such occasions, and had her dinner sent to her bedroom. She tried to restrain us from showing ourselves as well, but Roopa and I (not poor Sharmila, who was too timid) usually managed to escape. Afterwards, we would hear Biji vent her outrage at Paji. "Night after night serving food to unpurified men. I'm sure the cook is fed up, what if he quits in protest? Will you have me in the kitchen then, boiling cows' feet for them?"

Provoking Harilal wasn't the only reason—Paji was genuinely interested in the culture of his guests. "The Muslims might have been invaders, it's true, but look how incomplete we'd be without them. Imagine if we had never known what a biryani tasted like or died without seeing the Taj Mahal." Matters of religion didn't bother him—in fact, he was eager to cultivate the acquaintanceship of Muslims to emphasize his secular outlook. "Ram or Rahim, it's all a bloody hoax anyway," he'd say (though never to his Muslim guests, many of whom were quite religious). "If you're going to squander your time, what difference does it make whether it's in a mosque or a temple?"

Perhaps the one aspect of Muslim culture of which he was a true aficionado was qawwali. The inconsistency in this, the fact that such devotional songs should be at odds with his disdain for religion, never seemed to occur to him. Paji had one friend in particular, Salman uncle, with whom he often went to qawwali recitals. These events usually started late at night, and Salman uncle came to our house for dinner first, bearing gifts of almonds and raisins or the crumbly Persian vermicelli sweets that I loved so much. He enjoyed dressing in a stately silk sherwani for the occasion. The tunic ran all the way to his knees and was fitted with a stiff embroidered collar that brushed against his beard. His pajamas would be the tight-fitting kind, the white folds clinging closely to his legs, and on his head he wore the dark velvet cap that in later years came to be known as a Jinnah hat. In the summers, he hennaed his beard—to keep it cool, he said. Roopa and I took turns running our hands over it as if we were stroking a furry orange pet. Sharmila was intrigued by the color, but ran away each time we tried to coax her into petting it as well.

Salman uncle was the only one of Paji's Muslim guests with whom Biji seemed to be at ease, with whom she actually deigned to sit, even talk, at the dinner table. The main reason for this was his wife, whom he sometimes brought along. Yasmin auntie couldn't have been more different from the womenfolk of the rustic Muslim laborers who worked for Biji's father in their village. Not only did Yasmin auntie let her hair fly loose, or hold it in place with the flimsiest of scarves, but she also dressed in the most eye-catching outfits for which she went frequently to Lahore or Karachi on shopping trips. Her exquisitely tailored kameez had the sleeves cut to the precise length most fashionable at the moment, her salwars ballooned out or tightened up around her legs depending on the current trend, and some of her sandals had heels high enough to rival the ones the British memsahibs wore.

Biji turned all girlish and giggly in Yasmin auntie's presence, like a teenager with a crush. She was reticent when first introduced, but smitten from their very first meeting, by the end of which they were chatting and laughing like old school comrades. We were amazed to see the transformation in Biji—gone was the reserve and the comportment of the zamindar's daughter (maintained with all her Hindu lady friends), to be replaced by a startling impishness. We never saw enough of Yasmin auntie because Biji spirited her away as soon as she arrived, monopolizing her all the way to dinnertime behind closed doors, when they reappeared, scented with exotic attars and perfumes. Once, I peeked into the bedroom and saw Biji wobbling in Yasmin auntie's sandals, attempting to walk across the floor.

As a gift for one year's Eid festival, Salman uncle presented Paji with a complete outfit like the one he enjoyed wearing to qawwalis. Paji tried it out at once—the sherwani, the Jinnah hat, the tight pajamas, even a pair of gilt-inlaid shoes that came to a point at the toes. He emerged from his bedroom looking resplendent in the ensemble—like a nobleman from a Mughal court, or, as Salman uncle put it, "like someone whose ancestors had Persian blood."

It was true. We had never noticed the resemblance between Paji and Salman uncle before—they were about the same height and build, had the same aristocratic cheekbones, and standing together in their identical sherwanis, could have been mistaken for brothers. Biji, we could see, was quite alarmed at the sight. "Will you grow an orange beard next?" she asked Paji the morning after.

The next time Yasmin auntie came, she brought silk dupattas for my sisters and me, and an outfit for Biji as well. "Put this on and tonight we'll all go to the qawwali," she directed. Of course, Biji demurred at first, but it was clear her curiosity would win out. "I'll try it, but just for a moment," she said.

It was a salwar kameez, but one quite unlike the baggy type Biji wore about the house. The yellow color was one she would have never selected herself—it set off her darker skin strikingly, making an even more daring statement than orange or red. The kameez was cut snugly around the waist and stomach, pushing her bosom up, making her figure stand out. Sequins of tiny mirrors formed a pattern around the neck, they ran glittering down the arms and were inlaid in the dupatta as well. Biji stood in front of the mirror, looking at herself this way and that, pulling on the material to get the wrinkles out, tossing her dupatta carelessly around her neck.

"And now for the final touch," Yasmin auntie said, uncapping a lipstick from her purse and bringing it to Biji's mouth. But this was going too far. Biji drew her face out of reach and pulled the dupatta off.

"I'd love to join you, but I can't."

Our faces fell, because without Biji's company, we would have to stay home as well. Yasmin auntie, however, understood better than us that this was simply a ploy on our mother's part. She proceeded to administer the flattery and cajoling Biji craved, but never received from Paji. "What a shame if nobody saw you in that salwar kameez." "I was so looking forward to sitting together, the two of us." "It's only on special nights that women are allowed, you know."

It didn't take long for Biji to announce she'd come, "if only not to disappoint the children." She slung the dupatta over the nape of her neck, so that the two strands cascaded down her front, then looked at herself in the mirror again and wrapped one end fashionably around her throat.

Paji let out a "Wah!" of appreciation when he saw Biji's transformation, a reaction which so pleased her that she let him put his arm around her shoulders. I will always remember seeing the two of them descend arm in arm down the steps, like a Muslim couple on the day of Eid, dressed in their finest.

The qawwali was being held beyond the cantonment, on the other side of Mall Road—the mostly Muslim side, which we rarely frequented. We clopped along the gaslit roads, through neighborhoods that got progressively poorer, enveloped by the tonga's horse and old leather smell. Salman uncle explained the Sufi origins of qawwali to us, but I was too absorbed in the houses passing by to listen. I had expected them to be painted green or blue or some other conspicuous color to proclaim their Muslim identity, but there was little to distinguish them from houses in other parts of the city. The women in the courtyards also looked the same—they went about stirring pots over charcoal braziers, dressed in the usual baggy salwar kameez that everyone wore. Wouldn't it be wonderful, I thought, if up close, they were all wearing makeup like Yasmin auntie?

At the hall, what fascinated me inside was all the white. The ivory white ceiling, the lights blazing down from it, the musicians in their spotless kurtas, the snowy sheets covering the dais and flowing down to carpet the entire seating area. I sat on a sheet in the ladies' section against a white cottony bolster, my head covered by the dupatta as Yasmin auntie had instructed us all. A woman came around with a tray and served us glasses of frothy white almond milk.

There were several groups of singers ("qawwals," as Yasmin auntie called them) who performed in turn. The lead qawwal sang out each new verse to the tune of a harmonium, and then the rest of his group responded with the same lines, clapping lustily along. All around in the audience, people swayed to show their appreciation, or rose to offer money, or raised an arm and cried out "Subhan-allah." Biji squirmed around initially, and looked vainly around the room to see if she could spot another Hindu lady. She tried to pull her dupatta low over her forehead to cover her bindi, but relaxed soon after, when she realized nobody was watching. I remember being lulled to sleep by the sparkle and flash of sequins in Biji's kameez, as she and Yasmin auntie swung in unison from side to side in tune with the clapping.

Biji never wore the salwar kameez again. The increase in communal friction made it unsafe for Hindus to venture into Muslim localities, like the one where the qawwalis were held. Salman uncle and Yasmin auntie came a few more times to our house, but moved to Karachi soon after, which they said was more cosmopolitan. Years later, while rummaging through an old suitcase, I found the salwar kameez—Biji had brought the outfit along on the train to India when we fled Rawalpindi.

We did hear from Salman uncle three years later. A letter from Karachi somehow found its way via the Delhi refugee administration to Paji. "Both Yasmin and I are in good health," Salman uncle wrote, saying that he was planning a trip to Delhi that December to visit his brother Manmad. Manmad had been one of the refugees crossing in the other direction, leaving behind his burned-down cloth factory in Ghaziabad to flee to Karachi. However, he had missed India too much and returned a year later to take his chances in Delhi. "I'm looking forward to introducing my two brothers in Delhi to each other—I know you'll be good friends. Perhaps Manmad can even show you where the best qawwalis are." Yasmin auntie, he said, would also come on a future trip—she had already started buying up a collection of new salwar kameez for Biji in Karachi.

Both Paji and Biji kept waiting for the follow-up letter, which never came. There was no return address on the letter we had received, nor an address for Manmad, and we were never able to contact Salman uncle again.

ALTHOUGH INITIALLY it was harder, Paji did manage to build up a circle of Muslim friends in Delhi over the years. He even set up a special Hindu-Muslim group in Darya Ganj to foster such relations. He was able to renew his passion for qawwali, and Biji had to get used to having Muslim guests for dinner again.

In contrast, there were never any Muslims invited to Dev's house. Mataji would chat with Mrs. Ahmed over the wall, and Hema would sometimes include Mrs. Ahmed's son Rahim in a game, but the socialization seemed to end there.

On the day of the Eid festival, the Ahmeds sent over glasses of almond milk. "Don't drink it," Mataji shouted, running across the courtyard to pull a glass away from Hema's hand before she could have a sip. "How many times must I tell you, they're Muslim, they might have put a curse on it."

Mataji took the glasses into the kitchen and started emptying them one by one, pouring the milk down the drain. "I hate to throw it out, but what else to do? This way they won't be offended when I return the glasses, and also we can be safe."

chapter
eight

THE DAY BEFORE KARVA CHAUTH, MATAJI TOOK SANDHYA AND ME TO THE fair that had sprung up along the market street on the other side of the station. Every available nook seemed to have sprouted a stall, complete with cloth and bamboo walls and strings of colored lights. Mataji guided us expertly through the throngs of people, inspecting the mounds of vermilion and pooja ingredients, haggling over the boxes of sweets, making us try on bangles and gilt-edged slippers before buying them for us. "A small gift for my bahus," she told us. "It's the least I can do in return for making my sons live longer."

The "Chauth," it had been explained to me, referred to the fourth day of the waning moon, when wives fasted for the longevity of their husbands from the first sign of dawn to when they sighted the moon. It was the longest and most arduous of all fasts, since even a drop of water could void it, and it occurred usually in October, when it was very hot. "Sometimes you can't see the moon because it's obscured by the clouds," Hema said, trying her best to scare me. "Then you just have to go on fasting—even for days if necessary. I really hope that doesn't happen to you."

At first, I thought the name was "Kadva," or "bitter," to reflect how exacting this ordeal was. But Sandhya clarified that it was "Karva," not

"Kadva," which referred to a symbol of good luck, a sort of earthenware pot. *"Be sure to buy a karva if an old woman selling pottery comes to your door on that day,"* she sang, *"Because if you don't, she'll capture his spirit in it and steal your husband away."*

As the day of the festival drew closer, I noticed a change come over Sandhya. Her features, which were usually set in an expression of stoic perseverance, began to relax, even blossom into the occasional smile. Her hair broke free of its utilitarian bun and fell in shimmering cascades to her shoulders. Strands of jasmine appeared in it, and sometimes a hibiscus flower bloomed next to an ear. Green glass bangles clinked around her wrists, and the nails on her hands and feet acquired a coat of lustrous red. One morning, I heard her singing in the bathroom; another time, I caught her humming in the pooja corner. Even her rice turned less clumpy. It was as if she was becoming younger, more carefree, more radiant as time went by—as if she was reverting to the incarnation of a bride.

Arya noticed it too, because he seemed to linger every morning after she had touched his feet for her pooja, and just stare at her. There was never a kiss or any other outward show of affection, only this mutual gaze that mesmerized the two of them. Hema would caricature it for me when it happened by hanging her tongue out and rolling her eyeballs as if they had come loose in her head. At night, the long waits outside the bedroom door before Arya turned off the light inside multiplied from once a week to twice, then four times.

Perhaps it was the fact that I was the new initiate and she the experienced sister-in-law that made Sandhya's attitude towards me soften. I noticed it in little things—a sentence spoken when it was not absolutely necessary, a glance towards me without wariness or reserve, even an orange peeled for me when she peeled one for Mataji. "I used to be nervous, too, about the fast, but now it's my favorite day of the year," she volunteered one morning. "We'll go over all the steps beforehand, so you'll have nothing to fear." Hema got very jealous when she saw the two of us discussing the ceremony. She went around complaining that nobody talked to her anymore, wondering darkly if it was because the bahus were plotting a conspiracy.

In all my years of growing up, I had never seen Biji keep the fast. Paji had probably forbidden her because of the way it held women subordinate to men. I was unfamiliar with the steps Sandhya demonstrated for me—the right foot balanced on a grinding pestle, milk carried in a glass as an offering, the round sieve, the type used to sift flour, held up towards the moon. "Why should it be only women?" I wondered aloud. "Why don't husbands keep the fast for their wives as well?" It was as if Paji was inside, making me blurt out the words. "Shouldn't Dev be practicing these steps? And Arya as well?"

"I wouldn't know. It's not for me to say," Sandhya replied, her expression suddenly cold, her voice taking on a tone of formality.

She spoke to me again later, as we put away the sieve and the pestle. "Without Arya, I don't even know if I'd be alive. So it's not just that I'm fasting for his life, I'm also fasting for mine."

WHAT WORRIED ME MOST about Karva Chauth was Paji's attendance that evening to witness its conclusion. Sandhya had explained the sacred origins of the fast, how this was an opportunity for women to worship the mother goddess Parvati. Although I was not devout, I did not mind participating in such religious ceremonies. Whether listening to the mythological tales Biji used to relate, or singing songs at the temple, or making an offering to Lakshmi at Divali, it was easy to enjoy each observance as a cultural activity without pondering its deeper meaning. Paji, though, with his profound aversion to religion, was different. Like someone allergic to cats who starts gasping and wheezing at the mere sight of a feline, his face would turn purple and his eyes bulge when exposed to worship of any kind. He would tell us how as a boy he tied up his laces tight with such impossible knots that his shoes couldn't be taken off outside temples and he could escape going inside.

Even worse than the religious aspect of the ceremony, I was expected to touch Dev's feet before breaking the fast. "Some people just graze the ground in front, but it's the toes that one's supposed to touch—not the nail, because that's inauspicious, but the part just beyond," Sandhya had instructed. "And remember, everyone will be watching, so be sure to touch both feet."

I hadn't quite reconciled myself to the idea of performing this act. Why should I be bending down in front of Dev? Was he Gandhiji, that he should be bestowing a blessing on me? Why, to return to the question disturbing me all along, was I fasting for him in the first place? The way to go through with the whole affair, I had decided, was by thinking of it as a social custom—a harmless curiosity that Dev's family engaged in. One that didn't signify anything more, one that I could execute while taking my mind on a stroll somewhere. But what would Paji's philosophers say? How would I pull it off with him there?

The previous week, a letter had arrived for me from Paji. I instantly recognized the precise economy of the lettering in the address, inscribed in the dark blue ink he got from the stationer at Connaught Place. Even though the mailman made his final delivery by four in the afternoon, I found it only at night, propped up against the pillow on my talai.

I could tell right away that it had been opened. The edge of the flap was crinkled and bumpy, the line where it met the envelope yellow with clumsily applied glue. Paji's letters were always perfect in their appearance—he would get a new envelope rather than send one with the slightest blemish.

I had been waiting for a response from Paji ever since writing to him some weeks back. On the phone, I couldn't mention the letter I had sent because Hema would always be next to me, her ears twitching like a gazelle's. Paji never volunteered anything, not even an acknowledgment that he had received my note.

"Dear Meera," his letter read. "To say that I am speechless at your request would be an understatement. However, you are my daughter, and I feel responsible for you, as if all the mistakes you keep committing are in some way my own. We will discuss things when I accompany your mother to see you on the delightful occasion of Karva Chauth, in which I understand you will be participating. Love, Paji."

I knew that whoever had read the letter (my guess being Hema) would fail to detect the sarcasm behind the word "delightful." But the way Paji had referred to the impending event filled me with dread.

"Have you heard from your father recently?" Hema was unable to refrain from asking the very next morning.

—

ON THE DAY OF THE FESTIVAL, Sandhya woke me at five. "We have to hurry," she whispered. "Mataji was supposed to get us up an hour ago but she overslept. The sky is beginning to change already, we only have a few minutes left before it starts to turn red." Dev stirred as I rose, but did not open his eyes.

Mataji was in the kitchen, frantically heating the potatoes. "I can't believe I didn't wake up," she told us. "The prayers will have to come afterwards, there's almost no time to eat." She ladled the steaming potatoes onto three plates. "And to think I was going to make fresh parathas this morning. Now we'll have to make do with doubleroti."

Sandhya got the package of Britannia bread from the fridge and began to put slices to toast on the griddle over the fire. Mataji rushed over and plucked them off with her fingers. "We don't have time for that. Bring the doubleroti to the charpoy outside, we can make sure from there that the stars have not died out yet."

Outside, the sky was a reddish black. The iron rails were catching light from the lamps on the station platform to gleam portentously in their tracks. The three of us sat along the same side of the charpoy, facing the clearing for the new colony flats in the east, where Mataji said the first signs of dawn would emerge.

"Try to eat as much as you can," Mataji said, stacking our plates with slices of bread. "The moon won't show until at least eight forty-five tonight."

We began eating. The potatoes were very salty and Sandhya had put too many chilies in them—my stomach rumbled in protest at receiving them so quickly after awakening. I noticed both Mataji and Sandhya eating the centers of the bread first, which were easier to swallow, so I did the same. We ate quickly and efficiently, concentrating on getting the food in, not wasting any time on talk. Every few seconds, Mataji would glance up warily, as if on the lookout for enemy planes. There were birds beginning to chirp from the trees, announcing the brisk determination of the dawn to progress.

"Oh my God, I forgot the sev," Mataji said, and rushed towards the fridge. She came back with a bowl of sweet vermicelli and three spoons.

"I'm glad I remembered in time—it's part of the fast, you know—the ritual is not complete without it."

We began spooning up the creamy mixture from the bowl, alternating it with scoops of potato and bread from our plates. The food seemed to be taking forever to ingest—causing Mataji's sense of urgency to grow. "Fruit!" Sandhya exclaimed, and ran into the kitchen, returning with three bananas which she peeled with dexterity. The combination of bread and chilies and banana and vermicelli started making me a little sick.

By now, there was a definite redness in the east, though not bright enough to create shadows behind us. The stars above us had acquired a tired dullness, as if preparing, after a hard night's work, to retire for the day. I felt I couldn't eat another bite, so I put down my plate. Mataji and Sandhya stopped as well, and we all leaned back on the charpoy to watch the dawn progress.

The clouds above the horizon were just beginning to appear as brooding outlines when Mataji stood up, horrified. "The water. We forgot to drink anything. Hurry, we must have just seconds to spare."

We ran to the fridge, all three of us, and pulled out the whiskey bottles filled with water from the rack. In my hurry, the water streamed down my neck—Sandhya giggled as some dribbled over her chin as well. Babuji woke up with a start and watched us gulping down the contents, then turned over on his charpoy and went back to sleep.

"That's it," Mataji declared, like a headmistress signaling the end of a test, and we put our bottles down. She led us back outside and heaved a sigh of relief when above us, a star still twinkled feebly. A minute passed, and then several more, the dawn drawing closer but never quite arriving. Mataji looked skyward. "First you make us rush, then you go slow. What are you going to do, play games with us now?"

Sandhya climbed up on the charpoy, and I noticed how full of vitality she seemed today, from the glow on her forehead down to her feet flexing limberly against the ropes. She put a hand on my shoulder and one on Mataji's to support herself. Her hair hung free, her eyes turned luminous and the first rays curved up from the horizon to burnish her neck.

"I think I can just see it. The dawn," she said.

—

WE TOOK OUR BATHS later that morning, even though we were supposed to have done so before sunrise. "Remember, don't let any water pass your mouth by mistake," Mataji instructed. "If even a drop were to splash through your lips . . ."

Hema emerged sleepily at 9 a.m. "I haven't eaten yet. Can I join the fast as well?" She sulked when Mataji told her it was too late, then went to the kitchen to make herself a large omelet. "Oooh, this is so delicious," she said, taunting us with exaggerated smacking sounds from her lips.

"See this?" Mataji said, pulling out a squat pot with a stem from several folds of cloth. "This is the karva that my mother used—not even a crack in it after all these years." She started arranging the ingredients for the ceremony that night—rice, vermilion, saffron, and black gram, along the rim of a thali. Hema's eyes lit up when Mataji unwrapped the tissue from the glass bangles she had bought at the fair and put them on the steel platter. "Don't touch them," Mataji warned. "They're only for those who wake up early enough to keep the fast."

By eleven, most of the preparations were done. My bridal sari had been laid out on the charpoy in the bedroom, together with the gold I would be wearing that evening. For Sandhya, Mataji took out one of her own earring and necklace sets, whispering not to tell Hema that these were some of the pieces earmarked for her dowry. The mehndi man stopped by and decorated all our hands in delicate black-green filigree patterns. Hema drew her palm to her face and wrinkled her nose at the odor of the henna paste. "How can something that looks so beautiful smell so bad?"

The sun which had been in control of our lives since morning had long driven us indoors with its scorching rays. There was nothing much we could do while the mehndi set, so we lazed on the sofa under the ceiling fan. Sandhya occasionally broke into a snatch of song—I didn't know the words, but tried to hum along. Although my hunger hadn't returned after all the food that morning, the thirst had begun to assert itself. The dryness in my throat was spreading drought-like through my body—my lungs felt depleted, even my skin felt parched. "It'll only get worse in the afternoon," Mataji assured me.

The men came home for lunch after the mehndi man had left. "You must have made parathas for the fast. Where have you kept them?" Babuji called out, as we heard him searching among the thalis in the kitchen.

"I didn't have time. Today there's just doubleroti."

Mataji sat where she was, baring her neck to the breeze from the fan. "I remember how excited I used to be the first few years, sitting around waiting to serve Babuji his lunch, all dolled up from daybreak in my heavy bridal things. The kitchen would be like a furnace, but I would still make the chappatis fresh. Then one Karva Chauth I began to wonder why I was torturing myself—surely fifteen hours of fasting so that he could live longer should be enough. I kept making the chappatis until the dough had all been used up and waited until he had eaten his fill. Then I told him this was the last time—next year, he'd have to fend for himself."

Mataji sighed. "Of course, the following year I felt guilty, so I started making extra parathas for him in the morning when I made some for myself. But at least during the day I no longer go into the kitchen. And some years, when there are no parathas, he has to eat Britannia bread."

THE AFTERNOON BLAZED ON. We drew the curtains across the windows, which didn't help too much since the air inside was already hot. "The good thing about not being able to drink water is one doesn't sweat as much," Mataji said. She turned her face up towards the ceiling. "Thank God we have the fan." A few minutes later, the electricity went off.

We sat where we were, immobilized by this new adversity. The henna paste was still on our hands, so we couldn't even use newspapers to fan ourselves. Mataji stood up. "It's time to wash off the mehndi," she announced. "Let's use the water from the fridge before it gets warm. We can't drink it, but at least it can cool us off."

The water felt so cold and reviving against my palms that I splashed some on my face. Sandhya did the same, then playfully dribbled some drops down the back of my neck. Hema sneaked her bottle into the kitchen so we didn't have to watch her drink—since her taunts that morning, she had acquired a new sensitivity to our thirst.

Afterwards, we compared the henna patterns left behind on our hands. It occurred to me that the last time all our palms had been decorated like this was at my wedding, when we hardly knew each other. How amazing to be all related now—not just through marriage, but also through this shared experience of fasting. Sandhya sensed the intimacy as well, because she blushed when I caught her eye. For an instant, I wanted to take her hand in mine, press my lips against the design on her skin. "My mehndi is the prettiest, and Meera didi's is second," Hema declared.

The relief from the water was temporary—it soon evaporated, leaving my face feeling desiccated. The thirst was now a fire inside—I could monitor it raging through my body, trying to consume every thought in my mind. How did people go for days on end without water? I wondered. Gandhiji had done it for three weeks from his prison cell to demand freedom for the country. And here I was, doing it for a day, just so I could fit in.

I looked at the henna, a map of lines stretching across my palm. Could these be new fate lines, drawn to determine my future, these stylized shoots and twining flowers? I imagined myself in the midst of the pattern, tendrils curling around my ankles, ferns reaching out to caress my face. Leading me through a forest of strokes till I am standing at the edge of an orange lake. I cup my hands to take a sip but it is sand that they come up with. It is a desert I am gazing at, the waves simply furrows from the wind. Then the furrows deepen and shift, and I see wrinkles cut into human skin. It is the face of the woman from the station steps, telling me everything will be fine again. "God will grant you . . ." she begins to say, but then I see her in the door of a train.

"Meera didi, are you all right?" It was Sandhya, anxiously dabbing at my forehead with a wet cloth. Behind her, Hema was asking Mataji in an excited whisper if I had fainted.

"Yes," I said, even though I felt dizzy and disoriented.

Sandhya put her hand on my forehead. It felt cool against my skin. I looked at her face in wonder—instead of withering her, the thirst seemed to make her glow. "Only a few more hours. Time we started getting ready," she said.

AT THE FIRST SIGHT of my parents, I started crying. How extravagant my tears were, I thought, how reckless to be wasting moisture like this. I ignored the parchedness in my throat, the light-headedness from the heat, and fell upon Biji in an embrace. Paji hugged me as well.

"All those days I didn't see you," Biji wept. "Stay happy, that's all I prayed. I asked Devi Ma to bless my daughters with long-living husbands. What else does this old woman have to give?"

Mataji came out and accepted the offering of a silk sari that the bride's mother traditionally gave for the fast. "It's very modest, but come, let me show you around the house," she said. "All the gifts you've given us to brighten our lives—most of all Meera, of course."

Afterwards, Paji asked permission to talk with me alone. We sat on the courtyard charpoy where nobody could hear us. I felt feverish, but tried to smile and look alert for Paji.

"So this is the condition I find you in. Hands painted and fasting obediently like some fantasy Hindu wife. You look like you're about to pass out, so you can stop twisting your mouth into that grin. All those years I stopped your mother from degrading herself like this, and the first chance you get, you dive right in. Surely you know that medical science has found no evidence that starving yourself is going to prolong your husband's life? Couldn't you have told them no, if not for your own sake, at least for mine?

"And this hovel you're living in. Is this why you left your father's house? Two rooms for seven people—where did they set up your bridal suite, on the kitchen floor?" He waved his hand around. "Look at it all—that filthy toilet, that ramshackle door, that . . . good God, are those cow dung patties drying on the wall?"

I wanted to defend my surroundings, defend Dev's family, protest that the dung had been there a long time, and they didn't use it anymore. But I couldn't summon enough moisture to facilitate the words through my throat.

Paji ran his fingers over his brow and slowly exhaled. "I was afraid it might be bad, but I could never have pictured this. You can't imagine how it pierces a father's heart to see his daughter starved like a caged animal." He looked away from me, as if the sight was too painful to bear. "I have to blame myself too, you know. I could have tried to change your mind, I could have refused to let you go."

He turned back and earnestly grasped my hand. "When I got your letter, I was too stunned to respond. Greed has made her blind, I thought to myself. Or, more likely, the husband's greed. I now see how wrong I was—what a desperate situation you were writing from. There's only one thing that matters now, and that's for you to escape the life these barbarians have in store for you. Otherwise it will be like committing sati bit by bit while your husband watches on.

"So I've decided. I've decided you're going to Bombay. I'm prepared to pay what it takes. Over and above what they've already squeezed out, just to get you away from their clutches. If you must cart along that singer husband of yours, fine. That's your choice, not mine. The important thing is for you to break free, to make your own life. That's going to be my only condition. I've decided you're going to college, Meera. That you're going to study as I'd planned. That you're not going to sit at home and become fat like some bovine wife.

"Did you know that Roopa's pregnant? She called just yesterday with the news—the 'good' news I should say. Two months of marriage and already she jumps off the cliff. And here I am, looking for universities in Visakhapatnam for her to complete her B.A. All those promises I made to myself that if I did nothing else, I would educate at least one of your mother's daughters. Can you believe it—my own Roopa—disappointing me like this? And Sharmila's not bright enough, which only leaves you." Paji looked at me as if he had just paid me a compliment.

"But I suppose it's time for tonight's extravaganza. I shouldn't keep your relatives waiting, not to mention all the gods and goddesses they must have invited down especially from heaven. We can make the arrangements some other time. Why don't you call that husband of yours so he can hear my offer too?"

My mind whirling, I stumbled away to find Dev. He was thrilled. "As her husband, I couldn't agree more that Meera should study," he declared to Paji. "You have my word she'll go to college when we get to Bombay."

Dev was gushing to Paji about how grateful he was, how this was going to be such a wonderful opportunity. Had my mind been clearer, I might have anticipated his next action and had time to warn him. But after listening to Paji's plans for my future, I was as mentally drained as physically exhausted. Before I could stop him, Dev bent down to touch Paji's feet.

With the alacrity of a cobra, Paji's hand shot out to apprehend his wrist, twisting it so sharply that Dev cried out in pain. Hema, who had been spying on us from the kitchen, came running out. "What are you doing?" she exclaimed.

"Sorry," Paji said, releasing his grip. "It's a reflex action—I should have warned you. A custom I simply cannot abide." Paji's lips started curling into the familiar smile that was not a smile. "I suppose there's one more condition, then, to my offer. I don't know what type of ceremony you have planned for tonight. But if I see my daughter touch your feet, that'll be the end of your dream. I'll walk out that door and my offer will walk out with me."

BY EIGHT, THE GUESTS were all gathered in the courtyard. Mataji had invited her friends to share in the auspicious occasion of my first Karva Chauth. "There's Mrs. Sampath," Hema said, pointing at a woman sitting on the charpoy and kneading her chest. "She says she's going to get a heart attack since she can't take her blood pressure pills during the fast. Last year she fainted and the ambulance came and took her away, but people said later it was just to show off.

"And that's Mrs. Gangwal. She still keeps the fast even though her husband ran off with her niece four years ago. And next to her, Mrs. Pota, whose husband no one's ever seen. The rumor is he's dead."

I was having difficulty breathing. My jewelry felt heavy and constraining, the wedding outfit from two months ago tight and suffocating around my chest. My scalp was on fire, as if I had used chili powder, not vermilion, to decorate the parting in my hair. Even the bindi on my forehead itched so fiercely, I felt like scratching it off.

I sank down unsteadily on the special seat between Sandhya and Mataji to which Hema accompanied me. Round us sat the other women, and beyond them, the men stood about or watched from the charpoy. Thalis laden with offerings were circulated for everyone to admire, and my head swirled as I tried to follow the fruits and bangles and saris being passed from lap to lap. Mrs. Pota launched into a song about not sewing on Karva Chauth, and the women responded in a chorus about losing your husband if a stray needle were to prick him and drive him away.

There followed other songs, about a girl who fasted to bring back her beloved after he had been eaten by a crocodile, and about Savitri, who rescued her husband by tricking Yama, the god of death. Biji seemed to remember some of the words herself—I saw her swaying and clapping and singing along with the other women.

At some point, the singing stopped and the story of Karva Chauth was related. I tried to concentrate, even though by now my mind was listing and swirling. The tale was about seven brothers, who, moved by the suffering of their sister on Karva Chauth, shone the light of a lamp through a pipal tree so that she would break her fast early. She mistook the light for the moon as they had hoped, but the instant she took her first sip of water, her husband drowned. Fortunately, Parvati heard her cries of sorrow up in heaven. She came down to investigate, even though Shiva, her husband, sulked about being ignored over some weeping girl. When Parvati discovered how the men had interfered with this most sacred rite of womanhood to trick the girl, she was enraged. She threatened to assume her Kali image and destroy everything in sight. Shiva had no choice but to intervene with Yama, who reluctantly brought back the husband to life. It all sounded very familiar—hadn't Biji related a similar story to us years ago?

The women were just finishing a song in praise of Parvati when

Sandhya squeezed my hand. "Any second now. The moon will be unveiling itself."

I found it difficult to keep track of the ensuing flurry of activity—the lighting of the earthenware lamps, the pouring of water into the karva, the offering of rice and gram, the dabbing of red powder around the pestle placed on the ground. One of the women took out a small stone statue of Parvati which she had brought from Rajasthan. I did as the others did and used the third finger of my right hand to anoint it with vermilion.

"It's risen," Hema shouted, interrupting the ceremonies. "I can see it, over there, next to that house." It was indeed the moon, its rounded edge already beginning to clear the treetops—we had been too absorbed in the rituals to notice its stealthy ascent.

A hush fell over the congregation. Since I was the newest bride, it was my honor to be the first to break my fast. Sandhya helped me get up and bent down to arrange my foot on the center of the pestle. It felt cold and smooth against my arch, its convexity reassuring as I curled my toes around. Mataji handed me the sifter, and I held it up against the night. My vision swam as I did so—the moon looked a dirty white.

I took the glass of milk from Sandhya and prepared to pour my offering to the moon. But I couldn't summon up the silent words that were to accompany this action. The women watched me and waited for their turns as I stood poised with the glass. Should I turn around to ask them what I should be praying for?

Sandhya touched me at the shoulder and gently tilted my glass. I watched the thread of milk spill out and connect me to the earth. Dev loomed up in the sifter, his features curiously warped by the weave of the mesh. His nose seemed longer, his forehead too wide, the hollows under his eyes more pronounced. I looked at the blurred outline of his mouth and heard again the directions he had whispered. "Don't worry about Paji—I'll catch you in my arms before you can bend too much. It'll look quite natural—instead of touching my feet, we'll end it in a hug."

Sandhya exchanged the sifter and glass of milk in my hands for the fruit-laden thali I was to offer my mother-in-law. All that was required of me now was to follow Dev's instructions. He would catch me before I could complete my bow and feed me the first morsel to break my fast. Paji would nod approvingly from the charpoy upon seeing that Dev's feet remained untouched. Down at the station, the Frontier Mail would pull into the platform, ready to bear us away. Steam issuing out of its raring engine like from the nostrils of an impatient mare.

I looked into Dev's eyes and saw he could picture the Frontier Mail as well. Was Bombay within reach now, were his calculations proceeding as planned? Paji must surely have the same expression of self-satisfaction on his face. A daughter on her way to college, her life finally lived the way he wanted. Beside me stood Sandhya, her face shining with a serene beauty, like a moon bride descended to earth.

I'm not sure what exactly triggered my divergence from the script. Perhaps I could pin it again on Nehru, on his directive to assert myself. A clarity—calm, incisive—emerged from my hunger to reveal the action I had to take. I stared into Dev's eyes, and this time, his sureness faltered, his satisfaction dimmed. Realization flooded in and then alarm, as he followed the direction of my gaze.

I bent down before I could be swayed by the pleading beginning to distort his face. Too late, he tried to grab me, but I dodged my shoulder out of the way. I descended so fast that an orange fell out of my thali and rolled into the crowd. Dev couldn't pull back his feet even if he wanted to—there were too many eyes focused on them. He stood rooted where he was, his face ashen, his toes as vulnerable and exposed as a statue's.

I touched his right foot first, then his left, as Sandhya had instructed. The skin on his knuckles felt dry and surprisingly smooth. There was a quiver with each contact I made, as if my fingertips were delivering tiny electric shocks to him. I went through the motion of blessing myself by running my fingers through my hair.

Then I rose, my head still bowed, ready to accept my father's rage. Ready to accept the morsel that would release me from my fast for Dev.

chapter
nine

Hᴇᴍᴀ ᴅʀᴏᴠᴇ ʜᴇʀsᴇʟꜰ ᴄʀᴀᴢʏ ᴛʀʏɪɴɢ ᴛᴏ ᴘɪᴇᴄᴇ ᴛᴏɢᴇᴛʜᴇʀ ᴡʜᴀᴛ ʜᴀᴅ happened. She had read the letter from my father, but had been unable to decipher its significance. She had seen Dev so ruthlessly intercepted while trying to convey his respects to Paji. She had witnessed my father carry out his threat to storm out when I touched Dev's feet. But taken together, what did it all mean? What was the request I had made to render my father "speechless," the word he had used in his letter? What was his offer on Karva Chauth which had walked out the door with him?

Although tortured by her curiosity, Hema couldn't give in to the temptation of confronting me directly. That would mean admitting to having steamed open Paji's letter, which would lead to severe repercussions from Mataji. She had no recourse but to try and ferret out the information indirectly.

"If you had anything in the whole wide world that you wanted your father to get for you, what would it be?" she asked, mustering up all the innocence she could in her voice. When that didn't work, she tried another approach. "It's too bad your Paji had to leave so suddenly— wasn't he talking about coming back with some sort of gift for you and Dev?"

Somehow, she concluded that it must be an automobile I had cost the

family. "On the one hand, it's good she pays so much heed to our customs, but on the other, surely one can let things slide a little if it's a car
at stake." She wove more and more elaborate fantasies about this car,
right down to the brand (the larger Hindustan 14, not the more compact
Fiat), color (sometimes silver, sometimes black), and even a chauffeur
that Paji had supposedly agreed to. "There really wouldn't be a place to
put him up in our flat, but we could ask him to sleep in the car itself, as
drivers do." Even weeks after Mataji had ordered her to stop prattling on
about this nonsense, Hema still made wistful allusions to automobile
trips we could have taken to see the Qutb Minar and even the Taj Mahal,
had it not been for my rashness.

Dev spoke to me in monosyllables. He stopped wearing the open-
chested stripes and colored patterns he liked to flaunt so much, replacing
them with dark, drab shirts which he buttoned up to the neck. At night,
he lay on his talai with his back to me. Sometimes, he sobbed quietly in
the dark, with inhalations deep enough for me to notice, but not so loud
that Sandhya or Arya would hear. We no longer hugged or touched each
other. Mataji asked me why he seemed to always be moping, to which I
remained silent. "There's friction in every marriage," she said. "Men are
too proud, it's the wife that must adjust."

"It's not so bad," I tried to cajole him one day, "that you can't even
change that gloomy shirt. You've been wearing it so long that you look
more tragic than Saigal playing Devdas." Dev said nothing, just left the
room silently.

Minutes later, he returned to the bedroom and indicated that I follow
him outside. The house was empty—Arya and Babuji were at the station and the women had gone shopping. Dev held a small gunny bag, the
type used to store rice. In the courtyard, he pushed aside the charpoy
and slammed the bag down a few times on the ground underneath. He
held it up and shook it to assess the damage to its contents. Not satisfied,
he carried the bag to the toilet door and pounded it repeatedly against
the cement steps. Then he handed it to me. "This is what you wanted,
isn't it?" he said, before stalking out of the house.

I opened the bag and looked at the shards of record pieces inside. A few of the fragments still had the labels attached, and on one of them, *Saigal* stood out in clear white letters against the red background.

"EVEN GODS GET ANGRY SOMETIMES," Sandhya said, as she took the lid off the pressure cooker from my dowry. The earthy aroma of moong wafted out. "But who can explain their motives? Look at Arya—you might not know it, since he always appears so calm when you see him, but even he can have quite a temper." She laughed, as if at a private joke. "I don't know what the problem is between you and Dev— everyone can see there's something wrong—but I'm sure it will work itself out."

By now, the luster of Karva Chauth had faded from Sandhya's face. She no longer glowed like a new bride—her skin, so smooth and radiant just days ago, had begun to reveal its imperfections again. The polish had rubbed off her nails, the bangles packed away in a box like Divali decorations for the next year. There had not been a single wait in front of the bedroom door all week. The one thing that hadn't reverted to its previous state was Sandhya's attitude towards me. If anything, she had become warmer, so that she was now the person I felt the closest to in the household. We had started sitting together on the charpoy every morning after bathing, to let the sun dry our hair. Sometimes, I read out from the newspaper for her (she especially liked the horoscopes and the matrimonial ads). On other days, I showed her the letters of the alphabet on a writing slate.

Hema reacted to our friendship with dismay—a dismay somewhat tempered by the fact that I started to help with the cooking. Though I had never prepared rice before, mine came out so much fluffier that even Sandhya acknowledged it. "I don't know what it is—I keep wishing I was able to do some things better—Arya deserves it."

It wasn't the cooking that filled her with anxiousness, but her lack of children. She had been married for eight years already. "Sometimes I tell myself it's because I pray to Devi Ma just for a son. I know that's what Arya wants—a boy. So far, Devi Ma has only seen daughters in my womb, which is why she doesn't let them be born. It has to be only a matter of time before she looks in the right nook inside to locate a boy."

On Mondays, Sandhya kept the fast for Shiva, and ate only once, to ensure Arya's longevity. On Thursdays, she took no dairy products, to propitiate the goddess of fertility. She would go to the Lakshmi temple on Saturdays, and catch the train to Okhla to visit a holy woman on Sunday evenings. For a while, she had given up meat as a further inducement to the Devi Ma, resuming its consumption only when the doctor informed her that not eating it might actually cause her to become less fertile.

I was never bold enough to bring up the time she had emerged with a swollen face from her night with Arya. "He's my god," she would tell me, as if aware of what was in my mind. "And surely gods have the right to do what they want, don't they? Besides, it's in the nature of men to let things out once in a while."

I wondered about her parents, and about the rest of her family. I had noticed she never went anywhere, and nobody came to visit her. One day, as we were cleaning the stones out of the month's ration of wheat, she told me her story.

"My father was never very well-off. He had a small store in Lahore, selling notebooks and paper and odds and ends. Have you heard of Heera Mandi, the red-light area, Didi? We were right next to it, so close that tawaifs would drop by in groups during the day. They would laugh and talk and hold up the pens like pieces of jewelry against their skin. Sometimes, a costly item like one of those new ballpoint pens caught their eye. Then they returned in the evening, all dressed up in silvery dupattas and bright red lipstick. They always brought along a customer on such visits, to make the purchase for them. Do you know what I always wondered? What possible use could they have had, Didi, for all those pens they bought?"

Sandhya did not come out in front of the tawaifs, she said, but peeped out of the back room when they came. "My father hadn't forbidden me, mind you—I simply worried about what I wore. People sold parachutes in those days, left over from the war. I don't know if you ever saw them, Didi, if they sold them as cheaply in Rawalpindi as well. My mother would buy one and make outfits from it for all of us. The material was so light and tightly woven that it was quite comfortable for shirts and salwars. But I was young and silly back then. I did not want the tawaifs to giggle at me if they recognized the cheap material my clothes were made from."

I tried to imagine Sandhya as she described herself. She always seemed so quiet and measured now, so serious. Could she really have been carefree, even frivolous, as a girl?

"The morning we left Lahore, my father loaded all the wares he could onto a wooden handcart. Pens and pencils, diaries, bottles of ink, sets of crayons. Box upon box of all the things he carried, from key chains to rulers to glass paperweights—the kind with flowers stuck inside, that came from Iran." The only thing he left behind was the paper. "Bundles of it, tied in brown wrapping, which he piled neatly outside the door. It was amazing, he said, that he hadn't been looted like the other shops on the street. 'The paper is too heavy to carry, so it'll be an offering for all the luck we've enjoyed.' He tied things down as best as he could on the cart and sat my brother Anand on top. As he rolled the handcart down the street, I kept looking back. I wanted to see the tawaifs come out from their buildings and make their way to the paper. Finally, they would have something on which to use all their pens, I thought."

"You never told me you had a brother."

"No, I never did, did I, Didi?—he was a darling little seven-year-old. I was seventeen then, the eldest child. After me had come two boys, both of whom died of typhoid the year I turned nine. That's what made my mother have Anand—he was born ten years after me. He was the only son who lived, so naturally my parents doted on him. They treated him as if he was made of glass, as if he could break at any time. He was the picture of health though, always laughing and with the fat red cheeks of a Ganesh idol. My mother used to tell him that on his tenth birthday he would grow a trunk and then be complete. We all adored him, even my younger sister Chandini, born a year after Anand. She wanted to ride with him atop the cart. But my father said it would be too heavy to wheel them both, so she had to walk."

It took them the whole day to get through the smoldering streets to where the Grand Trunk Road left Lahore. "I still remember my first sight of the people. They were packed so close that I thought the road itself was alive. Like a snake crawling, or rather, two snakes, sliding slowly over each other in opposite directions. One moving away from us towards India, and the other side, the Muslim one, entering Lahore.

"The last time I had seen so many people was when we had made the pilgrimage to Katasraj temple on the day of Divali. Except that I knew nobody in this crowd was a pilgrim, they were all refugees. They walked along silently with their crying children. Sometimes a goat or dog followed behind. I saw people still bleeding from beatings they must have received on the way from Muridke. A few wheeled handcarts like the one my father pushed, even though everything they'd been carrying had been lost or looted. I could not bear to look at their eyes, so hollow and empty of life. There was a long line of trucks as well, filled with even more refugees. But the road was so jammed that it seemed faster to walk."

I thought of our own flight from Rawalpindi on the train. It was true, what Paji always said, about us being the lucky ones. Would we have ever made it if forced to walk?

"Anand was the only one of us who actually enjoyed the journey. 'Ganesh is sitting on his cart and being carried home,' my mother said. She made the trip a game for him. She told him a story about how Ashoka had the Grand Trunk Road built a long time ago. She tried to remember the names of the cities that lay along its route—between Kabul and Calcutta, she said. Every few miles, she asked him if he was hungry or thirsty, and pressed her hand over his forehead, to make sure he hadn't developed a fever. Whenever we came to a hill, she picked him up and carried him in her arms to lighten my father's load on the cart. I carried Chandini as well, whenever she began to slow. But my sister could see it was too much weight for me, so she tried to keep walking without complaining. Anand asked to switch positions with Chandini a few times to give her a rest, but my father always refused."

Twenty miles out of Lahore, just before another hill, Sandhya's father stopped. "He had been having difficulty with the cart. He would grunt as he tried to pull it one minute, then push it from behind when that didn't work. My mother suggested giving away some of the wares, but he would not hear of it. 'Each pen that I carry will buy one more kilo of flour for us when we get to India.' He rested for a few minutes, then pushed the cart all the way to the top of the rise without stopping.

"He was just about to start down, when Anand noticed that Chandini was far behind. 'Please, Pitaji, can't she ride on the cart instead?' I remember him asking. By now dust had covered over the red of his cheeks. But you could still make out how plump they were underneath.

" 'Don't worry, she'll catch up with us,' my father said, and began guiding the cart down the slope. He wove it between the people as it began to pick up speed. He was almost at the bottom when the right wheel hit a rock. The handles were wrenched from his hands and the axle broke in two.

"We all crowded around, first to stare at the damage, then to try and save the boxes being stepped on by the crowd. It was Chandini who noticed that Anand was not helping. He was sitting where he had fallen off, his head bent slightly forward. It looked like he was examining the Persian paperweights, which had rolled out around him.

"My mother called out his name, but he did not speak. She ran over, the crayons she had been gathering still in her hand. When she touched his shoulder, he fell over to the ground. We watched silently as he lay on his side with his eyes closed. His small chest rose and fell as if he was in a deep sleep. I remember the paperweights around his head shining in the sunlight. One of them had split open neatly into two halves. The flower inside was simply a curl of plastic."

Sandhya's father tried to stop the people going past. "He called to them to take what they wanted from his handcart, if only they could help. Notebooks that sold for four annas, crayon sets for eight, he offered for the price of a bandage. But what use were such items to people fleeing? They kept going past with barely a glance. Their only response was to circle around the area marked out by the paperweights. My father even tried to get the truck drivers to stop, especially the ones going back toward the hospitals in Lahore. He thrust brand-new diaries and expensive fountain pens through their windows. But they, too, drove on."

Finally, a doctor coming from Amritsar did an examination as best he could. "He must have been Muslim, but we didn't ask. 'The boy's still breathing, but the injury's gone to his brain.' He parted Anand's hair and showed us the thin red line starting above his temple. 'He won't last long—there's nothing you can do.'

"By morning, my brother was dead, as the doctor had said. We went searching for wood, but there was only scrub around. So my father broke up his cart and used that for the cremation. As the fire began to crackle, his eyes turned to Chandini, and I saw what he was thinking. If only he had let her change places with Anand. Then it would have been his daughter's body being eaten by the flames, not his son's.

"It was at that instant that I had a revelation. Arun and Alok, the two brothers who were born before Anand—surely my father must blame me, too, for not dying instead of them. The years of anguished looks from him, the bursts of anger for no reason. Suddenly, they all seemed to make sense. I stood there by the side of the road, watching my last brother burn. I vowed to make things up to my father by not letting myself become a burden when we got to India. As the smoke rose into the air, tears came to my eyes for Anand and even for Chandini. But I did not allow any for myself."

I put down my sifter and silently took Sandhya's hand in my own. Sandhya curled her fingers around mine. The uncleaned wheat lay forgotten, spilling out from its gunnysack.

"We remained there for hours. My mother had lost the will to move. In the end, a truck driver stopped. Perhaps he spotted the tiny pyre and felt pity. He let us squeeze into the crowd of people already in the back of his truck. When I looked at my parents, they stared back sightlessly. Their eyes were as empty now as those of the refugees from Muridke who had been beaten. Chandini was crying to herself, so I took her in my lap. I started telling the same stories about the Grand Trunk Road that my mother had related to Anand.

"We crossed the border at Wagah. I don't know what I had been expecting. Blue rivers and green plains, tigers and elephants, forest-covered mountains. All the wonders we had been promised about the Indian side. But the landscape didn't change. It had the same scrub and wild brush, the same dirt and heat. There were no sentries or guns or even a gate. All I saw were poles stuck into the ground, as if waiting for flags, and a row of upturned barrels painted white. Still, I felt a lump in my throat as we went over the line. I wanted to shout along when the cries of 'Long live Hindustan!' went up in the truck. But my parents didn't join in, so neither did I."

They stayed with the truck all the way to Delhi. "The refugee camp at Kingsway had too many people waiting, so we ended up at a smaller one on the other side of the Yamuna. Even then, they were out of tents, since so many refugees had already arrived. All that was left was a bare stretch of land, on which one of the camp workers marked out a rectangle in chalk for us. For the first week, we simply sat and slept in this rectangle, this piece of our new country. We let the rain soak our clothes and the sun dry them out, and waited for a tent. Little by little, we managed to gather pieces of wood and cardboard and tin and rope to build a small shack as the other refugees had done. Our plot turned out to be one of the worst ones, right next to the open field which served as the latrine for the whole camp. Even now when I press my nose against my skin, I think I can still breathe in the smell." I squeezed Sandhya's hand again, and she squeezed back.

"Twice a day, we lined up to receive our rotis and dal. I remember wishing I had some mango pickle for taste, or even a piece of raw onion. The drinking water was so dirty there was always the fear of cholera. Neither of my parents seemed surprised when Chandini fell seriously ill. They seemed to regard her worsening condition as part of her fate, as something to be expected. My father even talked about having a special ceremony at her cremation, where Anand's soul could be prayed for as well. But then some medical supplies were donated to the camp. Chandini's fever went away like magic with just a few pills.

"That's when I first saw Arya—he was the volunteer who brought the medicine to us. When Chandini recovered, my mother had my father search out Arya and invite him to our shack for tea. She paid a neighbor one paisa to borrow a teacup, and even managed to find a laddoo from somewhere to serve on the plate. When Arya came, Chandini was taken outside to show how well she'd recovered thanks to him. My mother told me to stay indoors for modesty's sake. I peeked through the rubber flap that served as our window. It was like being back in my father's shop and spying on the tawaifs again. I noticed how Arya took bites of just the right size, so that his laddoo lasted exactly as long as his tea did. Afterwards, he took out his handkerchief and carefully brushed the crumbs off his mustache. Even though the stool was too small for him, he sat on it with his back perfectly straight. Compared to everyone else in the camp, he looked very clean."

Arya seemed to adopt their family. "By now it was clear no tents were coming, so he would drop by with things for our hut. A piece of piping, a length of electric wire, and once, best of all, a sheet of plastic to stop the roof from leaking. I kept my face veiled during these visits and crouched in a corner with my mother. But it was impossible to keep my eyes from straying while he performed his repairs. A few times, when he caught me looking at him, I was unable to break my gaze. He had this way of drawing me in.

"It wasn't as if I started imagining I was in love. That was too far and fantastic to even enter my mind. My goal, what I thought about all the time, was to get married. I wanted my parents to be free of responsibility for me. If that couldn't be arranged, I had decided I would run away. Even if it meant ending up like one of the tawaifs who used to come to my father's shop. I knew there were a number of families like us who had lost everything in the Partition and were facing the same problem. It would take years to save up for a new dowry to get a daughter like me married. Many months back, my mother's cousin had written to us about a possible boy for me in India. However, that family had taken over a flat left behind by a Muslim neighbor in Delhi. This had greatly increased their worth, so a match with them was now out of the question."

Arya was the one who told them about a scheme being started by the HRM. "It was a marriage service. They were trying to match up unmarried girls with boys from the same community, to lessen at least this one worry of the refugees. My father didn't think anything could come of it, but I insisted he put my name in. Not surprisingly, there were many more daughters than sons whose names ended up on the list. Being completely uneducated, I had next to no chance of being picked.

"When Arya heard that they had run out of grooms before getting to me, he told my father that he would offer his own name as a match. After all, he said, he had been a refugee himself only weeks ago. It was just luck that they had arrived early enough to be moved into a small flat while all we got was a bare piece of land. His family was not pleased with his decision. One of the conditions of these matches was that no dowry would be exchanged. Being the father of a girl who had to be married off herself, Babuji was naturally upset. My mother had saved some earrings, which was the only thing she could give me as dowry. She had some rings as well, but I told her to save those for Chandini."

They got married at the end of September, about a month after the border crossing. "My family had to leave for Jabalpur the very next week. That's where the government had decided to resettle them—all my father had been able to do was delay it a little. I was the only girl married in the camp for whom a wedding procession came. There was no band or horse, just the doli—the same one in which you sat, which took me away.

"I never saw my family again. I was supposed to go visit them four months after my marriage. Babuji had even managed to get a ticket for me. But a few days before leaving, a telegram arrived from the Jabalpur refugee office. My family's cottage had burned down with all three of them inside. Neither my father nor my mother had ever recovered from the death of my brother. The job which the office had arranged for my father was that of a laborer—working to break stones for a new road. When I went there, the neighbors told me that the fire had started shortly after my father had returned that night. It was too early for the family to have been asleep, they said. The windows and doors had all been bolted from inside.

"Arya came with me to Jabalpur. They had found some charred remains, and he was the one who lit the pyres. On the way back, he sat the whole way while I lay with my head in his lap. I didn't sleep, but kept wondering what the point was of the long and difficult journey my family had made to India. Why couldn't we have just stayed where we were in Lahore and been murdered there? Then I realized that there had been a purpose after all—to deliver me to Arya.

"Now you see why it's so important that I not let him down. That I complete the task for which I was brought here, for which I was saved. Sometimes I see Anand, lying there peacefully as if asleep, the paper-weights twinkling like stars around his head. That's when I know my duty is to create another image just like him. For my family, to show them all that they didn't die in vain. For Arya, without whom I would have been in a brothel somewhere, or burnt to death along with Chandini in Jabalpur. I would gladly give him my life, but that's not what he needs. What my Arya requires from me is a son to carry on his name."

chapter
ten

Some weekends after Divali, the local HRM branch organized its annual exhibition event. We all went down to the public field behind the post office where Arya conducted his early morning exercises. Just two days before, the railway minister himself had come there to make a speech after inaugurating a set of new track relays at Nizamuddin, which Babuji had proudly informed us had been imported from Germany. Giant cloth hoardings with the minister's face still stared down from the middle of the field, interspersed with advertisements for industrial machinery from companies like Tata and Godrej and Siemens. There was also a billboard for Bata shoes among them, with the picture of a farmer holding a scythe, next to his wife and two children, all clad in village clothes with shiny new plastic sandals on their feet.

Large striped durries had been spread out over the grass. Sandhya led us to the very front, where a section had been marked off for special guests. I sat next to her, but Dev, still sulking, made it a point to sit next to Babuji, not me. Arya came over with a boy carrying glasses of tea, and I saw a quick flash pass over his face as he glanced first at his brother, then at me. "I'll send out some hot samosas," he said, and returned to the club building to see how the preparations were proceeding.

By ten, Kartik Babu, the official supposed to deliver the inaugural address an hour earlier, still hadn't shown up. Since the spectators at the edges of the sparsely seated durries were beginning to wander away, Arya gave the signal for the events to begin. The new recruits trooped out, gangly fourteen-year-olds in white undershirts and khaki shorts that looked like school uniforms. They did some marching exercises, but the recently planted billboards were a problem, and they had to keep turning around at the picture of the smiling minister. After the marching, they began performing calisthenics on the ground. Arya roamed through them like a general inspecting his troops, blowing the whistle in his mouth to indicate the count, occasionally prodding a boy's buttocks or spreading a pair of legs further apart with his foot.

Hema leaned forward in interest to watch the lathi duels that followed, her eyes widening each time the bamboo poles made a cracking sound. She seemed even more taken by the subsequent sword fighting, cheering at the more flamboyant thrusts, grabbing onto my arm when a boy got nicked. There was a wrestling display, for which the participants took off their undershirts and smeared their arms and chests with mud from a pit. Then came the last event, when Arya and one of the other instructors faced each other with lathis, bare-chested.

Arya's body, I noticed, was a lot thicker than Dev's—no naag on his chest, just a mat of wiry hair. He seemed to seek me out from the audience each time there was a break in the maneuvers, though perhaps it was Sandhya he was looking for. The fight ended with Arya pinning his opponent to the ground between his muscular thighs. He raised his lathi high in the air, then brought its end down to within an inch of the instructor's throat. This time there was no mistaking it—as he stood to take a bow, Arya's eyes locked purposefully with mine.

By now, Kartik Babu had arrived and the podium was dragged back to the front for his welcoming speech. He was older than I had expected, and was dressed in the saffron clothes of a sanyasi, with white ash marks on his forehead. "People ask why the HRM trains with lathis and swords. Why we make our boys get up before dawn and do push-ups on the ground. Why we teach them not to let the seeds of their life force spill out. The answer, I say, is freedom. We have to be vigilant and strong if we want to preserve the honor of our mother, this country.

"But that's not the Indian way, they say. We believe in nonviolence, they say, in turning the other cheek. To which my reply is to learn from the lessons of history. All the invaders who have swept across this country, from Mahmud of Gazni to Babar, from the Portuguese to the British, have been welcomed with turned cheeks. Cheeks that have been gouged time and time again. Remember this is our mother we are talking about. What kind of children are these who would stand by and see her bloodied and violated?

"I'll tell you who they are. These people living like parasites off our mother's body. They are the people who should have left for Pakistan a long time ago. Instead, they are still here. Why? Because the government needs their vote, that's why. The same government who forbids the HRM from going into politics, who says that rifles are too dangerous for us to practice with, that we should be content with defending our mother with sticks."

There followed a tirade against Muslim Personal Law, according to which Muslim men could have up to four wives. "Why not six or twelve or a whole harem?" Kartik Babu railed. "The government could get even more Muslim votes that way. And with all those wives, what about all the children they keep producing? The whole country has become a factory for Muslims, a breeding ground where they can multiply like mosquitoes, like flies.

"This year, the same government forced a Hindu marriage act down our throats that is a hundred times more restrictive. Next year, they plan to pass more. To preserve the rights of women that come from Hindu tradition, they say. Tell me, where in the Vedas does it say that widows should inherit their husbands' property, that daughters cannot be married until they're fifteen? And if they're so concerned, why don't they worry about the rights of Muslim women, instead of telling them they're worth only one-quarter of a husband? Why this discrimination, why this special treatment? Is this what Nehru means when he crows about his secularism?

"Which is why I say, learn to use your lathis. The enemy is all around. But there's peace now, people say, there's enough for everyone, there's prosperity. That's why we must be dormant now, like a datura seed buried deep in the ground, waiting to germinate when the rains return. The time may not be now when we need to wield our weapons. But it will come sooner than you think."

By the time the speech ended, I was dazed. Even more unnerving than the hatred gushing out of Kartik Babu's mouth was the way Dev's family seemed rapt at his words. Did Mataji and Hema, their brows furrowed in concentration, really subscribe to such ideas? What about Sandhya, with the glow on her face—surely her dreamy look wasn't due to the speech, but the lingering memory of her husband's lathi display? Only Dev was staring away in moody distraction, like a boy forced to attend school on a Saturday when he would rather be off playing cricket.

The congregation rose to its feet, and reluctantly, I did as well. Kartik Babu raised a fist into the air, then slammed it into his chest. The club members all followed—next to me, I heard a soft thump from Hema's breast. "Long live India," Kartik Babu shouted. "Jai Hind." The crowd responded after him, repeating the words each time he did. The new recruits were brought out one last time to sing the national anthem.

Dev slunk away, but I did not follow him. Instead, I tried to broach the subject of the coming Hindu Code laws with Hema, to educate her about all the protections she would be granted. "It's not only sons who will inherit property, but daughters as well." She barely listened, darting off to watch the recruits engage in an impromptu wrestling match.

I was trying again with Sandhya, who seemed more attentive, when Arya came up. I wondered why he had still not put on his shirt—the tangle of his chest hair glistened with sweat. "How did Bhabhiji enjoy the show?" he asked. Since I was his bhabhi, he followed the custom of not speaking directly to me, addressing the question to Sandhya instead.

"She didn't like your Kartik Babu's speech," Sandhya answered jovially. "Who can understand all this marriage act business anyway? But tell me, what about the fighting, Bhabhiji? Did you at least appreciate all that thwack-thwack?" She laughed, and I attempted to muster a smile as well.

"Where's Dev?" Arya asked me. "He seemed to leave in a hurry. I hope everything is all right." I felt myself turn red as he searched my face.

Mataji came up just then to pull Sandhya away for the preparation of the afternoon meal. Arya and I were left alone. Neither of us spoke. I resolved to keep looking down until he left, and began counting the red and brown stripes of the durrie. I was aware, just outside my vision, of the presence of his feet. I willed them to carry him somewhere else, but they didn't move. A waft of breeze blew the odor of his sweat towards me. It was pungent, like papaya, but with the sweetness removed, not at all like Dev's. The smell thickened around me, insinuating itself with the palpability of a cloth being wound around my face. I imagined it emanating from his armpits, from the pores on his back, from the soles of his feet, and shuddered. If only I looked at him, I knew I would be able to breathe again, but still I didn't.

"Meera," he said, and my head snapped up in shock. He had never uttered anything before to me directly—it was audacious for him to use something as personal as my name. "I want you to know . . ."

I tried to look away, but it was too late. He made sure my gaze was engaged, and with careful deliberateness, let his mask slip. The lust that he allowed to surface was so unvarnished it made me recoil.

"I want you to know how beautiful I think you are. If Dev ever—" Before he could finish, I rushed away.

ALTHOUGH I MANAGED to escape Arya then, it was harder to do so in the bedroom we shared. Suddenly his essence seemed to rise from the walls and permeate the air, as if something ripe and tropical had burst in the room. I tried to avoid looking at him, but my gaze, unwillingly, kept being drawn towards where he lay. At such moments, he stared at me with open desire. Each night that he saw Dev and me sleep apart on our separate talais seemed to sharpen his confidence, make him bolder. Once, as I squeezed by his charpoy, he turned so that my dupatta snagged on his elbow; another time, when the electricity went out, he ran a toe quickly across my abdomen while looking for candles on our side of the room. He accosted me in the courtyard to whisper my name, and loitered outside shirtless each time he saw me go into the bathroom. One morning when I unrolled my towel, a pair of his dirty underwear fell out.

There was nobody to whom I could complain. Dev was still not speaking to me, and the others wouldn't have believed what I had to say. What amazed me was that nobody noticed his behavior, or sensed anything amiss. Sandhya even relayed one of his overtures to me. "They're opening a new branch, the HRM. A shakha just for women, to get wives involved in the party as well. Arya asked if you would be interested in being the manager. You'd be working only under him all day, not to worry. They need someone who can read and write, or he might have asked me."

I told myself that since Mataji or Babuji or Sandhya were always at home, I would never be alone with Arya for him to try anything. But his constant advances made me increasingly jumpy and weakened my appetite. At night, I shrouded myself with my sheet, the way Sandhya did—it was the only way I felt secure. I had nightmares in which I was pursued across the empty platforms of Nizamuddin station and captured by malevolent presences springing up from the rail tracks. The slightest cough or scrape awakened me. Sometimes, when I uncovered my head to look at the time, I saw the whites of Arya's eyes gleaming through the darkness. I longed to cling to Dev, but he still shrank away when we touched.

Then my world changed. I found out I was pregnant.

chapter
eleven

THERE WAS ONLY ONE NIGHT IT COULD HAVE HAPPENED—A MONTH AND a half ago, just before Karva Chauth. It was during the week when Sandhya had been in her bridal bloom, the headiness of her scent making her irresistible to Arya. Dev and I had waited each evening for the light to go out in the bedroom, but that night, the delay was interminably long. For the first time, as we bid his parents and Hema a strained good night, I noticed the anger in his face beneath the surface. Perhaps it was this anger that made him throw aside his cover to squeeze in next to me under my sheet. He did not pull back when he usually did, but continued even when the rustling of our bedclothes grew alarmingly obvious. There was a cough as a warning from the other side of the room, but still, Dev pressed defiantly on. I gripped onto the sheet to keep us covered and sunk my head back into my pillow to blot out our sounds. Dev did not stop until he climaxed inside me, the one concession he made being not to cry out aloud.

When he first heard about our baby, Dev tried to show everyone that he was overjoyed. But at night, he still kept his distance, pulling his talai away from mine and keeping his back turned to me. It took some days for this to mend, for the wave of excitement in the house to lift him up in its swell, for his shirts to display some of their color again. One evening, he came home from work with a pair of baby socks and a tiny toy bell, another time he presented me with a new mother's diary and record book. Even when he placed his head on my belly and claimed to hear the baby singing inside, I sensed that his happiness was exaggerated. "Will it be a boy or a girl?" he said, without really trying to guess the answer. "What name will we pick?" he asked, but did not share in my laughter when I told him the names (all after favorite film stars) Hema had come up with so far. Sometimes, I found him sitting alone in the darkened living room after work, staring wistfully at the silent radiogram.

Mataji was more exuberant in her reaction—breaking coconuts in the temple in gratitude, performing ceremonies over me to ward off the evil eye, showering me with gifts of sweets and trinkets and toys. She started feeding me almonds crushed in milk every morning, and had a vat of mutton soup boiled for extra protein. Ten kilos of cotton were delivered to the house on her orders one Tuesday. Mataji sat on a charpoy in the courtyard and supervised the mattress maker himself to make sure he stuffed it all into the new talai he was sewing to better support my back. Every few days, she went to the market and returned with fresh pods of tamarind, their insides tart and sticky. "It's the one craving that was the same during each of my pregnancies—keep it by your bed in case you need some in the middle of the night."

Hema had already claimed the prerogative of naming the child. "I'm really good at it," she announced, pulling out her old dolls and reciting their names for me. "This one's Sweetie, and that one Dolly. The blue one I named Babloo, although without the head you can no longer tell it's a boy." She started parading around the house self-importantly in a sari, as befitted her approaching aunthood. Every afternoon, she crept into the bedroom and quietly nibbled off segments from the tamarind Mataji had left for me.

As I feared, Sandhya did not take the news well. She was in the kitchen when Mataji took me over to tell her, and looked up from her cooking shocked, as if she had been slapped. For the next day she didn't talk to any of us, but went around with her eyes rimmed red, the pain raw on her face. She seemed withdrawn for a long time after that—nodding whenever Mataji or I asked how she was, and quickly walking away so that she didn't have to speak. The writing slate remained untouched, and she no longer kept me company while I dried my hair.

Then one day I came upon her sitting in front of the shrine of holy pictures near the fridge. "For eight years I've been keeping every fast there is. At first all I could feel was jealousy, and anger at how I'd been betrayed." Sandhya turned around to look at me, and I noticed the flowers in her hand, the fresh mark of ash she'd applied to her forehead. Jasmine-scented smoke wisped up from a stick of incense, burning in front of several small pictures of incarnations of Devi arranged in a thali.

"I don't know if this will make any difference, since it hasn't for me. But for whatever it's worth, today I'm fasting for a son for my didi."

THE NEWS HAD ONE more profound effect—overnight, it put an end to Arya's advances. It wasn't just the reconciliation with Dev that did it, which Arya must have deduced from the sight of our talais nestling against each other again every night (one being twice the height of the other now, with all the cotton in mine). The fact that I was now with child made me exalted, inviolable—to prey on me would be to meddle with the forces of birth and creation, and this could invite unknown consequences. One evening, Arya came home carrying a paper bag which he placed respectfully in front of me. "Apricots," he said. "For the baby. For my nephew. Or niece." When I looked at him, there was no hint of the leer that I had become so used to seeing on his face—his expression now was serious, even contrite. I thanked him for the present, and he withdrew, satisfied. Even though I loved apricots, and knew they were quite expensive, I gave them to the ganga the next morning, much to her delight.

THE WEEKS WENT BY, and I waited impatiently for the baby to start showing. My fantasy was to promenade my swollen stomach around Nizamuddin, and have people compliment me on it. Every day I worried if my pregnancy was following the correct timetable—I looked in the mirror and wondered how to encourage the baby along. I still had no morning sickness, still hadn't craved the tamarind as Mataji had promised. My breasts hurt every night, and I was severely constipated, but other than that, I felt fine.

Mataji massaged my scalp with mustard oil every morning in the December sunlight. She brought me Ayurvedic powders and tonics and kept strict tally of what I ate—making sure that the heating foods like eggplant and mutton were balanced with enough cooling ones like yogurt and cucumber. More importantly, she was the arbitrator, the filter, for the streams of advice that came my way. "Eat bananas and milk and other white foods to ensure the baby is fair-skinned." "Sleep with a copper bracelet around your right wrist if you want it to be intelligent." "Rub your private area with fenugreek paste every day to ensure an easy delivery." "Eat lots of garlic, it will strengthen the baby's stomach." "Whatever you do, don't touch garlic or papaya—there's nothing more dangerous for a fetus." Hema, especially, like a bird foraging for bits of food and flying them to her nest, kept up a daily supply of suggestions gathered from her friends (although much to her disappointment, not one of her tidbits met with Mataji's approval). Even the ganga, perhaps to show her appreciation for the apricots, felt compelled to contribute by telling me what breast-milk-enhancing foods I could start eating to ensure a good supply.

For the first time since I had left Darya Ganj in a doli, I felt I could allow myself to relax—even, perhaps, be happy. The future seemed to be finally arranging itself in auspicious patterns, there was an optimistic tang to the air. The sun could shine in Nizamuddin as well, I now believed, the clouds drift away overhead, the sky become as clear. Dev's household might not have been what I had imagined for my life, but I had succeeded in the fight for my niche there. I had passed the test of Karva Chauth, and yet shown Dev he couldn't take me for granted. I had won over Mataji and Sandhya and Hema and even managed to single-handedly arrest Arya's advances. It was true I didn't agree with every opinion or custom of my in-laws, but with the arrival of the baby, I could slowly try asserting my own views more. My stature would rise, my position become more secure, especially if I gave birth to a boy. I found myself wishing for a son as I daydreamed on my talai, and had to shake the thought out of my head. This was exactly the mind-set Paji abhorred, one he had tried so hard to make sure we never embraced.

I had not seen or spoken to him since he walked out on Karva Chauth. My calls to Darya Ganj had petered out, since Biji used the excuse of my pregnancy to drop in several times a week unannounced. "Most fathers would be ecstatic at becoming grandfathers," she told me. "But who can try to figure out your Paji? He was upset when he heard about Roopa's pregnancy, and positively enraged when I told him about yours."

Although Paji's disapproval bothered me, it was Dev's lack of enthusiasm that was the real damper on my happiness. He dropped all attempts at pretending to be jubilant, and instead became subdued, even morose. Frayed old shirts in somber tones alternated with bright bursts of pattern—he didn't seem to care any longer what he wore. At night now, it was I who did the comforting, Dev who needed to be held. I was bewildered at first that he wasn't rejoicing the way I was, then hurt, then angry, then concerned. He was the father, after all—what effect would it have on the baby if he was so withdrawn? I kept asking him if there was something he wanted to talk about, and he kept answering that there was nothing wrong. "It's Paji's Bombay offer, I know," I finally confronted him with one night. "Isn't that what you're still in mourning about?"

"No," he said, after reflecting for a long time, which I knew signified that he really meant yes. "I just need a while to adjust. I'm not becoming a singer, you know—instead, I'm becoming a father. I should be happy that my clerking job at Hindustan Petroleum is so secure."

Looking back, I should have simply taken him at his word and left it at that. Perhaps all he needed was time alone to make the transition, as he said. But the glow of the baby inside me, the coddling from Mataji, the way everything seemed to be working out in my favor—all this filled me with a sense of good fortune that I wanted to share. I felt Dev and I had been playing a game of wills that I had won. Wasn't it my duty, as victor, to lift him out of his misery? It wouldn't just be magnanimity on my part—there was also the troubling issue of guilt. Hadn't I been the one to ruin the opportunity presented by Paji—what if Dev never became a singer due to me? At the very least I should try to make his Bombay dream come true—we could leave sometime after I had the baby. Giving up Mataji and Biji's help with the infant would be a sacrifice, but a small one in exchange for harmony. Besides, an even more unsettling question loomed in the background if I didn't make the attempt: what if Dev somehow held the baby responsible, instead of only blaming me?

That's when I made the fateful decision. I went to see Paji.

MATAJI SUMMONED A TAXI from the station to take me to my family's home in Darya Ganj. She had been unwilling to let me go by myself, but relented when I invented a Sawhney tradition requiring me to make the first trip back alone. "Are you sure you don't want me to accompany you?" she asked one final time, and I assured her I'd be fine. "Don't try to take some roundabout route," she warned the taxi driver. "We've been living in Delhi since before you were born."

I kept the window open, even though the wind blowing in was cutting and cold. Near the Old Fort, the familiar winter smell of pine nuts being roasted in cauldrons of sand was so strong that I almost had the driver stop so that I could buy some. There was a traffic jam as usual near Golcha cinema, and bullock carts being loaded with blocks of ice in the market lane. As I watched, a woman poured water over two boys sitting soaped-up on the sidewalk.

All through the ride, I kept rehearsing what I would say to Paji. I would apologize for my disobedience on Karva Chauth, of course, blaming it on the fasting that had made me too light-headed to think straight. "You were right, Paji," I would tell him, "I have to get away from their influence at once if I want to retain control of my life." Or perhaps, "If I want to live with a semblance of the principles you have taught me," is how I would put it. And now, it was even more crucial—not just a question of me, but also my child ("*Your* grandchild"). He had already seen how religious they all were, how orthodox—perhaps I would also let slip that Arya worked for the HRM. Did Paji really want to see his own flesh and blood being raised in that atmosphere? Could he stand the thought of his grandson bending down every morning to touch the feet of his elders? Scraping his forehead before priests at temples? Parading around with a lathi and doing push-ups every dawn as an HRM cadet?

Paji seemed to be in a jovial mood, which I recognized as a particularly dangerous sign. "I've sent your mother away," he said, leading me into his library. "Thought we could chat more freely this way." Even though it was the middle of December, the library air conditioner was still on. He shut the door behind me and circled around to sit down at his desk. I remained standing, my hands and face numb—either with cold or with dread, I couldn't be sure.

"Please," Paji said. "Tell me what's on your mind." He leaned back in his chair with an affable expression, as if having entrusted himself to my capable hands, he was confident of being regaled. As I blurted out the speech I had rehearsed, he nodded bemusedly a few times, even chuckling softly when I mentioned Arya was an employee of the HRM.

"I have some good news too," Paji said, after I had finished. I stood there, shivering, waiting to hear the verdict on whether he would help. "Did you know that what your sister's cultivating in *her* belly down in Visakhapatnam turns out to be twins? I should have bought a box of sweets, of laddoos, shouldn't I have—all this news to celebrate. Perhaps you can get in the game, too—have triplets, what do you say?" He gestured around the confines of the room. "A whole litter of grandchildren, like puppies running around—just think of how thrilled your Biji would be then."

"Paji, I—"

"Yes, yes, I know. I'm being unfair. It's the natural instinct to breed. All mammals find it hard to control—females, especially, who feel they haven't lived unless they lactate. But don't you think you could have stopped for a moment to lift yourself above your animal nature? Waited a few years? Is he so flawless, that husband of yours, that you had to lie on your back right away and reproduce another version of him?"

"But we weren't even trying to, Paji. It just happened."

"Ah, it was an accident. A mistake. And now you're asking me to help so nothing happens to it. This accident that you say is my grandchild. Tell me, why should I do anything, why should I care about it? Half its blood will always be your husband's, won't it? How do I know it won't *want* to prostrate itself in temples, march around in HRM parades? You don't come and tell me, 'Paji, please help me, I want to study,' or 'Paji, please save me, I want to be independent.' No, you spit on my dreams of sending you to college, just like your sister did. You let this man's seed sprout in your womb so you're forever tied to him. To a whole family of bigots, you announce to me today. Well, let me assure you, Meera, I feel nothing for this thing you're incubating in your stomach. I feel no relation, no responsibility towards it. It's only you that I care about, only your education, your welfare."

Paji got up from his chair and began looking through a row of books. I took this as a sign I was being dismissed, but he indicated that I should stay. "There's a remedy for everything now, you know—a smallpox vaccine, antibiotics, even a treatment for TB these days. What you have isn't so complicated that they don't know how it can be fixed." He selected one book, then put it back and selected another. "That novel by Dutta—why can't I find it?—about a woman who has the same accident you did. I thought you might read it, to know that life can go on—all one has to do is seek out the right cure."

I stared in incomprehension as Paji continued rummaging. "It's very different nowadays—not like Dutta's heroine who had to disappear for months. I'm sure Dr. Mishra could suggest someone safe and reliable in Darya Ganj itself. A person as young and healthy as you—the problem would be solved in an afternoon, before you even knew it. It probably wouldn't be worse than going to the dentist and getting a tooth removed."

Paji abandoned his search and turned around to face my blank look. "You have no idea what I'm talking about, do you?" he asked, and I shook my head. "I'm talking about you, Meera, your life, your independence, your self-sufficiency. Being prepared to accept what this world has to offer, being able to stand on your own two feet. Not flitting through life as the shadow of your husband, like your mother or her mother before her. I'm talking about you going to college, realizing the potential that's waiting to be tapped inside. Of getting away from your in-laws, of being free to forge your own existence. It's what you asked of me, it's what you wanted.

"But perhaps I shouldn't be the one to explain—perhaps it would be better if your husband did. Why don't you ask him to be here at noon tomorrow, so that I can talk to him? Tell him it'll be his last chance to make it to Bombay."

"I'M JUST SAYING IT'S an option to consider," Dev said the next evening. "I'm not suggesting we actually do it."

"An option," I repeated slowly. Paji had referred to the baby in my belly, the living, breathing being I was nurturing, as a "thing," as an "it." I supposed I should regard Dev's term to be an improvement.

"It's not like this is our only chance to have a child, Meera. We can always do it later, once we're settled in Bombay, once you've finished college, once I've broken into the music business. But this really is the last chance for an offer like this. He'll personally buy the flat for us, he promised, even give us money for another radiogram and fridge. All we have to do is let this one go, postpone things a bit."

"Let this one go. For a flat, a radiogram, and a fridge. That's about what Paji offered your family for me, isn't it?"

"I know how this must sound, Meera, but just hear me out on this. At first, I was shocked as well. This is your father, I thought—this baby would be his grandchild. I wondered if he hated you, if he was trying to take revenge. Could he still be angry over what you did on Karva Chauth, perhaps even over you marrying me? But then I looked into his face, and all I saw was sympathy. 'I know how difficult this is going to be,' he told me. 'But I'm thinking about the future, about my daughter's long-term happiness. You have to make her understand this.'

"Do you know what else he said to me? That I was wasting my time in Delhi. That my destiny lay in Bombay, nowhere else. 'Go there and make me proud to be your father-in-law. Go and become as successful as Saigal.' Even my own father has never given me such a blessing. And to think I imagined Paji didn't like me.

"He really does have our best interest at heart, Meera. It's much too early for us to have a baby. You shouldn't have to spend your life flitting around in your husband's shadow. You should be ready to accept what the world has to offer, prepared to be able to stand on your own two feet. There's too much potential inside you waiting to be tapped."

I recognized Paji's words from yesterday. In some corner of my mind I felt momentarily let down by Dev's delivery—it was nowhere as commanding as Paji's. Then the outrage caught up to me. "My father has already given me this speech—I don't need you to memorize it and vomit it back. Why don't you go back and haggle some more over the baby's price with him—demand that he throw in a pressure cooker as well."

"Please, Meera, just try to think about this."

"No, you think about it. How could you repeat something so ugly? This fatherly affection that you're talking about—why do you think he's suddenly showering you with it? Are you really so easy to hoodwink? If he loves you so much, why don't you try asking him to send you to Bombay by yourself? I'll stay behind here and have my child."

Dev went through every tactic he could think of over the next several weeks to change my mind. He tried to win my sympathy by telling me how defeated he felt, how drained and despairing, from mindlessly filing papers, morning to evening at his job. When that didn't work, he accused me of selfishness, of using the guise of motherhood to ruthlessly destroy every dream he had. He pointed out that my pride was to blame for the entire predicament—had I just gone along with Paji's directive on Karva Chauth, we would have been in Bombay long ago, with nobody to stop us from having a child now. On some nights, he pulled our talais apart angrily, on others he curled up next to my talai and stared at me pitifully like a pet denied.

Although outwardly I did not show any weakening in my resolve, my level of dismay was rising quickly inside. Every day of his campaign made it harder to ignore the fact that Dev did not want this baby. For a while I consoled myself with the possibility that he would have a change of heart when he actually saw the infant. But what if he didn't? How would I raise a child whose grandfather and father would have both preferred never to see it alive?

I thought several times of confiding in Sandhya, but the shame of revealing what my own father had prescribed, what my own husband supported, was too much to bear. In a corner of my mind, I worried also that she would tell Arya. The nightly antics between Dev and me had brought back the watchful gleam to his eyes. Although he had gone no further, I wondered if once the baby was born he would revert to his lechery.

Then one day, Dev received a call at his office from Paji. "Your father wants to see you tomorrow at eleven," he told me over dinner that evening.

BIJI WAS AGAIN NOT around when I got to Darya Ganj. "I sent her off to visit Varsha auntie in Agra," Paji said. "I haven't told her anything—it's best not to let too much emotion cloud the issue."

To my surprise, Paji ushered me into the drawing room this time, telling me how cold he knew the library could be. He even waited until I had seated myself first, before taking the chair across from me.

"Look, Meera," he said, leaning forward earnestly, as if by drawing closer, he could make me better understand what he had to say. "Dev tells me it's been well over four months already. When you first came to see me, perhaps some herbs or powders might have been enough to do the trick. But now it's getting so late that even Dr. Mishra's friend doesn't want to take the risk. It's all illegal you know—if he gets caught, he'll wind up in jail. Still, I've negotiated a price, that if you're willing, he can do it today."

I dabbed my throat with my handkerchief. This was my opening to recite the lines I had been crafting. That I respected my father's opinion and also my husband's, but only a woman could truly appreciate the life of a baby blossoming inside. That it would be the greatest sin of all to force me to "crush this bud before it got a chance to flower" (I had lifted the phrase from a sad love song by Suraiya). That as a parent Paji would surely understand what it meant to have the chance to love and cherish one's offspring.

Paji stopped me as soon as I began. "Yes, yes, Dev has told me all about what you've decided. But tell me, if he doesn't want it, how are you going to force it on him? Will you leave him and bring it up yourself, or will you stay and have him hate it all his life?"

"I'll do what needs to be done, Paji. And forgive me, but it was you who turned Dev against the baby by putting all that greed in his head."

"I merely tested him, and he failed. And if I dangle anything else in front of him, he'll leap at it, ravenously, every time. Is this the man whose child you want to be tied with? What if two or three years down the road you want to be free?"

"I'd never want to be free of my child."

"Oh, then you'd leave your husband and raise it yourself, would you? A married woman with an infant living alone in Delhi. This isn't Paris or New York that you can do such things. They'd circle you like sharks, they'd eat you alive.

"And even if nobody bothered you, what would you live on? Such willfulness is expensive, you can hardly expect support from Dev or me. At least if you had an education you wouldn't have to starve yourself, starve your own child. Is my idea so outlandish that you first go and study something?"

Paji got up and began pacing. "All my life I've tried to make sure I treated everyone fairly. Daughters as if they were sons, women equal to men. But what am I supposed to do if nobody wants to cooperate? If nobody wants to act rationally, if nobody wants to take responsibility for themselves? Your mother, fine, she's not educated, it's like trying to open a door by repeatedly banging my head against it. But my own daughters—first Roopa, then you? And tomorrow Sharmila?

"You wanted to get married to that bounder, I didn't object. To tie yourself to that gold-digging family, I gave everything they said. Even that slap in my face on Karva Chauth, I decided not to take offense." Paji nodded. "Yes, that was for my benefit, wasn't it? I thought Dev had forced you, but he explained you were simply *asserting* yourself. Good for her, I said to myself, I'm trying to run her life and she's not letting me get away with it. For once a woman's showing some mettle, getting her point across to her men.

"But not this time, Meera, this time it's not about control or revenge. Sometimes experience gives your elders more height to stand on, they're able to see further than you can. This is the moment to which you'll look back, five years down the road, or eight or ten. And be thankful, I promise you, that you listened to what I said."

Paji sat down on the sofa next to me and put his hand on my arm. "I know I can be harsh sometimes and blunt in how I speak. I know I've not been the perfect father, I know I've made mistakes. But don't take my love for hatred, don't punish me for it. Don't take it out on yourself by ruining your life like this."

Perhaps if Paji had stopped there, he wouldn't have succeeded. What broke through my last line of defense was something totally unexpected, something brilliant, shocking. Paji started crying.

By the time Dev came to pick me up, I was sitting in Paji's lap as I would when I was little. "My little Meera," he was saying, as he stroked my hair and squeezed his chest against mine. "I'm so sorry," he kept repeating, as I insisted he shouldn't apologize.

Paji didn't come with us. He said he couldn't bear to see me through it. He stood outside the taxi and gave Dev two rupees and eight annas for the fare. As we drove away, I was finally able to witness what I had craved so much from my doli—the sight of Paji standing in front of our house, waving goodbye to me. The taxi window was too dirty to make out if he was still crying.

WE WENT PAST DELHI GATE, then down the boulevard leading to Irwin Hospital. I braced myself for my nostrils to be assaulted by the smell of chloroform. But we drove right past the cluster of buildings, into the crowded bazaar behind Kotla Road. The driver stopped twice to ask directions from street hawkers. He finally pulled up in front of a shop selling bathroom fixtures. "It's upstairs," Dev said, leading me through the maze of ceramic toilets and washbasins spilling out over the pavement.

We climbed the staircase next to the shop. The door at the top opened just as we got to it, and a thickset woman in a salwar kameez peered out suspiciously. She had a dupatta wrapped around her head and tied in a knot behind, giving her a curiously bald look. "Yes?" she asked, and I caught a fleeting whiff of betel juice when she opened her mouth.

"Dr. Mishra sent us," Dev answered. The woman opened the door wider and wordlessly led us to a small room with green walls. She gestured towards a wooden bench, and sat down herself at a metal desk. She pulled out a notebook from one of the drawers and tore out a blank page on which she started writing something. I noticed the nail of her right thumb was black, her fleshy fingers devoid of rings.

"How old?" she asked Dev.

"Eighteen."

"Not her, what's inside."

"Four months."

"Not more? You're sure?"

"A little more."

The woman asked a few more questions about my weight and diet, continuing to address Dev, not me. "Wait here," she said. "I'll go get some tea." Dev began to protest that we didn't need any, that she was being too polite. "It's not for you, it's for her. To help her not feel anything." She disappeared into the adjacent room where we heard her mixing something.

I looked around the room. Scabs of green paint were peeling off the wall and ceiling. The floor needed a good washing, even though it had been swept clean. Next to the notebook on the desk lay a long screwdriver and hammer, as if someone had been about to carry out a repair. A strong meaty odor, like that from a fatty cut of mutton boiled in a curry, emanated from the door. It made me long for the smell of disinfectant, even chloroform.

I was about to remark to Dev that this didn't feel like a doctor's waiting room, when he pulled two tickets out of his pocket. "See this? The

Frontier Mail, next week. Babuji got us first class." A grin flashed over his face before he could suppress it.

"You mean you told your father?"

"I had to. But nobody else knows. Once we get to Bombay, we'll send them a telegram that you miscarried."

The woman came out with the tea. She handed it to me and gave Dev a folded bedsheet. "For her, after the tea. There's a charpoy in the second room through there. She has to take off what she's wearing."

"Is the doctor here yet?" I asked.

"What doctor?" For the first time, the woman spoke directly to me. "You don't need a doctor for this. I've been doing it for years. Don't worry, I'm not some village dai who uses mud to clean her hands." She smiled and I saw her paan-stained teeth.

Later, after I had begun to hemorrhage in the taxi back, after I had collapsed, blood-drenched, in Sandhya's arms, after I had passed the remaining chunks of fetus which Dev wrapped in a rag to dispose of somewhere, Paji would come to see me. "I had no idea," he would say, as he held his hand against my burning forehead and managed to cry for the second time that day. "Please forgive me." But back in that room, I quelled the uneasiness I felt, thinking that if Paji had arranged it, and if Dev hadn't considered anything to be amiss, it must be fine. After all my previous unwillingness, I didn't want to now appear as if I was making excuses and trying to back out.

I looked at the brown liquid in the cup. A swirl of white was floating on top, like some powder mixed in which had not quite dissolved. I took a sip, and it tasted like tea—lukewarm, and heavily spiked with ginger to mask whatever it was hiding, but tea, nevertheless. I was about to drink it down when a thought flitting in my brain since Darya Ganj articulated itself. "How was it that you came when you did to pick me up at Paji's?" I asked Dev.

"Your father told me. He said to come by at twelve-thirty, that he would have you ready by then."

I nodded. I raised the cup to my lips and emptied it.

PART TWO

chapter
twelve

SOMETIMES I THINK THAT THE FIREWORKS I DAYDREAMED ABOUT THAT evening in 1955 were heralding not Dev in my life but you. That they were sent up in the sky to preside over the coming decade and illuminate the way to your birth. Whenever the days grew too oppressive, I would see Gandhiji standing under a galaxy of starry rocket flashes, indicating that things would be all right. "Over there," he seemed to say, pointing at what lay unseen beyond the towering walls of the fort, his staff lit up in the night.

Did he somehow rig the flag that was still hanging over the platform at Bombay Central even though we arrived more than three months after Republic Day? As we circled around the station's manicured gardens, I noticed more flags affixed to the lampposts outside. I looked at the colored stripes fluttering in the gaslight, amazed that only a year and a quarter had elapsed since I had met Dev. How many lifetimes had I aged since that day?

But I had not aged, I reminded myself—I was young and healthy, as Paji had correctly declared. My body had pulled through the assault on it, the pills Dr. Mishra had given me had made my fever go away. "It's going to be a new city, a new beginning—forget what's happened here,"

Paji had said at the station. "You're only eighteen—just go to Bombay and pretend you're newly wed."

The taxi drove past the tall iron gates and merged with the traffic on the road. I stared at the women with saris tied in unfamiliar ways, the urchins drumming the backs of their brushes against their shoe polish stands, the hawkers vending peanuts and gram and sugarcane, the men balancing crates of tiffin boxes on their heads. Everywhere, people spilled from the pavements and swarmed towards the station like convoys of purposeful ants. A double-decker bus roared up threateningly behind a horse-drawn victoria, a burst of overhead sparks showered down as an electric tram rumbled along on its tracks. Was this the allure of the city, then, the therapeutic hubbub with which I was supposed to regenerate myself?

We turned into a road lined with apartment blocks—not the one- or two-story structures of Nizamuddin, but buildings that towered four and five and six times as tall. They were built so close that they looked glued to each other, like in a hurriedly assembled collage. Occasionally a temple entrance would emerge, decked with carvings and flowers, or a movie palace, moored by the side of the road like a glittering ocean liner. There were blinking lights and neon signs, and a billboard for cigarettes that changed into a cough syrup advertisement before my eyes. Despite all the cars, the atmosphere was clear, unlike the perpetual haze that hung over Delhi. Instead of dung, it was salt that I smelled in the air.

The flat Paji had bought us (from the brother of one of his qawwali friends, who sold it and migrated to Pakistan) was in Tardeo. Dev had been hoping for something in one of the more posh areas, like Malabar Hill or Breach Candy, perhaps even in one of the buildings facing the sea along Marine Drive, the jewels in "the Queen's Necklace," as he had heard them called. Not only did Paji purchase the cheapest place he could find, but he also left it in his name, to ensure I didn't stray. That I went to college and (a condition for which Dev assured me he would take nightly precautions) didn't have another child.

The taxi stopped in front of a building with an exterior so dark it looked charred. At first, I thought it might have been damage suffered during the riots in January. Nehru had announced Bombay would be centrally governed in order to develop it as the commercial capital of the country. Mobs of Marathi-speaking locals had rampaged across the city to protest it being wrested from their control. A front-page photograph had even made the Delhi *Times of India*, showing thousands of policemen battling the crowds on the worst day of the rioting.

As it turned out, our building had not been one of the victims of the public wrath. The burnt-looking exterior was actually a protective undercoating, painted on right before the monsoon one year. The rains had come early that season, and the project abandoned, without the surface layer of white ever being applied. When we stepped inside, the walls in the hallway, though cracked and peeling, were fortunately painted a less unsettling color.

Upstairs, the living room was cramped, the bathroom tiny, the furniture old and dusty. The balcony was so decrepit that it looked ready to shear off into the street two floors below. There was a filthy sink in the kitchen—when I tried to turn on the water, a cockroach crawled out from the tap. Dev carried his suitcase from room to room, as if searching for the door to a hidden, more commodious wing of the flat. He finally placed his bag on the bed and sat down next to it. "If I'd known this was all your father was offering, I would've moved us to Bombay myself long ago."

THE FIRST MORNING, after Dev left to meet a musician contact, I took my tea to the living room. The blare of horns rose from the road downstairs, and over it the call of a man going door to door sharpening knives. Dust streamed in through the open window, giving the sunlight a granular look. This would be my world from now on, I told myself as I sipped my tea—these rooms, these walls, this curiously humid heat. The village-like atmosphere of Nizamuddin dispelled by all the activity, the whistles of trains replaced by the sounds of traffic in the street.

What I longed for, though, were not the sights or surroundings I remembered from Nizamuddin, but the people I had left behind. For days, Sandhya and Mataji had taken care of me with such tenderness that in my delirium, I was never sure if it was my own mother ministering to me or one of them. Even Hema had attempted to sit awake next to my bed for a whole night (finally dozing off, still sitting I was told, at 3 a.m.). There had been so little time with them afterwards, so few opportunities to express how strong a bond I felt towards them. Barely had I recovered, it seemed, before I was being bundled up into the train—the compartment waiting to whisk me away to another life, like a second doli.

I closed my eyes and tried to transport myself back to Nizamuddin. There was the house in the railway colony, with the scraggly hibiscus bush growing outside. There were Hema and Mataji and Sandhya in the courtyard, their features slowly blossoming into color from black and white. Perhaps I had just walked in as well, because the three of them gathered close around me, as if in greeting. I saw the sun dappling our hair, smelled the hibiscus in the air, tried to get a snatch of what was being said. Then Sandhya turned, her hands streaked with red, her screams muffled as if coming through a windowpane, and behind her I glimpsed my bloodstained sari.

I went to the balcony to calm myself. Paji's words sounded in my ears—not to allow myself to think of Nizamuddin, not to regret what I had forever left behind. How meticulously I had followed his advice for a change. Pulling myself back from the brink whenever I felt tempted to relive the visit to the woman with the paan-stained teeth. Disengaging my remorse, my guilt, my shame, each time it began to clump around the part of me wrapped up and carried away that day by Dev. I had taken pains to stick with the story he and Paji advanced. Everyone from Hema to Biji believed I had miscarried.

My throat seized up. These days, it was the closest I came to crying. Even the sight of a newborn infant in its mother's arms could only coax up the tears so far. "Don't keep things bottled up," Biji had said. "You'll get eaten up from inside." But there was nothing I could do. I had lost the language of sorrow—even Dev singing "Light the Fire of Your Heart" couldn't wring anything from me now.

Below me, a man and woman were ascending slowly through the air. Their cheeks were afire in pink, their lips engorged in lurid pouts, their pupils floated up dreamily from milky seas of white. It was a film poster, hoisted for a rather seedy-looking movie theater called the Diana opposite our building. I watched as the edges were fastened to a metal framework, as the name of the film, *Love in Kashmir*, was inked onto the marquee. What a quaint notion, I thought, to be in love and frolic about in the snow in Kulu or Srinagar. I spotted the same poster in miniature clamped around a whole line of lampposts running along the sidewalk. *Love* blossomed improbably over and over again down the street.

DEV RETURNED AT TWO in the afternoon. "The water's as beautiful as they say it is. I caught a glimpse of it from the bus. Come, let's go take a look." He hurried me downstairs into a taxi as if the sea was in danger of evaporating.

It wasn't a very long ride. The water revealed its presence even before we got to it—the sunshine reflecting off its surface created a shimmer in the air. Suddenly the buildings parted to reveal an expanse of gleaming sand. Beyond lay the bay, the sea stretching to the horizon, the waves sweeping in gracefully to garland the land.

"Do you recognize it?" Dev asked excitedly. "It's Chowpatty Beach. From the postcard I had framed up in Delhi." He paid the driver and we got out of the cab. "See those tall buildings with the palm trees?—that's Marine Drive, where I had been hoping Paji would buy us a flat."

The beach was as lustrous as the floor of a marble temple in sunlight—I unhooked my sandals before stepping on it. When I looked up, Dev was already running towards the water. Perhaps he tripped, perhaps he flung himself down on purpose, but the next instant, he was tumbling on the ground, clouds of sand rising and cascading around his body.

"Look at this," he yelled, scooping up the sand by the handful and throwing it into the air. It landed on his arms, his chest, his face, but he didn't seem to care. "Isn't it wonderful?" I stared at the rivulets running down his head—tiny particles—mica, perhaps—sparkled in his hair.

Dev stretched out his legs and swished his feet luxuriously this way and that. "Did they used to make a children's beach for you at the Baisakhi fair like they did in Lahore? Trucked in all the way from

Karachi, they would say. To wait all these years and finally feel the grains sliding between my toes again." He burrowed a foot in, then watched the sand cascade off as he lifted it into the air.

Before I could sink down to the ground next to him, Dev was up and bounding towards the sea again. This time, he ran all the way to the water's edge. He stretched out his arms and thrust his chest forward as if expanding the cavity within to take in the deepest possible breath. "The sea," he shouted, twirling around towards me. "This is it. Finally." He turned back to the water. "Finally," he called out, and paused, as if waiting for an echo. He bent down to roll up his cuffs, but then simply kicked off his shoes and ran into the waves. "Come on in," he yelled, waving to me, just as a swell crested around his knees.

I stood where I was. Following Dev into the water seemed too forgiving—I was not yet ready to share with him the intimacy of the sea. "My sari will get all wet," I responded, but he was too absorbed in the waves to hear me.

I found a dry patch of sand to sit on. Dev frolicked around, falling backwards into the water, skimming the foam with his arms, tossing a coconut away from shore and then splashing over dog-like to retrieve it. The tide was not very strong, and the tallest of the waves rose lethargically only to his thighs. At one point, he disappeared headfirst into the water and I saw his legs rise and stick straight up towards the sky. Every once in a while he stood and cupped his hands over his mouth. I heard him call out something to the bay: "I love you," or "Beautiful," or "Finally."

In spite of myself, I decided that I, too, liked the sea. The salt in the air smelled curiously familiar, like something I had been breathing in all my life. I felt as if I had reached the end of a pilgrimage—the shore I was sitting on a frontier of opportunity, the sweep of water ahead ready to forgive, to absorb all memory. I could lose myself in this city, be a new person, start a new life, as Paji had said. Fate seemed to insist I remain tied to Dev, that I subordinate my will to his. It had taught me a lesson on how reckless it could be to resist. Perhaps it was time now to try leading the life it had limned out for me. Surely in time the salt would heal the wound inside.

—

IT WAS ONE THING to make my resolution at the beach, quite another to resist being pulled back under by the past. What kept me afloat was the responsibility of running a household. Each time I felt myself slipping into the darkness, I found a chore to distract myself. I counted the clothes for the dhobi's weekly wash and examined the floor for patches the ganga had missed in her cleaning. I haggled with vegetable sellers to squeeze out an extra apple or onion, and stood for hours to get our ration cards from the municipality. My resourcefulness surprised me, since nobody had ever advised me on how to perform such tasks. Each one completed made me feel more authentic in my newly assumed role as a housewife. Every hour I cooked or cleaned or shopped was another hour not spent wallowing in the disappointments and betrayals of my previous life.

The one area where my resourcefulness failed me was in the kitchen. For the first few weeks, I went through untold heads of cauliflower, since that happened to be the only vegetable Mataji had really taught me to cook. I was familiar with yellow moong, but the range of lentil colors at the bania's shop unnerved me. I managed to burn mutton and leave it uncooked inside at the same time. The chappatis I rolled had such intricate borders that they could have been the maps of countries.

Fortunately, the ganga walked in on one of my chappati experiments. "You have to add less water to the flour, and knead it more," she diagnosed, as she squatted to run her cloth over the floor. For mutton, she suggested mixing in yogurt to tenderize the more stubborn pieces. "Cauliflower is expensive," she told me another time, "you can cook cabbage the same way, you know." Although I could never summon the gleam of enthusiasm I saw in the ganga's eyes, I did follow her advice, and little by little my cooking improved.

Biji sent me a scandalized letter (dictated out as usual in Sharmila's handwriting) when I wrote to her about all the chores with which I was filling my time. "It's bad enough that the granddaughter of a zamindar is callusing her hands with such menial work. But to learn from a ganga, the same person who cleans your floors? I hope you have a big bottle of Dettol at home, to disinfect your utensils each time she touches them."

This was in addition to her lament that Paji's cheapness had landed us in the midst of a slew of Muslim neighbors. "Are there no Hindus left in Bombay, that he couldn't have found a more suitable building for his own flesh and blood?"

Dev had remarked on it while reading the residents' names at the bottom of the steps one day. ". . . Azmi, Hamid, Khan. Dr. Kagalwalla could be either Muslim or Parsi. But Afzan, Karmali, Hussain . . . ? All these people on all these floors—could we be the only Hindu family among them?"

There were even a few ladies in the building who dressed in burkhas. They glided down the steps in flurries of mauve or brown, their silk robes scenting the air with attars of jasmine and rose. Their veils were always drawn back over their heads and fastened in place, and sometimes I saw lipstick, even eye shadow on their faces. As I got to recognize them better, I realized they only donned burkhas for certain occasions, being perfectly comfortable at other times striding into the street like me in a salwar kameez.

Surely Arya, like Biji, would have bristled at being surrounded by so many Muslims. Dev didn't seem to think that way, and neither did I. Still, it did make it harder to assimilate into the life of the building community. I felt self-conscious as the only woman to descend the steps wearing a bindi on my forehead. Every day I glanced at the banisters leading up to unexplored floors, and imagined meeting one of the apparitions I had seen, floating down in her billowing attire. My fantasy was that I would ring a doorbell at random, and boldly introduce myself. Perhaps I would even be rewarded with a bosom friend—someone to address my aloneness, quench the longing to unburden myself.

Except I had always been reticent while making friends, even worse at opening up to them. Now, it was not only my shyness that held me back, but also the religious differences that might confront me after pushing the doorbell. *What if they were in the middle of their namaz, and the presence of a Hindu annulled their prayers? What if I interrupted a meal, and it turned out to be beef, which they invited me in to share?* Paji's secular guest list had not been enough to neutralize the years of wariness Biji had drilled in. I nodded at my neighbors and they nodded at me on the stairs, but months of such cordiality were not sufficient for us to progress from there.

Dev, unlike me, quickly tapped into a network of musician friends. I had little in common, and did not mix with them. It was good to be so isolated, I told myself—it would force me to appreciate Dev more when he returned in the evenings, make him easier to bear when he satisfied himself. Each morning, I turned on the radio to dispel the stillness that hung around the house, and waited for the ganga's visit to fulfill any need for company I had. When the cooking failed to ward off an impending attack of melancholy, a visit to Chowpatty helped. I considered a matinee at the Diana a few times, but the clientele looked too unsavory, and I always walked on to the sea instead.

My only significant contact with anyone other than Dev was through the mail. Biji sent me two letters a week, dictated to Sharmila, who always scribbled extra lines of her own at the end so as not to waste any of the blue inland sheet. Hema kept me apprised of all the news at Nizamuddin—a blanket of moroseness, she claimed, had descended over the entire colony due to my leaving. "Mataji is always irritable, and Babuji has started drinking so much that he's passed out twice on the verandah already. Even the radiogram broke down the day before when I tried to play cheerful records in the evening. Nobody seems concerned about fixing it—all they say is to stop nagging them about it." Compounding everything else, Pushpa's family down the street had bought a fridge (a Kelvinator at that), and people were going around saying how the ice it made was a lot colder than that of their Godrej. "It's getting so miserable that any day now I'm going to run away and come to live with you and Dev bhaiyya in Bombay. You can take me to the jewelry shops at Zhaveri Bazaar, show me the zoo." In one corner of each letter, Sandhya always painstakingly wrote out her name. It was her presence I missed the most—I wished there were some way for us to directly communicate.

A long letter from Roopa arrived in June, filled with details about the newly built naval quarters in Visakhapatnam and the glorious birth of her twins. "It's such an amazing feeling being a mother—to wake up with a glow every morning. You can't imagine how beautiful they look—the two lives I've created, sleeping side by side." I wondered whether she was gloating on purpose, or simply being her usual insensitive self. Dev pored over the letter all evening, holding it up against bulbs and lamps as if a secret love message, inscribed in invisible ink, would magically come to life.

It was Paji's missives, however, that made me the most uncomfortable. The same precise handwriting, the cursive letters so neatly formed, the envelopes all white and creamy, not hinting at the dangers they could be concealing. Most of them turned out to be quite benign. In one, he simply asked after the new radiogram and fridge he had bought as promised. In another, he sent me the certificates I would need for college admission the following year. But soon to come was a letter from Paji which once more would have a profound effect on our lives.

chapter
thirteen

DEV BEGAN HIS EFFORTS TO BREAK INTO SINGING FOR FILMS AS SOON AS
we got to Bombay. He came armed with two pages of contacts'
addresses, compiled from musician friends in Delhi, and methodically
started going down the list. None of these contacts had phones, and the
residences were often in the outer, less developed suburbs like Malad and
Borivili, so Dev had to take long train rides to get to them. Even when
it became apparent that the purported connections to the film industry
were quite nebulous, Dev persevered, determined to leave no name
uninvestigated in his quest.

His search eventually led him to a squat green building only a few
streets away, wedged between the Tardeo Medical Clinic and the distrib-
utor for A-1 potato chips. Famous Studios was where the songs and
background score for many movies were recorded. A friend introduced
him to the owner, who allowed Dev to spend his days in the lobby. But
despite daily sightings of music directors like Jaikishan and S. D. Bur-
man, and even the Mangeshkar sisters, fast becoming the empresses of
the singing world, Dev remained undiscovered. "So close, and I didn't
know how to approach them," he lamented to me in the evenings.

The only people who spoke to him were the musicians—maestros of
the traditional tabla and sitar, but also percussionists and guitar players,

who with audiences' westernizing tastes were increasingly in demand. Sometimes they dropped by our flat after a recording. Bottles of fluorescent fruit-flavored liquor invariably materialized on these occasions, and I hid in the bedroom as the congregation got rowdier. Once the alcohol ran out, they staggered back towards the recording studio, to the speakeasy called "Auntie's Place" in the alley next to the chip factory. Dev returned so intoxicated that I always wondered how he managed to find his way back home.

By September, more than half the money with which we had arrived was gone. Underneath Dev's optimism I noticed a jittery desperation begin to form. His musician friends stopped coming around—he spent long evenings with them at Auntie's instead. He knew his studio days were numbered, without a job we would not be able to go on.

That was when the letter from Paji arrived. He had addressed it, for the first time, to both of us—Dev's name before mine. The contents were brief. One of the men in Paji's qawwali circle was a good friend of Nawab Mohammed, the music director—the same one for whom a decade ago, Saigal had sung some of his best work. If Dev wanted, Paji could help arrange an appointment with him.

Dev folded up the letter and inserted it back into its envelope carefully. "Years from now, I want to be able to look back and read this letter again," he said, touching it to his forehead as if it were something holy. He placed it among his prayer things, between the statue of Sai Baba and the picture of Lakshmi. "Your father never had a son, but I feel he has adopted me."

NAWAB MOHAMMED LIVED in Bandra—not in the area which film stars had recently begun eyeing for their bungalows, but in the older, less trendy part of Pali Hill towards the church. Perhaps this reflected the fact that his heyday had passed—the golden period when producers lined up on the street in their Impalas to sign him up, when Saigal himself coronated him "the nawab of music directors," a title Mohammed soon incorporated into his professional name. Long after the movies themselves had been forgotten, and Mohammed's star had embarked on

its irreversible decline, the songs he had composed for Saigal still scin-
tillated over the airwaves, with a frequency that augured immortality.
His name adorned a movie only once a year or two now, but it was still
a name well recognized—the taxi driver at Bandra station knew exactly
which house to take us to at its mention.

The evening before, I had accompanied Dev to the Babulnath temple to pray for his success. Chowpatty was just down the road, so we
went there afterwards. "It's finally going to happen," Dev said, as we
walked along the shore. "I can feel it in the air, feel it in myself."

I stared at the serpentine contours marking the degrees of dampness
in the sand. Crusts of foam swirled around our feet.

"Don't think I don't realize what a difficult journey it's been. I'll
never forget the sacrifice you made—what Paji asked, what you agreed
to give up for me."

I looked up, astounded. Could I make Dev wilt by staring him in the
eye? But he was done with the past—it was the future at which he was
now gazing. "Can you make out that beige building—there, in the middle of Marine Drive? I think it's called Keval Mahal. Right on the top
floor—that's where we'll buy our flat."

After dinner, though, Dev's assurance began to crumble. "What if I
can't do it?" he said, his face drained of blood, a tremor in his neck.
"What if the words get stuck? It's been a year since I've competed, and
it's never meant so much."

It occurred to me that I could demolish his confidence completely if
I wanted. Here was an opportunity to convince Dev his pursuit was
doomed, the city a waste of time. A chance to exploit his vulnerability
and avenge my "sacrifice." But it was only numbness I found searching
inside myself, not an appetite for revenge. In any case, Bombay was
where all our prospects lay now—there was no advantage in precipitat-
ing a return to Delhi. The only practical course of action was to build
Dev's spirit back up that night.

"You have the exact voice he needs to start crafting hits again after
all these years. You'll sing so well tomorrow that he'll think Saigal himself has come back to life."

Nawab Mohammed's house was replete with all the trappings of wealth, or at least the ones used to depict it in Hindi films. Chandeliers glittered like ice sculptures from the ceiling, a double-banistered marble staircase swept majestically to an upper level, plush white rugs vied with extravagant Kashmiri carpets to adorn the floor, and on one wall hung an oil portrait of Mohammed posing heroically with his foot on the head of a dead tiger, as if he really was the nawab of some princely state. After waiting an appropriate amount of time for us to be impressed by our surroundings, a servant led us to a side room, where the Nawab reclined against a row of bolsters, sampling kebabs from a selection on a plate.

"I'm so glad you brought your wife along," he told Dev as we sat against the bolsters along the facing wall. "Sawhney sahib himself made another trunk call to me last night from Delhi. I understand you want to sing."

We sipped the rose sherbet the servant brought us, and took polite pieces of kebab from the plate at Mohammed's urging. His body seemed puffy, and his face had a pallor to it, as if he was not getting out into sunlight enough. Near his foot was a harmonium and, in case the carpets and kebabs and tiger were not sufficient to underscore his Nawab title, a jewel-encrusted hookah.

"Such an amazing talent, to be able to bring forth beauty from one's throat. And yet so rare to see it done well. I would have become a singer, believe me, had I half a voice. But I suppose people would say I've done my share to propitiate the gods of music." He chuckled softly, as if agreeing with himself. Abruptly, he raised his head to look straight at Dev. "So sing. Let me hear this Delhi voice with which you'd like to intoxicate our city."

I thought Dev would break into "Light the Fire," but he surprised me. He sang "When the Heart Only Has Broken," one of Saigal's last songs. It was a particularly soulful rendition—for an instant, all that had happened over the past year was left behind as I allowed myself to be swept away by the emotion in his voice. Could I have misjudged him, I wondered, could I have failed to understand this person I was living with? To recognize the sadness that must imbue his heart, to appreciate the pain that he, too, must be steeping in? I noticed that even the servant had padded back silently, and was listening from the doorway. Through it all, Nawab Mohammed leaned back with his eyes closed, his ring-studded fingers strumming through the air, as if plucking the strings of invisible instruments.

He seemed to enjoy the song so much that I thought he'd insist Dev perform his entire repertoire. But Dev had scarcely commenced the medley he had prepared when the Nawab opened his eyes and held up his hand. "Are they all Saigal songs?" he asked, with the air of a doctor convinced of a diagnosis, inquiring about lesser symptoms for form's sake. "Let's hear them some other time then.

"Do you know next year, it'll be a full decade since Saigal passed away? January 18, 1947—that's the day his drinking finally caught up with him. Even before his ashes were cool, people started saying the Nawab was finished without him. 'He'll never find anyone, poor man, who can sing like Saigal.' But that wasn't true. *Everyone* sang like Kundan Lal after his death, *everyone* wanted to be the next Saigal. Just listen to the first few songs recorded by Mukesh.

"But it's not what the listening public wanted. No, people were tired of melancholy, they were sated with pain. They wanted to laugh now, laugh and love and live in this new country. It was not as if sadness had gone out of style—it just had to be sadness of a happier, more uplifting kind. Mukesh was shrewd enough to understand this—he switched in the first year itself. Rafi was even smarter—he never even tried going the Saigal way—his sadness was of the mendable type—it came from the heart, never the soul. And the public loved it—these citizens of the new republic, these free, optimistic people who had been promised a dream that was finally within reach. It's just as well Saigal died in the same year the British left. If the drink hadn't felled him, Independence would have.

"So why didn't I change as well, you might ask? At first, it was pride. I was the Nawab, after all—hadn't Saigal himself said that? If the public didn't like what I was composing, it was the public's fault—I was the arbiter of refinement, of taste. Of course, I realized eventually I was wrong. I jettisoned the people I had trained to sing like Saigal. I tried to woo Rafi and the other young upstarts. But it didn't work. I wasn't as adaptable as Mukesh. I simply wasn't able to comply with the public's taste. Composing things I didn't believe in ripped into my core. I watched, helplessly, as Shankar-Jaikishan and all the other newcomers moved in. The industry sealed my fate by giving me a Filmfare lifetime achievement award at forty-eight.

"Since you've come to hear my opinion, here it is. Your voice isn't perfect, but Saigal would have approved of it. With practice and some training, it might one day come close to his. But the world doesn't need another Saigal, it already has enough songs by him. Which means my advice to you should be to learn to sing some other way. Perhaps like all the ditties that stir the teenage hearts of today. Except you're going to remain true to yourself—you're like me, not Mukesh. I can hear it in your voice, recognize it in your face. Go back to Delhi, is all I can say. Let your singing be a hobby to brighten your days. Give up this idea you have of singing for films. Neither you nor your wife deserves the heartbreak. It's the best advice, the only advice I can give."

Dev looked like he was in shock on the train ride back. I attempted to engage him in conversation, but he barely reacted. I tried feeling sorry for him, but the emotion that surged over everything else was relief—relief that Dev had finally had his fair chance, even if it hadn't gone well. Now, perhaps, he would stop squandering his time at the recording studio. I had accepted that my future, for better or worse, would be with him. Perhaps there would be an opportunity now to sit down and plan it rationally.

At home, I thought Dev would cry, or drink, or do something sentimental like listen to his Saigal records. But he simply sat at the dining table and stared through the window at the darkening sky. Finally, he turned to me. "If people hated Saigal so much, why would he still be on the radio? Why would I have won the competition last year? Why would I even be in this flat in Bombay with your father's blessings, and sitting next to his daughter?"

Something stirred in my mind. The trunk call that Mohammed Nawab had received the night before from Paji—could my father have had a hand in this? Could he have instructed the Nawab to be so thoroughly demoralizing that Dev would stop wasting his time?

"No, I don't believe what that Nawab Mohammed claimed," Dev

said. "He's just frustrated, that's what it is. He tried to make it after Sai-gal, and couldn't, so now he's bitter at the world. He'd rather discourage everyone who comes to him than take the risk of having to see someone else succeed."

A bottle of something green and illicit-looking had appeared on the table. "I'll show him," Dev said. "It takes more than a has-been like him to make me quit." He poured out a shot of the liquid, paused, then filled the glass to the rim.

I NEVER DID FIND out whether my father had been behind the audition, pulling his puppet strings and interfering once again. But if Paji intended for his son-in-law to give up singing in the pursuit of a respectable job, it had the opposite effect. The desire to prove Nawab Mohammed wrong strengthened Dev's resolve, gave him new tenacity. "I've convinced the owner of Famous to hire me as his new receptionist," he announced, showing me the box of tandoori chicken from Sher-e-Punjab he'd bought to celebrate. "The salary's quite pitiful, but now when the music directors walk in, they'll have to talk to me. And being a studio employee, I won't be so hesitant to approach the ones who might be able to help me."

Dev's strategy did yield some modest results. Under his badgering, a few of the music directors promised to have him audition. Roshan and Jaikishan actually came through on their word—though encouraging, neither gave him a song. Naushad hired him as an extra—sometimes as a chorus member, sometimes to sing a line or two in the background. His biggest success, one that received quite a bit of airtime, was a radio spot for Bournvita breakfast drink. Even Hema wrote that she had heard it in Delhi on the Vividh Bharati afternoon program.

As Dev became more of a fixture at the studio, music directors and film producers started relying increasingly on him. He was the one who knew whom to call to fix a microphone, the one to approach if the song needed the cry of an infant or the woof of a dog for a sound effect. He could arrange for a driver to go to Peddar Road when a Mangeshkar sister overslept, or get a battalion of violinists to be ready with their instruments on a day's notice. Once, he managed to switch an entire evening's schedule to Audio Labs, when a cat pawed its way into the utility box, shutting down the power and electrocuting itself. At first, he was happy to accept tips for these services, but gradually, as he became more indispensable, his name was added to the payroll. We could have been quite comfortably off, if Dev hadn't become addicted to his after-work stops at Auntie's Place. The cab fares alone (to get him home the few blocks in his drunken state) would have bought enough mutton to feed us all month.

One night, tired of waiting for Dev to show up drunk at the door, I decided to visit Auntie myself. I walked to the A-1 chip outlet, then entered the unlit alley next to it. The stench of garbage was so strong that I had to hold my dupatta over my face. It took some searching to detect the door built into the side of the A-1 building, stained as it was with countless streaks of paan. Inside, it was dark and smoky, with just enough light from the naked bulbs in wall sockets to make out the rickety tables. I saw only men there, sitting on benches at the tables, staring somberly into the liquid in their glasses. Dev sat alone on a stool at a bar at the back of the room. Behind him stood Auntie, her fingertips spread out on the counter, her multicolored dispensations glowing in rows behind her like bottles of orange and lemon squash.

The thing I noticed immediately was not the enormous vermilion bindi that covered half her forehead, but her hair. It had been dyed an emphatic black, both the tresses on her head and her eyebrows, though she had missed the eyelashes, which were white and furry. The light from the bulbs gave her hair a sheen that made her look like someone with an aura—a devi, perhaps. She took my hand in hers as Dev, flustered by my presence, tried to introduce us. "You're not here for what they all are—I'll get you some lemonade," she said.

That evening, I matched Dev glass for glass, as he poured the homemade brew from a bottle (pineapple, the label said) and I poured from a jug of lemonade. Auntie was very solicitous, behaving almost as if she were my real aunt. At one point, a man from one of the tables came and sat next to me. Dev was too far gone to care, but Auntie was there in a flash, yanking him out and depositing him back on his bench. "If they bother you, just let me know, Beti," she said.

Finally, when Dev's bottle was empty and we were at the door, Auntie pressed a one rupee coin into my palm. "For good luck, from your aunt." She brushed her hand in blessing over my head.

At the main road, I gave the coin to a man begging outside the A-1 shop. To think she could buy me for a rupee. I vowed I would never go back.

In time, though, I came to accept the role Auntie played in Dev's life. The nightly visits helped dull the keenness of his disappointment, blur the stark outlines of his lack of success. It wasn't as if there had been a paucity of effort on his part. Within months of joining the studio, Dev had begun voice lessons, continuing them religiously for over a year and a half. Every Tuesday and Saturday morning, he took the suburban train all the way to Jogeshwari, where his guru had promised him an entirely new singing persona, one that would give not only Mukesh but also Rafi a run for his money. On other mornings, he waited patiently for his hangover to abate at home, so that he could practice an hour or two before going to work.

But Nawab Mohammed's assessment turned out to be devastatingly accurate. Dev was never able to truly make the new voice his own, give it the conviction it needed, imbue it with tunefulness or soul. By the time he gave up on his lessons, there was rarely a night that he wasn't going to visit his Auntie. It was her libations that helped ease his way deeper into the responsibilities at the studio, whispering to him that this was not a slide into obscurity or failure but merely a step on the way to attaining his dream.

chapter
fourteen

THE ACADEMIC YEAR STARTED IN JUNE, SO I HAD TO WAIT UNTIL OUR SEC-
ond summer in Bombay to enroll for my B.A. Paji made the choice of
college easy. He recommended the highly reputed Sophia, followed by
St. Xavier's, or failing both, Elphinstone as a distant third. I immediately
struck them all off my list. Instead, I decided on Wilson, not only
because he hadn't mentioned it, but also because it was right across the
road from Chowpatty.

On the first day of classes, I walked the familiar route towards the
sea. It was the week before the start of the monsoon, and the skies overhead were gray and ponderous. In contrast, my mood was lighthearted,
even optimistic. This would be a welcome change, I was beginning to
realize, from the cooking, the shopping, the mindless haggling with
which I pretended to entertain myself. Even Dev had wished me luck as
I left the house, and said he would arrange for dinner that evening.

But my spirits settled as soon as the college came into view. I looked
at the dark stone buildings, at the Gothic arches over the windows, at
Wilson in Old English lettering spelled out above the iron bars of the
fence. I had walked past the college so many times before. Why did it
feel, as I passed through the gate today, that this was a prison to which I
had been sentenced?

Beyond the walls was a courtyard, with a central fountain of three nymphs spouting water from their mouths. Students sat on the grass and stood around in knots—a few hung up a sign announcing an annual Bazaar Day. I knew they must be sixteen or seventeen, only a few years younger than I, and yet I felt the chasm of an entire generation between us. Listening to their chatter, I was reminded of Roopa's girlfriends in college, whose parents were only educating them so they would be more marketable for marriage. (Wasn't that why Biji had relented about Roopa attending as well?) Once, I would have yearned for such company, for the chance to meet day after day to flirt and gossip. Now, after all I had experienced, what could I possibly have left in common with such classmates?

The first lecture, on Indian history, made me feel worse. I found it impossible to concentrate on the civilizations that had taken root along the Indus Valley—all I could think was how pleased Paji would be by the image of me sitting there. The weeks to come on these wooden benches, the months under the fans rotating lazily overhead—had he made me trade in my baby for this? I stared at the pages of my blank notebook, the ink glistening on the nib of my new fountain pen. Each word I jotted down in the next four years would be in accordance with what he had planned. I imagined him nodding in satisfaction—"Another new idea's been nudged into our Meera's head." The resentment was so sharp that I could taste it in my mouth—a bitterness, like the quinine we used to swallow in Rawalpindi for malaria. I tried to pull my mind towards the lecture, to the names of civilizations like Harrapa and Mohenjodaro, to the centuries before Christ when they flourished. But the chalk marks kept leaping and diving on the blackboard, the instructor's voice rising and falling like waves in my ears. A peon went by at last, ringing a large handheld bell to signal that the period had come to an end.

I rushed out of the classroom, through the hall, down the college steps. The waves were not only audible now but visible as well—I could see them flowering in blooms of white all along the arc of Marine Drive. I crossed the road and walked down the beach. The sea was engorged and foaming, as if the spirit of the monsoon strained inside, waiting to be delivered from its belly. Further up, a sand sculptor was smoothing out the previous day's deity carved into the ground, to start afresh. I thought about going back to attend my other lectures—English literature and civics, Hindi and world geography. But the clouds cast an irresistible melancholy over the beach, and the churning water kept me spellbound the whole afternoon. At three, I finished the lunch I had brought and started back home.

That week, I tried several times to sit through my lectures. But the classroom felt airless and suffocating each time, and the blood pounded so loudly in my ears that I thought my head would burst. Only the beach calmed me. I sat on the sand and imagined how different my life would have been with a child, how focused I would be, how active and happy. Perhaps I should simply go home to my chores, I thought, lose myself again in their vapidity. There would even be a sense of empowerment in not returning, in thwarting the future Paji had ordained for me. But then the idea of him shaking his head at the failure he'd been expecting all along stopped me.

The rains drove me back indoors. I looked into spending my time sipping tea in the girls' canteen, but the principal, Dr. Airan, often roved around outside, trying to catch students who were not in class. He was known for terrorizing not only the students but also the faculty, wielding not a timepiece or wristwatch but the very desk clock from his office each morning to check whether any of his professors were late ascending the staircase. I didn't want to attract his attention in case he knew Paji and started sending reports to Delhi.

The only alternative was to force myself to sit through the lectures. Fortunately, most of them were in Room 403, one entire wall of which consisted of a row of windows facing the sea. On clear days, the entire bay of Chowpatty opened up through the windows like in the panels of a painting. I found that glancing at this panorama from time to time helped me breathe. When the professor's voice became too oppressive, or my thoughts too claustrophobic, I followed the cars whizzing up and down the toy track of Marine Drive. Then I tried once again to turn to world economy or Shakespeare or the Indus Valley.

—

I INTERACTED WITH almost no one in college. Although some of the friendlier girls struck up conversations in class or the canteen, I was never more than polite. My feeling of otherness was too great, my sense of isolation too deep. Then, around the middle of the term, one of the male students started following me.

I first noticed him at the beach, reclining on the sand with his head on a blue cloth book bag. The monsoon had abated, and I had brought my lunch outside after a long time. I recognized him from history and perhaps civics as well—he always sat in one of the back rows monopolized by boys. As I watched, he propped himself to a seated position and bought a cone of peanuts from a passing hawker. I thought he glanced my way as he paid for his snack, but I was careful not to look back.

The next day, he came into the library while I was reading the newspaper, and made his way to a table a few spaces from me. I didn't look at his face, but I could tell it was him, from his nubbly blue bag. He opened a book and held it awkwardly in the air, so that it was in line with where I sat. I didn't wait for him to start eyeing me while pretending to read—I replaced the paper on its rack and left.

After that, he seemed everywhere. Gazing at the sand deity being carved on the beach, I picked out his face from the ring of onlookers tracking the sculptor's progress with me. He paced back and forth outside the open door as I sat in the girls' canteen sipping tea. Once, he showed up while I was haggling with a roasted-corn seller on Marine Drive. He now seemed to be in *all* my classes, not just in history and civics. I kept wondering if he would leave the safety of his bench at the back to try and come sit next to me.

By now, I had managed to take several good looks at him covertly. He was younger than I had thought at first, probably not yet seventeen. There was the faintest of fuzz sprouting from his chin, the galaxy of pimples on his face seemed to rotate every week. His hair was long, and stiff with pomade, as if he had tried to forcibly straighten out the curls. He wore a good-luck charm around his neck, the black cord wound so tight that his throat muscles strained against it when he coughed. There was a sweetness about him, an innocence, an earnestness, that came through even while he was stalking me.

Although every effort was made at Wilson to keep the sexes segregated, there was no dearth of furtive romance. Each afternoon, the alcoves along the balcony floor of the library were filled with couples pretending to study together (until one day Dr. Airan banned boys from climbing the stairs). Girls living in the hostel at Gamdevi were reputed to be particularly fast—some of them openly strolled around campus with male classmates, though even they weren't bold enough to hold hands. Was this the way these courtships started? I wondered to myself. Did my student think me unmarried, given that I didn't mark the parting of my hair with vermilion or wear a mangalsutra necklace?

I knew I should tell him at once to stop what he was doing. Hadn't such games, after all, led to my initial rashness with Dev in the tomb at Nizamuddin? But this student had never harassed me or even approached me in any way, so what sense did it make for me to initiate contact? Given how unlikely it was that I would ever speak to him or confront him, what danger could there be in carrying around some idle romantic notions to amuse myself?

My reveries about him were very different from my fantasies of Dev when I was seventeen. He was never shirtless or indecent in any way, I never followed him into a tomb, the cord around his neck did not metamorphose into a snake. Rather than amorous, my affection was maternal more than anything else. I wanted to cradle his head in my lap, rock him to sleep in my arms. I wanted to run my hands through the locks of his hair on days he allowed it to curl. If ever I pressed my lips against his, I wanted no wetness to taint our kiss.

The evening came when my student followed me after school. I caught glimpses of him loitering in front of a cigarette shop, examining newspapers spread out by a pavement vendor. At the Nana Chowk intersection, I paused in front of the window of the Bata shoe store to see if he would come up. But he stopped as well, pretending to be engrossed by the wares of a tea grocer.

I imagined leading him back home, walking up the steps, leaving open the door. Dev wouldn't be home from work for another few hours. What would I do if my admirer, like a stray dog, followed me up?

Perhaps I could pet him, lay out a plate of biscuits, and watch him eat. Fix him a cup of tea, the beverage that still seemed to have him entranced in its charms at the shop down the street. And after I have fed him and quenched his thirst, what then? Do I hug him and muss his hair to test my theory of motherly affection? Am I surprised when I discover the feelings he carries for me?

I could usher him into the bedroom after his feeding. Watch him take off his shoes and stand skittishly by the door in his bare feet. Do I boldly reach up to brush a crumb from the corner of his mouth? Catch a glimpse of his tongue as it nervously licks his lips clean?

And then? Do I go over to the bed and pull back the sheets? Does he waver a bit, then lie down next to me? His fingers too timid to make contact, but the desire so strong I can hear it thump in his heartbeat. I lie there and inhale the scent of his adolescence, let his presence envelop me.

Try as I might, I was unable to proceed further with this reverie. The image of his skin against mine eluded me. I looked at him watching the bins of tea so innocently. Wasn't I too young to have so disengaged myself from physical needs? Had my experiences with Dev drained all desire from me?

Even if I could complete my fantasy, where would it take me? How would my life be better if I were to cast my lot in with his? Would we run away together, settle down somewhere to begin again? What made me imagine he would be an improvement over Dev?

It was time, I decided, to confront my admirer. To disentangle myself from the game he was playing. "Hello, listen?" I said, striding up to the tea store. He looked up too late, unable to make a getaway. "Why are you following me, what do you want from me?" A flash of panic arced in his eyes. His complexion turned white, as if guilt was a lightbulb illuminating his face.

I could tell he was ready to bolt, so I softened my tone. "Did you want to ask me something?" He stared at me, his expression unchanged.

He swallowed so hard that I thought the cord around his neck would break. Each instant he stood there represented a separate trembling decision not to flee. I spoke even more gently. "You do know I'm married, don't you?"

He stared at me, then shook his head mutely. He swallowed again, and I thought he was going to say something. But he went back to examining the tea bins, perhaps to hide his disappointment. His gaze roved over them as if trying to identify the one in which the secret to happiness lay hidden.

It was his shyness that made me feel the stirring. The painful self-consciousness coming through, the discomfort he radiated at not fitting in. Without thinking, I extended my fingers towards him in empathy. As if we were in some foreign country where it was perfectly reasonable for a woman to reach for the hand of a man.

For an instant, he began to extend his hand as well, as if to clasp my palm and shake it. Then he realized what he was doing, what I had said. His neck stiffened, his eyes widened, and his whole body seemed to shrink from my fingertips. He began to walk backwards, first in small steps, then in more reckless strides, until he had cleared the tea shop, then the tire shop after that, and the restaurant that was next in line. He turned around and ran, weaving through the people shopping for shoes and tires and tea, then abruptly veered off the pavement onto the road. I caught my breath as a tram clanged by, but he sprinted nimbly around it, reaching the other side safely and continuing towards the police station at Gamdevi. I watched as long as I could for the white of his shirt as it bobbed down the street, the illumination of the lampposts coloring it yellow each time he passed underneath. Then, wrapping my untouched fingers in my dupatta, I turned around to make my way back home.

AT THE START OF the second term, Paji launched another of his letters into my world. "You never had very good study habits, so it's no wonder you did so poorly in your first-term exam. I have come to the conclusion that you need to spend more time with your classmates so that their work example will rub off on you as well."

A good friend of his, Dr. Jamshed Dastoor (the same Dr. Dastoor reputed to have been Lord Mountbatten's personal physician in Delhi), had just moved to Bombay. "By a fortuitous coincidence, his daughter Farida has joined Wilson this year. Please introduce yourself to her forthwith, since she could be just the role model you need for inspiration."

I had seen Farida—or Freddy, as she was called by everyone (even the professors reading out the roll call)—in two of my classes. With her startlingly pale complexion and the brazenly plucked eyebrows that climbed high up her forehead, she was difficult to miss—for good measure, she often appeared with an extravagant scarf tied around her neck, as if she had just breezed in from a Hollywood romance. Each morning, a gleaming white Mercedes pulled up to the front entrance of the college to deliver Freddy to her classes. The car remained parked all day under a tree next to the beach, the driver ready to whisk her away to where she wanted at a moment's notice.

I ignored Paji's letter. I had no desire to befriend Freddy. I reasoned that she was much too popular to approach anyway—there was no way to penetrate the protective circle of friends always surrounding her.

Paji must have contacted Dr. Dastoor as well, because one morning, the Mercedes pulled up beside me as I was crossing Laburnum Road. The door opened grandly, to reveal Freddy, in dark green goggles, waving to me. "I know it's only a short distance, but why don't I give you a ride?" I hesitated, then reluctantly got in—it would have seemed too rude to refuse, and besides, people were stopping to look and leer in the street. "I'm Freddy, as you must know—our fathers have decided we must meet. You're Meera, am I correct? Before I forget, do remember to vote for me in the election tomorrow."

Freddy was running to be the president of the English-speaking student union at Wilson—I had seen the cyclostyled handbills that her friends had been passing out. Although the lectures at Wilson were all in English, the college catered to a large population from poorer areas like Mazgaon and Dombivili, with a majority of the students having graduated from vernacular medium schools. Some of the teachers had even started peppering their explanations with Marathi and Gujarati phrases to ensure they were being understood. "Keep Wilson College English-medium!" Freddy's handbills urged.

"We made jokes about you being so quiet because you didn't know enough English," Freddy told me after we had chatted a bit. "But now that I'm hearing you speak, it's all so clear—only a convent school could have produced that accent. It's good I'm here—just in time to rescue you from the hordes of vernacs all around. Sometimes it feels like we're stuck in a zoo, with all these beastly languages and guttural sounds."

It seemed to take only hours for Freddy's solar system of friends to start orbiting around me as well. I was invited to play in the badminton courts, drink cups of tea in the canteen, assist in the annual play that the English Club put up (*Love's Labour's Lost* that year). The day the Cream Centre restaurant opened, I furtively hid my jam sandwiches in my purse and walked over with everyone else—Freddy wanted to be the first in the city to sample the sundaes they had been advertising all week in the newspaper. On Fridays, I trooped with the group to the Eros or the Regal or one of the other Hollywood theaters—I would have rather seen a film in Hindi, but was careful not to let my preference be known. Belying Paji's expectations, the only activity that never seemed to find its way onto the roster was studying.

DEV WAS QUITE AMUSED the first few times he spotted the Mercedes dropping me off. "I see you've made some new friends. Our Meera's moving up in the world." Soon, though, his mood darkened. He complained I was not paying enough attention to the meals I cooked and didn't have time anymore to iron his shirts. He was furious one evening when he came back from work without going to Auntie's, and found I hadn't returned. "This Freddy person with whom you've fallen in—does she have boys as well riding in that Mercedes of hers?"

Things came to a head when I told him about the class picnic to Elephanta Island. "Why not?" he said. "I can take the third-class train to Jogeshwari for voice lessons while you cruise off to the island. Perhaps in Freddy's own private yacht—does Mercedes make yachts as well?"

"If you don't want me to go, just say so."

"Since when have you needed my permission for anything? I thought you only asked your father for that. And why wouldn't I want you to go?—it'll be nice for you to cavort with all your friends from college, especially the men."

My first impulse was to respond in kind, to show I would not be cowed. But things had not been going well lately for Dev—despite his perseverance at lessons, even the newer music directors had turned him down in tryouts of his revamped singing style. Besides, there was my pledge to conform. I decided I would approach Freddy to explain that I was different from other students—being married, I could only go along on a picnic if my husband was invited as well.

"Oh, please bring him along. The more the merrier," she said. Perhaps I imagined the heavenward look she seemed to exchange with her friends.

We left for the island at 10 a.m. on Sunday, a boatload of English-medium college students and Dev. "Who'd like to sing a song for us?" Freddy asked, and Dev volunteered before I could stop him. He burst into "Awara Hoon," one of the new Mukesh songs his guru had been teaching him. People clapped politely when he had finished, but while he was singing, nobody joined in. "Who else—in *English* this time?" Freddy said, and I felt doubly mortified because Dev kept smiling without realizing the slight.

It was a long climb up the hill from the jetty to the temple caves. The weather was unseasonably warm for December—each step we ascended seemed to offer us up closer to the sun, to be withered by its rays. Dev appeared to have developed an obsession for Freddy in the time taken to make the water crossing. He hurried me along to keep pace with her, a foolish grin fixed on his face in case she happened to look back. Every time we passed a group of monkeys, he loudly mimicked their growls in the hope of attracting her attention. At one point, he asked me if I thought she might be thirsty, if he should buy her a glass of water from the girl winding her way down the steps with an earthenware pot on her head. "Freddy only drinks water that's been boiled," I informed him.

We had lunch before going into the cave. There were circles of people forming on the grass, and of course Dev wanted to sit in the one with

Freddy. "Would you like to try some kidney pie?" she asked us. "Daddy had our cook take lessons from the chef at the British Embassy."

I didn't want to accept, because we had only the usual jam sandwiches to trade in return, but Dev helped himself to Freddy's offering. "It's very good," he said, even though I knew how he hated non-Punjabi fare. "Tastes a little like mutton samosa," he added, and some of Freddy's friends tittered into their napkins.

Surely even Dev must have noticed the glances and winks that passed between Freddy and the other girls. He chose to ignore them all, lumbering on with his attempts to make an impression. Although clearly mocking him, Freddy made no effort to disengage herself from Dev's transparent courtship. Rather, she preened and flaunted herself under the attention, as if it was a waterfall cascading over her body. "Some more pie?" she purred, holding out the plate.

As we gathered at the entrance to the caves, Dev slipped away from the group. I spotted the shine in his eyes at once when he returned—I knew he had taken a few nips to fortify himself. I stood there mortified—what if Freddy or one of the girls smelled his breath? Fortunately, there was no obvious bulge or outline of a flask visible through the pockets of his pants. "Shall we go pay our respects to Shiva?" Dev asked, as if the congregation had been marking time just for his return.

One of the girls from my history class, Aarti, led us through the courtyard and up the stone steps. "My father's brought me here so many times that not only every panel but even the story behind is chipped permanently into my head." She paused at the top of the steps, each arm pointing towards one of the enormous reliefs flanking the entrance. "The two most opposite aspects of Shiva, as my father always declares. All his energy and action in the dancing Natraja on your right, and the stillness of his yogi pose on your left."

I tried to concentrate on the images, to tear my attention away from Freddy and Dev. Here was Shiva the yogi, seated in such a way that his lap seemed to be both emerging from and dissolving into the rock. Both his arms were missing and the stone was worn away from his nose and lips—his obliviousness to these mutilations only accentuated the trance he was in. And on the other side, another trance-like expression, but now the king of dance jumping out of the relief. Arms flailing around, legs crossing and uncrossing, his body in such exquisite balance that motion had to be inevitable. "The reason he looks so serene even as entire cities and continents are being obliterated under his feet is that he knows destruction will simply give him a chance to create once again," Aarti explained. Surely if I held my breath, and stared at Shiva's poised hand, I would catch a stirring, at least at his fingertips.

"Which one is your Dev more like?" Freddy asked, breaking my spell. Dev's face spread into a delighted grin—there was a chorus of giggles from her friends.

I tried to stay next to Dev as we followed Aarti into the cool interior of the cave. But it was as if Freddy had trained her friends, like a captain might his team for a soccer match—I found myself blocked at each step, and gradually, deftly, displaced to the outskirts of the group. "It's so dark in here. So romantic, isn't it?" Freddy said.

Aarti took us back and forth across the cave, showing us the tableaux on the walls in chronological order. Shiva marrying Parvati after years of asceticism, with Vishnu and Brahma and gift-bearing angels floating in to celebrate their cosmic union. The married couple playing dice, with Parvati closing her eyes to let Shiva win by cheating, so that he wouldn't sulk and stalk off and darken the universe. Shiva as the destroyer, teeth bared, sword raised, eyes white with anger, impaling his own son Andhaka for falling in love with his mother Parvati and trying to carry her off. "What Shiva's really destroying is the lust in Andhaka's heart—giving him an opportunity to conquer his passion and redeem himself. Which Andhaka does, finally, after a hundred thousand years of penance." Dev murmured something into Freddy's ear, and I saw her smile and coyly shake her head.

"And this is where the goddess Ganga descends from heaven and Shiva catches her in the locks of his hair. Notice the trace of unease Parvati displays at the arrival of her rival Ganga, who she knows will become Shiva's other wife."

Parvati's expression wasn't uneasy, but rather knowing, graceful, wise. She stood to one side of Shiva, her body arching elegantly away from him, a hint of indignation in the tilt of her head, and on her lips, the barest of smiles. "What I want to know is whether there's someone here for me as well, to catch me should I fall," Freddy said.

The most imposing statue in the cave was a giant trimurti next to the Ganga relief, towering several times taller than the copies I had seen made by the sand sculptor on the beach. Even Freddy and her friends interrupted their banter to gaze up at the three faces, crowned with intricate headgear rising into the darkness. Aarti reached up with her hand to show how she could barely touch one of the beads in the necklaces carved into the breast. "People sometimes claim that this shows the trinity of Shiva with Vishnu and Brahma, but it's really three images of Shiva alone. See the right face with the mustache, the lotus poised next to the one on the left—they're Shiva's two sides, masculine and feminine. And in the center, he's at his most contemplative, eyes closed, face devoid of expression, looking deep within himself. Imagine—he's been here since the seventh century—watching dynasty after dynasty pass by, his face always turned sightlessly towards the same patch of sea. Waiting for the right era to start participating in the universe again, when his eyes will finally open and he'll spring free."

I hung back as Aarti led the crowd away to see the image of Shiva as half woman, half man. The chatter died down and I was left alone with the trimurti. I looked at the diffused light burnishing a soft glow on its cheeks—was it trying to communicate a lesson to me? *Remain unperturbed by what might be happening*, it seemed to say—*accept my gift of serenity*. Even if Dev and Freddy grew more adventurous when they noticed I was no longer trailing them, why, the trimurti asked, should it really matter to me?

I turned towards the mouth of the cave to align myself in the same direction as the trimurti. Light filtered in from the outside and made the faintest of impressions against my shut eyelids. I followed this light, padding towards it through the dark, opening my eyes only when I heard the people admiring the reliefs at the entrance. Then I went down the steps and walked past the wooden fence, all the way to the railing that overlooked the motley collection of islands strewn across the water. Somewhere above me, a monkey made a strange rhythmic noise, like a bird chirping, then swung away through the branches. I stood there in the breeze, waiting for Aarti to lead the group out of the cave.

Dev and Freddy were the last to emerge. I watched as my husband offered his hand to steady Freddy, who seemed to be suddenly having trouble descending the steps. All through the boat ride back, she kept laughing at whatever Dev said—I had never told her my husband had such a sense of humor, she declared to me. I consoled myself that it didn't matter—I had been through more with Dev and Roopa, managing to keep myself above jealousy. "What was that expression again on Parvati's face?" one of Freddy's friends threw into the group, and I felt my cheeks turn red.

"Did you have to be so obvious?" I asked Dev when we got home. "At least you could have wiped the strings of drool off your mouth periodically."

"What a filthy mind you have," Dev replied. "Is that all you can think?" He went to sulk in the other room. Later on, I heard him hum the same Mukesh song from the boat to himself.

THAT WEEK, FOR THE first time since I had started going to college, Dev showed up after classes to pick me up. "I thought I could also thank Freddy, in case we see her, for that round samosa she brought, made of kidneys."

We ended up going to the Cream Centre for tea with Freddy's group. It was just like at the picnic—Dev as oblivious as before, Freddy leading him on, and the entourage giggling—not only at him, but now at me as well. I kept dreading another attempt by Dev to burst into "Awara Hoon," but to my relief, it didn't materialize.

I'm not sure how he got the time off, but Dev started showing up every second or third day after that. One afternoon, he came with us for lunch—on another, he accompanied us to see *An Affair to Remember* at the Regal. ("Next time we'll try to find you a movie with more songs in it," Freddy promised.) There came an evening when I glanced out of the balcony and saw him being dropped off at ten by the white Mercedes.

"It's really nothing," he said when I confronted him upstairs.

"Freddy wanted to see the studio, so we waited, but the recording didn't end. We'll try again on Saturday—I have the morning off—you can come along too, if you care."

I fumed all night. I would search out the boy who followed me last year, I told myself. Show up together at the studio on Saturday to let Dev know two could play the flirtation game. I actually looked for my stalker the next day in college—surveying classrooms from the outside, peering into the men's canteen, searching nooks in the library, but he was nowhere to be seen.

On Saturday, I told Dev I did want to be present at the studio. "As you like," he said, checking his nostrils in the mirror and tamping down a curl of hair behind his ear. He fastened his sleeves with cuff links in the shape of miniature eagles, then dabbed on the last drops from a bottle of Godrej after-shave.

The air-conditioning was off in the studio lobby. Dev's Godrej fragrance dissipated within the first half hour of waiting. Circles of sweat formed at his armpits, but he did not unthread the eagles to roll up his sleeves. "Perhaps the traffic is jammed at Nana Chowk," he conjectured when an hour had passed. "I should have told her the A-1 chip factory— her driver must be having a problem with the address," he said at 1 p.m. "There could have been an accident—I hope to God Freddy's not been hurt."

Freddy never showed. My first instinct, that Dev was not somebody she could be interested in, proved correct. Like a swirl of butterflies taking to the air simultaneously, Freddy and her friends left him behind, in search of the next bush on which to alight. The invitations to badminton courts and the Cream Centre ceased abruptly, the Mercedes stopped rolling around the corner of our street.

Although I was relieved to be no longer one of Freddy's projects, Dev took it very hard. I could tell he blamed me for somehow sabotaging things. He put away the eagles and didn't replace the bottle of aftershave for many months. On some nights, he seemed so forlorn that I wondered if I should be cheering him up—even, perhaps, trying to broker a meeting with Freddy. His ego had become more fragile, his confidence readily shaken, after months of drubbing at the recording studio.

He stopped going to Jogeshwari not too long after, discontinuing his voice lessons without telling me.

Freddy herself mostly ignored me after that, except for one brazen request to sign a petition against a move by the principal to hold some classes in Marathi. A few of her friends, though, took to making jokes about me. One of them even came up whenever she saw me, to address me as "Parvati." I started delaying my entry into classrooms to the very last moment so I wouldn't have to encounter the winking glances and knowing smiles. It occurred to me that I had three more years of joint classes with my tormentors ahead of me.

I needn't have worried. When the First Year Arts final exam results were posted that May, I found I had failed, and would have to repeat the year.

chapter
fifteen

PAJI SENT ME A SLEW OF SCATHING LETTERS WHEN HE LEARNT THE NEWS. In the first one, he informed me that I had not only shamed myself, but humiliated him in front of Dr. Dastoor as well. "Were you too proud to ask his daughter for help just because she's smarter?" When I couldn't think of how to reveal the flirtations between Dev and Freddy, he accused me of failing on purpose, just to anger him. "If that's how ignorant your thinking is, then just remember, you're only hurting yourself." I was composing a reply about how difficult my transition had been after the loss of my baby, when another missive arrived, listing all the money he'd spent on books and fees. "Perhaps I should have adopted a street urchin—I'd have been more appreciated had I sent him to college instead."

Something rose within me, something that made me tear up the explanation I had been trying to articulate. If that was Paji's attitude, then fine, I would absorb his anger, savor it, even find ways to provoke him further. Perhaps this was the way to soothe the injury inside, that still hurt so much every time I thought about it. I resolved to sit on the beach through all my classes in the coming year, picturing the money wasted every minute. It was unfortunate that colleges did not insist on uniforms—I would have enjoyed the extra coins draining from Paji's pocket.

The person who deflected me from this headstrong path, was, strangely enough, Sharmila. It must have been Paji's frustration with my performance that prompted him to turn to her in desperation. She had always been the least promising student of us all—lost in her own dreamy world, with an academic record as consistent as it was wretched. From the time she was little, she seemed serene in her vision of her future, one where Paji and Biji would hand over the baton of her care to a carefully selected husband. All she had to do was finish her schooling and matriculate, and the gentle burbling pleasures of a wife and mother would, soon enough, float her way. It was therefore a tremendous shock for her when this future suddenly vaporized in the intensity of Paji's attention. Over Biji's furious protestations, Sharmila found herself plucked from the living room viewings by prospective bridegrooms and deposited instead into the confines of Ramjas College (which just a few years ago Roopa had attended with Dev). Her letters to me were heartrending—filled with terror at this unforeseen turn of events, against which she had been too timid to protest.

But then she surprised everyone, not least of all herself. She took to her studies like a wick to oil, absorbing knowledge from books, from lectures, even, it seemed, from the university air itself. She woke up every day at 5 a.m. to pore over her notes and talked about her favorite subject, chemistry, with a fanaticism Biji found horrifying. She did so well in her first-term exams (science, too, not arts) that the college declared her a role model for their fledgling class of females in the sciences and even talked about awarding her a special new medal. Her weakening eyesight (due to all the reading she was doing, Biji charged) led to a pair of glasses which lent her appearance an older, more studious air.

The aftershocks of Sharmila's transformation made their way to me across the country through Paji's letters. "Can you imagine? She's aced the prelim in Physics." "My own daughter, a scientist—I can hardly believe it." "Did I mention they're going to fete her on Republic Day?"

Suddenly his exhortations for me to study waned—he no longer seemed interested in my dangling promises to improve. "I'll really have to think about it, Meera. Whether it makes any sense to pour in more money for another year if you happen to fail again." The looming threat of being cut off made me abandon my notions of non-cooperation and return to my books. In 1962, the same year that Sharmila blazed her way to an honors B.Sc. in chemistry, I managed to squeak across the finish line with a third division history B.A.

Sharmila's studiousness didn't end there. She went ahead and finished her master's in organic chemistry in just two years and then became the first woman to enroll in the newly instituted Ph.D. program in the sciences at Delhi University. The *Indian Express* even published a photo with a brief interview, in which the main question seemed to be when, exactly, she planned to marry. "Eve chooses test tube over family" was the caption under her picture, much to Biji's dismay.

WHILE SHARMILA SLAKED her unexpected thirst for knowledge, I wondered what to do with my degree. At the time I graduated, Paji, engrossed in Sharmila's M.Sc. efforts, distractedly suggested I get a job. "Why bother?" Dev said, each time I brought up the idea. "Surely what they pay me at Famous Studio is enough for the two of us." For a while, I did nothing, but I was no longer used to staying at home or content with a daily stroll to Chowpatty. Paji put me in touch with a publishing agency near Opera House, for whom I started translating historical books from Hindi to English.

It was not the most stimulating of jobs, but the proprietor, Mr. Hansi, was very solicitous. "Your father is an inspiration not only to every publisher, but every citizen in this country," he said. "You're lucky to be the daughter of such a great man." He gave me a desk in the largest of the three rooms, a room I shared with the two typists. It was hard to ignore their sounds at first—the zip of the cartridge, especially, set my teeth on edge. I wondered if I would have to ask to be moved, but fortunately, the noise merged into the background after the first fortnight.

Dev seemed unusually concerned that I not discomfort or tire myself. His solution, when I mentioned the typewriter noise, was that I simply quit. "Why get all drenched for a few rupees?" he said to me each time it rained. "Why go in at all, why can't you just sit at home and translate?" I told him there were too many reference books at work that I needed, too many words and phrases I couldn't process without Mr. Hansi's help. It wasn't the real reason and Dev was by no means convinced. "Be sure to let everyone know you're married—nobody expects a working woman to be a wife. Especially the men you see day after day—who knows what goes on in their heads?"

Dev's apprehension made me keep everyone at arm's length. I was always on guard, starting at even the most innocent of overtures as if an invisible line of etiquette had been crossed. I stole away each afternoon to the café in the courtyard of the Opera House movie theater to eat lunch by myself. There were tables set out under a canopy, and as long as I ordered a cup of tea, I could consume my jam sandwiches (egg on Wednesdays and Fridays) undisturbed there.

The day dawned when I received my first pay—Friday, the twenty-eighth of September, to be exact. A peon went from desk to desk distributing khaki brown envelopes with employees' names written across the top right corner in red. I tore mine open and counted twenty-five ten-rupee notes inside, two one-rupee coins, and sixty paise in change. I had started on the seventh, but Mr. Hansi had given me a full month's wages.

That afternoon, when the Opera House waiter brought my tea, I asked for a Mangola instead. He came back with my bottle and flipped open the cap, catching it expertly in midair. I opened my sandwich packet, and it being Friday, detected the slightly sulfuric aroma of egg. I had boiled it the night before, as I always did, and doused it with pepper precisely to reduce this smell. The thought of the chopped yolks and whites entombed in their mushy slices depressed me. It was quite profligate, I knew, but I had to call the waiter back. "Do you have pakodas on your menu?" I asked. "Or samosas, better yet?"

At home, I waited until Dev was sitting at the dining table before setting the khaki envelope in front of him. He rubbed it warily as if testing the paper, as if apprehensive he might find something offensive about the texture itself. "What is it?" he asked, finally, without looking inside.

"My first pay. Two hundred and fifty-two rupees." I took out the money, not just to show him, but also because I wanted to feel the crispness of the notes between my fingers again. "It was two fifty-two sixty, but I spent eight annas on lunch and gave the waiter a ten-paise tip."

Dev stared at the empty envelope as if his worst suspicions had been confirmed, as if the paper had been revealed not only to be disagreeable, but toxic as well. "Two fifty-two sixty," he said.

"I've been ordering tea there every afternoon and I'd never given the waiter anything, so I—"

But Dev had already put the envelope aside. "I have to get to the studio early tomorrow. The only time they could get both Lata and Rafi to show up for recording a duet was at eight a.m."

After that, Dev always became irritable on the last Friday of each month, when I was paid. We didn't talk of what I did with my salary, though he must have known that I deposited it into our savings account. I ordered not just samosas from Opera House, but mutton sandwiches as well. Sometimes, when it was very hot, I even splurged on a second Mangola.

One afternoon in January, I found the heavy iron gates to the Opera House compound were chained. Inside, I could make out the closed doors of the café—even the advance booking window for the cinema was shut. A watchman came up behind the gate and rattled his lathi against the bars. "There's a strike," he said, "haven't you heard? All the movie theaters in the city are closed, to protest the new government tax."

The next evening, Dev was at home when I returned. The actors' union and the musicians' guild had voted to join the protest (adding their demands for higher pay to the list of grievances). The studios had all shut down, and the whole film industry was now officially on strike. Dev could be out of work indefinitely—it would now be my salary that was crucial for our subsistence.

Dev took this as a direct blow to his ego. He started withdrawing my earnings in secret after I deposited them in our savings account, never asking for any of it directly. He became distant and moody, idling around in the dining room all day, drinking twice as much as before. A money order sent by Paji to help us out enraged him so much that he refused to sign the slip (I had to go to the post office myself the next day to retrieve it). Finally one morning, as I was about to leave for work, he barred my way by standing in front of the door. "I would rather dig ditches in the street," he said, "than continue living like this on the charity of a wife who works."

"Why don't you, then? It'll be better than staying at home drunk all the time."

"I see they not only pay you at your office, but also sharpen your tongue for free. Is this why I allow you to go, so that you can learn how to speak back to me?"

I tried to get past Dev, but he didn't move. "What will you do, write to your daddy if I stop you now? He's the one who first put this idea of working in your head, isn't he? Do you have to be such a good daughter that you always have to please him?"

"Don't forget that if it weren't for my father, you wouldn't have this house—you'd be living on the street. If you can gulp down all his money without a burp, why such pretensions taking it from me?"

"Yes, yes, keep telling me how worthless I am. How I'm a leech on you and your Paji—isn't that what you think? And as for your *respected* father—" He didn't complete his sentence, but slunk into the other room.

I went to work that day and every day after that, weathering Dev's taunts as best I could. My hope was that once his work resumed, he would calm down and revert to his earlier peevish but tolerant attitude.

But I underestimated the rage he would store up in the ten weeks the strike lasted. As soon as he started getting paid again, Dev disappeared every evening, coming back at 3 and 4 a.m, long after Auntie's had shut down. Thoroughly inebriated, he collapsed into the living room couch as soon as he returned. In the mornings, he was surly and ill-tempered and refused to answer the questions I posed. "It's none of your business—think you can still wave your money in my face?"

Finally, one night I confronted Auntie in her bar at 10 p.m. "What makes you imagine I keep track of my customers' whereabouts?" she snapped. Then she softened. "He only pops in here for a single drink these days—he spends most of the evening down the road, at Banu's place." She dropped her voice to a whisper. "It's one of *those* kinds of establishments. I can't believe I'm revealing this, but if we women don't come to each other's aid, who will?"

"You mean it's a brothel?"

"Not quite that sordid—only some dancing, or so I've heard. But a full rupee per glass she demands, this Banu does—imagine if I started charging that. I suppose she can get away with it, the way she struts around putting everything she has on display."

So this was what Dev had sunk to. I imagined going to Banu's place to retrieve him. Opening the faceless door to enter the hallway lit in garish pink. The drumbeat of a tabla starting up somewhere above, a woman clearing her throat and beginning to sing. Dev adding his voice to the suggestive lyrics, hands clapping, ankle bells chiming, a harmonium joining in. "Stop!" the hall attendant crying out, as I squeeze by the furniture and go running past him. My feet pounding on wood as I vault the steps, my breath coming in rasps as I part the strings of beads that screen the chamber upstairs.

What would I be greeted by? The scenes I had witnessed so many times in films? Clouds of attar-scented smoke, the gaudiness of painted-on gold, translucent curtains billowing in the wind. Courtesans reclining languorously around the room, customers leering drunkenly from the sidelines, musicians plying their instruments on the patterned linoleum floor. The thickly caked makeup on the dancing girl's face, the tiny white buds of motiya braided with tinsel in her hair. And Dev—Dev at her mercurial henna-painted feet, so rapt in his song that he doesn't even notice me there.

"But you shouldn't worry, Beti, he's a good boy, your Dev, not some modern-day Devdas. I think he must go there for the chance to sing, that's all it probably is."

Devdas. Could that be whom Dev was trying to emulate? The lovelorn alcoholic who was Saigal's most famous characterization, the role people said he was born to play? Dev certainly had the drinking down pat. Roopa could be his Paru, his unattainable love, and Banu could be the courtesan Chandramukhi, in whose lap Dev already seemed to be drowning his sorrows. And I? There didn't seem to be a part left for me to play.

"Why don't you just return home?" Auntie said. "I'll tell Dev tomorrow that you were here. It'll all be fine, just you see, your auntie will take care of it. You know you're like a daughter to me." I fought the urge to push away her hand as she stroked my hair.

That night, after he had returned, I crept up to Dev asleep on the couch, determined to uncover evidence of his transgressions. He still wore the clothes in which he had left for work—I sniffed them for attar, but all I could detect was a faint curry smell. There were no seductively long hairs that showed up against the white of his shirt, no incriminating petals of motiya or broken ankle bells in his pockets. In fact, he looked childlike as he slept through my search—as innocent as a slumbering Devdas, I thought to myself.

I never did act on my resolve to confront Dev at Banu's place. I was too apprehensive of bringing the matter to a head by barging in. The scene I had imagined—what were the ways in which it could climax? Would Dev be contrite, ashamed, or would he humiliate me in front of everyone, order me to return home by myself? And what if he and Banu weren't just dancing, but hidden behind another beaded curtain, locked in each other's embrace?

Perhaps Auntie kept her promise to tell Dev I knew where he went, perhaps she didn't. For a long time, there was no change in his nightly absences. It was only when I was forced to take a fortnight off from work due to too much accumulated leave that Dev began returning earlier— still swaying and tottering, but at a more decent hour. At the end of my fortnight, I sent a note to Mr. Hansi saying I wanted to use up the rest of my vacation time as well. When the final week was up, Dev had still not reverted to his earlier behavior. I understood then the bargain he wanted to strike for staying away from Banu—I resigned from my job.

FOR THE FEW DAYS THAT FOLLOWED, I felt aglow at my decision. Dev became very attentive, coming home straight from work, taking me to a play at the Tejpal one evening, and the next, to the Soviet Expo at Cross

Maidan. As an added bonus, Paji was beside himself with fury at my "self-destructiveness"—I waited eagerly for his letters to savor his gnashing. I didn't miss my job too much—translating the same facts repeatedly had become quite monotonous. The reigns of the Mauryas and the Guptas, the waves of Gangetic invaders—the problem with history was it never changed. Even worse were the technical volumes Mr. Hansi asked me to render—treatises on industrial growth since Independence, mind-numbing tomes on the rise in the use of fertilizers.

I was staggering home one morning, triumphant over the giant sack of onions I had haggled down to twelve annas, when a familiar white Mercedes drew up beside me. "My, so many onions," Freddy said, wrinkling her nose. "Looks like you need a ride—come in and sit beside me." The sack was heavy enough that I found myself accepting. "Only you, dear, not the onions—the driver will put those in the dickey."

Freddy was dressed immaculately in purple—right down to her fingernail polish and the scarf still tied dashingly around her neck. Since I had last seen her, the prosperity informing her features had acquired a patina of smugness—curiously, it suited her well. "I'll have our cook send you the recipe for a soup that the French make out of onions—I didn't know you were so infatuated with them."

Freddy insisted on taking me to lunch at Kwality's. With my onions held hostage in her trunk, she bombarded me with her post-B.A. accomplishments for an hour. The newspaper column she was writing, the speakers' bureau she organized for the Rotary club, the gallery show in which she had been invited to participate ("even though painting's just something I dabble in"). She had even formed her own theater company. "You remember Pesi and Keki and Judy from college—they're all so fond of acting—you must come and see us."

It was good that she kept talking about herself, since I dreaded the prospect of having to reciprocate. "But enough about me—what have you been doing with *your* life?" she finally asked as the bill came.

THAT EVENING, DEV dragged me to the Soviet Expo for one last visit before it closed. Clumps of people stood enthralled around the tractors and mechanical hoes, as if waiting for the machines to spring to life and start plowing the exhibition ground itself. There were gleaming models of MiG fighter jets suspended in a glass case, with a giant cloth backdrop showing Nehru and Khrushchev in a celebratory embrace. A woman sat at a desk in a stall, vending subscriptions to *Soviet Life* and *Soviet Woman*—twelve issues for a rupee, twenty-four for one-fifty.

Dev hurried me past everything—as always, it was the Ferris wheel that interested him. The sign claimed it was Russian-made, though it looked like the usual giant wheel, with yellow canopies attached to spruce up the cars a bit. Dev helped me into the seat and secured the safety bar over our laps. We rose into the air in spurts, stopping each time for the loading of the next chair.

"Look, you can see Marine Drive from here. And the Gateway, and the Taj Hotel." Dev swiveled around to point, and our seat tilted back dizzyingly in the air.

I followed the line of his arm, but the sights barely registered. What *had* I been doing with my life? I had mumbled something to put Freddy off, but her question still roiled in my mind. Why had I cut myself off from my job, from getting a taste of what independence meant? Why hadn't I taken college more seriously, established my own circle of friends? Why, for that matter, didn't I have my own newspaper column or theater company like Freddy had? I watched a trio of seagulls fly towards the sea, their white bodies receding into the dark. All my energy for the past few years had gone into resenting Paji or pleasing Dev. In the face of Dev's misbehavior, of his bullying, why had I let him get away with it?

Suddenly I no longer wanted to ride the Ferris wheel. I wanted to follow the seagulls and glide into the life I had not chosen. But the bar across my waist was locked in place, and the wheel had begun to descend, picking up speed. Dev squeezed my forearm and said something, but his words were lost before they reached me. The flags adorning the tractors came up to greet us, sickles and hammers waved in the breeze. I caught a flash of the attendant, his face a blur, his hand on the lever that controlled our speed.

What if he forgot to ease off on the lever? Perhaps there was still a chance to be free. I imagined us spinning faster and faster, so fast that the wheel broke loose from its mooring. Bulbs exploding, canopies crumpling, riders trying to hang on, as we began to roll across the grounds. The juggernaut flattening tents and tractors and cars alike as it barreled down the road to Flora Fountain. Its swath extending all the way to the dockyards, where it splashed with a final bounce into the sea.

But I remained where I was, unharmed and safe, but also undelivered to the liberating waters of the sea. The lights of Bombay kept swinging in their arc, approaching and receding under me. I lost track of the cycles—five, ten, fifteen—they seemed to stretch on to eternity. And through it all, as we whirled together through the air, Dev's fingers retained their claim on me.

"Wasn't that wonderful?" Dev said as we began to slow down. "Let's ride it again, shall we?"

chapter
sixteen

Four years after we moved to Bombay, Hema's wedding finally took us back to Delhi. I had tried, for quite some time, to get Dev to accompany me there, but he was always averse to it. "What will I tell them, with what face will I greet them, when I have yet to make the slightest mark to my name? Like a dog all beaten, returning with its tail between its legs, that's what people will say." Eventually I decided to go alone to see Biji, and twice requested Babuji to get a ticket from his railway quota. But perhaps Dev's unsociability was catching, or perhaps I was simply not ready to face Paji again. I made it all the way to the station platform one time, but changed my mind before the train left.

It was surprising how the distance between the two cities proved so much more insurmountable than an overnight railway journey. Despite all of Hema's letters threatening her arrival in Bombay on the next train, she, too, had never managed to visit. Sensing Dev's reluctance regarding family reunions, Mataji declared trains unfit for travel by a young unaccompanied woman. Besides, there was the task of finding a groom, which first had to be completed. Once the marriage was set, Hema started making all sorts of plans to come down with her mother before the ceremony—to shop where Bombay brides did, and visit all the shrines around the city for special blessings to ensure her firstborn was a son. The trip did not materialize.

Sharmila actually did visit once on a college trip with her classmates, though she didn't stay with us, and only spent a few hours in my company. Roopa's letters from Visakhapatnam (when not vaunting the adorable perfection of her offspring, a boy and a girl) occasionally mentioned that her husband would be transferred next to Bombay. Much to my relief, they landed in Madras instead, a posting still sufficiently far away.

The only person who came quite regularly to Bombay was Arya. He made a trip or two every year, first to establish a Bombay division of the HRM, and then to oversee it. On one of his visits, he even showed up at Wilson College, helping one of the vernacular groups set up a booth on Activity Day for recruiting students into the HRM. He always stayed with us on his visits. I tried to linger away from home when he was around, but it was impossible to completely escape him. Every morning when I came into the kitchen to boil the milk, it was as if I was back in the bedroom in Nizamuddin, stalked by his hungry look, and the smell of overripe fruit. The only reason to look forward to his coming was the hope that he would bring Sandhya along one day.

Although the intensity with which I missed everyone else eased over time, my longing for Sandhya only grew deeper. Perhaps it was because the only news I received about her were the occasional scraps Hema deemed important enough to send. Even though the words Sandhya scrawled out at the end of Hema's letters had, over the months and years, begun to clump together into the awkward sentence, it was hardly enough. On the one occasion that we had arranged to speak with Dev's family over the phone, she had been too overcome with emotion to say more than hello.

At my urging, Dev always asked his brother to bring Bhabhiji along the next time. But I knew these efforts were in vain. Arya would never want his wife around—she would just be in the way of what he still hoped to attain.

THE DAY WE ARRIVED for the wedding, Hema wasn't there to greet us at the station. "She's been practicing being mature the last few days," Mataji explained. "Like a married person should be, she says. You'll see."

Sure enough, when Mataji ushered us into the bedroom, Hema sat demurely on the bed, being measured for a new set of salwar kameez suits. She looked up with the barest of smiles, as if this was all she could muster, given the gravity of her situation. "Bhaiyyaji, Bhabhiji," she addressed us formally, "It is my hope that you had a comfortable journey."

Watching her walk was truly unsettling. She carried herself like someone with a very long neck, her body held in a stiff line and inclined slightly back, her feet apparently never leaving the ground. The effect was that of a statue being wheeled around at a stately tilt—one of a goddess or queen, perhaps. Mataji suggested she show us the thermos and cutlery set that would be part of her dowry. "It's this way," Hema said, leading us to the kitchen, as if we were guests unfamiliar with the layout of the house.

It had taken the four years since we'd left to find a groom for Hema. Babuji had rejected several suitors during the dowry negotiation stage. "When did everyone become so greedy?" he lamented to us. "Isn't it enough anymore to be from a respectable home?" He took a sip of his whiskey and shook his head. "If only I'd agreed when she was still eighteen—we could have escaped with half of what we're now paying."

Although the first ceremony was only the next evening, bushels of lightbulbs had already converted the lane outside the house into a glittering fairyland. Or rather, a movie set, what with loudspeakers tied to lampposts broadcasting film music to the whole colony. "It's going to be even grander than your wedding," Babuji boasted to me. "The most lavish Nizamuddin's ever seen." Gopal, the groom, was one of Arya's friends from the HRM, and the wedding enclosure was being set up on the same field where all the organization's events were held. "What's nice about having the ceremony so close to the house is that nobody in the entire colony can miss it. We'll parade the horse through each of the streets, and invite everyone to join the procession behind the band.

Arya's going to have the HRM tent put up, under which the brahmins will cook food for five hundred guests."

"I'm glad your mother dragged me there," Paji said to me during the music ceremony the next night. "It's so touching to see how my money is coming in handy to spare no expense."

Hema maintained her regal reserve through all the events. She barely spoke to any of her friends, displaying an ostentatious seriousness through all their jokes. "What happened to the rich old husband you wanted, the one who would buy you a car and a phone?" Pushpa teased, and Hema stared her down with an unsmiling look. Even Mataji, when she tried to get her to dance to the tune of a popular wedding song, was primly refused.

Thankfully, Sandhya found a way to get Hema down from her roost on the night before the wedding. She sneaked into Mataji's cupboard and emerged wearing a resplendent gold earring and necklace set, the same one Mataji had lent Sandhya on special occasions like Karva Chauth, but had now pledged as part of Hema's dowry. "How does it look?" Sandhya asked, turning around to model it for the assembled women. "Mataji said to wear it tomorrow—it'll go well with my red wedding sari, don't you think?"

Hema's reserve didn't stand a chance. She shrieked, unfolding herself out of her cross-legged pose and lunging at Sandhya in one fluid move. "Don't you like it?" Sandhya asked, running into the courtyard, with Hema bounding after her. Sandhya was able to take off the necklace just before Hema cornered her and toss it to Pushpa, who waved it in the air to get Hema racing, before relaying it on to Ranjana. Even Mataji got into the game, catching the necklace from one friend and lobbing it to another, while her daughter ran around screaming, trying to retrieve it.

By the time Hema finally caught up with the missing piece of her dowry, she was much too agitated to resume putting on her airs. She tried sulking for a bit, but then realized the inconsistency this presented with her earlier stance of poised indifference. She seemed confused at what to attempt next, when Sandhya sat down beside her and lovingly threaded the gold earrings through her earlobes. "There's nobody else on whom these could look better than my sister," Sandhya said, and Hema burst into tears.

After that, everything made Hema cry—the songs played, the sight of her wedding garments for the next day, the stray whistle of a train rumbling by, even the last mound of rice cooked by Sandhya, clinging to its tray. Watching Hema bravely choke down her dinner, Pushpa started sobbing quietly into her food as well, then Sandhya and Mataji and all of Hema's friends. Only my eyes, as always, remained ungraciously dry.

That evening Mataji cleared Arya and Dev out of the bedroom, telling them that the women would be sleeping together for Hema's last night in the house. Sandhya pushed the charpoys to one side and we lined the floor with talais and sheets to create a giant bed. By now, Hema had stopped crying—instead, her eyes were round and wide with a dawning dread. She clung to each one of us for minutes on end, as if trying to get her fill of our presence, as if storing up our hugs to last her into the weeks and months and years of her marriage ahead. "How will I live by myself?" she said.

"It's not even a half mile away—I'll come see you as soon as I can," Mataji replied.

"And Sandhya didi?"

"I'll bring her along."

"And Meera didi will come from Bombay?"

"Yes, yes, whatever you say. Don't worry so much. You're going to like it there." Mataji laid Hema's head in her lap and stroked her hair. "Remember your favorite story, the one of the princess who got married and never wanted to return home again?"

"No. You never told me stories when I was little—you only made that effort for Arya and Dev bhaiyya."

"Silly girl, of course I did. But I'll tell it again."

So Mataji related the story while Sandhya and I reclined next to Hema. It was a long tale, filled with brave deeds and princely suitors, a ravishing princess who bathed in the Ganges and a secret kingdom in the Himalayas. Hema's eyelids fluttered drowsily just as the princess was being transported to the mountains in a magic doli. "I've always wanted to ride a doli. . . ." she said, before falling asleep.

Mataji rolled Hema onto the farthermost talai. "Right from birth, she could always fall unconscious in a second. I hope she manages to stay awake longer tomorrow, on her wedding night." She sighed. "I suppose it's late, I suppose we should turn off the light." She stared at Hema, making no move towards the light switch. "All those years that she's been here—I can't believe this is the last night. That this old woman is sleeping with her little girl next to her for one final time." She lay down beside Hema and stroked her hair, then arranged herself so that her arm was cradling Hema's head. Sandhya waited for Mataji to pull a sheet over the two of them before turning off the light.

I stayed awake, listening for the sounds of trains, but there were none. The moon shone through the window to create its familiar pattern on the far wall. The same enigmatic shadow that had intrigued me on so many nights before—was that a house that the dark shape surrounded by the moonlight represented, or simply a box? Or maybe it was an automobile?

Today, I decided, it was a doli. The same doli that had brought me here on my wedding night, the very one borrowed by the groom's family to transport Hema tomorrow. I imagined her clambering into its dark interior, enveloped by the smell of wood and sweat that I could still summon to my nostrils. Would it lead her to a life different from my own?

"Are you awake?" Sandhya whispered next to me.

"Yes." I turned to face her.

"I can't sleep either. It's so hard to imagine she'll be gone tomorrow. She was not even eight when Arya first brought me here as a bride." Sandhya stopped, her face rippled by the shadows, her expression unreadable in the darkness. A wisp of light fell across her nose. "But I suppose that's how it has to be. One by one everyone leaves." I reached through the silence and took her hand in my own.

"Do you know, when you left, it took me months to be able to sleep again? Even when I did fall sleep, I would awaken in the middle of the night and stare at the blank space on the floor where you used to lie. I had become used to being reassured by your sleeping face—seeing it would make me doze off again. But now that you were gone, I started tossing and turning for the rest of the night. What I finally learnt was to imagine you asleep in your bed in Bombay. The bulbs from the movie theater you wrote about blinking on and off over your face, the sounds of the Bombay traffic rising up to your ears. I would hold my breath, certain that the light or the noise was going to wake you up. Only when I saw you remaining fast asleep through it all would I start to relax again.

"You know what my fantasy used to be? That you and I would get pregnant together. That our firstborns would both be sons, that we would bring them up like brothers, like twins. That by some amazing coincidence, they would even have their birthdays on the same date. Can you imagine what that would have been like—your son and mine—with the love of two mothers to shower them, not one?"

I pressed Sandhya's fingers and felt her thumb graze my skin in response. "When I first heard you were expecting, I was quite dismayed," she said. "I thought it was just jealousy, but it was really because my fantasy hadn't come true. I hadn't conceived like you. I suppose I had been wishing it so much that I had come to expect it. Forgetting that it was in my fate to never be so fortunate."

"Don't say that. It'll still happen, you'll see."

"No it won't. In fact, I sometimes wonder if what happened to you was because of me. Whether it was my inauspicious shadow that passed over your womb, whether it was—"

I covered Sandhya's mouth with my hand. She took my fingers away and kissed their tips. "Anyway," she said. "You're safe from my bad luck now, I'm glad you went away. It's good that Hema is leaving too. Sometimes I think I should go away as well—go to Benares, beg for a living, become a sanyasin. But then I think of Arya, how that wouldn't help him. I would want him to marry someone more fertile, more fortunate, but I don't think he'd be able to, knowing I was somewhere, still alive."

"Now listen—" I began to say, but it was Sandhya's turn to put her fingers on my lips.

"Don't worry. Don't pay too much attention to what I say. I'm talking so foolishly just because of Hema's leaving."

We slept under one sheet that night. It became quite chilly near morning, and I felt Sandhya get up to close the window. "I'm here, right next to you," I murmured, when she got back under the sheet. "So you can go right back to sleep."

She touched my forehead, as if to reassure herself, then traced her fingers down my cheek. "Your face is so cold," she said. "You're not used to the Delhi weather anymore. Should I get us a blanket from the chest?"

"No, we'll just snuggle up." I moved myself closer to her until my head was on her shoulder, just like Hema's was on Mataji's next to me. Sandhya unwound a part of her sari and covered my body with it. I pressed my face into her neck and felt her breasts, warm and comforting, against my own. "You'll just have to come back with me to Bombay," I said.

We stayed there for a while. I felt drowsy, but also curiously aware, as if something pleasantly stimulating had been released into my bloodstream. I wondered how the sensation of my body must seem to her, how my head and face and bosom must feel against her body. Was she surprised like me by how closely we could nestle, how each contour had an outline to unfold against? Did she feel the swath on her belly where the cloth between us ran out, where the bareness of my midriff caressed her uncovered skin? I imagined the two of us still enfolded in the liquid warmth of her sari, staring at the sky together through the window of a train. The stars watching our passage to a distant household where we could forever be with each other again.

Sandhya kissed my forehead, then slid down to press her cheek against mine. "I wish the night could just go on," she said.

SANDHYA KILLED HERSELF three years later. Officially, everyone said it was an accident, that she must have not seen the train. "To live right next to the station and be so inexperienced crossing the tracks," the stationmaster commiserated with the family on his condolence visit. It was true that Sandhya had just started delivering Arya his midday meal—she never had much reason to cross the railway lines before that. The empty tiffin box was found nearby in the grass, as if it was something precious, like an infant, that Sandhya had tried to save by throwing clear of the tracks.

When I first got the news, the impulse to rush to Delhi struck up within me like a physical spasm. Perhaps if I hurried, perhaps if I took a flight, I could still save her, there was still time. Dev's explanations that the body would have been already cremated, that I would be in no condition to see its mangled state anyway, did little to calm my irrational urges. It was only the arrival of Hema's letter that gave me a compelling reason to remain in Bombay.

Sandhya had been despondent for the past two years, Hema wrote, ever since Tony was born. When Hema's second son Rahul arrived the year after, it seemed to get worse. "Mataji said not to tell you, but there was a disappearance for an entire week last month. Luckily, Shilpa auntie spotted Sandhya bhabhi sitting on the steps of the Kalkaji temple— wrapped from head to toe in saffron and singing as if she were a sanyasin. She refused Auntie's attempts to get her to come back—Arya bhaiyya had to go fetch her himself."

Sandhya was disoriented and quite starved when she returned, according to Hema, and claimed not to remember how she got to the temple. There had been briefer unexplained absences in the past, and it was to keep tabs on her that Arya had suggested the daily trips to his office at lunch. "I should have guessed something was really wrong, when she suddenly became so impatient to learn to write. She always talked about how you used to show her the letters of the alphabet on a slate. She said she wanted to send you a complete letter—she told me not to tell you, that it would be a surprise. I asked Arya bhaiyya several times if he found anything, but he said no, she didn't even leave a note behind."

I realized I had to wait for the mail, to see if it might contain a missing message from Sandhya, composed to me before she died. Each morning, I dragged a chair to the balcony to sit until the postman trudged down the street with his khaki bag of mail. In the afternoons, once the sun had crossed over our building, I returned to wait for his second delivery.

Sometimes I glimpsed a woman from above with a red and perfectly straight line of sindhoor in her hair. Images of Sandhya would then swirl through my head. Here she was, shaking vermilion out onto the pooja platter, snipping hibiscus from the bush outside, waving incense sticks around Devi Ma. There she stood on Karva Chauth, balancing on the charpoy, as the sun turned the sky behind her red. I saw her emerging from her bath, her hair untied and dripping, her skin pungent from the nameless green soap Mataji bought in unwrapped blocks for the family. An herbal smell, a smell slightly oily, but nevertheless pleasant, that I still remembered from our last night, sleeping together on the floor. And with it, the moonlight in her hair, the contour of her breast, the soft heat of her belly as she snuggled with me. I imagined her practicing her vowels and consonants, drawing each loop of the *aa* and *ka* over and over again. Pulling out a piece of paper and putting the tip of the pencil in her mouth to moisten it, then beginning to carefully write out my name. Looking at her handiwork, deciding the strokes didn't look steady enough, taking a new sheet and starting again. I tried to make out the expression in her eyes—was that sadness, or love, or serenity in her face? But as the words slowly formed on the paper, I could read nothing beyond the letters in my name.

I kept up my vigil every day that week, then decided to extend it, just in case the letter had been delayed. April turned to May, the postman made his rounds twice a day, but what I was waiting for never came.

chapter
seventeen

AFTER SANDHYA, I THOUGHT I WOULD NEVER AGAIN BE ABLE TO BEAR the sight of Delhi. What took me back finally, was another wedding. During the very first year of her Ph.D program, Sharmila fell in love with a professor in her college.

She could not have picked a more unsuitable match. Dr. Munshi Afsar was not only eighteen years her senior, but also a Muslim. There were even indications, Roopa wrote (in the volley of missives she fired off from Madras), that unlike the qawwali connoisseurs it was Paji's hobby to befriend, this was someone who was a devout fundamentalist. That he prayed five times a day and donated most of his income to the mosque, that tucked away in some shady locality near the Red Fort was a secret household where he maintained not one but two former wives.

Biji was beside herself with fury. She put the blame squarely on Paji, for this, her worst nightmare. "If you keep bringing wolves into the house, encourage your daughter to play and eat with them, why be surprised now when one of their tribe carries her away? I'll never forgive this until my dying day." Of course, the number of things for which she could never forgive Paji till she died was by then already too long to list.

In a way, Paji *was* to blame. "It was his beard that I couldn't resist," Sharmila wrote in an embarrassingly overwrought letter she sent me together with her professor's photograph. After Roopa's allegations, I had been expecting the inflamed red eyes of a fanatic, the lecherous grin of a polygamist, but Dr. Afsar turned out to appear quite mild, even shy, his face somehow pulled back from his glasses as if he was trying to hide behind the lenses. Roopa, obviously, had allowed her imagination to get the better of her.

"Every time I went to his office, I was reminded of the beard Salman uncle had back in Rawalpindi," Sharmila wrote. "The one you and Roopa took turns stroking each time he came to take Paji for qawwali. The one I was tempted to touch, but was always too scared. What I really want Munshi to do is dye it orange with mehndi like Salman uncle used to. Except now I'd caress it with my lips instead."

For Paji, it was one thing to profess the secular outlook he had culti-vated over the years, quite another to abide by it where his own daugh-ter was concerned. He refused to give a blessing for the match. He was careful to never allude to Munshi being a Muslim, couching his objection in the age difference instead. As Sharmila's attitude hardened, so did his own, until the day came when he forbade her from continuing her con-tact. Which wasn't really practical, since in addition to being her sweet-heart, Dr. Afsar was also the mentor for her thesis.

What broke through the impasse was the death of Paji's idol. Nehru's leadership had been under a cloud for more than a year and a half, ever since the humiliating 1962 Chinese attack. Our troops had been so poorly prepared that in the face of the massive invasion, some of them simply fled. Having displayed their might, the invaders quickly declared a cease-fire and left. Paji watched in dismay afterwards as newspapers pilloried Nehru for having trusted China as a friend. The HRM seized the opportunity to denounce the prime minister's secular ideas as well. Suddenly Nehru's seventy-plus years began to show. He survived a stroke in the first month of the year, but not the heart attack that burst his aorta in May. The ultimate insult was yet to come—instead of the secular funeral he had decreed, religious leaders forced an elaborate cre-mation with full Hindu rites to be held.

With the death of his hero, something seemed to die in Paji as well. He sent me a long, rambling letter, filled with gloom and sorrow at the passing of India's golden age, at the end of hope and happiness and perhaps democracy itself. "Just wait a few months and see—these same scavengers who are vying with each other to praise him in the newspapers will soon be clawing and nipping away at his legacy. There's no one left to lead us into the future, nobody to uphold the ideals under which this country was born."

Perhaps it was this demoralized state of his that made him agree to Sharmila's Hindu-Muslim match. Or perhaps it was simply a sentimental response, a melodramatic tribute, to keep Nehru's ideal of secularism alive. Paji promised he would be there in person with Biji to see Sharmila wed.

When I first glimpsed Paji standing on the railway platform, he appeared unchanged from four years ago. His hair was still black, his mustache neatly trimmed, his bearing that of a colonel's, even though he had never been a military man. But then he started walking towards me, and I noticed how he moved more slowly and deliberately now, as if debating the necessity of each step. The idealism that shone in his eyes had faded, replaced by a milkiness that dated him even more than his sixty years. "Welcome home," he said, not only to me but also to Dev, and his words seemed free of guile, sincere. I almost wished that Dev would try to touch my father's feet again—it would have been reassuring to verify that one could get a rise out of Paji still.

We drove to Darya Ganj—Dev had wanted to be in Nizamuddin, but had changed his mind when he heard that Roopa was coming and would be staying with my parents as well. Biji was waiting for us all alone—she told me she was so angry with Paji that she had stopped accompanying him anywhere. Rage seemed to suit her well—enlivening her eyes with a healthy glisten, invigorating her cheeks with a wholesome flush. Her entire body appeared limber and well-exercised, as if she had been performing calisthenics in preparation for battle. "I don't even know how I will face the neighbors, much less my friends after this. If your Paji thinks I'm going to give my blessing by attending this travesty, this mockery of a wedding ceremony, he's mistaken."

But attend she did, not only in a red wedding sari but even with lipstick on her mouth, for perhaps only the second time in her life. Munshi's family was boycotting the occasion, so it wasn't clear whom she was trying to impress. The "travesty" itself took only a few minutes, it was the hour-long wait for the couples before us that seemed interminable. Munshi had suggested the idea of marrying in court—a wise one, since it preempted the fight bound to ensue over whether to have a Hindu or a Muslim ceremony. We almost got thrown out though, when Roopa's twins Dilip and Shobha decided to mount the benches—a constable appeared from inside the courtrooms to quiet them down.

They were cute, these children—they even managed to twist the expression on Biji's lipstick-covered mouth from a fume into a smile. What shocked me was how even Paji enjoyed their antics. He let them climb all over him and swing from his neck, calling them his darlings, kissing their foreheads. Where was his antipathy, his proscription against children now? How could he have performed such an about-face after insisting that I scrape out my womb?

We were finally called into the small chamber outside which we had been waiting. The clerk dipped the nib of his pen into a pot of ink before handing it first to Munshi, then Sharmila. Once they had signed, he picked up the register to examine what they had written, as if searching for an error that would allow him to annul the contract. Then, gauging our status by the clothes we were wearing, he decided on English as the language in which to recite his memorized pronouncement. "You are now becoming husband and wife," he said, and waited until Paji had tipped him two rupees before handing over the certificate. "I am congratulating," he added grudgingly, and nodded his head.

THE DAY AFTER THE WEDDING, when Sharmila and Munshi had left for their honeymoon in Kashmir, I found myself alone at home with Paji. Roopa had taken Biji and the twins to shop, and Dev had gone to Nizamuddin. I heard Paji rummaging around in his office, so I went upstairs. Even though it was the beginning of August, the air conditioner, to my surprise, was not turned on.

Paji was adjusting the plaque on the wall behind his desk. The inscription was his favorite quote by Nehru, and I still remembered the shop in Chandni Chowk where Roopa and I had accompanied him to have it engraved so many years ago. *"The spectacle of what is called religion, in India and elsewhere, has filled me with horror, and I have frequently condemned it and wished to sweep clean of it. Almost always it seemed to stand for blind reaction, dogma and bigotry, superstition and exploitation, and the preservation of vested interests."* The quote had been so long that the engraver had run out of space the first time he tried, and had had to start over with a fresh plaque.

Paji gave it one final swipe with his cloth, then turned around. "Do you think our new prime minister, this Shastri person, would ever be troubled by such sentiments? All he seems to care about is shoving his beloved Hindi down the throat of the south." He sighed. "I suppose I should be thankful—my new son-in-law doesn't seem too religious, it could have been much worse."

I looked at the box of papers lying open on Paji's desk. "Old report cards—Roopa's and yours and Sharmila's—I wish I hadn't thrown away the Rawalpindi ones when we fled. Now that you've all gone, it's only these memories that are left." He sighed again, then picked up the top sheet. "Hindi forty-one percent, English thirty-eight percent, science forty percent . . . that's Sharmila in the seventh standard—who would've thought she would ever get this far?" He chuckled. "I always thought Roopa would be the one to do well."

"But she did, didn't she? Look at the grandchildren she's given you."

"They're adorable, aren't they? Do you know what they call me? Paji the Great." This time, his chuckle turned into a full-fledged laugh. I stood there mutely, and finally he seemed to notice my unsmiling expression. His mirth faded, and he grimaced, as if something unpleasant from breakfast had just repeated on him. "I know what you're thinking, Meera, and believe me, I had no idea, believe me, I'm ashamed. The number of times I've wished you'd been surer, strong enough not to be swayed. If there was anything I could do to turn back time . . ." He stopped and stared meekly at the floor, his eyes growing milky once more.

"Why would you want to turn back time, Paji? I've graduated from college, haven't I? Not as illustriously as Sharmila, but surely you must be satisfied?"

"Meera, I never—"

"And look, no babies, either—look how scrupulously clean I've managed to keep my womb. It's your son-in-law who's made sure, of course. By myself, I probably couldn't have been trusted, but he's been exemplary in following your advice every night. And now that I've fulfilled all your conditions, surely you will be bestowing on me your permission to procreate?"

"You know I didn't mean it that way."

"Perhaps I should get it in writing from you, perhaps you can mail me a certificate. Or better still, mail it to Dev." I stared hard at my father, then turned around and walked away.

I DIDN'T WANT TO WAIT for Roopa to return with Biji and the twins, so I decided to go to Nizamuddin. I had not accompanied Dev there in the morning because I hadn't wanted to encounter Arya (it was a day of avoiding people). Now that it was after lunchtime, I could safely say hello to Mataji without running into him. Over the past few years, I had received bits of news about my brother-in-law from Hema—how he had thrown himself into the work of the HRM, how his hair had turned prematurely gray, how despite all of Mataji's attempts, he had stubbornly refused to remarry. "If not for himself, at least he should think of the family," Hema complained. "He's the eldest son, so it's up to him to carry on the Arora name. When God has given him this second chance, who is he to refuse it?"

Sandhya, I had written back angrily. It was *she,* not God, who had given Arya the opportunity to marry again.

Mataji was lying on a charpoy in the courtyard and staring at the wall when I came in. It took me a moment to realize that her hair was almost completely white—she had stopped dyeing it. She looked at me startled, as if I was an intruder she didn't recognize, then pulled me to her bosom and started weeping. "First you, then Hema, then Sandhya—nobody told me it would be this difficult." Her face looked curiously smaller, as if her teeth had all been pulled out, causing her cheeks to slump in.

Sandhya's presence hung over everything, strong and sweet and claustrophobic. It trailed me as I followed Mataji into the bedroom. "Arya doesn't come in here anymore, says he can't any longer," Mataji said. "After all these years, Babuji and I are the ones sleeping in this room." I looked at the talais on which Dev and I used to lie, rolled up and stacked neatly against the far wall. For an instant, I could almost feel Sandhya breathing in one corner.

Suddenly I had to leave, before I was completely overwhelmed by the air inside. "Where's Babuji?" I asked. "I should say hello to him as well."

"At the station, where else? Ever since he retired, he just sits on a bench and watches the trains go by. Dev's probably with him, too." Mataji shook her head. "Day after day, Arya remains at work, and Hema almost never drops in. I wish I had someplace to go as well—somewhere else to while away the hours of my day."

Babuji was not on the station platform—the watchman told me he was taking a nap inside. I decided not to wake him. I debated whether to go back to the house and wait for Dev, who must be still visiting his brother, or return to Darya Ganj by myself.

I found myself walking down the road, towards the scooter stand. There were goats grazing on the piles of garbage—I wondered if the brown and white cow was still around. The tract of land I used to cross while following Dev and Roopa so long ago was still empty, the colony that was supposed to have been erected there mired in a complicated dispute over electricity that Hema had once tried to explain. The row of shanty stalls was gone, however, together with the fruit and vegetable sellers and the metal parts shop—what stood there now were proper establishments with sturdy shutters and painted signs. Looming in the distance was the familiar sight of the moss-covered dome of Salim Fazl's tomb. Before I knew it, I was making my way through the bougainvillea, dense and blossom-filled after a July of plentiful rain.

Could it have been destiny that pulled me, or was it just nostalgia, plain and maudlin? Could I have divined, from somewhere deep in my consciousness, the sight that would greet me there? Weren't there a hundred different coincidences that must have all fallen into place for me to make my way through the surrounding wall at the right time? Had I lin-

gered with Mataji for ten more minutes, or found Babuji awake, would I
have escaped?

I pull a strand of bougainvillea from across my view, and for some
reason think of the last time I was here. It is like returning to the scene
of a crime, like looking through a telescope the wrong way to view my
life after it has been lived. There he is, standing in front of one of the
arches, his body lit up, sunlight dappling his hair. I look at his face, and
he turns it slightly in profile, as if to show me he is still handsome, that
every possibility still exists. Suddenly I know what I must do—reach out
to him and bring him to the present, erase what has happened, go on
from here. I think of the conversation I have just had with Paji—it no
longer angers me, I am liberated. I will share the news of this liberation
with Dev, tell him we can finally exult, we are free to create. Perhaps we
can even resume from the point where we left off, perhaps Salim Fazl
will let us use his tiles again.

Even then, I could have retreated, quietly retraced my steps back
through the thicket, kept the thought in my head and slipped away. But
instead I go forward, first one step, then the next, gliding through the
shrubs like some foliage-dwelling spirit.

Dev is looking away from me. I follow his gaze and see the color at
his feet—fabric nestling against grass, jewelry giving off a glint. I take
another step, and a sari billows up—the edge yellow and sinuous as it
rises in the wind. Too late, I realize the trap into which I have blundered—I want to turn back, but my body doesn't cooperate. My feet are
entranced, my legs bent on advancing, the fear that seizes my mind
seems to exercise no say. Even before the sari can subside to reveal the
figure it drapes, I know who it is, I know what I will see. There lies my
sister, her arms raised above her head, her body stretched out serpen-
tinely in the grass before Dev.

ROOPA SAW ME FIRST. "Hello, Meera," she said, as if there was nothing
wrong, as if this was something as innocent as a picnic for which my
invitation must have got lost in the mail. "Biji took the children home,
so I came here and happened to run into Dev." She sat up and looked at

me steadily. "Even a fool can see we haven't done anything. Don't make this into something bigger than it is."

For a moment I tried to work the numbness out of my lips. Perhaps she was right, perhaps I shouldn't make too much of what I had witnessed. Surely this transgression was no more egregious than the benchmarks set in the past by Dev.

Then an unfamiliar rage opened within me. A rage that rose up my throat and brought the heat back to my lips. "What exactly should I make of it then, Roopa? To see you and Dev cavorting like this? Perhaps I'm not smart enough, perhaps I need someone to help me, perhaps like your husband, what do you think? I promise you, Roopa, if I ever see the two of you together again, I'll tell Ravinder—let him be the one to make sense of it." Before Dev could begin stuttering his apologies, I stalked away.

All evening, the rage within me grew. It bloomed on my face with an efflorescence so brilliant and fiery white that it sent Roopa scurrying out of my path each time she spied me heading her way. She packed her bags the following night, and was gone by daybreak, returning to Madras a week earlier than planned.

Dev, meanwhile, tried to placate me, but after an insultingly short period, gave up and returned to Bombay. I lingered on, unable to transport myself back to my failed experiment as dutiful wife.

Biji was horrified, and kept trying to coax me to return, but Paji lost no time in enjoining me to stay. "You know I've sworn off trying to influence my daughters, but this much I feel it's my duty to say. Even the sturdiest of fabric unravels over time—there comes a point when it can no longer be mended, it has to be replaced. Just think of all the empty rooms in this house with all three of you gone away. What better gift could a pair of old parents expect than to have one of them reoccupied?" He began enumerating all the jobs in his publishing agency that were mine for the asking. "You could even try a different one every day of the week, until you find the one that's just right. Just make a clean break of it for your twenty-seventh birthday."

I was surprised by how easy my anger made it to decide. I bought a round-trip ticket to Bombay, to retrieve my belongings and leave Dev.

At Bombay Central, however, there was no sight of Dev on the plat-form. I sat in the taxi, fuming at him for having ignored my telegram (in which all I had intimated were my arrival details). The flat was a mess when I walked in—trash on the floor, clothes and paper strewn every-where, cockroaches lounging amidst the plates and glasses as comfort-ably as guests in a hotel lobby. In the bedroom was Dev, his eyes open, his lips dry, his forehead burning from the typhoid raging through him.

In the days and nights that followed, as I squeezed out ice water from handkerchiefs and laid them on Dev's head, the same thoughts went through my mind over and over again. Could this be some sort of ploy on Dev's part, could he have divined my intentions and purposely infected himself? But then I stared at his ravaged body, his gaunt face, the uneaten rice gruel beside him, and felt guilty. "Meera," he mur-mured through his delirium one afternoon. "I couldn't find the light-bulbs. It's good that you came."

It took him a long time to gain back his strength, and he needed me every step of the way. Each time I toweled him after a sponge bath, or walked him to the toilet, I wondered if he was pretending, and then felt ashamed at myself again. One evening, I came home to find him sitting on the bedroom floor, crying to himself. He had discovered the suitcase in which I had been secretly packing my saris, pulling it out from its hid-ing place under the bed. "You saved my life," he said, averting his head from me. "Don't leave me—without you, I'd be dead."

I didn't promise Dev anything. Even when he started suggesting that we have a child, I was careful not to commit myself. "Sometimes, when I see a baby being wheeled around in its pram by its parents, I feel so guilty. That could have been Meera and me, if only I had had more con-fidence, if only I had had more courage, I think to myself." He launched into these self-recriminations every evening, singing "Sleep, Little Baby Princess," and other Saigal lullabies—for his own sake or mine, I couldn't tell.

I took long walks through the city to clear my head. Sometimes, lost in my deliberations, I walked all the way to Colaba or Worli, and had to take the bus back. Every time I passed the intersection at Nana Chowk, a part of me always wondered if the nameless boy who had followed me in college might still be lurking around somewhere. I would see him dart between the buses and sprint down the street, but this time, I imagined myself running hand in hand with him. One day, after Dev had started venturing out of the house again, I brought down the smaller suitcase from its perch atop the cupboard and started stuffing my remaining clothes into it. But the sight of my toothbrush nestling next to Dev's in the bathroom made me lose my determination, and I unpacked everything before he returned.

As usual, it was Paji, finally, who precipitated my decision. His letters had become increasingly agitated after I had informed him about the delay in my return. I almost felt sorry for him—he had waited so long, and victory had been so tantalizingly within reach. I made the mistake of writing to him about Dev's proposition to become parents. The reply arrived that very Friday from Delhi, as if propelled in record time across the country by Paji's outrage. "Can't you see what the man is doing—this gush of paternal feeling that he's suddenly discovered within himself? You might as well let yourself be handcuffed to the bedpost, if you're going to submit to being impregnated by him."

By itself, the letter didn't quite do it—by now, I had learnt to automatically discount everything Paji wrote. If anything, it was reassuring to note that he had been restored to his old pugnacity, that he had fully recovered from Nehru's death. What caught me off guard, however, was the telegram that arrived a day later. THINK CAREFULLY, it exhorted. DON'T BE FOOLISH. SAVE YOURSELF. There were three exclamation marks, somehow transposed after PAJI, floating disengaged at the end.

That very night, I moved to Dev's side of the bed. His wrist still seemed frail when I took it in my hands, his cheek, when I stroked it, hadn't regained its fullness yet. I knew I should wait, but the exclamation marks were still flashing in my mind. "Paji just sent me a telegram. He agrees we should have a baby," I said.

PART THREE

chapter
eighteen

I ALWAYS IMAGINED YOU BORN OF THE SUN. AS THE SKY SWALLOWED THE stars, as Usha began to paint the dawn, as eagles were yoked once more to their celestial chariots and gods began to stir. The heavens would open up and beam a chute of rays down upon the earth. Vishnu himself would slide down, like a gold-decked movie star, bearing you in his muscular arms.

Though you might arrive under the moon instead. With Shiva, not Vishnu, bringing you into the world. Your eyes closed, your breath even, the dab of blue on Shiva's throat throbbing at yours as well like a brooch. Moonbeams, not sunlight, would transport you into my lap. You would open your eyes and gaze upon the twinkle of distant stars.

One thing I knew was that you would be beautiful. Your limbs as fleshy and plump as the Glaxo baby's, your cheeks as red as those of the infants chuckling from the calendar on the wall. I would press my lips over your mouth, your eyes, your nose, each perfectly formed digit of your hand.

It didn't happen that way, Ashvin. Bright day turned to twilight before you agreed to be born. I heaved and labored for hours, no golden chariot descended from the heavens to waft you down. Instead of the flapping of eagle wings, what I heard through the windows of Bombay Hospital was the rumble of trucks.

And you looked nothing like the calendar photos. When the nurse first laid you on my stomach, I felt a mistake had been made. Your nose was too flat, the eyes and mouth all wrong, like features carved out hastily from a vegetable kept too long. Smears of something white clung like cheese to your wrinkled skin. Had they pulled you out too soon, I wondered, was *this* what all my effort had wrought? Where was the neatly wrapped bundle I was expecting to be eased into my arms?

I lay on my bed exhausted, watching Shiva and Vishnu fade into the wall. Every tissue in my body felt sore, every muscle spent. The anticipation had all evaporated, what remained was the work stretching ahead. You lay so helpless and needy on my stomach, with your head elongated, your scrotum rudely swollen. What if I couldn't clothe you, couldn't feed you, couldn't bear to put you to my breast?

Waves of guilt, cold and briny, surged in over my despair. What kind of mother was I, to begrudge you my love? How could I deny you my milk? After what I had already lost, what if I lost you as well—wouldn't that be just what I deserved?

That's when I first felt it. Your heartbeat, but just for a second. Could I have imagined it? I closed my eyes, and pictured myself as a giant scientific instrument, dispassionately scanning your presence. I held my breath and there it was, faint and frog-like again, a heart beating through your chest.

Suddenly euphoria surged in. I felt lucid, I felt aloft, I felt myself borne along in its swell and carried over the edge. It was like diving through air, like plunging face-first down a waterfall, your visage shimmering in the pool below, emblazoned across the waiting earth. I realized how wrong I had been about your flaws—your skin was radiant, your nose the perfect size, your eyes shut tight communicated to me the peevishness you felt inside. I wanted to call out your name, to shout my love as I fell, I wanted to splash into your image and re-create it in a million sparkling drops.

The feeling vanished as rapidly as it had appeared. You started crying, and your body suddenly grew much heavier on my stomach. The nurse came in and lifted you off. "I'm sure you can't wait to feed him," she said.

I LAY AWAKE AS you slept in your crib. The walls around reminded me of another green room somewhere. I tried to clear my mind, to look past the curls of paint flaking from the ceiling, all the way to the starry sky beyond. Somewhere in this sky were the Ashvin twins. Biji used to point them out as we gazed at the clear Rawalpindi nights from our terrace. They were not too far from Rohini, the constellation after which she was named. The Ashvins were always together, she told us, linked by a bond that time could not break. They gave light and energy to all the bodies in the universe, even the ones in the furthest reaches of space. It didn't matter if you could only see one, since the other was always still there. The presence of the one obscured manifested through the brightness of its twin.

I lay in my bed, too far to be heard, and for the first time, whispered your name.

DEV TOOK US HOME in a taxi three days after you were delivered. Even though it was only the afternoon, I could tell he had poured himself a few. In the months since he had recovered from the typhoid, his strength had come back, and his thirst had too. As usual, he had gargled with Listerine afterwards—were you able to smell it too?

When we reached our building, I was reluctant to hand you over. But the staircase rose ahead, daring me to negotiate it with you in my arms. I told myself Dev was only glazed, not drunk enough to drop you. Listerine breath or not, he was still your father. He scooped you up with one hand and charged up in his renewed self, taking the steps two by two.

I felt strange, disoriented, as if I was dragging an unfamiliar body up to an unfamiliar floor. Dev came dancing up shirtless and handed me a balloon at the door. He had put on "House of Bamboo" on the gramophone, the only record in English he owned. Andy Williams sang about floors and walls and a roof all made of bamboo, and Dev sang along too.

Dev started doing the twist. He pointed to the ceiling, the walls, the floor in turn and mouthed the lyrics in his Punjabi English, translating some of the words. His voice was deep and sonorous, all wrong for the tune. Don't waste it like this, I wanted to tell him, don't insult a voice made for K. L. Saigal, for songs like "Light the Fire of Your Heart." But then I followed his hips swiveling from side to side, his shoes turning furiously on the floor, the snake on his chest black and glistening again, and lost my train of thought. I swayed uncertainly with the balloon in my hand and wondered if in my new body I, too, could dance.

Dev's eyes were shut tight in concentration. Was he trying to keep out everything but the music as he danced? Or was he conjuring up an image behind those closed eyelids? An image of the three of us, happy, protected, surrounded by the bamboo house he was going to construct. I wondered whether bamboo was a good material from which to build, whether such a house would endure. Perhaps I should have listened to the lyrics more carefully—maybe that's what the song was about.

Dev pulled my hands together and danced me into the bedroom. He took the balloon from my hand and fastened it to your cot. Balloons rose from ribbons tied all around the frame, bobbing up and down in the breeze from the ceiling fan. They looked like they were jerking their heads in tune to the music with Dev. He took me by the hands again and led me to the bed. Two balloons, one red and one blue, bobbed from opposite ends of the headboard.

I did not want to lie down. The sensations I was trying to contain inside might bubble up if I did. There was nausea to be sure, and disorientation as well, but also a rising exhilaration, as radiant as peppermint in my throat. Stabbing me gently through these feelings were spasms of despair.

I wanted to believe this was a new beginning. But the past was too unwieldy to hide, it intruded from every corner of my thoughts. "I've just come home," I said. "There's a thousand things to do, the baby to check."

Then I noticed the music still playing, and Dev's lips touching mine.

The Listerine had begun to wear off his breath. I let him kiss me, felt guilty, and clumsily kissed him back.

Dev kissed my face to the rhythm of the lyrics. His lips moved down to my neck. I tried holding on to his head before he could descend lower but he darted out of the way. "Bamboo door," he said, as he rubbed his face into my blouse, then pulled at it with his teeth.

I looked at his head. It was always handsome with hair, thick and black, but now the beginning of a bald spot had started to spread. I saw the tip of his nose, just visible between my breasts. His lips pressed against me through the material of my blouse. I imagined them leaving a mark, red with lipstick like the first time I'd seen them. How long ago had that been? The days when he tweezed the line of each eyebrow into formation. Worked the Vaseline into his pompadour and covered it with a cap all morning to set it in place. I remembered the bright floral shirts with the tops left unbuttoned for the naag to peek through. The tightly ribbed pants that spread down his legs like sections of pipe cut to fit. Everything about Dev was so dazzling then. How absurd it seemed now that I had been so mesmerized, like a chicken distracted by color and shine. I looked at Dev's hairless spot again and wondered how long he had before it claimed his head.

The record ended. Dev rubbed the sweat off his chest against my stomach and I felt him thicken against my leg. I grabbed his head in my hands as if to kiss it, then pushed it away from me. He looked up, startled at my vehemence. I kept my expression blank, though I was surprised as well.

"The doctor said six weeks, don't you remember?" I pressed my blouse back against my chest. "If you knew how sick I feel."

The drink began to falter on his face. Underneath the lingering bravado I saw the hope (or could it be fear?) he had been trying to hide. "I was just caressing you. I feel so good, so well again, as if I've got a second chance." He kissed my hand. "Perhaps the typhoid is the best thing that ever happened to me. All these years, and now this shining light in our lives."

"All these years," I repeated. "If he'd been born the year after we were married, he'd be nine now."

The keenness of my rancor surprised me. I studied Dev's eyes carefully to make sure he understood, that my words killed the hope in them. If there was to be reconciliation, it would be extended by me, on my terms.

The sound of the gramophone needle oscillating on the record came in from the next room. Now that the song had ended, faint strains of film music wafted in from a radio on some other floor. Not K. L. Saigal, but one of the newer ones, the upstarts, I noted.

"It wasn't my fault," Dev said. He buried his head against my chest, as if to speak directly to my heart. "I'll make it up to you. I'll do whatever you say."

Could I believe him? Did his words have enough heft to balance the weight of all I had endured over the years? He raised his head and I saw his eyes were wet. "Now that Munna is here, you'll see. I'll be a new person—we'll all be new—we'll have a new life." He wrapped my arms around his head and sobbed into my breast.

I looked up. The fan swirled cool air onto my face. A balloon had come loose and hung against the ceiling, just out of reach of the whirring blades. I watched its ribbon swish through the air like the tail of a dancing snake.

I imagined the ribbon entangled in the fan, the balloon pulled in and ruptured by the blades. Fragments of balloon skin rain down, and Dev looks up in alarm. You awaken crying and I run to your cot.

But every time the streamer got near enough to flirt with the blades, it darted away. I sat on the bed with Dev in my arms, looking at the balloon bob and push against the ceiling, but not come any closer to being ensnared.

AND THEN, SLOWLY, cautiously, I came under your spell. Night after night I responded to your silent summons, enticing me to the cot to admire your face. I watched the series of magic tricks you performed—the skin that cleared in the moonlight, the chin that miraculously emerged overnight, the head that resized itself to become proportional to your limbs. Sometimes, I felt an intense curiosity towards you, like a child might for a new pet or toy. I peered into your ears and nostrils, I counted your fingers and toes. I rocked you like a doll in my arms to see if your eyes flipped open and closed. The euphoria from the hospital returned each time I felt the tug of your mouth at my breast. The sensation of dropping, the feeling that your presence would transport me somewhere else. Sometimes, you opened your eyes while feeding and gazed at me with the sagacity (or was it lechery?) of a wizened old man. Secret smiles played on your lips as you slept afterwards, as if you knew you had me enmeshed in your wiles. I lost myself in these smiles, in these expressions of joy and sorrow and pique that shimmered across your face. My mood began to steady, my bleakness lifted, the stabs of despair went away. What emerged from the rustling shadows of those nights was an attachment I could almost not bear.

From where did this love spring? Was it biology pure and simple? The bond I felt because you were my child, the oneness I experienced when your body touched mine? Each time you clambered over me in your uninhibited exploration, I marveled that something so wanton could be so pure. Sometimes, I imagined you were a part of me again, as if the cord between us had regenerated to unite us once more. I felt your hands and feet cling warmly against my skin, and fantasized of pouching you like a kangaroo to watch you grow. My abdomen would be your playground, my chest your bed, I would offer you a breast when you were hungry and use it as a cushion for you when you slept. In the morning I would wait to see your smile—the sun would rise from my body when you lifted your head.

Or did my passion spring from the knowledge that for once I would matter the most in someone's life? Perhaps Biji and Paji had loved me, perhaps Dev did too. But with them, I could never be first, they had cared for Roopa more. You were going to be the star to reignite my universe, the light I was promised so long ago. As soon as you learnt to love, it would be me whom you loved the most.

You roused something else in me—the confidence that the years of marriage had dimmed. It was not just pride I felt at having created you, but also power. Each time you suckled, I became potent, invincible, an Amazon infusing you with strength. With you at my breast, we were a team of two, ready to challenge the world.

It must have been due to this solidarity that my thinking became no longer my own. Whenever I directed a thought to myself, it emerged addressed to you instead.

IT WAS ONLY NATURAL that I began to pay less attention to Dev. A shirt not ironed because of the diapers I had to wash. Rice not made fresh, or bread instead of chappatis, because you were not feeling well. A night turned away in bed so that I could check if you needed to be fed. Day by day I distanced myself from my old routine of chores.

Dev took it all good-naturedly, indulging me as never before. When I didn't cook dinner, he brought hot onion pakodas wrapped in newspaper with two kinds of chutney. When I was moody, he plied me with coconuts or squeezed oranges (once, even mangoes!) for juice. He made a chicken curry one day, which stained my teeth bright yellow from all the turmeric he added. At night, he took you from the cot and put you between us on the bed. He liked to play with your limbs, to pivot them about as if they were the movable parts of a robot.

It had not occurred to me that I would be competing for your affection with your father. Now, as I saw him kiss you on the nose or sing his nightly lullaby, I felt the first grinds of jealousy pepper my heart. On Thursdays, he marked ash from his pooja on your brow, then whispered special blessings from Sai Baba and Ganesh over your head. Perhaps it would be worth it to share you, perhaps we would really become a family of three in our own bamboo house, I consoled myself. Still, every time he held you, I made sure to pull you to my bosom afterwards to remind you how you were fed.

Dev's promise not to drink amazed me. He rounded up all his bottles of Indian whiskey (with names like "Diplomat" and "Aristocrat") as well as the brightly colored fruit concoctions bought from Auntie's speakeasy. He even fished out a quarter of gin hiding behind the sofa. He packed them all in an empty cardboard box which he hoisted onto the highest shelf in the bathroom. "A new start, for Munna," he declared. "And for you."

It didn't last. As he kissed you one night, I detected Listerine on his breath. Perhaps he had just gargled with it, I tried telling myself, but he seemed to gargle with increasing frequency after that. When I confronted him, he pulled down the cardboard box of bottles and showed me they were still filled. "I just like my breath to be fresh."

Of course, once my suspicions were aroused, he couldn't hide it much longer. I found an empty quarter bottle in his pant pocket, I noticed an unwashed glass smelling of alcohol by the sink. I sneaked out one night when he thought I was in bed and caught him pouring from a large bottle of fluorescent green sweet lime in the kitchen. There were no words exchanged. He looked at me, stopped, then lowered his eyes and resumed pouring.

THE FIRST TIME I ventured out with you in my arms, Mrs. Azmi, from the flat directly below, stopped to admire you on the steps. "All these years we've just been saying hello—what a darling baby you have." It wasn't only her, but the whole building, which, face unveiled, introduced itself. Dr. Kagawalla offered the name of a pediatrician, Mrs. Karmali and Mrs. Hamid invited us for tea. The Hussains, on the third floor, promised their son's old tricycle for when you were tall enough to pedal.

A second Hindu family had moved into the building, occupying the flat down the hall. Mr. Dugal, whose hair was prematurely gray, looked at you through large sad eyes as his wife patted your head. "So darling they are, at that age at least, reminds me of my Pinky in the first few weeks," Mrs. Dugal said. She thrust her daughter forward. "Tell Auntie how old you are." Pinky smiled chubbily, but didn't say anything. "She's three, but recites 'Jack and Jill' so well, you'd swear she was ten." Whenever we met after that, Mrs. Dugal attempted to make her daughter break into a nursery rhyme without success.

It wasn't just the building but the whole of Tardeo that saluted me for producing you. The street hawkers waved from the pavements as we promenaded by—my vegetable woman even learned your name. "Little

Baba," the shopkeepers cooed, and tried to wrap your uncoordinated fingers around candy that you were too young to hold, much less consume.

Paji sent a money order for five hundred and one rupees the week after I brought you home. "What joyous news you have delivered," he wrote. "Now that you too have made me a grandfather, only Sharmila has her duty left." There was no hint of the distraught letters or the telegram he had sent. "When are you bringing Ashvin to Delhi?" he asked instead. *Not until you account for everything*, I almost dashed back.

Perhaps his guilt opened the floodgates to his generosity, perhaps Paji had not forgotten the telegram after all. A second money order arrived the following week, to buy you a pram. Then came baskets of fruit, and a set of baby suits. Most extravagant of all was the offer to pay for an ayah. "Your mother was changing diapers for years—I want you to live your life without worrying about all that." Dev managed to convince me not to send the money back.

We went through a succession of ayahs. The first woman we hired was young and slovenly, with an alarming itch in her breast, which she kept scratching absently next to your face. The second attended to you with a wistful melancholy, as if having lost her own child, she was using you as a surrogate. She fussed over your booties longingly, like someone with a fetish, and finally disappeared with them one day, together with two of the baby suits Paji had sent. Maria lasted the longest. Clean, well-groomed, and Catholic, she told me that she had been taking care of babies in her family for fifteen of her twenty-five years. She knew exactly how to hold you, magically appearing to receive you from Dev whenever he attempted to pick you up in his clumsy way. You came out fresh and smiling every time she bathed you.

Soon, though, with Maria there to look after you, I started wondering about my own usefulness. She didn't like me watching while she washed you or changed your clothes, and often whisked you away to another room when I approached. Even feeding you, seemingly the only activity left for me, made her sulk. "Why do you have so much milk?" she demanded, when she saw me spontaneously wet my blouse. "It's better from a bottle," she remarked another time, and I told her it was no business of hers.

"You're being too possessive," Dev said, when I complained to him. "You should be thankful, not jealous, that we can afford someone to take such good care of Munna."

Two weeks into her reign, I finally summoned the courage to tell Maria we wouldn't be needing her anymore. She allowed a look of such contempt to flash across her face that I wondered how she had concealed it so long. "You memsahibs always think you can handle your babies, but you can't. Don't blame me if anything bad happens to your son." She wanted to hug you before she left, but I withheld you protectively in my arms.

Her threat echoed in my ears. I worried that she had cast a spell, that you would waste away with some incurable fever. I took your temperature twice a day and examined your body for spots. I watched you do pee-pee every morning to make sure the hole wasn't blocked. A few times, I thought I saw Maria on the street and asked Dev if the police should be called. Twice, I rushed you to the doctor—once, because your feces didn't seem the right color and the second time to demand why one testicle looked larger than the other.

On my third visit, the doctor took me aside. "I know you're a first-time mother, but these daily inspections have got to stop."

chapter
nineteen

War broke out. Emboldened by India's recent rout at the hands of the Chinese, Pakistan trained its own hungry eyes across the border at Kashmir, which it always assumed would be part of its own territory. Exploratory August skirmishes escalated into a full-fledged confrontation on the first of September. Bombay came under a blackout, against the dark cover of which rumors began to streak and flare and pop. An enemy plane had been shot down over the city, spies had parachuted down in the suburbs, the Pakistanis had decided to target Tardeo first, and would be dispatching a phalanx of American-built jets to blow it up that very evening. Daily media announcements instructed us on how to crouch under furniture or in the corners of rooms to avoid being annihilated by bombs.

Three years ago, when the Chinese attacked, it had felt quaint, almost serene, to eat by candlelight and watch the cars glide below with blackened headlights afterwards. Now I experienced a fear I had not known before, not even while fleeing the riots of Rawalpindi during Partition. I obsessed endlessly about airborne dangers hurtling down to do your four-month-old body harm. Wheeling your pram along Marine Drive, I kept an eye on the horizon, making mental notes on how to dodge the missiles that enemy ships might launch. This is where we would jump should the parapet collapse around us, this is how we would duck as the concrete bolsters began to spin and pirouette through the air. I tried to feed you nine and ten times a day—the feel of your mouth at my breast was the only way to keep myself calm.

Even more than the blackouts, I came to dread the wail of the air-raid sirens, so mournful that they may have been announcing the entire city's extinction. Each time they sounded, my instinct was to curl my body protectively around you in a ball. "You're going to suffocate Munna," Dev said, as he sipped his drinks in the dark. "Don't worry, nothing's going to happen—they're either for practice or a false alarm."

The sirens set you crying as well—one night, you wouldn't stop even when I offered you my nipple. Perhaps it was the setting of the blackout that inspired him, but suddenly Dev started singing "Light the Fire of Your Heart." He had given up the song years ago, even before his singing lessons had failed. Now his voice emerged afresh, the lyrics as buoyant as before, the melody sweeping like a river through the dark. A river that flowed around the two of us, lapping us with its rhythms, soothing away your tears, washing away my fears. I waited till he hit the climax to light a candle, just as I had seen the audiences do in college so many eons ago. You stayed peacefully at my breast after the song ended, entranced by the play of candlelight shadows on the wall.

Later, after the all-clear siren sounded, I carried you up to the terrace. Together, we watched the city emerge from the blackness, lights coming on dimly behind darkened windows, sounds blaring up from the horns of reawakened cars. Even though no shots lit up the Bombay sky, I imagined the atmosphere hazy, like after a fireworks display. For an instant, I even convinced myself I smelled gunpowder in the air.

Dev started accompanying us to the terrace after his song, carrying his drink in a metal tumbler to conceal it from the neighbors. He never stayed very long, returning downstairs when he needed a refill, leaving the two of us above. On these occasions, I waited for the other neighbors to drift back to their floors as well, one by one. Then I uncovered a breast in the moonlight and put the nipple to your mouth. The brazenness of this made me tingle—baring myself to the city, to the stars and the sky. This ritual we performed so openly, in view of the other buildings, in view of anyone chancing through the door. I waltzed the two of us around the terrace, the night swirling around us, the music swelling joyously, the breeze vaguely sulfuric against my face. A thousand enemy planes could not have sundered us—we were awash in the moon's protective rays.

PAJI SENT ME AN ENVELOPE filled with editorials about the war, as if concerned I might miss all the coverage in the Bombay newspapers. "Kashmir shows that there can be no starker contrast between the secularism of India and the religious doctrines propping up Pakistan," the *Indian Express* declared. "A territory indispensable to Nehru's vision of the nation, living proof that Muslims can prosper side by side with their Hindu neighbors in their own majority state." To which Paji added his own recommendation. "It's time for the Pakistanis to remove the *K* they added for Kashmir to their name—come up with a different acronym, because that's one territory which will never be theirs."

For years now, my father had given us a running commentary on the problem, as if delivering a play-by-play account of a football match between the two countries. "Foul," he cried, each time the Americans tried to push India into another UN resolution tilted towards Pakistan. "All they can think about is their favored player in the Cold War. If it hadn't been for the Soviets, they would have pried Kashmir out of our grasp and presented it to Pakistan as a penalty kick long ago."

The arrival of the war, after years of feints and scrimmages, energized Paji. He wrote almost daily, his letters filled with spirited analyses of the latest salvos on either side. His wrath at the U.S. grew with each successive report of American-made weapons being deployed against India. "All those Patton tanks that were supposed to protect Pakistan from the Communists—guess at whom they are being aimed now?"

The real danger lay not in American weapons, Paji said, but came from within, from all the guerrillas Pakistan had sent across the border to foment an uprising in Kashmir. "Listen to their talk of jihad—what they're hoping is that every Muslim in the country will feel a solidarity for the struggle and revolt. Now we'll finally see if Nehru's experiment comes true. Whether allegiance depends on nationality, or whether religion will be the trump."

Hema put it more blatantly. "Arya bhaiyya says that if the Muslims in Delhi start rebelling, we'll be the first whose heads they'll chop off. Not just because we're HRM, but because Nizamuddin's swarming with Muslims—it'll probably be the most dangerous place in all of Delhi. It's going to be like Ghazni or Gauri or one of those other barbarian massacres all over again. Bhaiyya has been handing out swords to everyone, to keep next to our beds. You should have one too—isn't your building crawling with Muslims on every floor?"

Even Mrs. Dugal did her bit to fan the paranoia. She pulled me aside on the steps after the blackouts began and declared Mrs. Azmi to be a spy. "I saw it from my balcony last night—the light shining out from her window—she's probably signaling to the hiding planes, sending secret messages into the sky. I'm not sure what to do—I didn't know who else besides you to confide in—why she wants the building bombed and all of us blown up, I don't know." She wanted me to accompany her to the police, but I refused.

Neither Hema's fears nor Mrs. Dugal's came to pass. The Kashmiris ignored Pakistani efforts to liberate them—for one, most of them didn't even speak the same language. Rather than deepening communal cracks, the war unified the nation—both Muslim and Hindu soldiers died defending their country. "If only Nehru were alive to see his dream come true," Paji wrote. "To see the nation he founded, the citizens he created, acquit themselves so."

Although the war ended in a stalemate, it had the effect of restoring the self-confidence of the military after their demoralizing defeat at the hands of the Chinese. Prime Minister Shastri became Paji's new hero. "Who knew that this little postage-stamp-sized man would prove himself so worthy of following Nehru's footsteps?" Paji found the fate of the American tanks particularly delightful. The gasoline-powered Pattons proved extremely vulnerable to fire, and perished in large numbers at the battle of Khem Karan. In fact, the U.S. soon announced it would stop manufacturing them. "How sad that we had to send all those American geniuses back to the drawing board," Paji gleefully observed.

On the last night of the blackout, with the approval of the UN cease-fire pact imminent, the terrace filled with people. Mrs. Hussain made kebabs, which she handed out to celebrate ("no beef," she assured us), while Mrs. Azmi brought along little cups of rice kheer, still warm. Pinky gulped down two cups, and then, with Mrs. Dugal's encouragement, helped herself to a third.

The sound of car horns trying to honk out film tunes came from the street below. People peeled the black panels off their windows and flung them off their balconies—all across the city, uncovered lights began to show. The Diana cinema even turned on the lights on its marquee. A small bonfire blazed on the terrace of the adjoining building—I could see the silhouettes of boys dancing around. There was the retort of fire-crackers, and then a bottle rocket zipped into the sky.

Dev took you from me and held you high in his outstretched arms. When you grew too heavy, he seated you on his head. "Look, little Munna. This is your country, this is your city." He began to slowly pivot around, pointing out the landmarks floating out like ghosts from the night. "And there," Dev said, looking towards a dark gap between the buildings beyond which lay Chowpatty. "There lies your sea."

More rockets rose into the air from some of the building terraces. Now that I actually saw fireworks, I couldn't smell the gunpowder anymore. Dev lifted up your hand and with it traced the arc of one of the rockets through the sky. It ended in a tiny explosion, which I caught in the reflection in your eye.

And then, the rockets, the people, the drama of the landscape spread out before us all coalesced in a wave of nostalgia. The only missing feature from my fantasy of years ago was the sound of Dev's song. I felt a sudden urge to stroke the back of his neck. "Why don't you sing?" I whispered instead.

For a moment I thought he would re-create my vision and burst into song. That Nehru and Gandhi and the nautch girls would materialize from the dark and pick up their number from the Red Fort. Instead, Dev handed you back to me, and picked up his tumbler to empty it. "I only sing for Munna now," he said, and walked away towards the steps.

—

MY SUGGESTION MUST HAVE planted the idea in his head, because Dev soon decided not to sing for you alone. He announced that, having gained his munna as a fan, he would try again to break into playback.

While your father focused his efforts on his voice, you concentrated on taking your first steps. I trailed you wherever you went, keeping track of the daily distance covered as if training you for an Olympic event. "Now that Munna's learning to get around, he can be my good-luck charm," Dev said, as you stumbled across the room. "I'll take him to the tryouts at the studio later this month."

Unfortunately, the plan to use you as a mascot didn't work, that time or the next. Dev returned home early on each occasion, irritated, undiscovered. "He didn't stop crying for one second. Thank God Sagar's wife was there to help with him, otherwise I don't know what I would have done."

Dev's new attempts allowed him to snag a few more choral parts, but not much else. One morning, he called us both to the studio, saying he wanted his son to witness "a historic occasion"—the music duo Laxmikant-Pyarelal had finally given him his break. But the song recorded as I stood with you in my arms outside the glass partition had embarrassingly little of Dev. Two lines in the beginning, and then one at the end, and a few "tra-la-la's" trilled in the refrain.

Confronted by his renewed failure, Dev cast around for targets to vent his frustration. "It's the music directors who've become spineless, pandering to the lowest depths of public taste," he railed. Another day he blamed Auntie. "I curse the night that she-devil entrapped me in her web of evil wares." He did not, however, reduce his visits to her speakeasy.

Then his discontent found an unexpected outlet. Dev had always appeared immune to the astrological dictates that governed life in Nizamuddin, the superstitions and old wives' tales. Perhaps he had subliminally absorbed them over the years, though, because now they suddenly burst forth and began to rule everything we did. The lunar calendar became indispensable to our very existence. No activity could be planned without a consultation, and one moonless night, he almost burst into tears imploring me not to take you out. Thursday was the most auspicious day of the week and Tuesday the least, I learnt—the former when new projects were to be embarked upon, while on the latter, it was dangerous to even get a haircut. Most bizarre of all, he developed a strong antipathy towards the ganga—not because of inefficiency or uncleanness, but because she was four feet seven inches tall. "Can't we get rid of her? Babuji always says that short people, and tailors, are repositories of bad luck."

It did not end there. A fellow musician introduced Dev to a holy man at Dadar who reputedly could turn around anyone's kismet. Dev started visiting him regularly. The guruji first decreed that no meat be eaten for a month to counter the evil eye. When this proved too austere, Dev gave up fish (which he had never been particularly fond of) instead. Next, the guruji prescribed a series of exacting poojas to be performed at home. Dev anointed each idol with a solution of saffron in milk and shopped for the correct flowers and fruits to hang as offerings. He gathered the ash from spent incense in a special pouch blessed by the guruji, transferring it into a brown paper bag every Thursday to consign to the sea at Chowpatty. Whereas before he occasionally came home with a discrete mark on his brow to indicate a temple visit, Dev now smeared, without the slightest trace of self-consciousness, enormous red and white tilaks on his forehead of the size a sadhu might wear (the ones with grains of rice stuck in them made me particularly queasy). One day, I returned home to find you ravaged by these religious marks—not just on the forehead, but even all over the chest and arms. I forbade Dev, in no uncertain terms, from involving you in any such future attempts.

But involve you he did. He came back from Dadar one evening and announced that Guruji had diagnosed the problem. "We've been remiss in our religious duty—there's only one way to change our luck. We have to perform Munna's mundan—shave the hair off his head."

chapter
twenty

For a long time after your initial fuzz fell out, you remained completely bald. When the new hairs finally emerged, I tracked their growth every morning, as if they were seedlings in a balcony pot. Just when I could imagine a field of long, flowing tresses, something unexpected happened. The strands began to curl.

Not curls easily straightened or weak of will, but the kind that shot out to wind snakelike around fingers straying too close. And stray close is precisely what fingers did in your presence—everyone, even strangers at the bus stop, felt a compelling attraction to your hair. They not only touched it, but luxuriated in it—feeling its suppleness, marveling at its gloss, losing themselves in the light leaping around to animate the whorls. I actually witnessed a tiny hand reach out from a pram parked next to yours and try to stroke your head.

Dev's proposal for a mundan left me aghast. I had seen the tonsuring performed on the son of one of Dev's cousins in Delhi. The boy, only two years old, screamed through the whole ceremony. He squirmed so much that his scalp became bloody from razor cuts. "If you think that's why we've let Ashvin's hair grow, you're wrong. I'll see how anyone harms even a lock on his head."

"It's to make it healthier when the hair grows out again," Dev said.

"Every family I know has it done—it'll ensure that fortune always smiles on him. It's not cruel or barbaric, not like the foreskin Muslims slice off. According to Guruji, it's even prescribed in the scriptures—a harmless haircut, that's all."

"I don't care what your guruji says or your scriptures. I'm happy with my son's hair as it is."

"He's my son as well."

Hema wrote me a letter to try and sway me. "At that age, they don't even realize it's gone. You should see the photos of my Tony—Rahul, too—afterwards. All bald and grinning, like happy old men." She detailed all the calamities that could befall you, that could ruin the family, if we didn't perform the ceremony. "Remember Pushpa, whose parents bought the Kelvinator? Her mother-in-law committed suicide after her brother-in-law drowned. All this bad luck, they finally realized, from delaying their four-year-old son's mundan too long. Unfortunately, it was too late—just as the barber raised his razor, the boy suddenly became bald—all the hairs decided to drop to the floor in one big suicide plunge. They've been to a hundred doctors, a hundred temples, but not a strand they've been able to coax back yet from his scalp."

Of course, Paji weighed in as well, framing his advice, predictably, in terms of Indira Gandhi. Ever since Shastri had died and Indira wrested away the prime ministership from her horde of rivals, he had worked her into almost every letter. "Truly a daughter worthy of Nehru—she's going to put India on the map," he declared, when she appeared on the cover of *Time* magazine. "All the chatter about women's liberation in the West—look who even this Betty Friedan person is lining up to interview now."

He began sending me articles about Indira in which he circled paragraphs in red—paragraphs which showcased her intelligence, or independence, or one of the other qualities of her character he felt I should emulate. Once, after being hit by a rock while campaigning in Orissa, I received a newspaper photograph of Indira's face masked in enough bandages to make her look like Batman (as she herself pointed out). "If only every woman could be half as courageous as her," Paji wrote on these clippings, as a helpful hint. Each time Indira foundered, however—

perhaps with a disastrous session in Parliament, perhaps with the inability to quell a rice crisis, the tone of his letters abruptly changed. "Thank God Nehru's not alive to hear people curse him for not giving the country a son. Maybe she is a goongi gudiya after all—the dumb doll that all those people call her."

When the mundan question came up, Paji's chart had Indira's star on the upswing. A few months before, a group of right-wing Hindu parties had launched an agitation for a country-wide ban on the killing of cows for beef. Some commentators called it a transparent attempt to create a vote-garnering issue for the coming elections. A mob of naked trident-carrying sadhus attacked Parliament House as part of a massive demonstration, quickly leading to looting, arson, and half a dozen deaths. Indira, though, did not capitulate. India was a secular country, she declared, and the poor had a constitutional right to this important source of protein. Beef would stay.

"All this religious nonsense, all these superstitious claims—if she could stand up to them so firmly, I hope my daughter will be able to do the same. Now is the time, too, before your husband's family gets their claws fully into Ashvin."

For a while, it looked as if for once, I would grant Paji his wish. I would emulate Indira's steadfastness, not let Dev prevail. Then I answered the door one evening when the doorbell rang. The first thing I noticed was the toy elephant—the one Sandhya had told me she bought years ago at the Baisakhi fair in anticipation of becoming a mother someday. Arya held it. "I've come to see my nephew," he said.

THE LAST TIME I had lain eyes on my brother-in-law was five years ago, when he visited on one of his frequent missions for the HRM. The venture did not succeed. The Bombay groups he courted were too busy with their language agitations to care about the religious agenda of the HRM. This lukewarm reception, coupled with Sandhya's death the following year, put an end to Arya's trips—an end I hoped would be permanent. I resolved, in fact, to never see him again—even managing, by some miracle, to avoid him entirely during the family trip to Delhi last

February (induced by Paji's claim—false, as it turned out—that he had suffered a heart attack). "May I enter?" Arya asked, and I silently stepped aside to let him in.

Dev rushed up to hug his brother, and you came toddling up behind to curl both arms around his leg. "Yara," you said. For a few moments, I could only stare—the ease with which he picked you up, the familiarity with which he covered your face with kisses, the way you laughed as he blew into your stomach, your delight as he rubbed your nose with his own. Nobody in Delhi—not Biji, not Mataji—had treated you with such intimacy. It was as if Arya had been your "Yara" not for minutes, but decades. Except for the hair that had turned gray as Hema had lamented, his appearance hadn't changed. A deepening of the lines around the neck, a thickening of the flesh around his waist, the shadow of unspoken menace still lurking behind his smile. I took you back into my arms and sniffed your hair to make sure you hadn't picked up his papaya smell.

"The hair a child is born with is unclean from the mother's womb," Arya said as I cleared the dinner dishes. All evening you had insisted on sitting in his lap, while I looked from his face to Dev's, trying to decide whether Dev had invited him, whether the meeting Arya claimed to be attending was a pretext. "It's to free Ashvin from the bonds of previous births that we must shave his head."

"Ashvin only had fuzz when he was born, not hair. And as far as I know, there are no previous existences listed on his birth certificate."

"It doesn't matter—the head must be shaved. It's a rite in our family that must be observed." His voice was calm and patient, as if trying to help a child access something advanced. "Surely you agree that it's our blood too that runs in his veins?"

"Is that what you came here to ask?"

Arya mussed your hair. You splayed your body against his stomach and smiled up at him. "Just look at this little one—he wouldn't mind, would you, Ashvin? Tell your mummy you want your mundan so your hair can grow out thick and strong from your head again."

"Yara head 'gain," you said.

Arya turned to me. "It's no business of mine if my brother allows you more freedom than he should in this house. But if he even forgets to remind you of your responsibility towards our only heir, then someone else has to pick up the task."

At first, Arya's visit only hardened my resolve against the mundan. How dare the Arora clan think they could bully me into submission? Paji's letters flared up in my mind—it was as outrageous as the Hindus trying to intimidate Indira into a ban on beef. But Dev seemed to go to pieces at the insult contained in Arya's words, polishing off a whole bottle of sweet lime each night after his brother left. "What kind of wife are you that you want to see your husband fail?" he blubbered. "That you're determined to make me a laughingstock in front of my own family? It's only hair, you know, it'll just grow back. When you know I love Munna so much, then why such stubbornness?"

In the end, pity for your father made me relent. I hugged you to my chest and buried my face in your head. Hating myself for what I would allow to happen to your curls.

ONCE THE PRIEST set an auspicious date for your mundan, I insisted we organize a big party for that day. I asked everyone to bring a present, two months in advance of your second birthday. I even went to Palmer's and Co. at Kemp's Corner to buy a birthday cake. I chose one in the form of a face, with pastilles for eyes and marzipan for ears. As a precaution, I had them create a hat out of icing, to tactfully cover the head.

Arya had instructed Dev to have an achkan stitched for you with gold thread. You started crying the minute you put it on—the jacket was scratchy and unyielding, the collar so high that it cut into your chin. You looked beautiful in your sorrow—your feet fitted into gold shoes that tapered stylishly (but uncomfortably) at the toes, the white pajama with embroidered cuffs so stiff with starch that you could barely flex your legs. Crowning it all was the doomed black resplendence of your hair.

I cared for it all morning. Washed it with Shikakai soap for the last time, savoring its thickness between my palms. Dried the whorls lovingly between towels, rubbed coconut oil into the individual curls. At noon, I fed you, then carried you into the living room where all the guests had gathered. The Dugals, the Azmis, several people from the recording studio, and the Hussains, who brought along their son's tricycle.

Dev lowered you into a dining chair decorated with flowers. He smeared ash on your forehead, then marked a tilak in vermilion. The barber picked up his scissors and waited for the signal to start. You saw the first few locks drop to the floor and looked at me, puzzled. Then you whimpered and tried to climb out of the chair. More hair fell past your eyes, in black clumps. Your whimpers grew louder, then subsided into sobs. I thought you might start kicking, but the gravity of the achkan and the faces around you prevented that.

Tufts rose from your head, like stumps in a forest leveled by a storm. Hair slipped in through the neck of the achkan, and you squirmed as if you had insects crawling up your back. I looked at the lifeless curls building up on the floor and felt like weeping myself. Somehow, I managed a smile to encourage you on.

The barber swept the loose hairs off your scalp. He selected the smallest razor from a set of three and sharpened it on his palm. I could see you wouldn't be still for it, so I took you in my lap. You held on to my hands and convulsed silently under the blade. I felt the crinkly material of the achkan against my body, its sharp edges jabbing at me even through my sari. At one point, you screamed—the barber had nicked your skin. The red spread across the edge of his razor—he asked for some water to swish it clean. Dev ran to get his bottle of Listerine and swabbed some over your head.

The barber finally finished shaving. I expected your scalp to gleam, but it looked bumpy and dull. Dev brought out the gold cap that matched the achkan and arranged it carefully to cover the cut. We tried to distract you with the face on the cake, wrapping your hand around a knife to cut into the hat. But you didn't stop crying. Pinky jumped up and down in the piles of hair, then grabbed two pieces of cake and disappeared. The clapping of the guests drowned out your howls, the flash of the camera lit up your tears.

The photographer kept clicking, eliciting louder crying with each flash. I picked you up and ducked into the other room. Pinky looked up creamily from the cake she was devouring on the bed. I shooed her out and closed the door behind her, then rocked you at my breast to arrest your sobs. I made clucking noises in my throat, and rubbed my nose against yours, but without success.

I leaned forward to kiss your cheek when my lips closed magically around one of your tears. It felt round and pearly, briny as the ocean. I gathered these pearls, scooping them up with my tongue, tasting the bursts of salinity as they dissolved one by one. When I had harvested all the tears and could see no more visible on your cheeks, I ran my lips down the salty trails to absorb the moisture that still remained.

Somehow this calmed you. You sniffled, then pointed towards the bed, where the presents lay. We unwrapped the gifts one by one—the tin of Cadbury's chocolates, the building blocks from Mrs. Azmi, the dog-eared Mickey Mouse coloring book, partially filled-in, from the Dugals. ("What to do? It's impossible to keep that girl out of anything," Mrs. Dugal later said.)

Back in the other room, the ceremony had degenerated into a drinking party for Dev and his friends. Mr. Dugal and Mr. Hussain had also been recruited. I cleaved through the group, billowing with fury, but nobody seemed to notice. Finally, on my third or fourth run, Dev intercepted us. "My wife and my son," he grandly announced, sweeping a hand over us. He thrust his face forward to kiss my mouth, but I turned so that he caught my hair instead.

"A picture," he said, and everyone joined in, hooting and clapping. Dev tried to take you from my arms, but I didn't let go. "With the two of you, then," he declared, and pulled me down to the couch. He landed on one of his seated friends, and I lost my balance and fell into his lap. The photographer clicked before I could stop him, and the flash lit up your unsuspecting face.

This time, you didn't stop crying. I tried rocking you, and gathering your tears as in the bedroom, but you kept producing more of them. I seethed as Dev tried it as well, imitating what he had seen me do. As he passed you to Mr. Hussain, I snatched you back. There was one thing left that might quiet you, one thing Dev could not mimic. I took you to the bedroom, feeling the heaviness in my breasts, and coaxed you into being fed.

IN THE MORNING, you had a fever. "It's probably the cut, all infected," I raged. "God knows from where you hunted down that barber. Are you satisfied now, or do you have some other family ceremony you would like to inflict?"

Dev said nothing. He got a fistful of salt from the kitchen and passed it around your body in a circle. "To draw out the evil eye, in case someone's put a curse." In the afternoon, just as I prepared to let my hysteria burst forth, the fever abruptly subsided. "See?" Dev said. "It wasn't an infection after all."

You did not smile or laugh even though your temperature was back to normal. Every morning, when you saw yourself in the mirror, you began to cry. You turned to me with the tears wet on your cheeks and only quieted down after I had captured them all with my mouth.

I did not forgive Dev. Even with the cut on your head almost healed, I kept asking for the Listerine to make him feel guilty. On the third day, I asked if he would mind sleeping on the sofa. "I'd like to keep Ashvin next to me until he's fully recovered. We can sleep outside the kitchen, though—I don't want to force you out of the bed."

"Why not put Munna in the middle so that we can all fit in?" We'd always had two single beds pushed together, so there would certainly be enough room to follow Dev's suggestion.

"He's become so sensitive after what's been done to him. It's not just your snoring that would keep him awake but also your alcoholic breath."

I could tell I scored a hit by the way he blinked back the hurt. He left the bedroom without complaint that night, pretending to be unaware of my intention to punish him. The next morning, though, he told me I was exaggerating the seriousness of things. "Munna's a lot more resilient than you think. It's you who's making him depressed." To prove his point, he asked me to watch as you laughed and played with him on the sofa. The minute I entered, your forehead wrinkled up and a troubled expression came over your face.

"See?" Dev said. "Besides, if you look, you'll notice his hair is already reemerging." I didn't give him the satisfaction, but turned away in silence.

That evening, I checked your scalp for myself. It was true what Dev said—I could see the follicles dotting your head. I ran a silk dupatta over it, and a chuckle burbled up from your throat when it caught. I scraped my fingers over the nubs and this made you laugh. Even more, you liked the feel of the tufts on your palms—you kept brushing your hands over your scalp as if sweeping things off.

In the days to come, the hair slowly lengthened and covered the egginess of your head. It grew out straight, however, the curls forever gone.

chapter twenty-one

Even after you had grown a full head of hair again, and seemed to have completely forgotten the mundan, Dev came into the bedroom only when necessary—to change his clothes, to get his pillow, to kiss you good night. He kept this up for months—too proud to say anything, waiting for me to retract what I had said. On some nights, as I lay on the sheets unable to sleep, I heard him singing softly to himself and almost called him back. But then I saw your closed eyes, your untroubled face, and decided not to subject you to your father's Listerine breath.

One day, as you stood in the yellow plastic bucket in the bathroom grasping the rim, you started calling for your daddy. "Dada, Dada," you repeated.

"Daddy has gone to work," I said, and emptied the red bucket over you. We were playing the bucket game, which had become the only way to lure you to your bath—you simply abhorred soap. "He can't stay at home like I do, to wash you." I started switching you between the buckets and pouring the water back and forth over you until it was all gone. Sometimes there was enough pressure for the shower to work, and you did a dance under the spray. But today nothing emerged.

"Dada," you said again, as I drained the residue from the soap dish into a mug of water and churned up some bubbles. I pulled back your foreskin and swished your shamey through the mug. Usually this made you laugh, but today, you seemed to have just one thought in your head. "Dada," you insisted, stamping your foot in the water for emphasis.

"Fine. Daddy can come and help on Sunday." I kissed your navel, and swished your shamey again, and this time you burst into giggles.

Sunday came, and you were all excited as Dev and I each held an arm and emptied mugs of water over your head. You jumped clumsily up and down in the bucket, splashing us all. I carefully maintained my stiffness towards Dev, though he looked so happy to be with us that I felt a twinge of guilt. You shook your body like a dog, your shamey swinging wildly from side to side—water sprayed our hair, our faces, our clothes, the wall behind.

Dev was about to dump more water on you when you suddenly yelled and raised your arms. The mug in his hand went flying into the air, then plopped down like a cap on his head. He looked so funny with the water spilling down his face that you began to roar. Even I joined in, which prompted Dev to take the mug from his head, fill it again and carefully overturn it on me instead. I gasped as the cascade streamed over my forehead, as the water soaked through my blouse and made it stick to my skin. Indignation rose inside me, raring and lucid, even as my vision blurred.

But then I noticed you laughing so hard that you had collapsed back into the bucket. Peeking out from underneath the uncertainty on Dev's face, I detected a playfulness I had not glimpsed for years. The same mischief I had seen so often on your own face—the crinkling of your eyes (like now), the pouting of the lips. I stood there, turning from your roguish expression to his, and felt my anger fade.

You were still laughing, so we lifted up the other bucket and emptied it over you, then sealed you between the two buckets, like in a red and yellow egg. When we cracked open the egg an instant later, you burst out with arms raised and teeth bared.

Afterwards, we held a towel over the bed and swung you hammock-style in it. Dev had taken off his shirt and undershirt, which were both wet, and I was clad only in a blouse and petticoat. I raised my end of the towel and sent you rolling to Dev, and then he raised his side, sending you seesawing back.

Finally, we played the powder game. Dev puffed you all over with talcum, then stood you up and rubbed it in. I aimed some puffs between your buttocks and you rolled your rump around in the air. You noticed talcum on Dev's chest, so we powdered Daddy as well, and massaged it in. Then it was Mummy's turn, and Dev shook the container all over me. I closed my eyes and felt your tiny palms and your father's fingers skim across my face, my throat, the neckline of my blouse.

When I opened my eyes, Dev, his skin smooth and white, had his face right next to mine. He kissed my lips and I tasted the talcum on his mouth, felt his fingers slide under my blouse. He kissed me again, longer this time, and I had to break away to remove your hand, which had followed your father's and was rummaging around under the cloth next to it. You looked up at me questioningly, and I could read the claim furrowed into your face.

I bent and kissed you as well. You reached up with your arms to surround my neck, then pressed your face into my bosom. "Mummy," you said, and I could tell that you were going to insist on being fed.

I unhooked my blouse and extracted an arm from a sleeve. Dev looked away, his gaze straying to the door. "Stay," I told him, suddenly bold, even though I almost never fed you in front of your father. "You'll be amazed at how efficient he's become."

You fit into your favorite position across my lap and raised your mouth for its practiced swallows. You looked up at me, I looked across the room at Dev. You pulled my head back toward you. "Look at *me*," you seemed to say.

Dev walked to me and stroked my hair. I felt a slow burn at exposing myself this way—embarrassment or exhilaration, I couldn't tell. There was nothing more natural, I told myself—the three of us anointed by the same powder, joined together in the same ritual. Your unclothed body, Dev's bare chest, and my naked breast.

"I'll leave you two alone," Dev said, and tiptoed out of the room.

—

THAT NIGHT, THOUGH, Dev returned, to end his exile from our bed. He picked you up from next to me, kissed your forehead, then carefully placed you in the half bed that had replaced your cot. "I thought you might have room for me," he whispered.

I saw he had taken off his shirt—the moonlight powdered the tips of his shoulder blades now. I reached out a hand to him and he kissed my fingers, then my wrist, then my elbow, following the curve of my arm to the bed. For a moment, we lay next to each other, staring at the ceiling as if trying to remember the next step. Then Dev propped himself up on both hands and bent over to kiss my mouth.

His breath was strong with Listerine, as I knew it would be. I tried to scrape this deceit away from his tongue, to taste the truth underneath. Perhaps that was the key to opening up—experiencing what he did, understanding what he felt. He pulled back his mouth and buried his face in my neck, then fumbled to remove my nightdress. I felt the cloth drawn back from my chest, his hands scooped out a breast. He rolled the tip in his mouth, then crossed his body over mine. His tongue felt strong and restless; his lips, firmer than yours, encompassed more of my flesh.

He tired quickly of my bosom. I heard him unbuckle his belt, felt him slide the pants down his legs. I tried to loosen my garments but his weight pressed the cloth to my skin. He raised my nightdress above my waist and it bunched against my stomach. He felt his way up my thigh with his hardness, then probed against my pubic bone. Finally, he caught the cleft he was looking for. "Meera," he murmured, and pressed himself in.

I remembered to take a deep breath to soften his entry. His weight pushed and receded against my chest as he retracted himself, then squeezed back in. His body, at an angle to mine, made his penetration more painful than usual. I didn't want to stop him, in case he lost his rhythm and had to give up, defeated. I tried to align myself to ease his thrusts but he held me too firmly in place.

As his speed increased, I heard the rustling of hair against skin. A sound as inexorable as the call of an approaching train engine, as the drumbeat of incipient rain. I braced myself for the final thrusts, against muscles locking in pain. I remembered not to look at his face when it happened—the pupil-less whites, the shuddering eyelids. Instead, I concentrated on the faraway thought that somehow, some part of this experience must be satisfying. I reeled this thought in, to crystallize it into awareness, into memory, as I felt him pull out and spurt softly onto me.

About a year and a half after we moved to Bombay, emboldened by my college-going worldliness, perhaps, I managed to quell my embarrassment long enough to ask Dev how it felt for him. He turned deep red, and didn't say anything, just nodded. About a week later, he mumbled the same question to me. I had all sorts of things I wanted to tell him, unuttered thoughts that I had fantasized about disclosing ever since the days at Nizamuddin. If he could start slower, if he could not press so hard, if he could caress me down there even after he had pulled out. But going to college had not quelled the awkwardness—this was still a new and frightening language in which I had no fluency. Panic reined in my breath and my windpipe started to close, suffocating the words in my throat. All I did was flush even more intensely than he had, and press my face into his chest so that he would not see the crimson. He must have interpreted this move as approval, because we never spoke of it again.

The discomfort no longer bothered me so much—like an affliction one finally accepts will be permanent, I didn't have to worry about curing it anymore. Now, it relieved me just to have the act performed to completion. It was not as if I enjoyed it as such, but still, there was the sense of accomplishment. Of contractual duties duly performed, of a long-standing enterprise regularly maintained.

Our transaction that night helped put the bitterness behind us, but also marked the beginning of a shift. We engaged in the act less and less frequently. Sometimes, it was the thought of waking you up that made us abandon the undertaking. On other occasions, the blame was harder to pinpoint.

Dev kissed me on the lips and I detected the staleness of alcohol seeping out from under his mouthwash. Perhaps I also detected gratitude. He got up and went into the bathroom. I felt around to locate the wetness he had left behind, then used an edge of my petticoat to wipe it up. I rinsed the edge off and squeezed it dry before going to sleep. No matter how much I wrung it, though, some dampness always remained.

IN THE CONTEST between the guruji's predictions and my expectation, I won handily—the mundan had absolutely no effect on Dev's playback attempts. Instead of giving up, however, Dev became even more obsessed with his rituals. Once he moved back into the bedroom, he emptied the top shelf of the cupboard and converted it into a miniature pantheon. In the center he installed his large picture of Lakshmi, with offerings of old ash-covered King George VI rupee coins at her feet. Next to it he placed the saffron-clad bust of Sai Baba brought back from the overnight pilgrimage to Shirdi. Around these, he arranged a baby Krishna painting from the 1962 calendar, a newspaper photo of Gandhiji, and even K. L. Saigal in a suit, looking young and dapper in his silver frame. From the roof of the shelf, he dangled an idol of Hanuman on a string, so that the monkey god seemed to swoop mid-flight through the air.

All the clothes on the other shelves started smelling of incense smoke, the bedroom reeking as well, and the tilaks Dev marked on his head grew more and more alarming. Your excitement on Wednesdays, when he allowed you to lead the pooja, disturbed me even more.

Past the sweet lime and coconut offerings in the corner, under his canopy of dried flowers, sat the idol you liked the most—your beloved Ganesh. You waved the incense over his elephant head so many times that Dev had to guide your hand away to propitiate the other gods as well. You always pulled the incense back to wave it some more over the mouse at Ganesh's feet. "Mickey Mouse," you called it, and only stopped waving when some of the fruit for the other deities had been offered to the mouse as well.

I imagined Paji hovering somewhere, engineering the twinges of dismay I felt every time I saw you lean into the cupboard with the incense. "It's not so bad, religion," Dev said. "There's a lot of peace in it—you should try it someday." Despite my resolve to remain disapproving, I felt myself pulled in. I allowed Dev to sprinkle the sugar crystals he consecrated on Thursdays onto my tongue again, the ones I had stopped accepting as a protest against your mundan. Each time you clamored to be taken to the temple, I accompanied you to Mahalakshmi, buying flowers for you to toss at the idols and lifting you up so you could ring the bells. I found myself relating the same mythological tales to you that I had grown up hearing from Biji. Kali crushed her husband Shiva under her feet again, Maricha appeared as a deer to tempt Sita, Krishna slew his uncle with a flying discus once more, Brahma blew out the universe in a single breath.

Your favorite tale came from Dev, not me—the story about how Ganesh got his elephant head. You clamored to enact it whenever your father was at home at bath time—it even replaced the bucket game. I pretended to be Parvati, the one about to bathe. "Little light of my life, Ganesh. Stand outside and keep guard—make sure nobody disturbs your mother while she washes herself."

You beat your chest ferociously. "I promise not to let anybody pass."

Then Dev, playing Shiva, lumbered in, demanding to be allowed through. "How dare you prevent me from seeing my wife? I don't care if she's your mother, get out of my way."

But you did not budge, and the fight between Parvati's son and her husband commenced. Dev tickled your sides and made sounds of "Dishoom, dishoom," as he pretended to strike you. You tried to pull him down, latching onto his leg and sometimes biting it. Finally, it came time for your favorite part—the beheading. Dev took you in his lap, and as you gurgled and guffawed, sawed your head off with the flat of his palm. You rolled around on the ground to simulate the head tumbling away. That was my cue to emerge from my bath. "What have you done to my son?" I screamed at Dev. "Don't come back until you have found a head to make him whole again."

You got off the ground and trumpeted like an elephant, and Dev put his hand to his ear. "There in the forest, what kind of animal could it be that I hear? Perhaps I can cut off its head and attach it to the boy." As Dev closed on you, you trumpeted even louder, your body all aquiver in anticipation at the prospect of being decapitated again.

At some point, Dev fashioned a pair of elephant ears from wire and cloth—he soaped you up and dunked you in the bucket a few times before crowning you with this contraption. "Ganesh had better be clean, or this brand-new head I've cut off from the elephant won't be able to stick." The bath was forgotten the instant you wore those ears—you ran through the house, whooping and trumpeting all day.

chapter twenty-two

AN ENTIRE MENAGERIE OF DISNEY CHARACTERS POPULATED THE DUGALS'
coloring book in addition to Mickey Mouse (each one duly slashed
through by Pinky in violent streaks of crayon). You learned to call them
by their names—Minnie and Huey, Bambi and Daisy. You made bark-
ing sounds when you came across Pluto, and asked if Dumbo (with his
own mouse Timothy, no less!) was the flying version of Ganesh.
Goofy's protruding teeth were so frightening that you turned the page
quickly so as not to see his face.

We found a potty at Crawford Market with a portrait of Donald
Duck on the backrest. You liked it so much that you sat on it for what
seemed hours—perhaps that's what made you so constipated from the
start. Sometimes you balanced on the footrests, standing unsteadily and
scrunching your face in exertion, but it didn't help. You made a quack-
ing sound with each success. "What has Donald Duck done?" I asked,
and together, we both said, "Laid an egg."

Mrs. Dugal boasted about her daughter's productivity—how Pinky
filled up her container, sometimes twice, every morning. She gave me a
bottle of oily green medicine for you. "Mr. Dugal swallows a spoonful
or two whenever he can't go, but for Munna, a few drops should do." I
opened the bottle—it smelled like rancid ghee, so I threw it out. "I mix

THE AGE OF SHIVA   245

in a little with Pinky's mashed banana every now and then," Mrs. Dugal confessed. After that, I detected a whiff of potty whenever Pinky was around.

I tried to keep you away from Pinky—I didn't want you to catch her potty smell. But no other children of that age lived in the building, and even though she was three years older, Pinky followed you around. In the afternoons, she rigged up a clumsy tent in the corridor using an old tablecloth and tried to lure you in. She especially liked playing with your hair. It was long and dense (and straight) by now, and Pinky kept sticking bows in it, tying it when she could, with a childish knot. I forbade her each time, but she stared at me blankly through eyes weighed down with kohl.

Coming up the steps one afternoon, I stumbled upon Pinky clutching you in her arms. I saw her lips pressed against yours, stars of adoration in her eyes. I tore her off your body and dragged her to the Dugal's door to complain. "Is this what you've taught her?" I shouted at Mrs. Dugal, and pushed her daughter forward. Pinky started sobbing, her kohl leaving black streaks on her cheeks. Mrs. Dugal slammed the door in my face. I heard the sounds of slaps and Pinky's crying rising to a wail.

You cried as well, as I washed your mouth and your face. "Chhee, dirty," I explained to you, but you only cried some more. After satisfying myself that Pinky's presence no longer lingered, I tried burying my face in your stomach, tickling your ears. But you did not relent, turning your face away even when I tried to capture your tears.

So I held you in my arms like Pinky had been doing, and kissed you. Your mouth was hot with anger and wet, but my lips smoothed away the indignation. I made exaggerated smacking sounds and blew air into your cheeks, until finally you laughed.

The next day, kohl back in place, Pinky rang our doorbell. "Can Ashvin come out to play house again?"

OUT OF ALL OUR NEIGHBORS, you liked Mrs. Azmi downstairs the most. I had befriended her ever since Mrs. Dugal had labeled her a Pakistani spy, not only to repudiate such charges, but also to put some more distance between us and the Dugals. Mrs. Azmi—Zaida, as she asked me to call her—had been married at the age of sixteen to her forty-four-year-old first cousin, Anwar. "I liked a boy in the next building," she confided to me. "Also a Muslim, but not from the same community. We wouldn't do anything, just talk and spend time together in secret. When my father learnt about it, he twisted back the little finger of my left hand until it snapped, and didn't take me to a doctor for a week. Anwar was well-known to my father, so it was the easiest match to arrange."

Now in his sixties, her husband suffered from indifferent health. Zaida came over in the afternoons, when he took his nap. There was something tantalizing about her visits, something conspirational—the signal tapped with a broom handle onto her ceiling, our floor, to inform us Anwar had fallen asleep, the vanishing act she performed right after tea, before Dev returned. She always had a toffee or hard candy on her person for you to find—hidden so skillfully (a Fruitee bar rolled into a whorl of her hair, a peppermint sweet taped behind her knee) that even I felt myself intrigued enough to join in the search sometimes.

She liked to listen to music when she came over. One afternoon, the radio broadcast a breathless number, the kind Lata Mangeshkar would never dream of singing, but her sister Asha had started specializing in. "It's Helen's cabaret dance from *Teesri Manzil*," Zaida said. "Quick, turn the music louder." She led you by the hand to the clearing between the sofa and the dining table and began to dance. Any notions I harbored of her diffidence were quickly dispelled as she swung and shook, mouthing the words, waving her dupatta and spinning you around in a pirouette. "You, too, Meera," she said, pulling me in when the next song came on.

After that, Zaida made dancing a daily activity, one that you eagerly awaited (as did I). Surprisingly, "House of Bamboo" became one of her favorites. "Even though I don't understand English, I can feel the lyrics in my heart." One of her nieces had taught her the twist, and the version Zaida performed between us in the living room sizzled with even more passion than Dev's rendition. "People keep talking about a band called the 'Beadles' or some such name—do you have anything by them?" A few months later, she presented you the "All You Need Is Love" single for your birthday.

On Saturdays, when her husband spent the day visiting his brother in Sewri, Zaida invited us to have tea at her flat. For you, she had a bowl of steaming rice kheer ready, with extra almonds and raisins fished out from the pot and arranged on top. You sat on the floor and savored each spoonful, watching the large hanging tapestry of women picking apples with baskets on their backs. "It's from our vacation in Kashmir—they really do pick apples like that. The only trip we ever took together, just the two of us without Anwar's mother."

Zaida's mother-in-law had passed away a little before you were born. "Sixteen years I spent in this flat living under that woman's thumb—peace be on her, but the only kindness she ever showed me was to die. All these years of being suffocated, all the catching up that remains. Can you believe it, I was forbidden to even greet anyone on the stairs!"

Sometimes your Zaida auntie swathed you in scarves of silk and nylon and fashioned a hat for you out of an old dupatta in preparation for the dance. "Please, please, will you make up my face as well?" you clamored, reminding me how I used to plead with Roopa to do the same. Unlike my sister, Zaida did not stint on cosmetics—she treated you to the full production—the foundation, the eyeliner, the rouge, the lipstick. The end result always stunned me—you could be a film actress, a Japanese geisha, a beauty queen. "Princess Ashvini," Zaida declared. "The most exquisite dancer in the whole of Bombay." You ran to the mirror near the door and stared at yourself, the dance forgotten as you stroked your cheeks and pouted your lips.

"I always wanted to have a baby girl. But after the two miscarriages, Anwar lost interest—perhaps he felt he was getting too old. He's not been bad, otherwise—I shouldn't complain. With his mother gone, I can do almost anything—listen to the radio, put on makeup, even go to the pictures, and he doesn't care."

I went quite often to the movies with Zaida. I even accepted her invitation to take us to a mosque. She extended it one Divali, when I took over a box of sweets, and she did not have anything to present in return. "Why not?" I said. "We've been to so many temples, it'll be good for Ashvin to see a masjid as well."

We caught the bus to Haji Ali. I had passed by several times, but never ventured to the mosque floating on its island in the middle of the bay. "There was a wealthy businessman who renounced all his wealth," Zaida told us. "He died on the way back from Mecca—this is the spot to which his casket miraculously floated." One could only reach the mosque during low tide, when the walkway that connected it to the mainland emerged from the waves. "The sea's only recently gone out—watch out for the puddles," she said.

We followed the crowds. A long line of beggars squatted along the edge of the path, holding out bowls clutched in bandaged hands or between the stumps of diseased limbs. Zaida gave you the small sack of one- and two-paise coins she had brought along. "A single coin for each one of them—it depends on their luck, what they get. Make sure you aim for the bowls—don't let your fingers touch their skin."

You were small enough that we could take you with us into the women's section. You stared at the marble floors, the decorated walls and ceiling, the women praying silently. As we approached the railing cordoning off the flower-covered shrine, a look of confusion came over your face. Finally, you asked, "Where's Ganesh?"

I tried to shush you, but Zaida laughed. "He's in there," she said. "They all are—you just can't see them."

That year, during Eid, I got to drink the almond milk that in Nizamuddin, Mataji used to pour down the drain. Zaida's version was garnished with a green layer of crushed pistachios and flavored extravagantly with cardamom and saffron. After finishing the jug she brought over, we did the twist.

HEMA FINALLY MADE her trip to Bombay, with her sons. She had put on weight, her face becoming full and fleshy, her chin peeking through like the nub of a particularly swollen mango. "What to do?" she moaned. "Both Rahul and Tony are such poor eaters, I'm the one who has to clean off their plates." Already she had acquired the manner of someone two or three times her age. "Tony, get me a glass of water from the fridge," she said, as she sat on the bed and sliced betel nuts for her paan. "Oh, my aching legs—Rahul, can you come give your poor mother a press?"

Between chewing on her betel leaf and instructing Rahul where to knead and for how long, she filled me in on the gossip from Delhi. "Guess who showed up unannounced at her parents' house? Pushpa. Said she was tired of being mistreated by her in-laws, can you imagine? Her parents sent her right back, of course—she was lucky her husband took her in again." She lowered her voice. "Babuji has some disease of the bowel—he doesn't even realize when he's gone all over himself. The washerwoman refuses to touch his clothes any longer—Mataji has to clean them herself now. Yet another reason for Arya bhaiyya to get a new bahu, to help her in her old age. Have you seen anyone in Bombay you can recommend?"

Before I could reply, Hema shook her head. "How could you?—all the people you ever see are Muslim."

Finally, Hema made it to the zoo—the wish she had expressed in so many letters before her marriage. This desire had long waned, but with two boys in tow now, she hardly had a choice. Rahul, who was seven, had a mean streak in him—he tried to prod the monkeys with a stick through the bars and I had to stop him from lobbing stones over the fence surrounding the giraffes. ("He's just trying to get their attention," Hema laughed.) Tony, a year older, was quiet and shy, and surprisingly friendly towards you, despite your age difference. He led you by the hand to the aviary cages and pointed out the birds for you one by one. Before leaving for Delhi, he gave you the largest of the shells he had gathered from the beach at Juhu. You cried so much as the train was about to pull out that we promised to take you to Delhi every year after that.

I could no longer avoid Arya on these trips, since we usually stayed at Nizamuddin. "See how good he is with children," Mataji said, each time he chased you around the verandah or showed you how to hold a cricket bat. "Rahul and Tony just dote on their uncle, too—but Ashvin seems even more fond of him." It was true—for some strange reason, you found Arya irresistible. I watched this rapport uneasily, unable to think of a seemly way to undermine it. You refused to go to sleep unless he had kissed you good night, you yelped puppy-like every time he invited you to run an errand with him, you even wanted to sit with him during meals and eat from his plate. A few times, I studied Arya's face as he played with you. Instead of the look of watchfulness, of masked menace, his features were open and unthreatening, his smile almost child-like. But then I wondered whether, conscious of being watched, he was putting on such a wholesome display for my benefit. "What an unjust world we live in, that someone like him would not be given the chance to be a father himself," Mataji said.

I wanted to correct her—the true injustice was what she had to bear. Every morning, she put an enormous pot of water on the fire to disinfect Babuji's soiled sheets and pajamas. I offered to help, but she brushed me away. "This is my lot in life. As long as these hands are able to take care of him, they will."

"But at least he could stop drinking. He'd have better control if he was sober, don't you think?"

Mataji gave me a look that warned me not to continue. "How are your parents doing?" she asked.

PAJI, ACTUALLY, WAS doing quite well—I hadn't seen him in such top form since before Nehru's death. "Do you know where I was this morning? At 1, Safdarjung Road—does that ring a bell?"

I looked at him, startled—it was the most famous address in the country. "Yes," he nodded, obviously pleased at my astonishment. "I was at Indira Gandhi's. First in the garden with everyone else, but then inside, to speak to her in person. She said that the country depended on publishers like myself. She hinted that the Congress Party might have things in store for me as well. Who knows, your father may even end up standing for election someday. Rajinder Sawhney, Minister of Information and Broadcasting, what do you think?"

Over the last few years, Paji had grown increasingly enamored of Indira Gandhi, applauding her each time she did something daring.

Snubbing the superpowers, nationalizing the banks, stripping the former maharajas of their titles and pensions, and through it all, ignoring the accusations of arrogance and high-handedness. The most recent act, where she formed her own breakaway Congress Party rather than take orders from the older politicians like Morarji Desai, sent Paji's opinion of her skyrocketing. "She's an example for all womanhood to emulate, I tell you—not afraid of any man. Any father would be proud to have such a daughter—were he still alive, she'd be able to stand up to Nehru himself."

By now I threw away unread the cuttings Paji sent me—I found politics not only tedious but irrelevant. How could antagonizing America or confiscating the maharajas' purses have any bearing on my life with you, notwithstanding the titillation these actions afforded Paji? The one exception concerned prices, which rose faster than we could keep up with on what Dev earned. The cost of food alone seemed to have doubled recently.

Biji blamed it all on Indira Gandhi. "I'm supposed to be illiterate, so what can I say? All I can tell you is that when I give the servant five rupees to go to the market now, he asks for ten. What people like your Paji never talk about is how prices are crushing people, how families have so little that they can't even keep their cattle from dying." It startled me to discover this sudden interest in politics Biji had developed, even more so to be apprised of her newfound empathy for the common man. "I'm a zamindar's daughter, remember—it runs in my blood—my ancestors have tended their villages for centuries. There's no honor in warming your behind on the throne if you can't even keep your population alive."

Paji brushed aside such objections. "Look at all the respect India is gaining in the world for being so independent, for not kowtowing to the West. She's only been in office for a few years—it takes time to solve problems of the economy. It'll all be sorted out by the time my grandson's up to my chest, won't it, Ace?"

Paji had started calling you by this truly strange nickname. I complained to him that it sounded like a fighter pilot in the British air force, but he persisted. "Tell me, Ace, what would you like to be when you grow up? Not a singer like your father, I trust?"

Although you adored Biji, who ordered a full crate of Coca-Cola especially for you on the first day of each vacation visit, you always remained a little wary of Paji. Perhaps you sensed my own mistrust. He tried to lure you with candy or coins to come talk to him—enticements you would snatch from his hand and run. Each time you lingered, he lectured you on one of his pet topics—the evils of religion, the worthlessness of prayer. Sometimes he got quite aggressive, even towards you. "Perhaps you're not quite an ace after all," he said, when you told him about feeding Mickey Mouse, at the foot of Ganesh. "One can't expect to breed a prize rose if it has stock mixed in from a pedestrian strain."

This attitude towards you convinced me to take my chances with Arya at Nizamuddin rather than stay at Darya Ganj. I didn't want Paji's shadow to cast a pall over your life, like it had mine.

PAJI WASN'T THE ONLY PERSON I tried to make sure didn't influence you too much. There was, of course, Arya as well, and also Hema's husband Gopal. I worried about them brainwashing you with their HRM propaganda if my vigilance faltered. Already Hema's younger son boasted about watching the new recruits wrestling in the mud—I saw him marching around the house one day, a stick propped against his shoulder as if it were a gun.

I also kept a wary eye on Roopa. She had managed to find out in advance about two of our Delhi trips, and shown up each time on the train from Madras, with her twins. Although Dilip and Shobha, being nine years older, already inhabited their own separate world, you fell instantly in love with your "Roo auntie," much to my chagrin. "Darling Ashu," she kneeled down and called to you, and you ran across the room to fling yourself into her arms.

Your Roo auntie bought you all sorts of expensive presents—a windup tank that spewed sparks when it ran, a toy gun that shot Ping-Pong balls. (Back in Bombay, you used these to terrorize poor Pinky with particular gusto—lodging a Ping-Pong ball in her mouth, setting fire to her hair with sparks from the tank.) When Roopa heard about Zaida's makeup skills, she brought out her own bottles and brushes and did your face up so extravagantly that for two days you refused to wash it off. The night we slept over at Paji's, she told you stories we had heard in our childhood—mangling the scenes, confusing characters and events, but managing, nevertheless, to tantalize you—she could have read you the telephone directory, and you would have still been rapt. The next morning, you wailed that you wanted her to bathe you, and I reluctantly gave in. After that, you insisted I lather you in the ears like Roo auntie did, that I float the Ping-Pong balls in the mugs of water poured over your head. "Roo auntie didn't wash my shamey—she told me I was old enough to do it myself."

"Did she show you how?" I asked, and you shook your head. "Then you're not old enough." I swished it as usual through the water in the mug.

I did not understand Roopa's motives. What was behind this attempt to charm you, to make this new inroad into my life? That last time in Delhi, I had gone as far as threatening to inform her husband Ravinder if she ever repeated what I had witnessed between her and Dev. It didn't quite seem like she still lusted after my husband, though I remained alert whenever they met. Perhaps I still intercepted the occasional wistful look or fleeting glance, mostly from Dev, but I could no longer be sure of it.

I tried to delve into this, the night you insisted you wanted to sleep close to your Roo auntie again. "You've certainly put the charm on Ashvin. All those presents, all this attention—he's going to think that you're his mother, not I. Are you trying to steal him away?"

Perhaps I was reading too much into things, perhaps this was the way an aunt normally behaved, perhaps I was being too jealous or possessive, like Dev always complained. Roopa didn't rise to the bait. "I'm lucky to have such a wonderful nephew," she said, brimming over with a sweetness that made my jaw ache. "He reminds me so much of you, and a little bit of Dev."

THE DAYS GO BY, much too fast, like the pages flying off a calendar to denote the passage of time in a movie shot. A jumble of memories, photos spilling from a brimming album, overwhelming me each time I try to keep the years apart. There you are, peeling litchis by the half dozen, trying to shoot them out of your Ping-Pong gun. Squatting by the Ashoka pillar at Hanging Gardens to have your picture taken, smiling enigmatically, like Mona Lisa might, because you are secretly doing number two in your shorts. Is that on the same page that you dance on the bed, your very own moon surface, as the radio announces the first step by Neil Armstrong? Or the day that Montessori begins, when I stand outside listening to you howl, then go back in, defeated, to take you back into my arms?

Perhaps the pictures are arranged by theme, not chronology. With an entire section reserved just for all the times you land in trouble. The week you steal into the bathroom and cut your face while trying to shave like Daddy. The time you spray pedestrians with color left over from Holi as they pass below our balcony. The afternoon you wrestle with Pinky and she breaks your tooth accidentally, the dog at Sharmila's house that bites your thigh when you try to ride it like a pony. How many times alone did you fall from the swing to bloody your chin at Mafatlal Park?

And next the images that include your father. The night we found ourselves huddling together in the hotel bed in Khandala under a single frayed mosquito net. We had barely enough room to balance on the edges of the bed without falling off, the way you had your arms and legs splayed. Neither of us could sleep, with the heat and the lack of space, and the mosquitoes diving unhindered through the holes in the net. Then you made a sound so alarming and strangled it made us both sit up. We looked at each other and began to laugh—we had just heard you snoring for the first time.

The album has another section, one I have named the "bamboo house," in which this image could have also fit. The section with the three of us always cozily absorbed together in some activity, every frame a tinted photo capturing an instant of domestic harmony. We are playing the Ganesh game before your bath, or negotiating the waves at Chowpatty, and in the background above us, the bamboo eaves hover protectively. Riding the giant wheel at the Dassera fair, or tucking into

a Cream Centre sundae with three spoons, the slats of bamboo all polished and gleaming like ivory.

Did I imagine our future would look like this? The pages of this section fluttering open one after the other, ready to archive, to celebrate,
every incident in our lives?

But then other images come into focus, and I see a darker reality
emerge. One in which bamboo houses simply get blown away and even
the Beatles split up. This flurry of scenes is from a different part of the
album, one marked by confrontation, conflict. The occasions when Dev
gets so drunk that I send you in to plead with him to stop. The nights he
stays out somewhere and you keep waking up to ask if he has returned.
The fights over tilaks smeared on your head each time Dev drags you to
his Dadar guruji. The time he slaps you when you break the clock, and
I warn him never to touch you again.

The last scene remained fresh in my mind for weeks. I hugged your
head, trying to leach the hurt away with my body, and kissed your eyes,
your cheeks, your nose. I sat on the bed and rocked you in my arms—
you looked into my face and neither cried nor spoke. I kept you by my
side that night—Dev slept on the sofa, something he did more and more
as time went on. You touched my face as I kissed you good night, and
unfurled your fingers to show me they were wet. For a moment I
couldn't believe it—my vow of so long ago not to cry—even though
this time, it was for you, not myself. I tried to turn away, but you tugged
me back by the arm and told me that I had to close my eyes. I felt your
mouth dab the spot under my eye—uncertainly at first, but then with
more assurance. You pressed tiny kisses like an angel might, first into the
left cheek, then the right. I squeezed my eyelids shut tighter together,
forcing out more tears for you to scoop up. Each fleeting contact so soft
and pleasurable that I didn't want the sensation to end.

Perhaps my inventory of images contains nothing so egregious to
justify a future so bleak. A lawyer pleading Dev's case might claim that
by no means have I proved he deserves his fate. Except doesn't the
album contain yet another section in the back, its pages yellowed, its
edges all bleached? With something dark and unformed beginning to
stir again unseen?

I know, of course, of this section's existence—I have clasped it firmly shut to lock away the memory it contains. Of the sibling who went before you, the twin to your Ashvin, the one with whom you share your name. Somehow, after all this time, I can feel him reawaken inside me, preparing to press his claim again.

It takes a while before I realize what is happening. That he is the one whispering to me silently, all those times my lips start quivering unexplained. That it is his presence, wafting silkily through my being, which makes me want to get up each time I am joined in bed by Dev. We are laughing over some joke, the three of us, and I suddenly want to stalk away. Dev brings home a tandoori chicken, or my favorite pakodas, and it is all I can do not to throw them away.

I never quite understand why he has reappeared. Perhaps to guard against forgiveness, to mount a campaign against the past being erased. Perhaps we are becoming too much of a family, and he wants to ensure I don't sign on to the bamboo future with Dev. I find myself fighting your father on trivial matters, getting more contentious over every decision that has to be made. The emotion overloading my nerves, the resentment ratcheting up inside, until I am ready to turn you against Dev.

But right now let me show you a scene from the front of my album—a walk on the beach to search for Ganesh. We are on the sands at Chowpatty, on the morning after the annual festival has ended. You run along the edge of the water, pointing at the bits of colored clay that have begun to wash up already. We have done this for the past few years—joined the crowds to watch Ganesh and his entourage of gods and leaders and film stars immersed. And then, come back the next day, to look for what the waves have put on display, what the tide has returned. You find a few small parts—a trunk with a tusk attached, an upturned palm imprinted with an auspicious swastika, the tapering ornamentation of a head. But you seek something more awe-inspiring—the truncated bust of a movie-star hero, or perhaps a half-dissolved face, still recognizable as a Gandhi or Nehru.

Today, though, the waves are big and foamy and leave little behind. We should have come when the tide was going out, not flowing in. The sand is smooth and cleanly swept—even the sculptor has not resumed his carving after yesterday's crush of people. You pick up a shell and toss it into the water, disappointed by the paucity of the treasure on the beach. "Let's go to the aquarium," Dev suggests, and you cheer up at this prospect.

We never make it. About halfway on the walk there, we encounter a cluster of people on Marine Drive. Some are milling around on the pavement, others stand on the parapet, still others watch from vantage points atop the concrete tetrapods shoring up the land. Dev pulls us through the people to see what they are gesturing at. An enormous Ganesh idol, twice as large as life size, reclines faceup on the tetrapods down by the water. The two right arms have broken off, the lower extremities dissolved, but otherwise the statue appears remarkably intact, with the conch still in its lower left hand. A look of serenity graces its face, as if oblivious to the people around or the waves breaking at its base, it is completely engrossed in contemplating the sky. A small bird perches on the belly, equally absorbed in its rumination of the sea. The bird pays no heed when someone tries to shoo it away.

Nobody seems to know how the idol could have got there. "It must have been lying here since dawn, it must have floated in overnight," an onlooker says. "Clay is too heavy, it can't float," someone counters. "Even if it could, how did it reach so high?" "Not to mention so far from the beach where it was immersed."

"This is Ganesh we're talking about," a young man in a loincloth says. "Remember, he can do whatever he wants."

People are even more divided about the meaning behind this sighting. A good omen, some claim, that Ganpati has returned to bless the land a second time. Others are so disturbed by the unsuccessful immersion that they clamber down to the statue, braving the waves to try and pry it loose. You strain to join them, so Dev raises you on his shoulders to afford you a better look. Between waves, somebody attempts to lift the statue by one of its remaining arms—the clay is so wet that it crumbles off.

A volley of large waves come crashing over the idol, and water surges up through the tetrapods. The wind whips the spray all the way to where we stand. More waves churn in, like warnings from the sea to stand back as it pulls out all the stops in its high-tide display. The last few people trying to set Ganesh free retreat to the safety of the parapet. "He's coming loose!" someone shouts. Sure enough, the statue, no longer encumbered by its arm, has begun to rock and shift. The bird teeters on the belly, trying to ignore this change in circumstance, then calls it a day and flies off. Another wave envelops the idol, and then the sea seems to lift it up. Ganesh rotates lazily, his head still gazing upwards, his eyes still focused at infinity, his trunk furled neatly above his mouth. For a moment, he rests on the last of the tetrapods, then begins his seaward journey. "Ganpati baba maurya," the crowd calls out—someone throws petals, but they flutter back in the wind. The women all cover their heads with their dupattas—feeling self-conscious, I join in. "He's going home, finally—look how buoyant he is." Ganpati does appear to be floating through the waves, like a graceful swimmer doing the backstroke—perhaps it is a miracle after all.

For some reason, melancholy, not happiness, engulfs me as I gaze at the departing statue. I try to cheer myself up, to tell myself that Ganpati is returning home, that he will venture far into the ocean and even seek out the goddess who lives in the sea. But I can't seem to shake off the feeling of loss. All the bereavements in life—I think of my unborn child, of Sandhya, and even her baby Ganesh brother. Whom am I destined to lose in the future?—I hold my breath to stop myself from completing the thought. I tighten my grip on your arm as you stand between Dev and me, shouting "Ganpati baba maurya."

"Don't think like that, Didi," Sandhya tells me, whispering into my ear. "It's an auspicious occasion, be happy like everyone else here." Her presence wafts around me, I smell the herbal green soap she uses on her skin. "It's a day to mark the passage of time. All three of you will return here to marvel at how much Ashvin's grown year after year." Ganpati rises above the water, the sun glinting off the edge of his golden crown, and the crowd cheers.

But it is my premonition that is right, Sandhya's optimism is misplaced. We will never see Ganesh immersed into the Arabian Sea again, not the three of us together, you, Dev, and I.

chapter
twenty-three

PAJI FILLED HIS LETTERS WITH DRAMATIC ACCOUNTS OF THE COZINESS HE was supposedly developing with Indira Gandhi. First the invitations to her garden, then the talks indoors, then breakfast one day, lunch another, until he had garlanded himself with the mantle of someone in her innermost circle. "Good breeding always shows," he enthused in one letter, going on ingratiatingly about her poise, her elegance, her appreciation for beauty. "Such a remarkable person—she could have been a poet if she hadn't become prime minister."

In another letter, Paji boasted of inviting Indira to come visit them at home for dinner. "Your mother, can you believe it, asked Sharmila to help her prepare a list of questions on the economy. Instead of worrying about cleaning the house or planning the food, Mrs. Home Minister of Darya Ganj wanted to demand an explanation on how the country is run. Thank God Indiraji couldn't come, otherwise I would have never lived down the shame." Paji had started attaching a respectful "ji" to Indira's name, ever since the possibility of his standing in an election had been suggested.

That December, when Indira called a surprise midterm election for February 1971, Paji was all agog. "They're trying to decide which constituency should be mine—whether they'd like me to run from a district near Patna, or some spot in Himachal Pradesh." It soon became clear, however, that the Congress Party would extend no such invitation—they had earmarked the sizable donation extracted from Paji to fund someone else's campaign. Paji hid his disappointment well, making it sound as if he had personally advised the party to get someone more experienced, for the greater good. "All these supposed freedom fighters like Morarji Desai, showing their true colors by jumping into bed with the HRM. When they chant for Indiraji's removal with *Indira hatao*, we should shout back, *Garibi hatao*—Remove poverty—instead."

I never found out if Paji had really coined the "Remove poverty" phrase as he seemed to claim in his letter, or if he'd heard it from someone else. The juggernaut of *Garibi hatao* swept through the country, resonating with city dwellers and farmers, Hindus and Muslims, the poor and the middle class (but not, of course, the rich). It obliterated the HRM and the rest of the coalition that had tried to bring Indira down, handing her a victory so complete that she now had enough seats to even amend the constitution at will.

On the evening of the victory announcement, we watched the revelers in the street, as they danced and set off fireworks and distributed sweets. The sense of jubilation became so infectious that I found myself doing the twist with you on the balcony. Down below, all traffic had come to a standstill, halted by a spontaneous rally that had taken over the road. "The mother of the nation," a voice cried out. "Indira Gandhi," the crowd responded. "The keeper of our destiny." "Indira Gandhi." We looked down at a man wielding a megaphone—behind him swirled a giant portrait of Indira sprouting enough weapon-bearing arms to rival Durga. "She'll return us to prosperity," he shouted. "Indira Gandhi," came the chant from the crowd.

As it turned out, that night marked the end of our prosperity, not the beginning. We were going to bed when Dev revealed to me that he had lost his job.

IT WASN'T EXACTLY ACCURATE, the way Dev phrased it—he wasn't let go or fired, but had stalked off after a fight. One of the music director duos who had kept promising to let Dev sing had decided to give the opportunity to someone else. Enraged, Dev told them to set up the recording for their new golden boy themselves. It took a week for his pride to run its course, a week he spent sitting at Auntie's all day. By the time he was ready to apologize, Vasant, the studio owner, refused to speak with him, sending out his secretary to say they'd hired someone else.

Although I immediately felt the grip of anxiety, Dev remained quite relaxed. "Where are they going to find someone who knows the ins and outs of the place, who can pull together a recording like I do every day? Wait another week or so and Vasant himself will be crawling up to me with an apology. That'll be the time to inform him he's not going to get me back without a raise."

The week turned into a fortnight, then two, and yet Dev didn't seem too concerned. "Don't worry," he said. "It's not like there's only one recording studio in the whole of Bombay."

But there might as well have been, because Vasant spread rumors all over the city—how Dev picked a fight with Kalyanji and took a swing at Laxmikant, how he spat at new singers coming into the studio and cursed at the high priestess Lata Mangeshkar herself. For all practical purposes, this finished Dev's career in the music industry—he found himself blacklisted everywhere. "Why not go to Vasant, plead with him to at least clear the air?" I suggested, a step Dev refused to take.

He spent his days at home, as if on an extended vacation, with the living room sofa his hotel. Room service for breakfast, when I fried him an egg, followed by a leisurely bath and perhaps the newspaper, then room service again for lunch, and then a nap. He woke up in time for the two-thirty listeners' choice program, asking me to turn up the radio for his favorites. In the evenings, he took some money from my purse to go to Auntie's, returning only when he could barely find his way back.

Each time I raised the question of our dwindling finances, he looked at me, offended, as if I had breached some rule of etiquette. "So hard I've worked all these years. At least don't deny me this temporary rest. Besides, didn't Paji say he might help?"

As a side effect of all this rest (to which his body was perhaps unaccustomed), a host of ailments soon afflicted him. His neck got stiff, his gallbladder hurt, he massaged his kidneys daily to relieve the pressure in them. He stopped eating onions because they upset his stomach, coconut and yogurt gave him "the chill." He spent hours in bed doing exercises to straighten his spine—it became a form of entertainment for him. He went to the doctor every third or fourth day, returning with bottles of chalky pink suspensions the compounder had mixed.

But for you, he would have sunk into a complete state of torpor. You got into the same holiday spirit as your daddy, jumping on him while he napped, riding him like a horse around the room. He neighed when you pulled his hair, galloped when you tweaked his ears, and threw you off each time you dug your elbows into his back. Soon, he began taking you on walks downstairs, dropping you off and picking you up from school. In the evenings, you sat and played cards with him, and shared his tea and snack. You announced you wanted to wash up with Daddy every morning, even though ever since turning five, you had insisted on bathing without my help. I stood outside, listening to the two of you laugh and shriek—much more than I remembered when we played the bucket game.

Was it wrong of me to begrudge Dev this idyllic existence? Churlish to nurture the resentment in my breast? It wasn't jealousy, I told myself—I just worried like any mother would, about all the time you spent together day after day. What if your father's influence proved harmful? What if you ended up like him? Your only ambition to sleep ten hours each day and make it to Auntie's for your drink?

I tried to compensate whenever I could. Each time Dev started his ritual of soda and ice, I lured you to the kitchen to have hot puris fried in oil. I took over from Dev whenever he toweled you dry, or combed your hair, or pared your nails. I insisted on taking you to school some mornings, despite Dev's assurances that he didn't mind. When he folded sheets of papers into boats, I taught you how to construct more elaborately folded planes. I bribed you with Fruitee bars, and bought you icy cola drinks—the more I tried, though, the more you attached yourself to him.

And then came the day I realized what I was up against. It started with you frisking around on the bed with your father while I tried to put up the curtains leading to the living room. Dev had come up with the brilliant idea of taking them down the night before to wrap them around you and Daddy as saris. Suddenly the two of you began wrestling—first on the bed, then on the floor. "I'm Superman," Dev said. "I'm King Kong," you countered, trying to catch your father in a scissor hold. Dev always took care to use only a fraction of his strength when he tumbled with you—today, he allowed you to wrap your legs around him and pin him down. I'm not sure what happened next, but your body came crashing into the chair on which I stood, knocking it out from under me and dumping me on the floor. The rod bent in the middle, the curtain ripped in two, and a few of its rings clattered across the room.

"What kind of hooliganism is this?" I cried out. "Do you think this is a wrestling pit?"

Neither you nor Dev responded—you stared silently at each other. I threw the piece of torn curtain at your father in anger and struck the ground with my fist. "Answer me," I shouted. "Is this how one behaves at home?"

To my amazement, the two of you, still looking at each other, started giggling. Dev picked up the curtain fragment and swished it at you, and you fell over backwards in laughter. He wrapped it over his head as he had yesterday, pretending it was the edge of a sari. He got to his feet and started dancing, the curtain rings sounding against his forehead like the chimes of a tambourine. You sprang up from the floor, clapped your hands in elation, then began to dance as well. *"My love has got me a sari from Bikaneer,"* Dev sang, tearing off a piece of the cloth for you and draping it over your head.

I stood there, overcome by the unreality of the situation. The fun you and Dev seemed to be having—what should I do—join in as well? Then I remembered the ruined rod, the destroyed curtain, the mocking of my words. I strode to where you were dancing and ripped the fragment off your head.

It had the desired effect. You clutched at your bare head, shocked. Dev stopped his song in mid-sentence.

"This is all very well," I said, managing to strike an even tone. "But there's only dal in the house, and Ashvin's school fees are due. You're wrong if you think wrestling and dancing makes you a good enough father. Why don't you get a job, instead of spending your life being a fool?"

I watched with satisfaction as Dev's face crumpled. He turned to face the wall, the curtain still dangling ridiculously from his head. The rings jingled a little as he took several deep breaths. When he turned around again, I saw he had managed to make his eyes wet.

"What sad and sensitive tears. I'm sure they'll impress Ashvin. Perhaps you should save them in a vial and pull them out each time he asks why you're still unemployed."

Dev staggered out of the room. You looked at me, wide-eyed. "I'm sorry," I said, as I held out my hand. "Mummy and Daddy might fight, but we still love you." Instead of coming to me, you retreated, turning around and running through the door, as if I might try to harm you.

For a while, I just stood there silently, still holding the cloth from your head. Then I righted the upturned chair and ferreted out the curtain rings that had rolled under the bed. At the door to the other room, I stopped, immobilized by what I saw. Dev sat on the sofa, his eyes closed, his neck craned like an expectant pet. You knelt in his lap, holding his face in your palms, leaning up to kiss the tears off his shaggy dog head.

PERHAPS IF I HAD BEEN NOBLER, perhaps if I had been less wronged, I could have been more generous, reacted with equanimity. But understand, Ashvin, your father was also my husband, the man who had robbed me of my firstborn, the man who was preparing to again usurp my claim. You were the sum total of my life's accomplishments, the reason for my existence—there could be no question of giving in. Never before had I seen you framed so clearly as through that doorway—you were the prize in a contest I had to win.

You must realize I didn't want to be cruel, that evening, or in the days and nights that followed. I was preoccupied, strategizing, wondering how I would fight to retain what was mine. I knew you sensed my remoteness—the way you whimpered, the way you followed me around to engage me, the way you clung to me in apology. It was not you but your father, remember, towards whom my disaffection was directed.

The bamboo house vision, where I could gradually realign your affections, was, I decided, too fraught with risk. Instead, I began to imagine a future without Dev. I confided this idea to Zaida to gauge her reaction. "Perhaps I'll run away with Ashvin, bring him up in a small unknown town somewhere. I'll start working again, not mention it even to Paji—we'll subsist on what I can make."

To my surprise, she was aghast. "He's lost his job—how can you think of abandoning him at a time like this? Just think of how selfish it would look, just think of what people would say." I tried to argue that Dev had never been a good provider, that he lacked drive, that I could no longer bear his drinking—an activity that surely expressed his dissatisfaction with me, his disappointment in life. But Zaida only scoffed at this. "Did you see the ganga yesterday, with her bruised eye and her split lip? At least your Dev mellows when he's drunk, it's not like alcohol is a fuel that propels his fist. And look at Mrs. Dugal, sitting there unperturbed as her husband downs peg after peg. He tends to drool when he's drunk, so she carries a handkerchief in her purse to dab off the spit. Your Dev might be out of work and have his bad habits, but he's still a good father, you have to admit."

I saw what she meant. People were hardened by husbands who beat, who broke skin and bones and teeth. They would mock my pampered complaints, laugh that my disappointment could hardly compare. Perhaps I'd have had a better shot if Dev occasionally slapped me around, punched out a tooth, darkened an eye. At least then I could point to my bruises as I left, giving the world a reason why.

I never did get anywhere with my plan. Zaida pointed out a flaw that made it unworkable. A married woman could hardly expect to survive in a small town away from her husband, she said. "They'd rip you for sport, come after you like wolves."

Dev must have sensed something amiss, because he tried to squeeze out sympathy by putting his wretchedness on display. He started inexpertly frying his egg himself now every morning, gazing at me with sad, jobless eyes each time the yolk spilled out and hardened against the pan. He stopped listening to the radio or taking naps during the day, spending silent hours on the sofa staring worriedly at the calendar instead. He wore the darkest shirts he owned, with pants that were charcoal black, to show me how solemn he felt. One day, I even found the newspaper had *Positions Available* ads circled in red—he never followed up on them, though, as far as I could tell. He hugged you often and spent time playing with you as visibly as possible, in a misguided attempt to appeal to my motherly instincts.

You understood the dangers better than your father. You wriggled out from his demonstrative romps each time you sensed they might trigger my remoteness again. Whenever a fight broke out, you hid in the bathroom until the shouting subsided, to avoid being pressured into taking sides. You learnt to divide your affection so scrupulously you could have been in training to be a diplomat. Sometimes I felt guilty when I saw your growing cautiousness—your antics always guarded, your laughter no longer carefree. But I was unable to shake off my anxieties, unable to rescue you from having to tiptoe around my needs.

One afternoon, I came back from my shopping to find neither you nor Dev in the flat. On the landing, Pinky was skipping rope, one of the many new girlish pursuits Mrs. Dugal had nudged her towards. "Uncle's teaching him to fly a kite on the terrace," she said, her healthy cheeks jiggling as she skipped. "Another useless boys' activity." She rolled her eyes as I went up the steps.

How long was it (five and a half years already?) since those blackout nights on the terrace? When I waltzed around with you in the moonlight, your mouth at my breast? Now, as I gazed across the same expanse, you seemed so grown, the kite string grasped with such determination in your hand. "Pull!" your father shouted, launching the kite—paper rustled, slender ribs flexed through the air. Just when it looked like the kite was going to enjoy a graceful ascent, the nose did an about-turn and dove back towards earth. "Let out more string!" Dev yelled, but you were too mesmerized by the spectacle of the plunge to react. The kite hit the terrace and lay there like an injured bird, a triangle of paper protruding like a broken wing.

Surely I could teach you to control the string better than that. Our servant Kesar had secretly introduced us to this male pursuit at Darya Ganj. I remembered the afternoon Roopa had engaged my kite in a duel, and much to her shock, I had severed her string. How surprised you would be to discover that your mother had some proficiency in this activity as well.

"Mummy's going to teach you today," I announced the next afternoon, as you gathered up your kites and reel. "You might not believe it, but in her heyday, she used to be quite the ace."

My heart lurched as your face fell. "But I always go with Daddy. He was going to show me the trick of how to fly the kite in a circle through the air."

"Daddy's a little tired today," Dev said. "Mummy can show you as well." He looked at me hopefully, glad for the opportunity to be of help.

On the terrace, we knotted the string to the kite, and I ran back to you once it was aloft. As I helped you tug and reel out, your reserve began to dissolve. The kite ascended into the sky, soaring past the tallest buildings, rising even higher than the sun, it seemed. When it was barely a patch against the clouds, the riffle of its paper no longer audible, you squinted at it through narrowed eyes. "It's so high," you whispered, as if suddenly realizing how distant was the other end of the line that sprang from your hand.

"Don't worry, sweetie. You've seen aeroplanes in the sky, haven't you? Those fly even higher than that. One day, you'll see for yourself— we'll go up there in an aeroplane together, travel to some new and wonderful place. Wouldn't you like that?"

You stared at the kite, your brow furrowing. Then you turned around. "Won't Daddy get lonely all by himself?"

I felt my cheeks flush. I tried to keep my voice singsong, carefree. "We'll take him along, of course. I wasn't going to leave him behind."

You examined my face, perhaps to decide if I could be trusted. Just when I thought your next question would slice like a scalpel to expose my innermost intentions, your expression relaxed. "Where will we go?" you asked.

FOR A WHILE AFTER THAT, I still managed to cling to my fantasy of the two of us running away together from Dev. But you wiped out even these lingering traces on the night before your sixth birthday, when I asked what present you would like. "I wish you would kiss Daddy," you replied. The earnestness of your expression could not hide the tide of insecurity shored up behind.

Guilt rose inside me. What kind of mother had I become to keep putting you through this? I pressed your face to mine.

The next day, we stood on either side of you, Dev and I, and helped you guide the knife through the cake. After you blew the candles out, I gave your father a peck as you had requested. "Nothing's going to happen," I told you, squeezing you in my arms to make you feel safe. "Mummy and Daddy are fine, so you can stop worrying your little six-year-old head."

But I was not fine. My resentment against Dev had not abated, it bided its time inside. I felt increasingly in the grip of your unborn sibling from fifteen years ago, his phantom presence come to haunt me. He did not manifest himself in my nightmares, creating grisly images of the room above the plumbing shop, or visions of blood and gore. Rather, he infiltrated more subtly, more insidiously, sending questions bubbling up through my consciousness each time I saw Dev at play with you. *How could your father hug and kiss and wrestle with you so breezily, without the slightest inkling of guilt? Why should someone be allowed to enjoy such affection from you after snuffing out the life of your twin?* I tried to calm myself with arguments—hadn't Dev been contrite, wasn't I culpable as well? But your twin always had the perfect counter to my reasonableness. *What if you ended up loving your father more than your mother—where would be the justice in this?*

In June, you started first standard at St. Xavier's. We had managed to get admission for you through one of Paji's contacts. The fees were three times what we'd paid for pre-first, and now there were uniforms and books to buy as well. I had to ask Paji for a supplement to the monthly check he had been sending ever since Dev had quit. "There are some very promising leads Dev's found," I wrote. "He's bound to have a job again any day now."

In response, Paji cut out a newspaper article, which spoke about how the prime minister's "Green Revolution" had proved to be a success.

"This begging-bowl image of us that Indira's putting an end to—let's hope you'll soon be able to match her example as well."

By now, Dev seemed completely at ease with his unemployed status—settling in for the long haul, it appeared. One night, he even asked me if I thought we should have another child. "Munna seems so alone sometimes, I feel we're depriving him. Just think when both of us are dead and gone, he'd still have someone to call family if we gave him a sibling."

I stared at him, stunned. "We can't even afford to buy Ashvin a second pair of shoes—how do you think we can afford another child?"

"There's always God to provide. Besides, don't you think your parents would be overjoyed if we gave them another grandson?"

It took me a moment to figure out Dev's meaning—a second child would make Paji amenable to sending more money. "Maybe one of them could be an engineer—an astronaut, even—the other, a physician. He'd like that, wouldn't he, your father?—his grandson the doctor he never could become?"

I turned around, pretending I hadn't heard Dev's words. *Tell him,* the voice within me urged. *Tell him that we would have already been two, Ashvin and I. If he hadn't* . . . I concentrated on the edge of my pillow and willed myself to be silent.

"And of course if it were a girl, there would be nothing like it. She would be our little princess—we'd all dote on her—Munna, you, and I."

chapter
twenty-four

THE WAR THAT RIPPED THROUGH OUR EXISTENCE ORIGINATED AT THE border with East Pakistan, hundreds of miles away from where we lived. I had been reading about the events there for months—the elections where the East Pakistanis voted against years of exploitation, the brutality with which West Pakistan repressed the resulting rebellion, the millions of Bengali Muslim refugees who streamed into India as a result. How could I have ever imagined that something so distant could cause us such irrevocable change?

It took a while for the conflict to reach us. As the atrocities against the East Bengalis by their countrymen mounted, the calls for Indira to march in became increasingly shrill. "She's getting the world to accept us as liberators, not aggressors, so that America can't come after us in Pakistan's defense," Paji explained. He claimed the trouble had been building even longer, ever since the Partition. "Yet another sign of British genius, to lump together such far-flung regions with not even a common language, only because both were Muslim. *Now* will people realize just how worthless religion is?"

In the beginning of December, the Pakistanis blundered in with a preemptive attack against India. It was just the excuse Indira had been awaiting. "There is no option but to fight," she declared.

1962, 1965, and now 1971—preparing for wartime felt so familiar, it could have been a way to mark the passage of years. I had saved the panels of blackout paper from '65—I took them out from under the birthday decorations and put them up. The previous routines started up again—offices closing at 4 p.m., night shows cancelled at movie theaters, sugar and kerosene disappearing overnight from grocers' shelves. Police advised pedestrians to wear white shirts so as not to be run over by public buses in the dark. "Only confirmed drinkers make it to speakeasies," the newspaper reported, a caption worthy of a photo of Auntie's place.

By the second night, the rumor mill was grinding in earnest—Pakistani agents swarming undetected all over Bombay, reports of enemy planes sighted (as usual) at Madh Island. Mrs. Dugal muttered again about suspicious goings-on in the building, but quieted down when I reminded her that this time our East Pakistan allies were also Muslim.

Although the war went on for two weeks, for all practical purposes, it ended for me on the fourth day. The fall of Dacca, the liberation of Bangladesh, the drama of Nixon deploying the Seventh Fleet against India—all these could have occurred in a different era, on a different continent. The only memory that somehow lingers hazily from that week's newspapers is a picture of a Soviet spaceship landing on Mars.

The day before, a Sunday, started out innocently enough. You insisted on sharing Daddy's egg, so I fried an extra one for him. He was feeling a little groggy, so instead of tea I made him coffee, which he also let you sip. It being a holiday, Dev didn't take his bath until noon—he spent the morning in his pajamas, wrestling with you on the bed. At one point, while I rolled out the chappatis in the kitchen, you dragged your father in, to show me how well you had lathered his face for him to shave. A few minutes later, you ran in again, to show me how Daddy had lathered your cheeks in return. You came a third time, with an ash mark on your forehead—Dev had sent you to rummage around for a fruit offering for Ganesh.

At lunch time, Dev pulled out one of the oversized bottles of beer he had stored in the fridge. "Just this one," he told me, when confronted with the look I gave him. "To clear out the kidneys—I feel I'm not urinating enough." Ever since he had stopped working, he always claimed some therapeutic reason for drinking during the daytime—beer for urinary health, whiskey to ward off an impending cold, rum to cure the ache in his neck. I snatched your hand away when you tried to hold the glass for him while he poured.

Afterwards, you wanted to go to the terrace to look for enemy planes, but Dev convinced you it would be too dangerous, directing you to the balcony instead. He rolled a sheet of paper into a telescope and asked you to keep a watch on the sky while he took a nap. Zaida showed up a half hour later and put on an old Beatles record she found at her cousin's place. You barked in accompaniment as they crooned about working as hard as a dog.

That evening, more cars jammed the road below than I had ever seen before on a Sunday. Perhaps people were already getting claustrophobic after two nights of blackouts. We watched them from the balcony, the Fiats and Ambassadors crawling by the unlit streetlamps, the drivers blowing their horns more aggressively than usual to compensate for their painted-over headlights. At seven, the air-raid siren sounded. You ran inside to turn off the lights—you were still enthralled by the novelty (all false alarms, so far). Even after the all-clear siren sounded, you insisted we keep the candles lit and sit in the dark.

So Dev began singing, reprising his Saigal performance from the last war. For a moment, I was transported back to when you were an infant in my arms, when I could see his voice fill your luminous eyes with calm. Now, as you sat in your father's lap, you fidgeted and drummed against the chair, out of sync with his words. One foot pivoted around on the floor, as if doing the twist with a life of its own. "Can we put on the Beatles now?" you asked, the moment Dev's lyrics died down.

We actually had to turn the lights on to make you sleepy that night—the darkness had excited you too much. The next day, the sixth of December, was a Monday. I didn't know if your school would be open, but dressed you up early in your uniform all the same. We waited at the corner until nine, but the school bus never came. Dev was still asleep when you burst into the bedroom. You woke him up, yelling, "No class today."

Perhaps it was providence that kept you home to spend one last day with Dev. Although, had you been away, I might have been less rankled, and things could have turned out a different way. Something oozed inside of me that morning when Dev let you break the yolk of his fried egg again. I felt a slow burn spread into my chest when you lathered him and wrestled him and ran around once more with ash on your forehead.

"Still having beer for your problem?" I remarked as Dev poured his second glass at lunch. "Perhaps one doesn't need to urinate quite as often as you think."

Dev set the empty bottle down on the table noiselessly, as if the slightest clink or scrape might propel my anger to a higher level. He sat where he was and stared at the crumbs on his plate as if waiting for permission to touch his beer.

"What's the matter, something else wrong now? Your elbow, perhaps, or is it your neck? I forget, should I get you rum or whiskey for that?"

Still, Dev did not speak. You looked at him, then me, hiding your face behind your tumbler of lemonade. "Well?" I said. "Are you going to answer me, or do I have to call Auntie to come make the diagnosis?"

"Just once," Dev said softly, shaking his head. "Just once."

"Just once what? Speak up, maybe your son wants to hear as well. Just once can school fees not be squandered on alcohol? Or just once can Daddy digest his food without having a drink?"

"It's *you* who can't digest your food, not without having a fight with me after every meal." Dev threw back his chair and stood up so abruptly that the beer bottle toppled over and rolled off the table. "Just once I wish you wouldn't talk down to me. Day after day you train your tongue to speak only in taunts. If not for me, at least think what Munna must feel."

"What *must* Munna feel? Watching you loll around the house unemployed every afternoon, gulping your drinks. Is that the model you've set for him to grow up as?"

"Yes, yes, go on. Tell him how useless his father is, how he can't even get a job. Don't think I haven't figured out your scheme. You've been trying to turn Munna against me since the day he was born."

Dev wrapped a protective arm around you as if I was about to pull you away, and this further infuriated me. "I'm not the one who's turning him away, *you* are, with the behavior you keep displaying. He's six years old now, he has eyes and ears and a brain, he can see for himself what his father is like."

"And what about his mother, does he see through her preciousness? So refined, so much too good for everyone, always strutting around with her nose in the air, always doing what her father directs. Instead of coming after me and ruining my life, why didn't she marry her Paji instead?"

I'm not sure how long the fight went on. I remember you disengaged at one point and disappeared into your usual hiding place in the bathroom. I remember dredging up every grudge I could think of, from Roopa to Freddy to my dowry, and Dev doing the same. Only the shadow within me, the phantom presence of your unborn sibling, remained uninvoked.

The bell interrupted us. It was the postman, delivering a letter from Delhi, which had arrived with Paji's usual impeccable timing. By the time I returned from the door, Dev had stalked off to the balcony.

The fury within me was so centering that it held me in a state of heightened clarity for the rest of that afternoon. I felt like an actor during the intermission, charging myself for the second act of a play. While Dev smoked cigarette after cigarette on the balcony, I decided on eggplants for dinner and blistered them over the gas. I sliced tomatoes and cucumbers, and onions as well, arranging them precisely on a platter in an enormous burst of salad. At one point you asked me for help on using a compass, and I bore down so hard that the needle pierced your notebook. I read the letter from Paji with its sheaf of clippings rubbing in the news of Indiraji's latest accomplishments. Neither the usual accompanying gibes nor Paji's meddling suggestions left much of an impression in the spate of my rage.

The siren went off promptly at seven again. You kept sitting at the dining table, drawing circle after circle as if hypnotized. I switched off the lights myself and used a single match to try and ignite all the candles.

As they blossomed into flame, a snatch from some familiar tune swirled unidentified through my head.

I sat in silence and waited for Dev to come in from the balcony. Your compass pencil rasped against the paper as it crisply etched out its curved lines. The traffic outside seemed less noisy compared to the day before. I remembered reading that between sirens, cars were supposed to come to a standstill at the curb. Every now and then someone took advantage of the cleared road and I heard them zooming through the night.

Dev finally appeared, and for a moment, I wavered. I could feel the afternoon's events weighing down oppressively—did I have the stomach to complete the unfinished fight? Then, through the darkness, Dev's defiant eyes met mine. I felt instantly electrified. "Look, Ashvin," I said. "Daddy's come inside."

Even then, we had a chance. I could have vented my sarcasm, which Dev could have chosen to ignore. He might have gone back to the balcony, or braved the blackout at Auntie's like one of those *Times of India* souls. After all, we knew the options, we had played out these roles so many times before.

But then the unplaced tune surged back into my mind. It unmasked itself, overrunning my consciousness, garrisoning the centers of my brain. "Daddy's going to sing for us," I heard myself say. "The song he's been singing for years now to make Mummy his."

I had never thought myself mean or sadistic, always staying behind a self-imposed cordon of restraint. But now I felt compelled to try cruelty as an experiment, see what effect it would have on Dev. I wanted to summon up something truly venomous, experience the thrill of it issuing from my lips. "You know the one I mean, don't you? The one Daddy likes to sing every chance he gets? The one he's spent his whole life singing and done nothing else? The trouble is, nobody's thought his voice good enough in all these years to make a record out of it."

I didn't discern any visible reaction from Dev, so I thrust in deeper to make sure I reached him. "Come, let's hum it together—it looks like Daddy's forgotten, but we can remind him. I know you prefer the Beatles, but I promise we'll play them after Daddy's finished." With that, I set the tune free, humming it loud enough to drown out your protests that you didn't want to sing. I picked you up and twirled you around in a show of affection for Dev.

A voice inside urged me to retreat, but I continued, unable to stop myself. "Looks like even this isn't ringing a bell for poor Daddy—perhaps he needs to hear the lyrics as well. Come, Ashvin, this is fun, you must join me in helping him." I started crooning the song, twisting around the words, inventing new lines, exaggerating the tune as mockingly as I could. *"Will you light the darkness of my heart? To dispel the fire in my life. Nobody wants to hear this song. So I keep singing it at home every night."* You struggled as I grabbed your hands to clap them along with the words.

I brayed on for a few more verses, until Dev shouted for me to stop. "Can't you see he's crying?" He strode over and lifted you out of my arms.

The act of having you physically taken from me crystallized all my outrage. I went on the attack instinctively. "So much concern you have for your son," I said, the presence inside me furiously typing up the script. "Before he gets too attached to you, why don't you tell him what you did?"

"What are you talking about?"

"You know perfectly well—the one you forced me to drop, the one whose life you traded for this house. Do you want to reveal it to Ashvin or should I be the one?"

"Are you mad? Have you completely lost your senses?"

"Ashvin, listen to me, Mummy has a story to tell you. That man holding you, he's not only your daddy, but also the daddy of another."

"How can you cling on to such rubbish after all these years? *You* were the one, not me, who—"

"Listen to me, Ashvin, a sister or a brother that was in Mummy's stomach, do you understand? We'll never know what it was, because before it could come out, Daddy had it killed."

"Shut your stupid mouth," Dev said, and, still holding you with one hand, grabbed my arm with the other. I screamed as if I had been struck, and tried to get away, losing my balance as Dev let go. I toppled towards the floor, striking my head on a corner of the dining table along the way. For a moment I sat there dazed, feeling around with my hand where my scalp felt sticky. When I looked, there was blood on my fingers.

"Meera?" Dev said, uncertainly. "Are you? I'm sorry—I didn't think . . ." He remained standing where he was.

I felt more blood seep out from under my hairline and brushed at it with the back of my hand to wipe it away. You started crying, then wriggled to get out of Dev's arms. "It's okay, shhh," Dev whispered. "Mummy's fine, she just scratched her head—Daddy didn't mean to."

But you began screaming and flailing, and Dev was forced to set you down. You came running across the floor and buried your head in my chest.

"Daddy didn't mean to," Dev said again, kneeling down beside us. "Munna, look at Daddy." But you kept whimpering against my breast. Dev turned to me, speaking with a different tone. "Are you going to tell him I didn't do it on purpose or are you going to make a big drama out of this? Perhaps you can convince him that I'm trying to murder his mother as well."

"Just leave him alone, will you? You've done enough as it is."

"And you, as usual, are completely innocent." Dev got up. At the door, he tried to get your attention one more time. "Daddy loves you, Munna, you know that, don't you?" In the candlelight, I could just make out the line of his chin, the curve of his lips, the shine of his pupils against the whiteness of his eyes. "Does Munna love Daddy?

"Ashvin?" Dev said quietly, one last time, and I felt you stiffen against me. By the time you turned around, your father had left the flat and closed the door behind him.

WE HEARD THE SOUNDS even before I had a chance to put something on my wound. They were delicate, like balloons burst underwater, like kernels of corn popping in an adjoining room. "It's outside," you said, and ran to the balcony. "Mummy, come quick—there are lights floating in the air."

I stood with you and stared at the festoons high above the buildings. They were neither gun flashes nor bombs, but surely something connected with the war—I had to tell you I didn't know what. They reminded me of pictures of cells under a microscope—each light a nucleus of luminous purple surrounded by a plasma of magenta glow. A string of them shot up, then slowly came apart, drifting through the sky like fireworks that had forgotten to explode. For a while I wondered if these *were* some strange new fireworks—could India already have won the war? Perhaps if I watched long enough, they would bloom in plumes of orange, white, and green, to shower the country below.

Then the guns started. Shadows jumped and the outlines of buildings reverberated in white. The skies lit up as if from sheet lightning flashing through the night. "The Pakistanis, they've come," you cried out. "They're going to throw bombs on us." You turned to me, horrified. "Daddy. I didn't stop him. He's outside."

"Daddy can take care of himself," I began to reply, as you darted into the bedroom. "Ashvin," I shouted. "Stop, didn't you hear what I said?" But it was too late. You ran out of the flat, leaving the door open to the corridor outside.

I raced after you. I had to slow down on the staircase, which was dark—I could hear your feet stumbling down the steps ahead. People were milling around on the pavement, pointing to the sky, watching the aerial events as nonchalantly as a shooting star display. "Ashvin!" I cried out as you dashed out on the road to avoid the crowd.

An oncoming Impala almost ran me over as I stepped onto the road myself. I saw your figure ahead, zigzagging between the cars that had heeded the regulation to stop. Every few seconds, you glanced up into the night as if to keep a lookout for bombs. "Daddy will be fine," I kept calling out, even though I knew you wouldn't look back. "Let's go home—he's probably waiting for us, wondering where we went."

Another car emerged from the maze of motionless vehicles on the road, blinking its painted-over headlights at me as it careened past. The sound of the antiaircraft guns was almost constant now—their echoes bouncing off the building façades. In the sky, the orbs still hovered, peering down at us like purple eyeballs.

Something flamed down from the sky and crashed ahead in front of my eyes. People scattered, but I charged towards it, mindful only of you. By the time I got there, a knot of onlookers had cautiously advanced to watch. A metal tube, still smoking, lay punched into the road. Someone said one of the purple lights had crashed down from the sky, another claimed it was an unexploded bomb.

Peeping in waist-high between two of the men, I saw your face. Instantly I was upon you, grabbing onto your shirt, your belt, your arms, so you couldn't get away. I tried to lead you homeward, but you caught hold of a lamppost and struggled to break free. "I have to find Daddy, let me go," you yelled.

There was a whistling sound, and then something smashed behind us. A man lay bloodied on the pavement, a woman sat screaming beside him. An instant later, an even louder sound, almost a shriek, filled the air. As we watched, the cigarette shack at the corner of Lamington Road seemed to burst in two.

Suddenly projectiles were falling all around. While most people ran, some stood rooted to the ground, staring at the orb-dotted heavens, waiting, it seemed, to be struck. I dragged you into a building, and we huddled in the vestibule together with others who had ducked in for refuge. "Ram, Ram," the building watchman chanted, but his voice was drowned out by the clanging of fire brigade trucks.

There was a window high above the door, through which I could see the outside. The night seemed smokier than before, faraway flashes still flared out of sight. A purple light meandered across the window frame, followed by another. I imagined the heavens flowering in bursts of color, rockets exploding up high. Gandhi appearing beside me in the vestibule to remind me of my destiny, pointing once more at the sky.

Then I heard you crying softly to yourself in the darkness. I lifted you up and pressed my mouth to your cheeks. The clanging and sirens faded into the background as my lips encircled your tears. The sky remained unadorned by fireworks, the vestibule ungraced by Gandhi. It didn't really matter what happened to the world, I thought, my destiny was safe in my arms.

chapter

twenty-five

FIFTY PEOPLE WERE HOSPITALIZED THAT NIGHT, TWENTY OF THEM JUST from Lamington Road. Many more sustained injuries all over the city. A woman died in Matunga, two boys lost their eyesight watching the spectacle from their balcony, and a man was hit on the terrace of a building in Sewri ("He gave his life defending the country," a neighbor declared). Several eyewitnesses reported sightings of enemy planes—one had them swooping in from Marine Drive, another swore they almost crashed into the skyscrapers on Malabar Hill, before swerving just in time. These reports all went unsubstantiated. The actual explanation came later—a short circuit triggered off a false alarm which resulted in the deployment of the antiaircraft guns. The mysterious purple lights that lured people out were tracers sent up to scan the skies. What rained down on the spectators to maim and kill them were empty Indian shells, not Pakistani bombs.

Dev was not one of the victims of the falling fragments. He was killed on the bridge leading towards Bombay Central well after the all-clear siren, according to the police officer who came to our door the next morning. Someone had noticed him minutes earlier, singing along the middle of the road, his arms open as if raised in welcome to the stars. "What with the dark shirt he was wearing, and no streetlamps or headlights, neither he nor the taxi driver must have seen each other," the officer said. "You should go claim the body today from Nair Hospital. It'll be harder once they send it on to the municipal morgue."

The officer left, and I stood there, too shocked to close the door. You emerged from your hiding place in the bathroom. "Did the policeman tell you where Daddy went?"

ZAIDA PULLED ME through the morning. The war had caused a nine-hour delay for trunk calls booked to Delhi, so she sent telegrams instead. She told me to change my orange sari, reminding me gently that it was white for mourning. You sat dry-eyed in her lap in the hospital waiting room while I went to identify Dev. Given the uncertainty of wartime transport, and the fact that the remains were supposed to be cremated within a day, there seemed little point in waiting for anyone to try and make it from Delhi. She arranged for the body to be driven to the crematorium at Marine Lines, and we followed in a taxi.

You had not cried at all since hearing the news. Each time I hugged you and you didn't react, I felt the anguish in my chest. Would you blame me for your father's death?—even worse, would you blame yourself?

You stared at the fence of the Queen's Road park going by, with the sculptures of the tortoise and the hare fable, the fox and the stork. A boy climbed to the top of the metal sputnik, as you had done so many times yourself. I caught a glimpse of him sliding down the pole in the center, heard the laughter of his parents encouraging him on. "Ashvin," I said, but you kept looking intently out the window, your hands clasped around the edge of the glass.

We passed by the long wall with the crudely painted signs for rat poison and table fans, the absurdly muscled torso of Dara Singh advertising a wrestling match. Behind, I knew, lay the burning ghats. As our taxi crept along, a procession of men with a corpse held aloft proceeded up the pavement next to us. The face was withered, the body shrunken and decked with flowers—people danced and beat drums to celebrate a life lived so long.

When I had seen Dev earlier in the hospital, the sheet had draped peculiarly over his body, as if his chest was slumped in underneath. As we entered the chamber with the raised concrete platform on which he lay, I saw that the shroud and the flowers made him appear uncrushed again. You went running between the chairs and mounted the steps to the dais—for a moment, I thought you were going to throw yourself across the body. But you stood staring at the closed eyes and the cotton peeking out of the nostrils, and made no attempt to touch your father.

"Is this your babuji?" the priest Mrs. Dugal had hired softly asked. With his black-framed glasses and untrimmed beard, he had more the air of a poet than a pundit. "Come, let's have you wash your hands and your feet," he said, and took you by the arm to the adjoining room. I sat down uncertainly between Zaida and Mrs. Dugal, thinking that I should have kept your socks and your shoes. About a dozen chairs in the rear were occupied by people who looked like they might have wandered into the wrong funeral—I had no idea who they were.

When you returned, I got up to join you on the platform, but the priest motioned for me to stay where I was. "There are some things that have to be done alone in this world," he said, "and it is to the son that this duty falls." I sat back and watched anxiously, as if you were about to perform the leading part in a school play.

It was the ghee that made you cry. You followed all the priest's directives capably until then—repeating the mantras after him, sprinkling the body with sesame and dates, replacing the sprig of basil in Dev's mouth each time it fell out. Even the ghee, you managed to squeeze out of its bag as instructed, first over one eye, then the other, then the mouth, and the remainder over the heart. But you began to shake when you stood back to look at the thick white puddles, spilling over from Dev's eyes as if he was crying streams of molten wax. The priest pried the empty bag out of your clenched fingers as you broke into convulsive sobs.

Zaida restrained me from flying up to the stage and sweeping you into my arms. Already the priest was moving you on to the next ritual. He set a shovel on the floor above Dev's head and asked you to sprinkle it with water. Still gasping, you lifted the earthenware pot he gave you and brought it down on the blade.

The pot smashed as it was supposed to, sending pieces clattering across the floor. A few spun over the edge of the platform—one of them struck me lightly on the foot. Your gasps subsided into a steady weeping as the priest's incantations rose to fill the chamber. The only word I recognized from his stream of Sanskrit was "moksha"—I tried to form a picture in my mind of Dev's body liberating his soul.

After dragging the bamboo staff around the body, you sprinkled the red and vermilion powders and completed the last of the prayers. Then you fit your head in the curve between your father's chest and chin and lay there, closing your eyes and pressing against his neck. Sesame seeds stuck to your cheek, the streams of ghee melted into your hair. I had seen you so many times in this position, balancing contently on Dev's chest, as he read to you, sprawled out on the sofa or bed. The priest eased you up and handed you the final offering of a garland.

One by one, the audience members got up to also lay flowers—the Dugals, the Hussains, Zaida, and the two musician friends of Dev she had managed to contact. The people at the back of the room remained seated—an old man, I noticed, had fallen asleep with his mouth open. I stood on the dais, holding a string of marigolds. Should I fall at Dev's feet, weeping and refusing to let go, the way widows in movies behaved? I remembered the stories of wifely devotion that Biji used to relate— Savitri arguing with Yama, Sati immolating herself when her husband Shiva was insulted. How many women had actually followed Sati through the ages?—thrown screaming into the pyre, or love ushering them voluntarily into the flames?

But I was unable to even bring myself to touch Dev. I tried to recall him from the first time we had met, the allure in his smile, the chest hair curling provocatively into a snake. But it was difficult to look past the rivulets of ghee now, the basil in his mouth, the smears of vermilion and red, the sesame dotting his face. It was as if death had transformed him from a living, breathing person into a temple shrine at which offerings were made.

And now the bamboo mat on which Dev lay had been carried into the furnace chamber. The furnace door opened to paint Dev's forehead gold and give the flowers on his chest the same tint. Two attendants heaved at a lever to push the pallet on which Dev's mat had been laid. As I bent forward, the pallet hit the ridge of the furnace opening and came to an abrupt stop. The impact sent Dev sliding on his bamboo mat head-first onto the slab inside the furnace. He lay there unmoving, his face upturned, his arms by his sides, as if holding his breath in an X-ray machine. Then the furnace door began closing and I heard the whoosh of flame. I bent down lower, to catch one last glimpse of Dev, to see the inside of the womb that had swallowed him. The walls were a brilliant orange, the air was beginning to scintillate, and for an instant, I saw myself inside, reclining in the fire next to him.

WE COLLECTED THE ASHES the next morning. The attendant who took my receipt referred to them as "flowers." My first thought was to open the iron box and look inside for some sign to confirm they were Dev's. But I kept the thin white gauze cover on and gave you the box when you asked to carry it.

Mrs. Dugal had declared that one must travel to Nasik or some other holy spot for the final immersion. "You can take Ashvin with you and stop at all the temples to make a pilgrimage of it." When I pointed out that it was Chowpatty where Dev was fond of immersing his weekly pooja offerings, she laughed. "The water around Bombay is so impure that even fish, before they expire, try to slither away."

The priest said that water was water, and anything that connected to the ocean was equally holy. "If you think it would have made him happy, then feed a cow an apple or a banana every day for a week afterwards. Otherwise, simply send him to his next life with joy in your heart."

I suppose I should have waited to hear what rituals Dev's family wanted to have performed. Both Arya and Hema were arriving the next day on the Frontier Mail—the telegram had been delivered before we left. But something within me insisted that the ceremony be more per-sonal, that the two of us immerse the ashes at Chowpatty ourselves.

The Americans had just condemned India at the UN for instigating the war, and there were thousands of people rallying at Chowpatty against them. I had the taxi take us to Nariman Point instead, at the other end of Marine Drive. The first time I had come here was fifteen years ago with Dev, right after we moved to Bombay. I remembered how we had walked past the point where the buildings ended, until we stood at the very edge of the newly reclaimed land. Since then, the reclamation had encroached a lot further into the sea, with several construction sites strewn with trucks and cranes. We walked past the newly completed Air India building, and next to it, the five-star Oberoi hotel still being built.

The day was warm and sunny, the sky untroubled by enemy planes. The bay stretched out on our right, the waves lapping against the shore tastefully, as if in a watercolor. The road ended as abruptly as it had fifteen years ago, the pavement suddenly giving way to a mass of the ubiquitous tetrapods tumbling down to the water. Where was the spot where Dev and I had paused, to listen for the sea thundering below, to imagine the first Portuguese ships sailing in?

"There are so many seagulls here," you said worriedly. "Will it be safe to empty the box?" We were standing at the base of a set of rocky slabs that led to the water's edge. I had taken the box from you so that you could better keep your balance. Every once in a while a wave bobbed gently over the lowermost step.

"They won't bother us. The important thing is that the water should carry Daddy away." I bent down with the box. "Here, take the gauze off and let it go." The wind plucked the covering from your hand the instant you released it.

You hadn't spoken much since the cremation. At night, you had insisted on sleeping on your father's favorite sofa, burying your face in the pillows as if trying to breathe him in. I crept in several times to carry you to the empty space next to me in bed, but you were always awake. Finally, I sat on the sofa myself and spent the night cradling your head. At dawn, you raised your head from my lap, suddenly alert. "You weren't crying like Dugal auntie was. Aren't you sad that Daddy is dead?"

"Of course I am," I managed to reply. "But sometimes grown-ups get so sad that they can't even cry."

I tried now to muster the tears that would comfort you, but they did not come. The vow to never cry again, from the day I married Dev, still held me in control. You uncovered the box to reveal the fine gray ash inside. Mixed in were long black filaments of carbon and bone fragments bleached white. All I could think of, even with the streams flowing down your face, was how comfortably the contents filled the contours of the box. To be purified this way, to end up so compact—it was what I would want for myself when I was dead.

The wind picked up and some of the ash blew out. Perhaps it was Dev, trying to pull my attention to him. *Remember the time when I first held your gaze? Think, Meera, think, was I really so bad? Did you wish me to die, is this the way you wanted it to end?* I tried to match the voice to an image in my head. My eyes remained dry, my tears unshed. There was never a time when I had wished this, I could honestly reply. *Think, Meera, think, the life that you led.*

I still held the box, but now your hand pulled urgently on my wrist. "Mummy," you said, and I could see you wanted to immerse the ashes yourself. For an instant, I hesitated—wasn't this the duty of the wife as well? But then I relinquished my claim. You clambered across the rocks, the box pressed to your chest. I saw you close your eyes and fold your palms in prayer. The words were too far away to hear. I knew you wanted your privacy, so I forced myself to look away.

How many times must Dev have performed his Thursday afternoon immersions? The shriveled sweet limes from his cupboard temple, the dried flowers, the ash from his incense. Sometimes a piece of fruit or stale chappatis we weren't going to eat also added to the brown bag. Once, even an idol of Sai Baba that broke in half, an expensive wristwatch which failed to work after the first month. "It all goes back to the ocean, just like Ganesh," he would tell you. "The sea goddess knows how to fix the things we return this way." He would touch the bag to your head and mine in blessing, and sometimes take you to Chowpatty with him. I never saw him actually throw the bag in. Would he do it from the edge of the waves, or toss it down from the road rising up to Walkeshwar? *It wasn't that I never took you, Meera—you never came.*

When I turned around finally, you were standing at the lowest level of the rock, the box held poised. A wave skimmed over your shoes, leaving a gray line of wetness on your socks. You tipped the box halfway, and a cloud of ash fell out, swirling back to encircle you in its embrace.

A few of the filaments wafted all the way to where I stood, spinning like seed husks through the air.

You stood there for a few moments, watching the ash settle over the ripples and be carried away by the current. Then, in one movement, you turned the container upside down. A cascade of ash came billowing out. And with it the fragments of bone, white and gleaming, that tumbled towards the water like seashells returned to the ocean.

THAT NIGHT, YOU SLEPT next to me. For a while, you felt guilty about not being able to doze off on the sofa, like your father used to on so many nights. "Do you think Daddy will mind?" I assured you that your sleeplessness was only because it was a little chilly outside.

You had shown little reaction to anything since we had come back from Nariman Point. I tried to interest you in your aunt and uncle arriving the next day, but you didn't brighten up. Zaida brought over a bowl of your favorite dessert, rice kheer, but you hardly touched it. Even Pinky appeared at the door (bearing, of all things, a kite), but you refused to see her. You sat on the balcony all evening, your chin resting on the railing, and stared outside.

You know how much I loved him. You know I would have died for him. Is that why you tried so hard to keep us apart? Is this what you wanted, Meera, are you satisfied?

I hadn't been able to turn off Dev's voice. He had whispered to me all day, in tones alternately reproachful and benevolent, sometimes telling me how much I had misunderstood him, sometimes reminding me how dependable he had been as a father. It was as if the phantom within me had departed, appeased, and Dev had taken over instead, determined to revamp my feelings towards him. *Did you know how much you meant to me? Do you miss me now that I'm gone? Don't be sad, Meera, I don't want you to feel regret at all.*

Already Dev's image was starting to acquire a dignified sepia tone, the edges all smoothed, the blemishes airbrushed out. Was this what happened when people died? What would the picture look like after a few weeks, or a few months? People coming around to tell me what a martyr he was, no one aware of the injustice I had borne? Who was to say that in time even I would remember any of the wrong? The memories of our better moments together welling over everything else?

It's the best way, Meera, believe me. Not only for you, but for Ashvin as well. Something for him to cling on to, something for his memory. You emitted a soft sound from your throat as if sympathizing with your father in your sleep.

It wasn't as if I was glad that my husband had passed, I felt like protesting. I would bring him back in an instant if I could, if not for myself, then certainly for my son. Everything was still too raw, too new; there would be time enough for grief to come. *Understand, Meera, I'm not blaming you. All the years for Munna to grow—I just wish I could have remained around.*

Somewhere, the empty pages of an album flapped open. There were entire sections that would have to be filled now by the two of us alone. How would I pull us through, playing the role of both a mother and father? To whom would I turn if I couldn't do it all? *It's not going to be easy, Meera, you being the only one.*

But then, I came upon an unexpected clearing in my mind. What if I were to accept what had happened as an opportunity bestowed upon me? To view Dev's death not as a tragedy, but as a bequest. The bequest of freedom, of liberation, to bring you up exactly as I thought you should be. Without the pressure or influence that would constrain you into following in his footsteps.

I remembered the first time Dev had related the Ganesh story to you. About how Shiva kept refusing Parvati's pleas to give her a child, how lonely she felt each time he became an ascetic and escaped married life. Hadn't she gone into the forest and created a baby herself? Mixed together sandalwood paste and bath oil and flakes from her own body, fashioned the son she was molding just the way she wanted him to be? So enchanting was her creation, so perfect for her needs, that she soon forgot all about Shiva, as she frolicked through the days in her son's company.

Could this be my invitation to mold you just as Parvati had done? Affirm my motherhood in the coming years as joyously as her? Hadn't

I always known that you would be the promised one? Entrusted to you the key to my future even before you were born?

A siren wails somewhere in the distance. You stir, as if trying to decide whether to remain asleep or heed its sound and awake. "It's okay," I whisper. "I'm right here." I pull you closer to myself.

PART FOUR

chapter
twenty-six

THEY SAY ONE PASSES THROUGH FOUR STAGES OF MOURNING AFTER bereavement, or perhaps it is five. My experience was different. In the weeks after Dev's death, I found myself seized by a keenness of mind, a lucidity, that I had not known before. I felt as if a wind had blown in from the ocean to clear away the cloudiness lingering for years. I remained oblivious to the workings of the world beyond, to the battlefield successes of Indira Gandhi, or her liberation of East Pakistan. But within my own sphere, everything seemed to intensify—sounds becoming sharper, colors more vivid, smells more pungent, as if I had suddenly acquired the faculties of a feline. I felt capable of absorbing the broad sweep of my life in a glance, of springing nimbly across the chasm between the future and the past. My powers of concentration seemed so enhanced that I might have solved algebra problems in my head had I tried.

I did, in fact, perform several mathematical calculations, as I appraised our fiscal condition. I pored over passbooks and records and the jumble of receipts that Dev had stuffed under the mattress over the years. Just after you were born, Paji secretly took out an insurance policy on Dev for one lakh and twenty thousand rupees with me as the beneficiary. Undoubtedly, he meant to use it someday as another hold on me, not knowing that the company had mailed us a copy of the statement by mistake the first year. My mind raced as I imagined a future free of financial worry—I could invest the money in the government's Unit Trust, we could subsist off the interest, I wouldn't have to go back to Delhi to live with Paji (as Mrs. Dugal had already started suggesting). It was true my father still had the flat in his own name, but even he wouldn't dare press this to his advantage against a widowed daughter.

With the racing of my mind came an increase in energy as well. I scrubbed the floors and washed the walls, even dragging a chair into the bathroom to rub the stains off the ceiling with a rag. I emptied the cupboard of all of Dev's clothes, sorting them into neat bundles of underwear and shirts and pants. Then it felt unseemly to be giving them away so soon, so I put them all back. I collected his comb, his toothbrush, his shaving set from the toilet, and stored these in a separate box. I even found myself dismantling his pantheon of gods—you looked so stricken that I simply gave each idol a good dusting instead.

Interspersed with these bursts of manic activity came bouts of guilt. Could I have prevented Dev's death? Wasn't my inability to love him enough what really killed him? And now that he was gone, why was I in such a rush to get on with the rest of my life? What evanescent delights did I expect to be waiting around the corner for someone like me, someone who had just established her own unworthiness? I stared at myself in the mirror every morning, at my eyes inflamed with sleeplessness.

Sandhya appeared behind my reflection in the mirror, offering words of comfort. "Believe me, Didi, you loved him quite a lot, even if you didn't know it yourself. It's only natural to keep so busy that you don't have time to face regret. But you must find the sorrow inside and let it out, not be so hard on yourself." I wanted to tell her that I couldn't afford the luxury of following her advice. I couldn't risk being immobilized by grief when what you needed was my strength.

I found it calming to play the roles others had scripted for me. I ushered mourners into the drawing room and served them subdued cups of tea. I acknowledged condolences from the vegetable hawkers with a silent nod of my head. Wherever I went, whomever I met, I learnt to hide the frenzy I felt. When Hema and Arya finally arrived (three days late due to war-related delays), I met them at the station, dressed irreproachably in widow's white.

Although I submitted dutifully to the mourning ceremonies Arya organized, drama and unpleasantness broke out at the end. Hema threw herself across the flowers and the urns and the pooja paraphernalia as if it was Dev's body underneath. "Come back," she loudly wept, "come back for one last glimpse. For your sister to feed you one more time with her hands, to tie one last rakhi on your wrist." As Arya helped her up, she suddenly turned on me. "First you snatch him away from us and bring him here to Bombay, then you kill him? Even his ashes you couldn't wait to get rid of, has your thirst been finally slaked?"

She apologized at the railway station, as we waited for the train to depart for Delhi. "He taught me to play marbles. I would cheat, and he would let me, pretend not to notice. I was so terrible in those days—always hiding shoes, dropping freshly ironed clothes into buckets of water, stealing schoolbooks and pencils and whatever I could get my hands on. Arya would chase after me with a cricket stump, but Dev would just shrug it off. I was always his little Hemali—do you know he used to make up a new song for my birthday every year?" She rested her head against the window of the train. Light filtered down on her face, erasing the pounds to make her look ten again.

"Tell me," Hema said, and now the innocence in her eyes was replaced by something more worldly. "All these white saris you've been wearing—is this how you're going to dress for the rest of your life?" She leaned forward, and behind her, I saw the silhouette of Arya's figure on the adjoining seat. He was reading the Ramayana as part of the rites he had undertaken to complete for Dev. All through the duration of the visit, he had been scrupulously proper, dignified—I couldn't have faulted his behavior if I'd tried. He had taken you on long walks to Chowpatty, to three different temples, and even, upon your insistence, to Dadar, in an unsuccessful attempt to locate Dev's guruji. You had been so upset at his departure that you refused to come to the station. "There's Ashvin to consider, too, after all," Hema whispered, as if able to peer into my mind.

Before she could connect the dots any further, the whistle blew. Hema squeezed my fingers tightly through the bars as from behind her, Arya nodded succinctly to me. Then the train started moving, and Hema's face, with its round mixture of mourning and curiosity and childish intrigue, started receding. I stood on the platform and watched it grow smaller and smaller, until it melded into the blur of the compartment wall. Too late, I realized that my sari had been blown off to my shoulders, and lifted the white edge to drape it befittingly over my head.

I DIDN'T WEAR MY AURA of widowhood at home. My regalia of white protected me in public, but I shed it as soon as we were alone. Could you have interpreted my self-preservation as duplicity, is it why you became so reluctant to tell me what you were going through? Day by day I saw you become more distant, retract further into your carapace of grief.

I poured my newfound energy into trying to coax you out. I wooed you with Mickey Mouse and Donald Duck, but it became clear they no longer held you in their thrall. I recruited Pinky to entice you with her games of rope, but she gave up when you didn't respond. Even Zaida couldn't get through—you rebuffed both her offer to make your face up and to play her Beatles records. You went to school every morning and came back in the afternoon silent and withdrawn. "Ashvin needs to talk to the other children," your first standard teacher called me in to say.

It was only natural for you to need time to make peace with Dev's death, I told myself. Hadn't I experienced your awkwardness firsthand, when on Parents' Day I was the only mother from your class to show up without a husband? But as the months went by, your self-isolation did not diminish—it seemed only to intensify. You stood alone on the balcony and stared at the traffic for hours on end. You bolted to your hiding place in the bathroom each time the doorbell rang. "He still refuses to make friends," was the remark in your April report card.

Hema's husband Gopal popped in one morning to pay us a visit on his way to Poona. You scurried into the bathroom upon hearing the bell. After seating him, I knocked on the door to insist you say hello, but you had sneaked out by then. I found you in the bedroom, in a picture-perfect pose of sleep, complete with deep, even inhalations and a sheet drawn up to your neck. No matter how much I tried, you wouldn't get up to say hello—when I shook you, you snored in response. "No need to rouse him," Gopal finally called from the other room—you awakened just after he left.

There was one silver lining to your shyness, which I felt a twinge of guilt about. If you refused to interact with others, the bond between us had to grow.

You began the second standard in June, when you were seven. Even though the monsoons were failing in great swaths of the country, Bombay, paradoxically, endured some of its most ferocious downpours. The sky ranged in mood from petulant to raging, battering the city with sudden torrents even while pretending to be on the verge of letting the sun emerge. The ganga claimed she had seen the new skyscrapers at Nariman Point actually sway in the winds from the Arabian Sea. Tardeo flooded repeatedly, as did Nana Chowk and Gowallia Tank—trains stopped running, cutting off the suburbs completely. I bought you a pair of gum boots to negotiate the water flowing through the streets, but it swirled easily over the rims and filled them to the top.

You loved this wet tromping, smiling for perhaps the first time in months. I looked away immediately—had you caught me, you might have pulled down a curtain of gloom on your delight. The next morning, the school bus didn't show, and we had to walk to the BEST bus stop. You sloshed along at my side, your boots getting heavier with each step. "Wait," you cried periodically, stopping to empty them one by one. The next morning you even wore socks, just so you could squeeze them out when they got waterlogged.

On the worst day of flooding, our double-decker BEST bus got stuck at Nana Chowk. Usually the drivers would barrel through recklessly, trying to generate the largest possible waves to douse the pedestrians wading along the sidewalks. But a momentary lapse of nerve had thwarted our driver—the engine died and water came streaming in across the floor of the bus. "Look, it's covering my feet!" you exclaimed—precisely the reason why you had hedged against riding on the upper deck this morning. Outside, the water stood so high that I had to convey you to safety on my shoulders like the mothers of the other schoolchildren. "That woman's carrying her daughter so fast," you said, trying to spur me on in a race. One of your rubber boots came off—the bus conductor managed to grab it as it floated past.

A protracted volley of thunder broke out, like long and roaring laughter at my idea of taking you to school. The wind picked up, shooting bullets of rain directly into our faces. You shrieked as the wave from a more intrepid bus almost knocked us over. "Let's go all the way home piggyback like this," you proposed. But by now I was wobbling under your weight, and had to set you down.

Miraculously, the sidewalk vendor occupied his usual spot by the Irani hotel—perched on a stack of crates, huddled under a sheet of plastic, but still selling his wares. I bought you twenty paise worth of sugarcane. You tromped along happily through the shin-high stream of water, biting into the segments and watching the chewed-out fragments get swept away. We even stopped at the wall near Bhatia Hospital to search for snails. You had started a collection, storing them in a tiny old aquarium with an ill-fitting lid which Zaida had once used to hold goldfish, feeding them scraps of vegetable peelings retrieved from the trash bin. Today, however, they seemed to have decided not to wait around to be captured in the driving rain.

At home, you refused to get out of your wet clothes. "I want to go downstairs again to search some more for snails."

It had been so long since I had seen you in such high spirits that I relented. "But first you have to have something warm to drink."

"I think I need coffee to warm me up today," you informed me gravely, knowing I never allowed it to you, unlike Dev. We settled on Ovaltine and I went into the kitchen to warm the milk.

When I returned with the glass of Ovaltine, I could see your mood had changed. You were sitting in front of your snail aquarium, watching one of the captives try unsuccessfully to escape. As it explored the gap between the lid and the case, you pushed it with a pencil, so that it fell down to the bottom again. Instead of a smile, your expression was bleak, pinched.

I tried drawing you to myself but you were stiff with resistance. "Look at how brown Mummy's clothes have become," I said, hoping to distract you with the mud on my sari from the water I had waded through. But you didn't turn around, even when I attempted a kiss— you kept jabbing the pencil through the gap in the aquarium top again and again.

Wrestle with him, Dev whispered from nowhere. *He'll like that, Munna will.*

I hadn't heard Dev's voice since the days right after his death. He would have simply grabbed you from behind, locked your shoulders in an arm hold, twisted your body to the floor to sit on you. Why did these maneuvers seem so awkward for me to perform, so forward, so inappropriate, so masculine? How could I be both your mother and father if something as innocuous as wrestling made me hesitate?

I imagined rolling around in the heat of the bout, your thighs encircling my neck or my knees around your waist. What if clothes got torn, if flesh spilled out, if there was bare skin? And yet, wasn't it only a few years ago, when you clambered across my body to feed from the nipple of your choice? When I stood you up naked to dance your tiny feet across my belly and clap your hands in the air?

"We're going to wrestle, you and I," I announced, in a tone I hoped sounded playful. I grabbed your legs to swing you around, but my own legs came in the way. When I attempted to lock you under my body, you offered so little resistance that I rolled right over. You lay on the floor, your face turned to the ceiling, your arms limp and splayed.

"Don't you want to wrestle with Mummy?" I asked. "Come, it will be fun." I knocked with my knuckles against the door of your chest, like I'd seen Dev do. In reply, you began to cry. Soft tears at first and then sharp convulsing sobs that thrust deep within my soul.

I took you, still crying, into my lap. You turned over to hide your face in my leg. I draped my muddied sari over the two of us like a tent. The Ovaltine cooled silently on the table, thunder sounded periodically outside. I kept my body curled tightly over yours, rocking you ever so slightly, waiting for your tears to be spent.

Afterwards, I threw away the Ovaltine and made some coffee

instead. We sat together on the floor, tented again in my sari, and alternated sips from the cup. When it was empty, and you had licked the rim clean, we went into the kitchen to look for some dinner for your snails. The spinach was all gone, and there were no leaves left on the cauliflower, so I peeled some carrots into a plate.

We watched the snails together all evening, leave behind their glistening wakes as they crawled along. You attached each one to a carrot strip, then put your ear to the glass—to hear them chew, you said. "Will their caca be orange tomorrow?" you asked, just before going to bed.

BY THE END OF JULY, the monsoon was still setting records in Bombay, even though many regions of the country teetered on the brink of a drought. A cartoon in the *Times of India* showed a man drowning in the rain from a solitary cloud hanging over him, while all around, people crawled about with bulging eyes and parched tongues. "Why don't you come to Delhi to get away from it?" Paji suggested. "It's 1972, remember—they're having a special ceremony for twenty-five years of independence at the Red Fort. With all the money I've been donating to the Congress Party, they had better give me seats in the box reserved for Indira Gandhi herself."

I recognized this as another of Paji's efforts to resettle me in Delhi. He had been tactful and restrained in his campaign, making his first attempt only a full four months after Dev's passing. I had parried all his invitations. I knew I needed time to be alone, and didn't want to risk being sucked in by venturing too close. I also wanted to decide first on how to proceed with the insurance policy. Should I confront him with it, or should I leave the money untapped, in reserve? Right now, Paji took care of all our needs with the check he sent every month. Wasn't there a danger in making a demand for the money—that he might use the excuse of my self-sufficiency to cut off all future assistance?

As it turned out, my response to Paji's latest invitation was determined by something totally unrelated. While cleaning the aquarium, I forgot to replace the lid, allowing most of the snails to escape.

The first inkling of the getaway came when I sat on one of them. It had somehow dragged itself all the way to the sofa to meet its doom, and made a soft crumpling sound, more felt than heard, under my weight. After that, we located snails all around the room—sometimes trailing slime along the edge of a book, sometimes clinging to shirts or underwear, but much too often by the telltale crunch when they perished underfoot. You became so distraught that you stopped talking to me. At night, you stalked away from bed—whisking the dusty covers off your old half-mattress in the corner of the room to lie down.

I pleaded for you to come back to bed, but you pretended to be asleep. I sat on the floor in the dark for more than an hour, but you did not relent. Finally, I got my pillow and stretched out on the tiles next to your mattress. When I awoke at dawn, you were lying curled up next to me on the floor, your head against my chest.

That day, I braved the rain all afternoon to search for snails while you were at school. There were none to be found at Bhatia Hospital, so I prowled around the neighborhood, sneaking into the building compounds to scour the walls. The watchman at Sheetal Towers came running up to shoo me away, but then joined in the search when I explained what I needed. By that evening, I had your aquarium stocked again.

Although you accepted the new brood, you remained wistful for the ones lost. Surely a week in Delhi would make a good apology, I thought, especially since it meant an unexpected week away from school. We left the aquarium with Zaida, who invented an excuse why you couldn't take it along. "Snails don't like being in a train because the rocking makes their caca get stuck," she said.

I packed only white for the trip—not to appease my in-laws, but for Paji's benefit. At the station, I noted with satisfaction his shock at seeing me dressed in the tradition of a widow. To his credit, he kept his dismay to himself. I had not seen him after Dev had passed, and he hugged me with a warmth I had not realized he could muster. "It's at times like this that I envy the believers among us," he said. "They can blame it all on God's will."

Biji had been checking the windows of the train on the other end of the platform. Arms outstretched, tears streaming, she walked, then ran towards me. "My Meera, my darling, how could life be so cruel?" she said, wrapping me in her embrace. "Already in white for your thirty-fifth birthday—it breaks my heart to see you in these clothes. Every morning I awake and think, what has life left you with?" She burst into full-fledged weeping, refusing to be consoled when I tried to convince her my fate wasn't quite that tragic.

I took you that very afternoon to Nizamuddin. A flock of maudlin feelings arose in my heart when I spotted the top of Salim Fazl's tomb from the taxi. The station itself was in the throes of renovation, new buildings being built and a sleek new bridge rising over the tracks. In the midst of the construction, the familiar garbage pile, with its obligatory attendant cow, had migrated to despoil a fresh wall.

Mataji had deteriorated as much as Hema had warned. Her left eyelid drooped, her mouth curled in on itself, her frame bent into a startling S shape with a pronounced central hump. She was surprisingly composed. "There's only so much sorrow one can show—I learnt that when Sandhya died. After a while, the tears simply take care of themselves—they learn to drop quietly inside. Still, I should have gone before Dev—it was a shock no mother should have to bear." A visible twitch ran through her body as she spoke her son's name.

She took us in to say hello to Babuji, who lay in a charpoy with his mouth open, his hands twisted at the wrists against his chest. "It's Meera," she called, as if shouting down a well. "Dev's wife. She's come from Bombay with your grandson." He did not respond. You pulled at my sari to get away from the smell of feces and urine. After all the care Babuji used to take to tighten the knots every week, the ropes of his charpoy were now depressingly slack. "Arya offered to hire a ganga to take care of him, but I refused. I'd lose the one focus of my life. All the time I have—what would I do with it?"

Mataji shuffled outside to the kitchen to make some tea. "Remember this?" she asked, pointing to the center of a row of blackened pots above the gas. I saw it was the pressure cooker from my dowry. "Hema wanted to take it when she married, she had been coveting it for years. But I told her it was to this house that it had come, and refused to give it up. Arya likes his mutton, so I still use it from time to time. He's been looking forward to seeing you both—he should be here very soon. It'll be good if you can get his mind off his aging parents for a while." She looked up at me, and I noticed her left lid no longer drooped as much, that the cloudiness in her eyes had cleared.

Fortunately, Arya showed up not alone, but with Hema. He had bought a car, a secondhand Fiat, and Rahul and Tony sat in the back. Everyone clustered around you—Hema kissing you repeatedly all over your face, Tony shaking your hand with grave formality, and Arya lifting you up into the air. Rahul darted around with his pea-shooting gun, taking aim without firing, at each person in turn.

Your cousins whisked you away to show you a pack of wolves they'd found living down the street. "Don't worry, they're only dogs—puppies, really," Hema said. She looked at me, then Arya. "I'll go help Mataji, let the two of you catch up."

The frown on Arya's face stopped her. "Why don't you show Bhabhiji where she can rest instead?" he said. "I'm sure she must be tired after her train."

Arya kept up his careful politeness towards me all that evening—in fact, through all the times I came over to Nizamuddin on my visit. Hema and Mataji made increasingly blatant comments about how he and I had each lost a spouse, but Arya ignored them, thwarting all their attempts to leave the two of us together alone. I was never sure if he was simply trying to make a good impression, or getting my guard down for some future ploy. He did convince me of one thing— the affection he showed you was genuine—you were his favorite of the nephews. I felt some concern about the times he took the three of you wrestling at the HRM pits. But Hema assured me the military exercises for the cadets were held in the morning, that this was strictly for play.

If Arya put a smile on your face, Tony transformed you. I took you to Nizamuddin every evening at your urging, and as soon as Tony came home from school, he walked over the half mile from where they lived. The two of you were very furtive about your games—with secret codes involved, and a mysterious hidden fortress somewhere. You didn't even take poor Rahul into your confidence—he spent the time hunting pigeons with his pea gun or sulking by himself. Tony started you on the hobby of collecting stamps, and you reciprocated, much to Hema's dismay, by teaching him about snails.

I succumbed one evening to my memories. Mataji sent me to buy coriander and I found my feet treading the well-remembered path to the tomb. I did not know what self-destructive urge led me there, what irresistible temptation the place held for me. Hadn't I come to grief on every occasion I had blundered onto its inauspicious grounds—the time I saw Roopa stretched out on the grass eight years ago, the time even earlier when I first sealed my fate with Dev? The bougainvillea grew thicker than I remembered it, obscuring most of the structure that lay beyond. My breath quickened as I pushed through—*Turn back,* I thought to myself, *don't venture in.* Why did I feel so certain there would be some malignant new discovery lying in wait within?

The walls inside were less adorned than I remembered them—even the last remaining tile fragments having been gouged out in the intervening years. The ground had been colonized by a shadow-loving plant of some sort—I kept brushing against its luxuriant fronds. I waded in as far as I could into the interior, as if immersing myself ritually in a river. Memories of Dev came swirling up from the darkness to greet me— would I stumble into the grave in which we had lain?

I heard a tinkling sound, like a coin being dropped, and came to a stop. Was there someone else besides me—could Dev have somehow returned in ghostly form? Suddenly the tomb was filled with his presence, his breath traversing audibly through the air, his eyes gazing at me unseen from somewhere. I took another step in—tendrils of vegetation rubbed insinuatingly against my legs.

And then they came charging at me, two shapeless apparitions bursting across the floor. I screamed, then turned and ran, but was felled before I could reach the door. A glint of silver rose above me, a mask came off each head. Tony waved his toy sword triumphantly in the air, "Nobody enters the fort without the secret password," you said.

THE EVENING BEFORE Independence Day, I came back from Nizamuddin to find my parents in the midst of a tremendous row. "Next time, I'm going to let them leave you in for a few nights with your hoodlums," Paji was saying. "To teach you that jail doesn't mean having tea and biscuits with the officers while you wait to be driven home in a limousine."

"They're not hoodlums," Biji shouted back. "They're college students from good families, with a conscience. They care about jobs and prices, they care about how your Indira Gandhi is ruining the nation."

"And you? Have you started caring about prices as well? Answer me this, Rohini, have you shopped for vegetables even once in your life?"

"I'm a zamindar's daughter—it's my duty not to be selfish, to not think only of myself."

Biji had gone that morning with a group of students from the college at which Sharmila taught to gherao the minister for home affairs. I was stupefied by this news—that Biji would participate in such a protest, with college students, no less. I imagined them surrounding their target, bringing all business to a standstill, shouting slogans and singing songs of resistance like Gandhiji had. There had been some puzzling references to student rallies in the letters Sharmila still wrote occasionally for Biji—could this have been what she meant?

"Last month it was to rail against foreign policy, and before that some crazy protest against nationalizing the insurance industry," Paji said, turning to me. "This hobby of politics she's suddenly developed at sixty—ask your mother if she even has an inkling what nationalization means. Always some knee-jerk reaction against Indiraji, always something to embarrass me. Doesn't she realize these people are taking advantage of her just because she's illiterate?"

Apparently the police had been waiting for the protestors, and drove them all in a van to the Kailash lockup. ("We sang 'Vande Mataram' the whole way," Biji proudly declared.) The Congress Party secretary for Delhi city personally phoned Paji. "He said there'd be no problem, nothing would enter the records or the press. The press, can you imagine, *the press*? They dropped her back here in a black Ambassador—I hope she realizes how much that ride is going to cost me."

"Yes, yes—he can give lakhs of rupees to put that woman back in office, but ask him to spend a few rupees on his wife and see how he screams."

Later, after Paji shut himself in his office and slammed the door, Biji explained how she had entered the realm of student politics. "For years, Sharmila's been observing how your father treats me—taunting me with names like 'Professor Rohini,' or 'Mother India,' or 'Darya Ganj Prime Minister,' beating down my every opinion just because I can't read. So your sister took upon herself the task to educate me—she labored for months to teach me to read." Biji shook her head. "Unfortunately, it's true what they say—once a dog's tail begins to curl, it can never be straightened. All the years I had resisted your father's attempts to educate me had left their mark—now even my own daughter was unable to succeed."

Paji's mocking grew worse once he learned about this failed attempt. "Wear it as a badge of honor," he told her. "Six months and you still can't spell your own name? That's wonderful!—surely it will prove to everyone you're still a zamindar's daughter."

Whereas before Biji could just shrug off his taunts, now they made her feel old and useless. "I knew I had to find a way to bite back at him to regain my confidence. Your father had just started sniffing around Indira Gandhi and her Congress Party, dreaming of a seat in Parliament. What easier course of action, I thought, than to come out in support of the opposition?"

Biji took to peppering her comments with praise for the Swatantra Party and the Jan Sangh, two groups she'd heard Sharmila mention. She vigorously criticized Indira's policies like the devaluation of the rupee, without the slightest understanding of what they meant. "Your Paji's reaction was infuriating—amusement and nothing else. He even offered to go over the opposition politicians with me so I would stop mixing up their names."

Biji's growing frustration prompted Sharmila to propose her curious scheme. She had seen the student group, armed with anti-Indira placards, waiting outside to use her classroom every Friday after her lecture. Being a professor herself by now, it wouldn't have looked right for Sharmila to sit in on one of their meetings. But she told them that her mother was very interested in learning more about the opposition and asked if they would mind having Biji come one day to attend.

"The first time your sister dragged me to the classroom, I was petrified. A sixty-year-old woman, unable to read or write, meeting with college students, no less! I wanted to climb the rows of the lecture room until I rose so high I was out of sight, perhaps into the arms of Krishna himself. But there were too many eyes watching my every move, so I tried to shrink into a corner of the first empty bench I could find.

"Don't ask me what they talked about—the Communists, most probably, were arguing as usual with those from the HRM. At the end, a girl remembered me and brought over some tea, saying, 'Here you go, Auntieji.' I'm not sure what gave me the courage to open my mouth, but I replied, Not *Auntie*, I'm old enough to be your *nani*. My words fell into a lull in the arguments, and the students all looked up and laughed.

"So I became their Naniji, their grandmother, their tea-drinking mascot, who began sitting faithfully through all their meetings. What more can I tell you about them? They're all quite muddled, even I can see—they spend half the time fighting with each other, and the rest plotting their protests. I'm not sure if they really want to change the world or simply rebel. At first I used to nod at everything, but now I've found that I can have some useful ideas as well. The Communists, especially, keep congratulating me—for rising on the behalf of the workers, they say, after the disgrace of being born to a zamindar family.

"And your father? He sulks a lot and blames me for killing his chances with the Congress Party, even though they were already quite dead. He's careful, though, not to challenge me so recklessly now. If I say that the price of onions has gone up or it's more difficult to get a job, he doesn't demand to know in which newspaper I've read that. He might even be a little scared of these grandchildren I've found—if he tries to press on me in any way, he knows I can retaliate."

PAJI WAS NOT HAPPY when he found that his seats for the Independence Day celebration were located at the furthest edge of the reserved section. To make things worse, he had been assigned hard wooden benches, not the cushioned chairs designated for VIPs, and even these were being occupied by people from the adjoining unreserved enclosure. Although the trespassers quickly fled in the face of Paji's red-faced rage, he sat there fuming afterwards. I wasn't sure which woman he blamed more for his diminished seating status—Indira Gandhi or Biji.

My mother had been quite clear she wouldn't be joining us this morning. "Isn't it bad enough that they bring in people by the truckful for all Indira's rallies? Why should I be one of her cheering masses just for some news documentary?" Instead, she planned to attend a party organized by her "grandchildren." "It's not only Indira who loves her country—the rest of us celebrate Independence Day too, you know. Tell your father it's nothing political—I'm not going to get arrested, so he won't have to pay this time."

When Indira took the podium, Paji simply sat there, refusing to clap. Instead, he muttered on about how he had been hoodwinked out of his seat. I thought he was being overly sensitive about our seating arrangement, but Sharmila whispered that he now meant the electoral district from which he was supposed to stand—the Parliament seat he maintained the Congress Party stole from him.

All around us the crowds stood and cheered, like extras on the set of some epic like *Mughal-e-Azam*. Indira waved back as the air force band started up, as helicopters dropped rose petals, as battalions of schoolchildren marched past. Thousands of color-coordinated balloons rose into the air, to form a giant aerial Indian flag. Finally, even Paji got up to applaud. After all, this was the leader who had united the country and carried it to such an overwhelming victory, something no one could deny. The papers had been full of how Hindus and Muslims had together restored the nation to its rightful glory, how secularism had triumphed, finally, decisively. "Let nobody ever say again that the Nehrus were wrong in their vision," one editorial proclaimed. The costs of the Bangladesh war were forgotten, the droughts all over the country somewhere far away. *The mother of the nation*, people had called Indira in the last election, and nothing could be truer, I thought, as I added my applause for the documentary films.

Afterwards, Paji tried to salvage what remained of his pride by taking us to the VIP enclosure, where they were serving tea and pakodas. He flashed his special Congress Party donor card, but the policeman standing at the entrance was unmoved. "Only a green VIP pass," he said. "Otherwise who knows what kind of people from the street we'd have to let in?"

Had Sharmila not been there, Paji would have surely gotten himself arrested (paying for his own release this time, instead of Biji's). He took a swipe at the policeman, and only her quick reflexes managed to deflect his hand and make him miss. As the calculations ground along on the policeman's face, she hustled our sputtering father away. A whistle blew behind us, but by then, the swarms of people had closed around us and we had blended in.

We returned home to a party in progress. Two college-age men chatted in the verandah with a woman holding a glass of orange squash. More youths stood around in the drawing room, boys on one side, girls in a row on the other, a platter of samosas on the table between them. "Have you met my grandchildren?" Biji asked, bustling in. "The college was closed for the holiday, so I invited them here instead." The servant handed Paji a samosa, and he looked at it, stupefied.

"How was the parade?" Biji asked. "Did your Paji get you in close enough to the goddess to touch her sari?"

For a moment, Paji kept staring at the samosa clutched between his fingers. Then he hurled it across the room at the server. To the accompaniment of Biji's screams, Paji started chasing people out—snatching the samosas from their mouths, knocking their glasses of squash to the ground. One of the boys called Paji a dirty capitalist—Paji pushed him so hard he went tumbling across the floor and rolled into the verandah. "This idiocy of yours has gone far enough," Paji shouted at Biji, once the room had cleared. "I never want to see these hooligans of yours again in my house."

"It's my house as well," Biji yelled back, and Paji strode up so close to her that for an instant I thought he meant to slap her.

Instead, he stared hard into her eyes, his face red and inches away. "Don't bring them here again, Rohini. I'm warning you." He turned on his heel and walked up the stairs to his office.

Biji glared after him. "It's my house as well," she shouted again, once he had slammed shut his office door.

—

PAJI MADE HIS PITCH to me the next morning. He started with the guilt-based approach. "You've seen what's happening to your mother. Going on her crazy protests, adopting those rascals as her own. Day by day she becomes more unhinged. And who can really blame her? When she has nobody to talk to, when her real grandchildren live hundreds of miles away. She should be hearing the word 'Nani' from Ace's mouth, not from those delinquents. I keep asking myself—what could we have done for Meera to insist on living alone so far away?

The carrot part of the campaign came next. "You've grown accustomed to the sea, that's fine, but we have the Jamuna here, and the Ganges isn't so far away. I'll get Ace into Model school—St. Xavier's in Bombay can't compare. I'm not going to push too much, because in the past you've punished me for speaking my mind. But a whole floor to yourself at home, a job whenever you ask—tell me, what else is there to say?"

When I didn't answer, Paji lunged into the final stage, to remind me he also carried a stick. "Sometimes I can't help but wonder what would happen to you if the checks from me stopped. If I fell ill, or suffered financially, or some other disaster occurred. I shudder to think how you would manage, how you would even find money for food." He made an attempt to visibly shudder, but it came out looking like a shrug.

"To tell you the truth, with Bombay prices so high, it isn't a bad time to sell the flat. It's quite an extravagance for me, you do realize—to run this household in Darya Ganj and pay for yours as well. Besides, I have to be fair to Roopa and Sharmila—there's a limit to what one daughter should expect. Don't get me wrong—I'm not saying anything for right this minute, that I'm stopping the checks."

"Actually, it's fine if you do, Paji. I found out about Dev's insurance policy—the company sent us a copy by mistake. One lakh and twenty thousand rupees, I think the notice said. If I invest the money, the interest should more than cover your check."

I had meant to be cautious, to not fling the policy in his face. Now that I had given in to the temptation, I savored the surprise around his mouth, the series of astonished blinks. He opened his mouth as if to contest what I had said, then closed it.

He found his voice soon enough. "It's been so long, Meera, but I really did mean to inform you about it. Your Paji's getting old—to have forgotten something like this. Except you don't really need it, you know—that's what I'm trying to say. If you come live with us, you won't have expenses anyway."

"I can think about it, Paji. Once the policy has been processed."

He made one last attempt as I left his office. "Why don't you let me hold it in reserve until Ace turns eighteen? I can even invest it for him if you like, make sure the money doesn't get frittered away."

BY THE TIME WE drove to the station on the last day of our trip, Paji had fully recovered from my discovery of the insurance policy. "Believe me, Meera—I'm glad that you have your independence now. You're all set financially, so no one can tell you where to stay. But you know as well as I do that there's no argument left for you to continue living in Bombay."

Biji, I could see, was trying hard not to cry—for once, she was in complete agreement with my father. "You've been away for far too long, Meera, and I don't know how many years remain for your parents. It's cruel of you to deprive us like this."

There was more campaigning at Nizamuddin station, where Arya managed to have the train make an unscheduled stop through Babuji's railway contacts. Even Mataji made it to the platform—as I hugged her, I could feel the individual bones leading up to the hump in her spine. "Go home, pack a bag, and come right back," she said. Arya raised you on his shoulders one last time, then swung you back onto the steps of the train. "Your Bombay adventure is over," Hema called out as the doors were closing. "It's time to return to the people who care."

As you played in the train with the other children in the compartment, I recalled the images I used to have of the Frontier Mail. Its engine thundering across the country, smoke billowing from its stack, the sound of its whistle—a call to freedom, to liberation—rallying through the air. I wondered when the rail line had first been laid—wasn't it in the previous century, under the British? I imagined laborers toiling under the sun to make the connection—digging the beds in the ground, filling them with rocks, laying down the slats, welding the rails in place. The line progressing from one center of the country to the other, mile by mile, village by village. The yellow mustard fields of the north, the desert millets grown in Rajasthan, the trading cities of Gujarat, the plateaus and the plains. How had they bridged the mighty rivers of the Tapti and the Narmada? How had they blasted through mountains that had been impassable for centuries? How many people had lost an arm or a limb, perished while trying to ford a river or dig a tunnel through a hill?

And what if they had never succeeded? The two cities never linked—no easy train connection for people to effect such momentous change? Or if the cities had ended up in two different countries—Bombay falling to Pakistan, say? I wouldn't be facing the dilemma now on where to live. In fact, there might never have been a bustling film metropolis by the ocean to lure Dev from Delhi in the first place.

Sometime during the night, I awoke as we went over a bridge. The rumble of wheels passing over the suspended rails reverberated from the chasm below. The engine sounded a single whistle, mournful and desolate, as if its promise of a new life had been defeated. You looked so vulnerable, so trusting, asleep in the berth next to me, bands of light cycling over your upturned face.

The next morning, the dusty, monsoon-deprived landscape dógging us all the way was gone, replaced by fields, green and wet, dotted with palm trees. Pockets of sea winked at us from the distance, as women standing on the shores of lagoons cast giant fishing nets through the air. One by one, the suburbs of Bombay started appearing, their names flashing by on wooden blocks of yellow and black. Jogeshwari, where Dev took his singing lessons, Bandra, where we'd gone to see Nawab Mohammed, Mahim, with its familiar smell of sulfur and low tide, Dadar, where Dev's guruji had lived. The buildings grew taller, the streets more crowded, the masticating cows and buffaloes gave way to buses and lorries and taxis. I watched the excitement build in your face, as you pressed against the bars of the windows as if trying to break free.

Suddenly Paji's offer seemed further away—wasn't it his control that I had spent my life trying to escape? And Arya—how long would it be before he used you to make a move on me—surely someone like him could not be trusted to change? It was true that you had seemed happier in Delhi, but taking a weeklong vacation was very different from living somewhere. Given that you had managed to perform well in school even with the trauma you had undergone, wouldn't uprooting you be risky at this stage?

A more troubling thought surfaced—how, if we moved in with Paji, would I keep him from taking over your life as well? His designs had already been plain on this visit—the way he tried to sabotage your daily temple trips with Biji, the toys he dangled as inducements to make you comply with his wishes. On Sunday, you had been teary and uncommunicative all day. I finally learnt that Paji had caught you praying in your room that morning, and unleashed one of his punishing silences—the kind I still remembered so vividly from my own childhood. "I know it's not even been a year, but have you thought about switching your name back to Sawhney?" he asked me that same evening. "That way, you could also change Ace's last name."

I knew I could never betray Dev in this way. Whatever our differences, Dev had always been a good father to you—I would not endanger this link, which Paji wanted to obliterate. As the last few stations before Bombay Central passed by, I began to feel a growing loyalty, an incipient tenderness towards Dev. I thought of how eager he had been to come to this city, what endless fascination the sea had held for him. Wouldn't this be where he would have liked you to grow up? To walk the streets he loved, to visit the temples at which he prayed, to take advantage of every opportunity he might have missed?

The train started slowing. The engine hissed and puffed into the terminus, its confidence restored, its whistle full of promise and cheer again. Even before we halted, the coolies came bursting in, swooping bedrolls off racks, fighting each other to carry bags. I looked through the window at the platform outside—Bombay, the black and yellow signs proclaimed.

chapter
twenty-seven

THE FIRST NIGHTMARE CAME IN SEPTEMBER. I AWOKE TO FIND YOU
flailing your arms beside me, calling to your daddy. I warmed you a glass
of milk and let you snuggle up tightly to me. When that didn't put you
to sleep, we played Ludo, followed by snakes and ladders, until you
finally dozed off at three.

The next week, the nightmare recurred; four nights later, it came
back again. You were so exhausted in the morning that I kept you home
from school that day.

Although I never quite determined what you saw, a guilty suspicion
began to grow within me. The words to which I gave wing on the day
Dev died had flapped around in my mind like bats ever since. Had they
found a way to burrow deep into your head as well, to hibernate? Could
they be haunting your dreams now, having, for some reason, been
stirred awake?

I still remembered my charges. That Dev was the father of another
child, one that had been in my belly but perished inside. Had I gone so
far as to accuse him of murdering your sibling? With all the emotion and
turmoil of that moment, could it have been something you had understood, retained?

Each time I thought about those odious utterances, my face colored with shame. Dread seeped into my stomach whenever you seemed pensive. It would be foolish to remind you of what I had said, to try and jiggle the dream out of your subconscious. All I could do was squeeze you to myself in bed, let the nightmares run their course. Which they did eventually, though the cure did not come easy.

It started with a single pimple at the center of your forehead, something so insignificant that I took it to be the bite from an insect. By that night, when your fever hovered around a hundred, the boils had spread all over your face. I went to the fourth floor and brought down Dr. Kagalwalla. "They're chicken pox—like mosquito bites, but bigger—from chickens," he teased. "Have you been bothering the chickens again? Don't worry, they'll go away—there's nothing to do but wait."

Mrs. Dugal suggested washing you with neem leaf water—you moaned weakly as I dabbed at the pustules. Oozing and angry, they covered every inch of your body—the roof of your mouth, the soles of your feet—even, incredibly, the tip of your shamey. "When did the chickens bite me?" you asked. "If they come when I'm sleeping, will you chase them away?" I assured you the boils had nothing to do with chickens, just the toxins in your body being cleansed. All the evil humors that had built up in the past unlucky year being drained.

A week later, I felt a pimple above my lip while applying cold cream to my face. It couldn't be, I thought to myself—hadn't Roopa given me chicken pox when I was eight? By the next morning, I found myself covered as well—I could barely swallow, or walk, or urinate. Dr. Kagalwalla reappeared, summoned by Zaida this time, to assure me that I couldn't pass it back to you again.

All that day, I screened my face from you, trying my best to keep you away. I imagined you horrified by my appearance, recoiling at my blisters—I didn't want you to carry around the image of a mother with an ugly face. Perhaps I could arrange for you to spend the night with Zaida—would her husband mind if you slept over for a few days? I lay by myself in the darkened bedroom, my mind feverish, my body aflame.

The door opened and you walked in, holding the Ludo board. "Do you want to play a game?"

"Mummy's not feeling well," I said, relieved that the room was dark enough to hide the unsightliness of my face. "She needs to rest."

You clambered onto the bed. "I could bring you my snails to look at then," you offered, pulling up as I vainly tried to shrink away. You peered with great interest at my boils. "Did the chickens come and give you bites as well? Don't worry, mine went away." You straddled the edge of my pillow and sat there cross-legged. "You can put your head in my lap."

It had been your favorite position—lying in my lap—whether you were having your temperature taken, or being told a story, or having custard spooned into your mouth. I hesitated, feeling awkward at the idea of playing along. "Wait, I have to get something," you said, and bounced off the bed. In a moment you were back, your legs refolded, your hands lifting my head, and with a grunt of effort, arranging it to rest between your thighs. Before I could protest, you popped a thermometer into my mouth. "Remember, you have to keep it under your tongue." Then you attempted to take my pulse. You pressed your fingers into the flesh of my palm, looked at the wall clock, and nodded to yourself. "It's very good," you declared, and pronounced my temperature to be excellent as well. The thermometer read a hundred and one degrees when I checked it for myself.

In the days that followed I felt an agony that contorted my mind and exuded from my pores. And yet, I recognized it as an opportunity to forge a bond with you that might never come again. How many times would I get to relive an experience that so closely duplicated one you had just gone through? The heat under my skin, the swellings on my tongue, the soreness of every inch. Each morning, I imagined your body where mine was now, awakening to an identical map of pain.

You took over the role of the mother completely. Cradling my fevered head in your bird-sized lap, bringing me bits of bread spread clumsily with jam. One evening, you even got Zaida to boil you some water with neem leaves. You laid a towel on the bed and carefully sponged my face and my neck. I watched your face hover over me in concentration, lost myself in the soothing sensation. You wanted to continue all over me like I had, but I stopped your hand as it neared my chest.

For weeks afterwards, once my fever had gone, we pointed at each other's speckled faces and laughed. Mrs. Dugal announced she would finally send Pinky over one evening. "Now that you're fine, it'll be safe for her to see Ashvin again. She did have chicken pox when she was two, but why take a chance, I thought to myself."

Just before Pinky was due, I highlighted both your face and mine with red lipstick dots. The minute she entered the flat, we sprang at her. She screamed, and tried to escape, but we slammed the door shut behind. We chased her around the drawing room, until she finally realized it was only lipstick we were afflicted with. She seemed fascinated by the dots—"Could you make me up too?" she asked.

So we gave Pinky chicken pox as well, then went to drop her off at her mother's. When Mrs. Dugal opened the door, she shrieked so loudly that even Zaida heard it one floor below.

PINKY, AT TEN, HAD moved past her mother's efforts to feminize her, and entered a tomboy phase in her life. She insisted on having her hair cut short so that ribbons could no longer be braided in it. She stopped skipping ropes and lopped the heads off her dolls—her interest turned to cricket and kites. She played house with you again, but this time she made you the wife.

I would pass by the two of you sitting under the table next to the staircase, and see you serving her dainty pieces of bread. Sometimes she toted her plastic school case as if returning from work, while you cooked inside. She gave you play money, with which you tried to buy jam from our fridge; she pretended to drink, so that afterwards, the two of you could have a fight. One day, she slapped you for speaking back to her—you ran crying back to our flat, saying you would no longer play her game.

But you didn't give up on Pinky completely—you went up to the terrace together to fly kites. I always made sure that someone was present as a chaperone—I didn't trust Pinky, with the heft she had acquired, not to fling you off the parapet. In time, she became quite an expert at cutting other people's strings—going aggressively after any other kite that dared enter her domain. Mrs. Dugal, who had shown nothing but distress at Pinky's tomboy status, now started gushing about her daughter's prowess at aerial warfare. She cleared an entire wall in their flat to hang as trophies the remains of downed kites that landed on the terrace.

By the time she was twelve, Pinky had pulled together her very own gang of children from the neighboring buildings. Complaints poured in about their delinquent escapades—guavas lifted from vendors' carts, windows broken while trying to knock mangoes from trees, and once, all the steps in the adjoining building, from the ground to the second floor, covered with cooking oil. (Much to the children's disappointment, nobody slipped—the coating was more sticky than slick.)

Thankfully, you stayed at the periphery of this pack, limiting your participation to the occasional street cricket match. Meanwhile, your teachers kept reminding me that you remained too aloof. I tried a few times to intervene when I brought you lunch. "Why don't you ask Sunil to play hide-and-seek with Ashvin?" I suggested to the mother of a classmate one day. Before she could respond, you turned red with embarrassment and ran away.

In truth, you didn't strike me as unhappy. I never let you be too alone—you could always depend on my company when needed. I taught you rummy and pairs and all the other card games I knew, and even played cricket with you in the corridor between the flats. On some nights, we cleared everything off the dining table to have a Ping-Pong match.

Still, there remained periods when you withdrew, when you became silent and disengaged. Unable to concentrate on anything, you moved food listlessly around your plate. I wondered then if you thought of your father, what these broodings were that you could not share. I wanted to be close enough to you to X-ray the innermost thoughts in your brain.

But I learned to restrain myself and accept your need for solitude. Perhaps these bouts were necessary to maintain your peace with the loss you had sustained. Perhaps they were indicative of a Tagore or an Einstein inside, developing unseen, like in a chrysalis. Didn't you usually bounce back by bedtime, and want to cuddle with me again?

SOMETIMES, WHEN YOUR mood didn't lift so readily, I took you to the beach at Juhu. Although Chowpatty was much closer, its waves were too sedate, the water increasingly polluted. We rode the train to Santa Cruz, stopping along the way at the park with the concrete Air India plane. The sight of the beach instantly cured your spirits—you raced across the sand to jump into the water, shirt and all. I remembered how your father had done the same, the first time we came to the sea after moving to Bombay.

The tide flattened you repeatedly, but you quickly got to your feet, pounding your chest for the next onslaught. I knotted my dupatta around my neck and waded in as well. You liked me to stand behind you. Each time a wave came thundering in, you raised your arms at the last instant for me to lift you above the crest. Sometimes, I underestimated the tide and got knocked over myself. Then we rolled together in the foam, a mass of arms and bodies and legs.

Afterwards, I bought you an ice gola from the cart parked next to the Sun 'n Sand hotel. We watched the man grate the ice into a pan, and then form it into a ball around a stick. You agonized endlessly over the color of the syrup, even though they all tasted the same. When it was very hot, I bought one for myself as well. We sat on a bench and licked our golas as the sun dried us off.

One Sunday, a girl got carried out to sea. The parents had equipped her with an inflatable life ring decorated with cartoon characters, clearly imported from abroad. All the children looked at it in longing as she paraded up and down the beach, rotating the ring slowly around her midriff, to show off the cartoons equally. The wave that took her wasn't even particularly big—one second she was clambering onto the ring, and the next instant she was rolling away, as serenely as a coconut. She ended up a few hundred yards from shore, a colorful shape bobbing in the whitecaps, waving invitingly, it seemed, to the onlookers on the beach. While her parents ran around and pointed frantically, some of the children waved back, and asked if they, too, could venture out like that. By the time a fisherman was recruited to negotiate the waves to fetch her, the girl had slipped out from the ring and appeared to be beckoning people into the water instead. She was carried glassy-eyed and ringless to a spot where the sand was dry, and a crowd gathered around to watch if any water would come out as her chest was pressed.

I held you to myself, imagining you swept away from my life while I watched as helplessly from shore as the girl's parents had. After that incident, I never felt at ease taking you to Juhu again.

THE INSURANCE MONEY for Dev finally came. Paji delayed it as much as possible. "I can't find the papers—who knows where your mother has misplaced them?" "The death certificate you sent must be lost in the mail—could you get another one made?" "They've found a misspelling in Ace's name—I'll have to start all over again." I deposited the check immediately, before Paji could dream up some reason for recalling it, then went to the shops at Opera House selling TV sets. The broadcasts had finally started in Bombay at the end of last year, even though television had been inaugurated in Delhi twelve years ago. For months now, you had been sighing each time we passed an electronics store, and making wistful references to shows like *Here's Lucy* and *The Count of Monte Cristo*, which the children at school all talked about.

I settled on Televista, an Indian brand (since foreign ones smuggled into the country started at ten thousand rupees on the black market). It blew a valve on the very first day—in the coming months, we got to know the repairman quite well. The only channel, the government-operated Doordarshan, broadcast endless hours of propaganda films. Each night, the news slavishly detailed the prime minister's day—following her around as she visited hospitals or greeted foreign dignitaries. The shortages and strikes due to a second failed monsoon could have been plaguing a different country. "Even if the Soviets and Americans launched a nuclear attack," Zaida said, "they'd still show Indira cutting the ribbon to a fertilizer factory."

You sat rapt through everything—even the shows in Marathi and

Gujarati, which you didn't understand. The TV remained on from the wailing sign-on tune at six-thirty until ten o'clock, when, with a final flash of the snail-like Doordarshan logo, the transmission went off the air. The most popular show was the Hindi movie on Sunday evening—when shops closed early and even public buses mysteriously vanished from the streets. Wild rumors circulated all week about the next telecast being a recent hit like *Guddi*, or *Amar Prem*—the films actually shown had either flopped or were quite old.

It hardly mattered. Viewers streamed into our living room on Sundays —Zaida and Pinky and Mrs. Dugal and Mrs. Hussain—even the ganga, who squatted on her favorite spot by the door. I found myself transported back to my youth, when movies formed such a big part of my life—the familiar tales of doomed love, of twins separated at birth, of prostitutes with hearts of gold.

One Sunday, they showed the classic *Mother India*. The heroine, Nargis, had caused quite a scandal by falling in love during the filming with Sunil Dutt, the actor playing her son. In the movie, Nargis shoots her son for bringing dishonor to her family—the mother goddess Kali killing off her offspring, a reviewer said. In real life, much to everyone's shock, Nargis had married him. The fact that he was a Hindu and she a Muslim only fanned the controversy.

I felt a strangely familiar, yet almost forgotten pressure behind my eyes when Nargis's husband died, leaving her alone with two young sons and a mound of debt threatening their very lives. "Go ahead," Zaida said. "What's the use of watching a movie if you don't let it out?" So when Nargis tied herself to a plow to till the land and feed her children, I let the tears wet my cheeks. And when Sunil Dutt lay bleeding in her arms and called her "Mother" for the last time, I allowed the deluge to come.

After that, I let myself cry every Sunday—a weekly amnesty of sorts from my pledge of so long ago. When Madhubala sang "When One Has Loved, Why Should One Be Afraid?" before being bricked up in a wall; when Meena Kumari was murdered and buried under the floor by her drunkard husband's family in *Sahib, Bibi, aur Ghulam*. Tragedies revolving around maternal love made me weep the most. Movies like *Aurat*, where the mother, like another Kali incarnation, is also forced to kill her criminal son after a lifetime of sacrifices for him. Or *Aradhana*, where she confesses to the murder committed by her boy and emerges from jail to find he has grown to look exactly like the father she loved.

Even though I knew how overheated these stories were, I couldn't help falling under their spell. A part of me wanted to suffer like the heroines, to be tempered by the same fiery tests of motherhood they underwent. What would it feel like to yoke myself to a plow and fight the unyielding earth for food to put in your mouth? The dirt mingling with my sweat, the muscles straining in my neck, the rope marks burning proudly on my chest? I watched Nargis and Sharmila Tagore and lost myself in fantasy—of hardship and survival, of tribulation and self-denial. Opportunities for sacrifice burst forth to rise like mountains around me, waiting to be scaled, step by arduous step, as proof of my love for you, my devotion, my all-encompassing passion.

WHAT ELSE CAN I SAY about those first few years after I was left alone with you? The section they inaugurated in my album of memories was the happiest I had ever known. It was like the first chapter of a book I couldn't wait to read, the trailer of a movie starring the two of us destined to be a masterpiece. I held on to your hand as you let me accompany you through the landscape of your childhood.

It became my second childhood as well—or perhaps my first, since I was always discontented with the one I had lived before. All the toys Roopa got to choose and play with first, all the comics of which Paji disapproved. All the foods Biji deemed too arousing—the sour candy drops and the jamun berries—even the coffee. I now had the power to indulge you with everything (and myself, simultaneously). To concentrate all my attention on you and have it all reflect back only on me.

Perhaps this had been my deepest unfulfilled craving—to have more attention lavished on me. Now I felt this need being slaked, through all the things you did for me. You peppered my egg every morning, sprinkling enough to completely cover the yolk the way I liked. At night, you checked that I had taken my vitamins, and filled a glass with cold water for my bedside. Each time I wore a salwar kameez, you found the right dupatta from the cupboard; for saris, you laid out the matching blouse. You always made sure I kept enough for myself when I tried to heap your plate with the last of the kheer.

Do all mothers get to be such close friends with their sons, or was this a blessing only for me? The way our family album brimmed with so many images of shared activity? The time after I had taught you to ride a bicycle and the shopkeeper suggested I also rent one for myself. It felt a little low, but I managed to remain astride, taking care to wrap my dupatta several times around my neck so that it did not get entangled in the spokes. We rode up and down the side streets, going by the back way almost as far as Gowallia Tank. Then we spotted Mrs. Dugal emerging from the Sai Baba temple, aimed our bikes at her, and pedaled furiously. She screamed not once, but twice—first when you buzzed her, then when she was buzzed by me.

Or the visit to Hanging Gardens when you discovered your first keri, nestling in the shrubs under a mango tree. "Is it a real mango?" you asked, holding it in your palms like something newly hatched, the sap still oozing out of its navel.

"Yes," I replied. "It just fell before it was ripe. It's sour, but taste it, go ahead."

You took a tentative bite, and I saw the stars in your eyes—suddenly I wanted some myself. "Come, let's gather a few more. Mummy will show you what she used to do with them in Rawalpindi."

At home, I found an empty jam jar into which I chopped the keris. By now the pungent raw mango aroma had intoxicated you as well, so I let you mix in the salt. "It takes a few days for the skin to turn dark," I warned, and you shook the jar to hurry things along.

By the next evening, you had agitated the jar so frequently that the keris were suspended in a thick white froth. I knew you wouldn't be able to last another day, so I let you open it. "They're maha-tastic," you pronounced, your highest compliment, and I nodded in agreement as I felt the tickle in my throat. We sat at the table and fed the pieces to each other until the acid turned our teeth numb.

That week, you seemed to notice the boughs of the old mango tree in your school grounds for the first time. They carried so much fruit that parrots fluttered around constantly, trying to peck at it with their red beaks. You started spending both your short and long recess rooting for keris in the plant beds underneath.

On Friday, I found you moping when I came to pick you up after your cub scout meeting. Too many other boys had heard about the treasure hunt and the day had gone by without finding a single keri. I remembered the guava tree that grew in the compound of our Darya Ganj house—the ripest, most tantalizing pieces always seemed to be out of reach. I had often been tempted to lob stones at one of the clusters, but the time Roopa tried it, she ended up hitting a neighbor, and Biji gave us both a beating. The guavas had mocked me all through adolescence, until one year the tree was cut down.

I'm not sure what prompted this nostalgia to translate itself into action, but suddenly I found myself taking aim at a mango with a stone in my hand. Before I could sober myself with responsibility or consequences, I felt a satisfying ripple in my arm muscles, saw the stone arcing through the air. A lime green parrot flew squawking out of the tree, and a mango, plump and heavy, dropped to the ground. "Did you see that?" I shouted as you ran to retrieve it. "If the wind doesn't knock them down, your mummy can."

Within a few minutes, there was a fusillade of stones bombarding the tree. The boys who were your rivals, the servants who had come to pick them up, even some of the hawkers selling candy in the compound, all joined in. Keris started raining down one after the other, turning the shrubs underneath into a free-for-all. Then the inevitable happened—a rock strayed far from its course and crashed through a window in the rectory behind, where the principal and the other fathers lived.

I ran with you, as my instincts urged—not pausing to worry about principles or propriety. By the time the vice principal, Father Bernard, charged down looking for someone to cane, we were crouched safely behind the wall at the edge of the grounds. "I can see everything from up there," he yelled, wielding his stick, his white robes billowing around his shoes. You giggled together with the boys hiding next to you, and I began to giggle as well. On the bus home, you reached into your pockets and laid six keris, fat and fragrant, in my lap.

Afterwards, I felt uneasy. Why I had been so quick to set a bad example, so reckless in my determination to be your friend? Could this have been something I imagined fathers would do—something, perhaps, to make a bolder man out of you? You had come a long way in the past three years, but there was still something amiss. The way you took out the box under the bed on Sundays to touch each implement in your father's shaving kit. The long silent prayers in front of the pantheon, the continuing pilgrimages to Chowpatty to immerse pooja flowers. There was a gap in your life, I could see, a hole I knew I would never feel adequate enough to fill. Did Dev make me launch my stone, his absence for which I had tried to compensate?

I even gave wrestling another shot—this time, better prepared, I managed to keep awkwardness at bay. But I was too apprehensive of causing you hurt. You wore the disappointment plainly on your face— the bout hadn't matched up to your encounters with Dev.

So we replaced the wrestling with games of tickling. You lay down first, pretending to be asleep, as I started on your sides, just above the hips. I moved gradually, teasing you with bare hints of pressure, until my fingers had inched up and were poised at your armpits. There I let them linger, grazing occasionally against your skin, until your eyelids began trembling and the suspense fluttered across your face. Just as your eyes popped open, I lunged in—tickling you until you bucked and flailed on the bed and the room filled with your shrieks. We switched roles once you were spent—it didn't take long for you to learn that my ears were the most sensitive, not my armpits.

One May afternoon before your ninth birthday, I took you to Chowpatty to fling your final milk tooth into the sea. On the way back, we ran into a giant procession at Nana Chowk. At first, I thought it was a demonstration by railway workers. Over a million of them had gone on a national strike, paralyzing transport for a fortnight, spreading food shortages everywhere, bringing the country to a standstill. But then I saw people dancing, flashes of firecracker bursts, plumes of colored powder rising into the air. It was a celebration, not a protest—India had just tested an underground atomic bomb in Rajasthan. We watched the national flag being waved, large tricolors with the central wheel replaced by the prime minister's face. From the chaos of all the domestic problems confronting her, Indira had managed to give rebirth to herself as Durga again.

All that evening, one could feel an elation, as galvanizing as electricity, crackling through the air. We would be rubbing shoulders with superpowers now—no longer would Pakistan dare make its territorial forays. Zaida, the Dugals, the Hussains, even the ganga came to crowd around the TV set—it could have been Sunday movie time again. The blast came on, the ground shook in Rajasthan, and a cheer went up in the room. "Boom!" Pinky went, "Maha-boom!" you shouted. You threw your arms up together, and jumped in unison off the bed.

chapter
twenty-eight

EVERY ONCE IN A WHILE, SOMETHING HAPPENED TO PULL ME OUT OF THE idyllic routine into which we had settled. To remind me there existed a far crueler world outside our front door. Most disquieting was Zaida's news, the afternoon you kept trying to coax her into dancing. "It's Anwar," she finally said. "He's announced he's going to take a second wife. At age sixty-nine."

Unbeknownst to her, he had been seeing a woman every Saturday for all these years—each time, in fact, that he had claimed to go visit his brother in Sewri. "And here I was, thinking he was in such poor health, trying to tiptoe around him while he rested in the afternoons. Now I know why he took all those naps—it was to build up his energy for the end of the week."

At first, it had seemed so unbelievable as to be almost amusing. "Suddenly the mouse who's not even peeked once down the mousehole for all these years decides he's a tiger after all." But she had soon realized the seriousness of her situation. "It's his right, he tells me, to marry again. Not just once, but three more times if he wants. He says he's going to bring her here, that he wants me to take all my things and move into a corner of the living room. And if I make any trouble, he can throw me out—he says the law is clear."

The law was, indeed, clear. For Hindus, it was so difficult to get a divorce once married that people had been known to change their religion to prove the clear grounds they needed for dissolution. Zaida, though, had been wed under Muslim personal law, for which the rules were different. Not only was Anwar legally allowed four wives, but he could divorce Zaida for any reason, simply by repeating the word "talaq" three times. "Everywhere, even in Pakistan, they're getting rid of this instant talaq divorce, but here the mullahs just won't let it go. Even Indira, can you believe it, is too scared of them to touch the issue."

In fact, all Anwar had to do to be free was to support Zaida for three months in return for the twenty-five years she had spent with him. "Not even three months, mind you, but three menstrual cycles, the way the rule is framed. I told him if he was so worried about the money, he could keep track of what I did in the toilet to make sure he didn't overpay."

In the coming weeks, Zaida became more hopeful, and even started dancing with you in the afternoons. Though it was legal, many Muslim communities, including her own, strongly discouraged the practice of three-talaq divorce. "He's just using it as a threat—let's see the mouse actually say the words to my face. He's wrong if he thinks I'm going to fall for his bluff and agree to share this house with that whore of his." She actually sat down face to face with Aneez, the woman in question, at a meeting arranged by her father to try and smooth things out. "A fifty-five-year-old widow, no less. With two grown children, imagine! My own father telling me that I should accommodate her, that I shouldn't put this to the test."

"Don't listen to them—they're just trying to break your will," I responded. "A woman that age who knows she's not welcome won't come rushing in."

For a few days, it looked like Zaida's strategy of holding firm was going to work. Then, late one afternoon, she burst in. "Anwar's given me an ultimatum. Either I agree to all his conditions to make this widow of his welcome, or he's going to utter the words this Saturday. Right after his bath—he says one has to purify oneself first—he'll probably go see her afterwards." She paused to catch her breath. "What he doesn't know is that I'm going to make it more difficult than that. I want you to come and be a witness—let's see him open his mouth then."

"Of course," I nodded. "But why just me? Why not summon the rest of the building as well?"

When Anwar emerged from the bathroom, he was confronted not only by Mrs. Dugal and myself, but also by Mrs. Hamid, Mrs. Kagal-walla, both the Hussains, and even Mrs. Karmali, who rarely ventured out of her flat anymore. I noticed Pinky had slipped in as well and was watching from behind the kitchen door. "What kind of foolishness is this?" Anwar shouted. "This is not some circus, but a private affair."

"Why? Are you ashamed? Don't you want your neighbors to know? If you're prepared to say them to me, you can say the words in front of them." Zaida turned towards us. "Look, he's even taken the bath that's prescribed. This should only take a minute—do stay for tea afterwards."

For a moment we all looked on silently. Then Mrs. Hussain prodded her husband to speak. "I'm sorry, Mr. Azmi," he said. "We weren't going to come, but your wife requested us to—she's like a sister to us. A man your age—perhaps you could give it some more thought?"

In response, Anwar pushed roughly past Mr. Hussain into the bed-room, and slammed the door. "What's the matter?" Zaida called out. "Are you going to disappoint all your fans? They've come to hear you teach them the word, have you forgotten how it's pronounced?"

Zaida's strategy produced the desired result. Aneez withdrew her acceptance within a week—there was too much gossip in the commu-nity, making the prospect of marriage too humiliating. "She sent me a note—on perfumed paper, no less, our Aneez memsahib did. That she's asked Anwar not to get a talaq—can you imagine the gall? Perhaps she's expecting me to go pledge my eternal gratitude to her, waiting with a martyr's look inside her cave."

The matter didn't end there. Anwar was so enraged that he refused to speak to his wife, and would not even look at her when they were in the same room. One afternoon, as Zaida and I were sipping tea, he appeared at my door. His eyes were bloodshot and his kurta pajama stained. "I've come to say something to my wife, and I want you to be a witness." I had no choice but to let him in.

He spoke to Zaida in chaste Urdu, using the formal honorific to address her. Things had been poisoned between them, he said, due to her selfishness and her unwillingness to obey the law of God as set down in the Koran. She had made a mockery of him and herself in public. Instead of trying to preserve the sacredness of the marriage between them, a marriage which clearly allowed him to take another wife if he desired, she had defiled it to a point where it could not be saved. There was no point any longer in showing pity or consideration to such a she-devil, such a churail—it was time to do what he should have from the start. "Talaq," he said, the *q* sharp and reverberant as it cut through the air. "I promise that the remaining two pronouncements will be forthcoming soon, at a time of my choosing."

"If you're man enough, just spit them out now and be done with it," Zaida responded, but Anwar ignored her. "I'll divorce you myself, if you don't," she called after him as he calmly walked out of my living room.

For a while, Zaida looked into getting a khula, the kind of divorce that could be initiated by the wife. In addition to the conditions being much more onerous, however, it also meant that the amount of money promised to her as meher in the marriage contract would be lost. "Besides, it's probably what he's hoping to provoke me into. If I'm the one to ask for a divorce, then I'm the guilty one. Nobody can point a finger at him, can they then, for going and pursuing his fifty-five-year-old?"

Her father made it clear that whether it was talaq or khula, he would not accept her back. "Get these extravagant ideas out of your head," he said. "You've already dug yourself into a hole with your obstinacy—think very carefully whether you can afford to continue this behavior."

"I'd rather be dead," Zaida told me, and I tried to think of advice to give, tried to imagine what I might do in her place. I felt terrible at having little more than sympathy to offer after all the difficult periods she had seen me through. I started keeping her with me as long as I could each afternoon, filling her up with the bonbon biscuits she liked so much to cheer her up. When she looked tired, I insisted she lie on the sofa while I massaged her head. You got into the act as well, trying to distract her with solos danced to Beatles records. But our efforts were overwhelmed by the direness of her situation. "I can't live like this—live under this sword hanging over my head."

Except she had few other options left. She was too proud to move in with anyone, declining each time I proposed she share our flat. Her husband knew she didn't have a penny to her name with which to fend for herself. "You've disgraced yourself too much to continue as my wife," he announced. "What you need is to learn some humility first." He would take her back, he said, provided she agreed to obey all his demands, like a servant would. Any rebelliousness, and he would not hesitate to utter the two words that separated her from the street. "Think of it as training. A mare who's become too used to running around, being reminded of the leash for her own good."

Anwar started Zaida's "training" slowly, doing things to irritate her more than anything else. He complained no matter what she presented him for dinner, railing against cauliflower one day and specifically asking for it the next, sending her back into the kitchen to bring him rice if there were chappatis, and chappatis if she had cooked rice. He critiqued her cleaning and washing and ironing like a finicky house mistress—his goal to identify at least three tasks every day for her to do over again. Some of his tactics were impish—setting her bath soap to dissolve under the tap, hiding her glasses so she couldn't read, secretly drinking up all the milk so that there would be none left for her early morning tea. "If that's the worst of it," Zaida told me one afternoon, "then fine, I'll tolerate it with a smile, until his dander subsides."

Unfortunately, she miscalculated—in the face of her equanimity, Anwar just became meaner, more humiliating. He forbade her from visiting any of the neighbors or even chatting with them, like his mother had done when she was alive. Zaida would steal in for a few minutes while he was asleep to tell me what new indignities he had dreamt up. I tried again on these visits to convince her to move in with us. "Not just myself, but think of how overjoyed Ashvin would be," I said.

But she again refused. "I can't give in now. I have to see this to the end."

Anwar started haranguing Zaida about money, accusing her of theft if she couldn't account for every paisa he doled out for groceries. Each time she returned from her shopping, he patted down the clothes she was wearing to check for hidden coins and rupees. He dismissed the jamadarni and ordered Zaida to clean the toilet every morning herself— "I can't afford to have two servants in my employ," he said. Always a fastidious man, he suddenly started coming back from his walks with his shoes smeared with mud and cow feces—he took them off at the door, where he made her sit and polish them. He let her cook only enough mutton or chicken for himself—when he was done with dinner, he scraped the dregs of the gravy into the remainder of the custard they had for dessert every night, and left that mixed up in a bowl for her to eat.

It was only the exchange of Eid greetings that gave us a pretext for a proper visit to Zaida in her flat. The Hussains were already there, sipping glasses of almond milk. Zaida was just about to pour you a glass when Anwar complained the milk had too much sugar in it. "Go back to the kitchen and make it again," he ordered.

Zaida laughed nervously as if he had just made a joke. "I think the sweetness is just right. I'll give some to Ashvin—perhaps he can be the one to decide."

"Didn't you hear what I asked you to do?" Anwar said. "Go prepare another batch. Right now." When Zaida made no move to obey, he raised his hand to strike her in front of us all.

It happened so fast there was little time to react. One instant, I watched in shock as Anwar's hand began its downward descent. The next, Zaida's fingers shot around his wrist to arrest his slap. "It was a divine moment, a revelation," she said afterwards. "My arm propelled forward by Allah himself. After you all had left—everyone, incidentally, making sure to finish their milk in my support—I told Anwar it might indeed be his right to divorce me or not. But it would be a sin to allow my mistreatment to continue any longer—not only for me, but also for himself."

Anwar's response was to throw his almond milk at her face. It was not too hard to avoid, she told me—a little fell on her dupatta, but most of it splashed harmlessly off the wall. He then hurled the empty glass towards her, which she also managed to dodge. The glass bounced off a lamp and fell intact to the floor—for some reason, the fact that it didn't break seemed to infuriate him. "Pick it up," he shouted, stomping his foot on the ground like a child trying to intimidate a pigeon or cat. Zaida stayed where she was. "Pick it up," he shouted again, "or I'll speak the words that are waiting to leap off my tongue."

"I felt nothing. Perhaps it was God's presence still inside me that made me so tranquil. I was prepared for any eventuality—I knew that if I stood my ground, He would take care of me no matter what happened. Anwar kept repeating his threat, but the more he reiterated it, the more it became clear to both of us that it was empty, that he wouldn't be able to bring even one of the two remaining 'talaqs' to his lips. By now, I was feeling so strong, so righteous, that I could almost feel the light shining from within me and radiating through my skin—like one of those pictures of Christian angels, or Jesus or Mary with their hearts aflame. Perhaps Anwar saw this glow within me as well, because his words began to falter, his eyes became large and fearful. He emitted an anguished cry— of terror, almost—and went running into the bedroom."

For a while, Zaida just sat on one of the chairs and waited. "Had my clothes not been in the bedroom cupboard, I may have packed them and left, though I probably would only have come here, to your flat. I noticed there were ants already beginning to be attracted by the milk on the floor, so I dampened a cloth in the kitchen to wipe up the spill. I examined the glass Anwar had thrown—it had chipped very slightly around the rim. I kept looking at it for a long time after I had rinsed it, unable to decide whether to return it to the cabinet or throw it out. Finally, I set it on the counter, opened the bedroom door, and went in."

Anwar was lying absolutely motionless on the bed. "As if he were a patient on an operating table, and I the surgeon to whom he had entrusted his fate. His face was so bloodless that I thought he had suffered a heart attack. I imagined letting him lie there as I watched the life ebb out of him. He gasped, and I drew closer—so close that I could feel his breath on my hand, though I didn't touch him. I realized he was trying to say something, but I wasn't sure I wanted to hear it. What if he was using the last of his energy to dredge up the words he had been unable to summon earlier? But there must have still been some remnant of the noble presence within me—or perhaps I just felt pity, now that his last moments seemed near. In any case, I found myself smoothing out his forehead, holding his hand, telling him I was there. His eyes opened, and they were surprisingly clear—I drew back, startled by the realization that he was not quite on his deathbed. He started whispering again, and this time I put down my ear next to his lips. 'Aneez,' he was saying. 'I'll never be able to marry my Aneez, thanks to the churail.'

"I suppose the presence inside me must have abruptly vanished, because I spat in his face. He made no move to wipe the spittle off, but stopped whispering for a moment. Then he started repeating Aneez's name once more, over and over again, as if he were chanting a prayer. I watched the dark hole of his mouth open and close, framed by the thick fleshiness of his lips. I spat at him again, repeatedly, striking not his nose or his lips or his cheeks, but the flowing white beard that made him look like a mullah, that he took such fastidious pride in. I spat until I could work up no more spit. He neither winced nor made any attempt to protect himself. Then, even though I could see that he was no longer a tiger but a mouse again—an older and frailer one at that—I slapped him. It was the only way I knew by which I could stay married to him.

"After that, he was silent and still. When it was time for dinner, I thought about eating all the chicken myself, and serving him a mixture of gravy and custard with crusts of bread soaked in. But I couldn't make myself do it. Instead, I divided the meat between two plates, though I gave the smaller piece to him. He didn't touch his plate. I tried to spoon some rice into his mouth, but he turned away. I was never quite sure if he was still lamenting Aneez, or if his need for penance was too great."

It took a week for Anwar's paralysis to end. Zaida came by to visit every day, giving me updates. "He seems to be hungering for further mistreatment, but I don't feel the need anymore. As long as we both understand each other now, and the bluff of his two hanging words has been forever swept away." She rehired the jamadarni that very week, then got a ganga to come in as well, to cook the food and clean the floors.

Two months later, I was surprised to be invited to Zaida's place again on a Saturday afternoon. Ever since things had been straightened out, Anwar stayed at home that day, listening to the radio or puttering around the flat, and Zaida came over to our place instead. "I sent him out," she said, as she opened the door. "I couldn't stand his restlessness."

"But where?" I asked.

"To visit his 'brother' in Sewri, where else? It was more than I could bear to watch his long face every week, to follow his pitiful shuffling movements as if he was a hundred years old. If it's a mouse hole he needs, then fine, let him have it—now that we both know I can be the only wife. I can ensure he's well-fed and take care of him when he's sick, but affection is not one of the obligations I'm going to fulfill."

Then, before I could ask her any further questions, Zaida showed you the Beatles record her cousin had just lent her. "Come, Ashvin, I'll put it on so we can twist."

chapter

twenty-nine

Barely had Zaida's crisis been resolved than Roopa decided to pay us a visit, jarring us once more out of our day-to-day tranquillity. "Ravinder's being posted on a ship for a month and the twins' college starts again next week. I feel so guilty not having come earlier to be by your side, but this is the first chance I'm really getting to be alone. Tell darling Ashu that his Roo auntie can't wait to see how he's grown." I almost wrote back asking her not to come, but then relented, remembering how fond you had been of her the times you'd met in Delhi.

At the station, Roopa hugged us both simultaneously to her chest, telling us how shocked she had been to hear about Dev. There were tears in her eyes, which puzzled me—should I remind her that her condolences were three years too late? I soon understood the real reason behind her visit—she had pledged to make an offering at Sai Baba's shrine in Shirdi. "I told Sai Baba I'd visit, but he had to give both Dilip and Shobha good marks at the college in exchange." There was no easy way to get to the remote town from most parts in the country—Bombay was one of the few accessible starting points for the overnight bus trip. She tried to convince the two of us to come along, suggesting we make a proper excursion of it by spending the night there in a hotel room (something she was afraid of doing alone). "If not for yourself, then come for Ashu's sake—even more so, for Dev's. Remember, Sai Baba was his favorite saint. It would give such peace to his soul—how he would have cherished you making the pilgrimage for him!"

"I'm sure you'd be much better at getting Sai Baba to bless his soul than I would," I replied. "Dev himself might appreciate it more to hear the prayers from your lips."

I did offer you the choice of accompanying your Roo auntie. But it was apparent you didn't want to go—in fact, you were relieved to see her leave. The two days Roopa spent in Bombay had not passed well. You were disappointed to get clothes as a present (two pairs of pants, stitched specially for you, Roopa claimed, but which didn't fit). You no longer had any interest in having her make up your face—the experiences of being Pinky's wife had cured you of that phase. The very first evening, you brought in your aquarium to give Roo auntie the chance to feed your snails, and were offended by the look of revulsion on her face. You missed your school bus two mornings in a row because she occupied the bathroom too long. ("Just a minute," she'd say, and then take ten more.) You didn't even like being called "Ashu" now, but she laughed it off each time you reminded her of this. "You're too young, Ashu, to mind about such things. What is it, nine now?—you couldn't be becoming an adult so quick." What galled you even more was that at the same time, she declared you too grown-up to sleep between her and me on the bed, banishing you to your half mattress instead.

I felt just as frayed. Somehow I had reverted to being the obedient younger sister—the role Paji and Biji had ingrained in me when I was a girl. I found myself preparing Roopa's breakfast, heating the water for her bath, waiting to hear what she wanted for lunch. "I've never had so many bananas in my life," she complained, upon my return from the market. "It might be a bit late in the season, but did you bother to check if they had any grapes?"

By the time Roopa returned from Shirdi and stayed another two nights, the whole house was in disarray. The bathroom cabinet overflowed with her toiletries, the fridge festered with foods I had bought that she refused to eat. Her clothes (including, much to your embarrassment, two brassieres) were strewn everywhere, just like when we were young. The ganga had still not returned after Roopa scolded her the first morning for not sweeping out the floor under the cupboards. You, meanwhile, were also chafing, over a quiz your aunt had taken it upon herself to administer to you the previous morning, to test your preparedness for a geography test. When I informed her you hated to have your studies supervised, she replied that it was something I should start doing, something she had done for *her* children. "And look, it works— they're now both in college, aren't they?"

"When is Roo auntie's train?" you asked, the Saturday she was supposed to depart.

When Roopa had left for Shirdi, I noticed that the two twin beds were pulled apart. Thinking nothing of it, I pushed them back. Now, as she finished packing her first suitcase, she told me to help her separate the beds again. "It doesn't look right for them to be connected, as if it's the same bed. Ashvin's a growing boy—he's getting much too old for that."

Before I could demand to know what exactly she meant, Roopa continued. "You're spending much too much time with him. A boy that age needs space to breathe, to make his own friends. I almost feel like I've blundered into the house of an old married couple—all these routines with him in which you're so set. I went into the bathroom and couldn't even tell your toothbrushes apart—they're both red." She looked at me as if she dared me to refute this damning piece of evidence.

"What are you talking about? Ashvin's toothbrush is half the size of mine, and it's the only color they keep at General Stores—red."

"Look, Meera. Ravinder's been posted on a ship before. I know how lonely it can get. It's a terrible thing, loneliness. Especially if you're staring at a whole lifetime stretching ahead. But there's no reason you should think you have to lean on just Ashvin. There's no reason why, with some luck, you shouldn't find someone else. I know Dev would've wanted you to."

"What do you know about what Dev would've wanted or not? You weren't the one married to him for sixteen years. Throwing yourself at someone every once in a while doesn't make you an expert on his soul."

Roopa sighed. "Let's not do this, Meera. I didn't come here to fight.

If it makes you feel better, you can hurl all the insults at me you want. But you have to let these things go. Otherwise the resentment will burn a hole through your gut. So what if Dev loved someone less or more? You can't keep plunging into this pool of jealousy. The thing is, he's gone now—it's time to let the bitterness drain from your heart."

She patted my hand. "Now listen to me. There's someone I know— the brother of our neighbor next door. He has two children—he cremated their mother only a year ago. He's a typical Madrasi, short and dark, but surely you shouldn't let that make so much of a difference now. Come out and visit us—I think he'd be agreeable—but even if he refuses, what have you lost?"

My first reaction was to fling Roopa's short and dark Madrasi back into her face—to tell her she ought to marry him herself, so that he could keep her company while Ravinder was away. But then I realized something momentous had transpired. Roopa's slights over the years had just crossed a line, brimmed over a threshold beyond which I felt free to disown her as my sister. I no longer had to worry about what she thought or said or did. I would take her to the station and never see her again.

"It's settled then," Roopa said, as she filled her second suitcase with all the shopping she'd done—the perfume bottles from Crawford Market, the purses from Colaba, the salwar kameez suits, the georgette saris, the Kolhapuri footwear. "You'll come and visit as soon as Ravinder is back. We'll have a lunch, invite my neighbor over with her brother. It might be a good idea to buy something less dowdy than the outfits you go around in."

Roopa's train was at three-thirty, but there was no longer any reason to endure five more hours of this. "Come, Ashvin, it's time to get dressed. We're taking Roo auntie to the station earlier than I said."

ALTHOUGH I TRIED to put Roopa's visit out of my mind, it was difficult to dismiss everything she said. Was I letting my own needs get the better of my judgment? Was I being too overbearing, too suffocating with my love? Even if she had ascribed more to my affection than there was, what effect must the constant limelight of my attention have on you? Already you were always kissing and hugging (and tickling!) me. Was this more than other children your age?

I found myself staring at the beds while you were at school, and finally shifting them away from each other—not as far apart as Roopa had done, but so that a conspicuous gap opened between them. All afternoon, I agonized over reasons to explain the change—the beds would shake less this way when one of us turned, it was easier to change the sheets and the bedcovers. But although you must have noticed the difference, you simply seemed to shrug it off.

I decided to stop sitting in the balcony every day, waiting for you to return from school. It was too easy being lulled into a sense of hopelessness, to spend my time plowing through the disappointments of the past. I found a simpler remedy than Roopa's suggestion to get remarried—I went back to work.

It had been over a decade, but the publishing company still had its office at Opera House, with Mr. Hansi still the proprietor. He was overjoyed to see me. "I must warn you, though, we've had some changes. We don't do anything historical anymore—our target audience is a little different." He beat about the bush some more before confessing sheepishly that they no longer published books at all. "What we've come to realize is that our strength, basically, lies in comics."

Mr. Hansi assigned me Casper and Superman and Richie Rich—I translated them into pirated Hindi editions. The comics were crudely reproduced, by photographing the originals, whiting out the balloons, and manually typing in the translated words, before sending them on to the press. Occasionally I also performed more legal translations—tales from the Ramayana or Mahabharata, from Hindi comic books into English. To your delight, the company soon added Mickey Mouse and Donald Duck to their list of pirated clients.

During my previous stint there, Dev had always worried about the loose impressions people might form about a woman in their workplace. Nobody paid attention to me back then, but now that I was a widow, every second look I received from my male coworkers seemed to be a leer. Several mornings, I would find a heart-shaped piece of paper stuck into my typewriter, sometimes with 'I love you' typed in red. Mysterious calls for me came in on Mr. Hansi's number, with nobody at the end of the line when I picked up the receiver. Both Mr. Phadke and Mr. Malkani invited me to eat lunch with them outside—I finally said yes, provided they also brought their wives. Even Arun, the baby-faced print setter, offered shyly to blow on my tea one afternoon break, to cool it for me.

I suppose I should have expected such behavior, given how things had changed, even in my neighborhood, after Dev died. The shopkeepers downstairs lost little time in becoming markedly more familiar in their manner—the General Stores proprietor tried to woo me with free bars of soap twice. The bania at the ration shop winked at me one evening while I shopped for lentils—in the face of my fury, he called me his sister and claimed there was something caught in his eye. Dev's long-lost musician friends showed up sporadically for months, to offer their condolences and to see if I was sufficiently recovered to accompany them to tea.

The most blatant attention, though, came from within my building. Each time I ventured outside, somebody's husband seemed on the prowl, waiting to accost me on the steps. Mr. Karmali and Mr. Hussain exchanged strong words one day as they vied with each other to carry down the radio I was taking for repair. Mr. Hamid almost broke his collarbone rushing down from the floor above to help hold open my door.

More invitations for tea accompanied these encounters, each one dropped so casually that it had to be rehearsed. My suitors invariably suggested one of the cheap Irani restaurants around to rendezvous, throwing in some convoluted reason for not inviting their spouse. Not that I would have agreed, but couldn't they have made their overtures more imaginative? Lunch somewhere, perhaps at the newly opened Caravan Grill—or even the modest Cream Centre, for an ice cream sundae? Instead, the only unusual proposition I received was from Mr. Hamid, who offered to take me to Borivili for a viewing of his factory, where they manufactured prosthetic limbs.

In the contest for the most preposterous of my would-be paramours, Mr. Dugal emerged as the winner. I had always considered him a little wan before, someone whose personality made him fade obligingly into the background. All this changed the night he came knocking, ostensibly to borrow some sugar—"just a tea's spoon." Tea, however, was not the beverage of choice for the evening—his breath was so laden with alcohol, it seemed syrupy. I came out of the kitchen with the sugar bowl in hand, to find him in the living room, holding on to a chair for support. "Your husband was always such a good friend of mine," he began, but was soon complimenting me on my teeth. "They're so white and shiny—what toothpaste do you use?"

Before I could nudge him out, he plopped down to the floor. "My wife has grown too fat, she doesn't pay the slightest attention to her appearance anymore. It's good you're still maintaining your looks after what happened, it's the sensible thing to do. Look at me—even though I feel so young inside, I know I'm almost bald." He leaned his scalp forward. "It's the amoebic dysentery, you know."

He started reeling off the remedies he had tried unsuccessfully—the ayurveda, the homeopathy, the colonics. "I was always sick, even as a child, all the bronchitis I used to get." Interspersed through his ramblings were wistful comments about my figure, my face, my clothes. "That's such a pretty nail polish," he said, swiveling towards my feet, and I drew back as he tried to pet my toes.

I escaped by sending you to summon Pinky from her flat to come tell him he was needed at home. In the morning, Mrs. Dugal seemed unsurprised when I apprised her of her husband's visit. "Oh, he just likes to come by and chat—don't mind anything he says."

"This wasn't just chatting—he was drunk, and sitting on my floor."

Mrs. Dugal laughed as if it were all a big misunderstanding. "No, no—he only has a tiny peg at night, so he can sleep. Don't worry, it won't happen anymore." She couldn't quite hide the embarrassment in her eyes.

The next evening Mr. Dugal was back, but this time I was more prepared. "Your wife told me she just bought a big bag of sugar for you this morning," I said, and closed the door.

THE ONE PERSON, surprisingly, who didn't cast his lot in with these crude attempts was Arya. He started writing to you soon after we came back from our 1972 Independence Day trip to Delhi. He wrote his letters in

Hindi, because it was important to know the national language, he said. Since you hadn't learnt to read in Hindi yet, I read them aloud to you when they came.

In the beginning, his letters were routine and dry. He updated us on Babuji's condition and the construction of the new Nizamuddin station. He spent whole paragraphs enumerating everyone who sent their love from Delhi. At the end was a checklist of questions to fill up the page— what sports you were playing, how your studies were faring.

But he soon opened up, writing about things that he thought would interest you—a trip with Rahul and Tony to Connaught Place, the new children's train inaugurated near Okhla station, the red-haired dog that came by every evening to eat leftover scraps. How these days he was learning a new subject, cooking, from Hema auntie, to give Mataji a break on some evenings. He told you about the role of Dashrath he had agreed to play for the reading of the Ramayana dur- ing the Dassera festival—he was having difficulty memorizing his lines, he confessed. His letters arrived from such far-flung states as Orissa and Tamil Nadu, where he traveled to set up new offices for the HRM. "Today I sat in the train all day with my Ramayana in my lap and watched this vast nation of ours go by. Sometimes I imagine I'm truly one of the characters in the epic, making the same journey as our Lord Ram did." All the travel was exhausting, he wrote. He wished he could turn the clock back to conducting the recruits in their morning exercises as he used to long ago. "There's nothing I miss more than the mud and sweat of the wrestling pits."

For a while, he related stories about your father. "He was always such a happy baby, laughing more than he cried in the crib." Even when he was a boy, their parents invited the neighbors to come hear Dev sing. "On some Sundays, my mother used an old sari to convert the balcony of our flat into a stage. Your father held his head under a stream of cold water—to awaken the music cells in his brain, he said. He emerged on the balcony with his long wet hair curled into a knot like a prince, and gave the signal for the curtain to be raised. A cluster of people gathered on the street, and soon there would be twenty or thirty or even fifty spec- tators watching the concert from two floors below."

The lyricism that emerged in Arya's letters surprised me. He described a field trip to Kashmir with his colleagues and spoke of flower-strewn lakes and valleys carpeted in green. He filled an entire page writing about a misty mountainside in Assam, where women appeared and faded "like angels" as they harvested tea. He started adorning his text with snippets of poetry. Sometimes he became reflective and wrote of the vagaries of life and perseverance in the face of tragedy. "People change all the time, but it's up to those around to recognize this. Your uncle is no longer the same person he was ten years ago, or even five."

These last philosophical musings, I guessed, were meant for me. They were written in a refined and flowery Delhi Hindi which even I had trouble deciphering. Living in Bombay for all these years, where people spoke a pidgin version, had stultified my vocabulary. I brought in a dictionary once I went back to the translation agency, to keep handy while reading his letters.

When it came time to reply, it was once again I who had to transcribe the response for you. Each word I formed, each page I filled, further wore down my resistance, made it feel less bizarre an idea to be corresponding with him. I addressed the letters to Yara uncle and signed them "Ashvin," but it was impossible to ignore that it was my handwriting on the paper, my sentences running down the page.

Must Arya have become as used to my letters, as I did to his? The cream-colored prepaid envelopes with the embossed blue stamps—must he, too, have learnt to recognize them instantly when the mail came? Were there bundles of old letters saved for some reason, sitting in a box on his cupboard shelf as well?

I took you to Delhi during almost every vacation now, where Arya remained as proper and formal towards me as before. But the letters communicated a more intimate set of feelings. "Every person harbors an image of perfect beauty within," he wrote once. "It's only when that idea is captured that the person can become truly fulfilled."

IN ONE LETTER, ARYA pointed out a curiosity he discovered in the English spelling of your name. One could rearrange the first five letters in

"Ashvin" to form "Shiva." But also, replacing the first letter *A* with a *U*, your name became an anagram of "Vishnu" instead. He wove elaborate tales about Shiva and Vishnu competing to claim you as theirs. Each time you were lost in your own world, Shiva would point out that you were meditating, to be more like him. But then Vishnu would counter with occasions when you were energetic, even mischievous, in emulation of his own incarnations.

Your favorite story had the two gods descending to Tardeo to have a fight over you. Shiva grew even taller than the building we lived in, so that with one foot planted in the street in front, the other foot reached all the way to Bombay Central. He struck his trident into a cloud to charge it with lightning, so that he could envelop objects in giant fireballs just by pointing the prongs at them. Not to be outdone, Vishnu appeared as an enormous eagle, whose wings stretched from Colaba to Mahim. He attacked Shiva with his talons, tried to rip him apart with his beak—in the ensuing fight, half of Tardeo was destroyed. In the end, neither god won—each realized he was fighting himself, they were simply two faces of the same being. "That's why Ashvin should be so proud that be brings Shiva and Vishnu together in his name," Arya wrote. After that, you insisted on "Ashvin" whenever Paji tried calling you "Ace."

chapter
thirty

I FOUND MY JOB AT MR. HANSI'S EASY BUT NOT VERY COMPELLING—
translating cartoon blurbs could provide only so much variety. Coupled
with that, my male coworkers continued harassing me—I felt myself
worn down brushing off their advances. As it turned out, I didn't have
to work there very long. Four months after I started, the *Indian Express*
published an exposé on the thriving copyright infringement industry in
India. In response, the police raided the sidewalk hawkers selling pirated
Jacqueline Susann and Harold Robbins novels near Flora Fountain.
They also appeared at lunchtime one afternoon, to arrest Mr. Hansi and
close down our office.

After the *Indian Express* exposé was forgotten, with Jacqueline
Susann back on the street, I learnt that Mr. Hansi had diversified into
book pirating himself, at his reincarnated outfit in the faraway suburb of
Bhayander. Just as Paji was looking for another job for me, your school
offered to hire me as a teacher for their new program of nursery classes.
The hours were about the same as yours, which meant we could ride
together on the public bus. Even more appealing, I would face no more
leers—the only male teachers were Jesuit fathers.

Perhaps all my motherly instincts had been expended in bringing
you up, because I found other people's children a lot less endearing

than my own. One of the tots got into the habit of flinging his note-books at the board—another had an accident in his pants like clock-work every day after lunch. I especially hated accompanying them downstairs to the playground—the way they swarmed around me like a shoal of tadpoles, bumping into my legs, pulling at my hand, using my sari to wipe their sticky palms. A coworker suggested I ask to be transferred to a class with older children, but for that one needed qual-ifications I didn't possess.

Still, I kept at it until the term ended in April. I managed to procure a key to the terrace above the statue of St. Xavier's, and that's where we began to go for lunch. We sat on the shaded part of the parapet, looking over the top of the mango tree, the shrieks of the children playing in the compound below barely reaching us. You enjoyed my parathas the most—peeling them apart and finishing all the potato filling first, then rolling up each half and eating it dipped in ketchup.

I never gave back the key to the terrace. Long after I quit my nurs-ery school job, we continued to sneak up on the days I brought you lunch. Sometimes, after a rain shower, we sighted rainbows over Metro Cinema, shimmering in the sun as they rose and plunged. The city sparkled before us, the air itself smelling as if it had been scrubbed.

Finally, one day, our lunches on the terrace ended. We carried our parathas to the top, and found a new lock in which my key no longer worked.

BY THAT SUMMER, the student violence from Gujarat and Bihar had swept over the whole country. I read about riots almost every day in the newspaper—sometimes sparked by high prices, sometimes unemploy-ment, sometimes corruption (the news on TV carefully omitted all such reports). For the first time that I could recall, a strong and charismatic leader had emerged from the opposition—Jayprakash Narayan, or JP as the former freedom fighter was called. "Total revolution," he declared, a struggle which would not end until Indira was removed from power. He managed to form a coalition that outlandishly combined both Hindu and Muslim fundamentalists. Paji fired off enraged letters, complaining how Biji had outdone herself in ruining his reputation by participating in the JP protests. No denial by Biji came in the mail—she didn't seem to have time to dictate her letters to Sharmila anymore.

We went to Delhi earlier than usual, because of rumors of another railway strike. The city was baking when we arrived—several people had already died in the heat wave sweeping the north. The Loo wind seemed to have set its rudder to blow in from the Thar Desert precisely to the center of Delhi every day, its blasts wilting tree leaves as they hung from their branches, withering any patch of exposed skin. In the afternoons, normally bustling areas looked as if a curfew was in place—people emerged only in the morning, before the strong gusts started, or after the sun had set.

Despite this, Arya chose 4 p.m. at the Coffee House in the middle of Connaught Place to meet. He sprang the invitation on me one day in Nizamuddin, claiming he wanted to discuss something important. "Their cold coffee, you might still remember, is the best in the city." Perhaps I felt the bond of our correspondence obligated me. There could be no harm in meeting at such a public place, I thought, and agreed.

By the time I found myself pushing open the door of the Coffee House, I dreaded what would transpire inside. The orchestration of letters over the years, the subtly endearing messages they contained—surely they pointed to only one motive. The air-conditioning made me feel a little better, as did the sight of the dark-cushioned chairs inside, the walls covered with the soothing coffee-colored drapes. Paji used to bring us here for special occasions—I recalled the square-tipped dessert spoons, the tall ice-cream-topped drinks.

"I wasn't sure you'd come," said a man, walking up to me. It was Arya, clad in a suit and tie. My first reaction, which I managed to stifle, was to laugh. This person, who I had seen so often in loincloth and undershirt, who was most at home covered in mud from a wrestling pit, was attempting to make a good impression on me by becoming westernized (that too, in this heat). His tie was all wrong, his coat too tight and poorly stitched, and yet he managed to pull it off better than I would have expected. It was the gray temples with the clipped gray mustache, the rimless glasses he had begun to wear, which gave him a distinguished air. I half expected him to pull my chair back for me, but he led me to the table and gestured at it, then sat down before I did. "Their cold coffee is very good," he reminded me again.

It was indeed very good, served with a generous scoop of ice cream floating in the frothy liquid. I tried to concentrate on what Arya was saying—for some reason, he wanted to give me an overview of the HRM. "People say we're against Muslims because we protest their special rights, or against Christians because we speak out when they convert villagers through bribes. But we're not against any group or sect—we're Hindus after all—a religion that's always believed in coexistence, never conversion. You must understand this—we're here to help people, not hurt them—protecting the rights of other Hindus, that's the only goal we have."

He went on to enumerate the offices he had opened for the organization—it seemed like he had been to almost every state in the country. "After Sandhya died, I accepted any assignment that would take me away from here, take me away from her memory. I stayed in huts in Assam, ate what the tribals ate in Nagaland, traveled standing up in third class unreserved all the way from Nagpur to Bhopal. I carried an extra pair of laces in my pocket, because with all the walking I did, I was worried the ones in my shoes would break." He told me he lost count of all the stomach ailments he suffered—for weeks, he was delirious with malaria in Bihar. "It's taken more than a decade, but now I finally feel the network is in place. And some of the offices I've managed to open have left even the people at our headquarters amazed. Seven in West Bengal alone—can you believe it, the Communist state? It just shows that even Communists can get fed up when they keep having their jobs stolen by Muslims from Bangladesh.

"The point is that I'm back now. As long as I was traveling so much, it was impossible to even conceive of a future for myself. But now—now, the time has come to stop running away. To let the wheel of my life stop spinning so I can ease into my place in the world again."

I watched his hands as he spoke. They were thick hands, but their coarseness seemed curiously restrained, as if smoothed out by a manicure. Were these the same hands that had hit Sandhya hard enough to bruise her face? Could they have somehow reformed themselves, shed their brutality as easily as dirt being cleaned out from under their fingernails?

Perhaps Arya read what I was thinking, because he started to speak of Sandhya. "It's been twelve years now that she passed away. A week doesn't go by that I don't wonder if I could have done anything to stop what happened. I console myself that perhaps her need to provide me with a son was too great. Even when she was alive, I felt she sometimes wanted me to do the things I did, that it was the only way she could live with her guilt. Not that it's any excuse, or that I'm not ashamed."

Arya stared at the ice cream melting into his coffee, his expression clouded—with repentance or self-pity, I couldn't tell. Then he looked up at me. "I asked you here to show you something. Something I've been carrying around for a long time." He took out a folded-up piece of lined paper, the type one tore out of a notebook, and handed it to me. "Over the years, I thought several times of talking to someone about it—showing it to Mataji or Hema. But I was never ready—I knew what they'd try to force me into, I knew what they'd say. Of course, when Dev died, I thought of sharing it with you. It took all my self-control to wait until today."

I could see the impressions in the paper from the pencil strokes on the other side, the writing arranged carefully between the faint blue printed lines. I felt uneasy unfolding the sheet—if Arya had concealed this for so many years, there would surely be something unpleasant waiting inside. To my surprise, the sentences confronting me were scrawled out in the uneven hand of a child.

"You do recognize it, don't you?" Arya asked, but I shook my head. "Look carefully at the handwriting." I scanned over the lines—the letters were so raggedly formed that it was hard to understand the words. Then my name jumped out from the text, and I stopped. "It's Sandhya," Arya said, something I realized the instant before he uttered the words. "She left it under my pillow—I found it the day after she died. I remember how anxiously she was trying to learn to write from Hema—it must have taken her forever to form those lines."

He took the paper gingerly from my fingers, as if it might crumble if not handled carefully enough. "See how she's erased the first line? She never called me by name, so she must have had a difficult time deciding how to address me—she left it blank, finally. Isn't it amazing—to be married to someone for all those years and never once hear your name in their voice?"

He handed the paper back to me. "She'd have wanted you to read it. I have it memorized, anyway—*I'm going away now. I want to meet Devi Ma and ask her why she didn't answer my prayers.* Look how much care she took—it might be hard to read, but the grammar, the spelling, are both perfect.

"*Please forgive me for all the years I've disappointed you. Please forgive me for any mistakes I've made. After I've gone, please marry again. I know there are many sons still waiting in your future. This time, marry someone like Meera who's more educated than myself. It will make you happier.*" Arya stopped, and looked away. "Every time I read that line, I feel so ashamed. She must have known, mustn't she? Caught my stares in your direction, seen all along what I thought I hid."

I read the last sentences of the letter myself. *I pray your life gets filled with as much happiness as you have filled mine with. I will always worship you as my god.* She had not signed her name at the end.

"There's not so much else to add," Arya said, still not looking at me. "I've already told you I'm no longer the person you knew from before. Loss has a way of mellowing you, making you more mature. What Sandhya would've wanted—what you can read her wishing in the last thoughts in your hand, is, as you must guess, what I want as well. You know I already think of Ashvin as my own son. That will never change, whether or not you decide to complete my world.

"I'm not proud of the side I've shown you in the past. I know I will never meet anyone as refined, as beautiful, as cultivated as you. The only way I can prove that I've changed is if you give me a chance."

I could certainly not claim that his proposal took me unawares. Still, I was stunned by how easily the obliqueness of the letters had been stripped off in a few plain sentences. "I'm not sure what to say," I managed to respond.

Perhaps Arya read the apprehension in my face, because he leaned towards me over the table—so far that the straw from his glass brushed against his jacket pocket without him noticing. "You don't even have to move to Delhi. I can start working for the Bombay branch of the HRM. Ashvin could continue going to his school, and you could keep the friends you've made. I'd have to find some way to look after Mataji and Babuji, but it wouldn't be so hard with Hema living a half mile away."

He sat back in his chair and began toying with his glass, looking at me carefully, as if trying to decide if he could trust me with a secret. "I don't know if you've been keeping track of what JP has been doing for the country these days. It's just a matter of time, you know, before he forces Indira to quit. When that happens, the HRM is going to be in the forefront—we're one of the few groups, he knows, who's supported him since the beginning. All the years the government has tried to keep us down—the pot is going to finally burst from the pressure under that lid. I warn all the new recruits to be prepared for changes in this country that no one can even imagine. All this corruption you see now, this kowtowing, this favoritism—the HRM is going to simply wipe all of it away. I could tell you more about the plans we have, but perhaps it's bad luck to talk at this premature stage." I was glad to have him to go on, glad for the chance to hide my distress, to bring a noncommittal expression to my face.

"The point I'm trying to make is simply this. On at least this one issue, I can clear away any misgivings you might have about me. God willing, my best days are just around the corner. It wouldn't be such a bad time to link your star to mine." He said this not boastfully, but with sincerity. The suit kept the scent of his body contained as he sat there— the air was heady with coffee and nothing else.

Could I really have been serious when I told him I would think about it, or was it just a way to be polite? Did I really keep flashing back to the earnestness on his face as I rode the motor rickshaw back to Darya Ganj, or was it just the heat playing tricks? "There's nobody else in the world I'd rather leave him to," I heard Sandhya say. She held out her arms lovingly for me, inviting me to press my head against her breast again.

The next time I met Arya in Nizamuddin, he was again as proper and reserved as before. He was no longer attired in a coat, though, and his hair didn't seem as perfectly trimmed.

BY THE TIME I got on the train to Bombay, the intensity of Arya's proposal had subsided in my mind. It was one thing to find his letters pleasant reading, quite another to entrust my fate into his hands. Marriage, as I had found out, was all about physical responsibilities. This was not going to be some platonic union or meeting of minds.

For years, a part of me had waited for the day that Dev would make love to me in a way that left me fulfilled. The longer this hope remained unrealized, the more the actual need within me had faded. After Dev died, I had wondered if the physical side of me might, in some glorious renaissance, flower again. Perhaps I would run into the boy who followed me in college and actually carry out my reverie of spending the night with him.

I revisited all the fantasies I'd had about the boy over the years, and tried to imagine their consummation. The heat flowing once again through my lower self, like it had so long ago in my life. The craving magically returning, so that the two of us could be united in its embrace through the night. I was only in my thirties, Hema had reminded me (and Arya barely forty, she had lied). There were many more years of sexual activity ahead of me, according to the *Femina* issue on women's sexuality Sharmila had mailed.

But the renaissance hadn't come. The yearnings of my body remained dormant, only in an abstract sense did they seem still alive. I wondered if it could be true, what *Femina* was claiming about female gratification, or a myth cooked up in the reporter's overheated mind. And not just *Femina*, but all the references that cropped up with increasing boldness in books and songs and films. The way Sharmila kept rhapsodizing about Munshi, the way Hema made sly references to Gopal. Even Zaida shocked me with her fantasies one afternoon when she talked about the neighborhood boy she had loved.

Surely all this enthusiasm about sex must be exaggerated. There was little I could remember to recommend it from my experiences with Dev. Even were I to feel moved enough by such considerations and seek a husband again, I would hardly expect Dev's brother to be the best candidate. I tried to imagine Arya's mouth on my lips, his hands on my breasts, his body on top of mine, and shivered.

There was also a nagging question about Sandhya's note—why had it been unsigned? I remembered all the letters I received from Nizamuddin on the corners of which she had laboriously scrawled out her name. If this was to be her last communication, wouldn't she have wanted to do the same? Could Arya have written the note himself, to push me towards accepting him? Could he have omitted the signature, realizing I might recognize it as fake? In the end, I decided he probably hadn't, but the last bit of doubt remained.

It hardly mattered, though—once I was back in the flat with you, I realized how little need I had for someone else. I always avoided characterizing our existence as a happy one for fear of having our luck turn, of attracting the evil eye. But with each day of contentment that went by, it became harder not to admit it. I decided to write Arya a nice letter declining his proposal. I told him that with all the loss his parents had been through, it was important he stay with them now. I complimented him on his gentlemanly behavior towards me ever since Dev had died. "Wherever she is, the kindness you extended to Ashvin and me must have filled Sandhya's heart with joy. I can never stop thinking of you as her husband, as the one she truly loved. As Dev's brother, and hence my own. And of course, you will always be Ashvin's Yara uncle to me." The result was quite satisfying, I decided—reading it, he could not possibly be offended. Nor could he be left with any hope that it would be fruitful to pursue me further. I mailed it just in time—a few days later, on the twenty-sixth of June, 1975, to be exact, the whole country came to a standstill.

chapter thirty-one

Mrs. HUSSAIN KNOCKED ON THE DOOR AT 8 A.M. "COME QUICK. IT'S your Paji on the phone. A trunk call from Delhi." Then, seeing my alarm, she added, "Don't be worried—he probably just wants to talk about the Emergency that Indira Gandhi's declared."

She elaborated as we hurried up the stairs. "It's on radio and in all the newspapers. JP and the rest of the opposition—Indira Gandhi's rounded them all up and thrown them in jail. She did it last night, after her own cabinet ministers were all sound asleep. Plus, she's suspended freedom of speech—not just that, but right to property, everything. All the news is being censored—*the Indian Express* left its editorial page blank in protest."

Paji quickly filled me in on the rest of the details. How the crisis had been brewing for two weeks, since the judge in Allahabad found Indira Gandhi guilty of election fraud and banned her from holding office. How a Supreme Court judge ruled that she could remain until her appeal was settled, but not vote in Parliament until then. "Of course, the opposition went wild with the scent of her blood in the air. Did you see JP's rally yesterday, when he called for a blockade of the prime minister's house? I suppose this was the only way she could stay in power, though she claims she did it because JP urged the armed forces to revolt."

The morning newspapers in Delhi hadn't even been printed. "She had the electricity cut off to every press in the city, including my own. What's sad is that the original election fraud charges were so laughable. Do you know, the London *Times* called them no more serious than a traffic offense?"

Someone seemed to be screaming in the background on Paji's side, and I heard a series of muffled thuds. "In case you're wondering, that's your mother. I've locked her up in her room, and she's trying everything she can to get out. She was all dressed up to go on a protest march with her student hooligans this morning, can you imagine? What she doesn't realize is how much trouble she's in already—it'll be a miracle if I can prevent her from being carted off to jail."

As it was, the police came that week not only for Biji but, much to his shock, Paji himself. It was only through the intervention of his Congress friends, and a promise to print two lakh free copies of a pamphlet entitled "The Many Boons of the Emergency" that Paji managed to secure his (and Biji's) continuing freedom. "The amazing thing is that your mother still seems to think that what she did was reasonable," he wrote. "She spends all day threatening to go to Tihar jail to visit her incarcerated friends."

Paji wasn't the only one forced to resort to such tactics to save himself. All sorts of people found themselves entangled in the giant nationwide dragnet that was supposed to capture "antisocial elements" (smugglers, black marketeers, and, presumably, opposition politicians). The dowager princess of Jaipur was kept in jail until she signed a declaration in support of the Emergency. The editor of the Communist-leaning weekly *Blitz*, who had denounced Indira at every opportunity, suddenly appeared on television to laud her boldness and integrity. Mrs. Hussain told me of industrialists lining up to garland Indira, or even throw themselves at her feet for forgiveness, depending on how errant had been their politics.

A few mornings after the declaration of the Emergency, I saw a list in the newspaper of twenty-six "antipatriotic" organizations that had been banned. As Paji pointed out, the groups spanned the political spectrum, from the Marxist Communist Party to all sorts of right-wing communal Hindu factions. Foremost among the latter was the HRM. Arya went into hiding that very first week, just before the police came to arrest him under MISA, the ominously titled Maintenance of Internal Security Act.

June turned into July, then August, then September. With each month, the nation backed away further from the anarchy into which it had seemed ready to plunge. It was tremendously soothing to wake up every morning and read about nothing but all the benefits we were enjoying. MISA had cleansed everyone from tax evaders to drug dealers to, we were told, wife beaters, from the country. Both sugar and kerosene were suddenly in plentiful supply at the ration shop downstairs. I went to get the television license renewed, and to my shock, the clerk greeted me with a smile. Nobody had an inkling as yet of the forced sterilizations and other atrocities Indira's son Sanjay was planning to unleash.

By October, giant cloth posters of Indira hung all over the city, perhaps painted by the same artists who made the posters for Hindi films. They were so large that ripples ran through the image of her face, from the tip of her nose through the waves of white in her hair—a superheroine flying intrepidly above us, ready to tackle any adversity that came our way. Her countenance became familiar, reassuring—whereas previously she had been ubiquitous only on the television news, now Indira truly was everywhere. One of these posters was even erected for a rally held in your school compound—it listed the entire twenty-point program the Emergency was supposed to accomplish. Afterwards, Indira remained smiling benignly over the playground, as if, undeterred by the twenty listed tasks already on her plate, she had generously tacked on the guardianship of the schoolchildren as the twenty-first.

Inspired by this vision in their backyard, the school organized a drawing contest—each student was to pick one of the twenty points and make a poster about it. You picked point number fourteen—"controlling the prices of essential commodities." The poster depicted a gaggle of children cheering and dancing around a mound of sugar, with rupee notes sticking out of some of their pockets. The prize, however, went to an entry on point number seven, "limiting land ownership among the wealthy."

WE DIDN'T MAKE OUR usual trip to Delhi that year for the Divali festival. On the one hand, you missed the activities with your cousins, especially the gambling at vaguely understood card games, using potato chips as stakes. On the other hand, you had forgotten how much fun it was to light rockets from our terrace. Pinky was particularly outrageous, being at the peak of her tomboy phase. She lit "atom bombs" under cans, kicked ground wheels like footballs, flung live whistle rockets at children in range. Once, she set fire to the curtains in Mrs. Hamid's flat on the floor below. I noticed she was always protective of you—never subjecting you to the same rough play she employed to keep a hold on her gang.

The newspapers predicted an unusually subdued Divali this time due to the Emergency, but shops seemed packed as usual, and worshippers spilled out of temples into the street. I was apprehensive about Divali eve, when I would be the one responsible for the pooja for Lakshmi that Dev always used to perform. The year after he had died, we had not celebrated, and after then, we had always gone for Lakshmi pooja to Nizamuddin.

When it came time, I got several of the details wrong. You reminded me of the coins that were supposed to be dabbed with milk for prosperity, the saffron with which I neglected to mark the forehead of Lakshmi. I couldn't remember the prayers Dev used to recite—you were resentful of my impromptu substitutions. At the end, you brought the sugar for me to sprinkle in your mouth and my own, but without Dev, it wasn't the same. I tried to get you upstairs to the terrace to distract you with the fireworks, but you pouted that you preferred to stay in and watch a TV program on the Emergency.

When the doorbell rang, you let me be the one to answer it. It took me a few seconds to match the unshod person before me, clothed grimily in a loincloth, with the one I had seen only some months before, so spruce in a tie and coat. "I didn't think you'd turn me away on Divali,"

Arya said, his face barely visible through a mass of knotted hair, his body reeking of dirt and sweat. "So I waited until today before knocking on your door."

You must have recognized the voice even with the TV on, because you came running up, shouting, "Yara uncle!" The sight of the disheveled figure at our doorstep, still waiting to be invited in, made you stop. "Yara uncle?" you asked, uncertainly.

"Yes, it *is* your Yara uncle." Arya took the opportunity to stride in and lift you up into the air. "Don't you recognize him under this beard?"

"No, I don't. It looks awful, your beard. Why are you dressed like that? And what's that smell?" You wrinkled your nose.

"Your uncle has been hiding because bad men are chasing him. He's trying to look very ordinary so no one recognizes him. You have to promise not to tell anyone you saw me here, understand?" Arya put you down. "Understand?" he repeated, staring into your eyes until you nodded.

He turned to me. "I hope you don't mind—I'm sorry to barge in like this. With everyone celebrating, I felt too alone—I just couldn't resist coming over today. It's only for an hour or two—I won't spend the night—I'll go right now if you say."

It wasn't just his appearance that made me nervous, or the way his eyes roved about the room behind me, as if searching the corners to make sure nobody would spring out. His sudden presence here in Bombay, in our building, at our doorstep, the way he used to materialize all those years ago, also brought back uncomfortable memories. But I could hardly ask him to leave. I told myself that the issue between us already stood resolved by my letter, that all I had to do, if needed, was to remind him of my discouraging response. Perhaps in a way that was firm, yet not harsh—a way that acknowledged the compliment he was paying me with his continuing interest, even held out the possibility of meeting again, innocently someday, for ice cream at the Coffee House. "Are you hungry?" I asked.

Arya nodded. "It's been a while, especially, since I had chappatis cooked at home. Although Yara uncle can only eat if Ashvin here feeds me with his own hand."

"But the smell," you said, scrunching up your face again.

We decided he would first take a bath, before I served dinner. As the water heated, Arya told me how he had spent the last several months. His words tumbled out rapidly, with deep inhalations between them, like a man who has been running, speaking between gasps to catch his breath. "I was lucky—they made the mistake of going to Hema's house instead. I think they mixed me up with Gopal—they took him to the station, but then let him go—I suppose they didn't think him important enough. I left Delhi that very night. All the traveling I had done paid off—I knew exactly where to hide, whom I could trust. Of course, the police was shutting down HRM offices everywhere and locking up the same people who had helped me set them up, so I had to keep moving. They almost captured me, too—once in Patna, where a constable fired a rifle after me, and then again at the station in Nagpur. Someone had lent me the change of clothes I have on—the police thought I was a villager fresh off the train and let me walk out." He paused to thrust a greedy handful of the peanuts I had laid in front of him into his mouth. "I must be quite high on their list, I think. Not like George Fernandes, whom they've still not caught—not as famous as him, but still." I did not miss the note of pride in his voice. As he chewed, a little of his hunted expression seemed to dissipate.

I expected him to mention my letter, but he didn't. Could he not have received it? There was no point bringing it up myself, so I kept my silence.

You carried in a box from the bedroom and ceremoniously laid it down on the table next to the nuts. "What's this?" Arya asked. "A present for Yara uncle?" Inside were Dev's toiletries and shaving set. Arya pulled you into his lap. "Yara uncle can't get rid of his beard, you know. Otherwise the bad men might recognize him."

In the end, though, perhaps against his better judgment, he did shave. I was startled to see him emerge from the bathroom. I had shown him to the cache of your father's clothes you had insisted we keep. Arya had helped himself to clean undergarments, a kurta pajama outfit, a pair of chappals that were almost the right size for his feet. With his suddenly clean-shaven face and the way he had slimmed down on the run, he resembled Dev more than ever before, despite his gray hair. He even had the same Cinthol soap smell on his skin, the same Godrej after-shave scent emanating from his face. You noticed it too, because you wrapped your head in the shirttails of his kurta, and tried to burrow into him.

At your insistence, Arya performed the Lakshmi pooja again. This time, Lakshmi had her forehead properly anointed with saffron, and the appropriate incantations were recited while moistening each coin with milk. Arya sprinkled the consecrated sugar in our mouths—his manner, from the closing of his eyes to the tilting of his head, was so reminiscent of Dev, that I had to look away. You pulled your Yara uncle to the pantheon, to have all the other gods appeased correctly as well, after the years of negligence to which I might have subjected them.

After dinner, you wanted to go up to the terrace to set off rockets, but Arya shook his head. "Yara uncle isn't ready yet to meet your neighbors after shaving off his beard. He's going to teach you three-card flush instead. It's more important on Divali than setting off fireworks—to gamble and test your fortune for the coming year." Even with the five-paise stakes, you raked in more than six rupees—your uncle called it beginner's luck, but used various shuffling tricks to make you win.

At some point, you put on "House of Bamboo" on the gramophone. Arya was reluctant to dance, but you latched onto his kurta and dragged him out on the floor. He was slow and ungainly, not at all like Dev. He settled into a peculiar cycle of steps, alternately raising each arm to form a right angle at the elbow, then twirling clumsily. I clapped along, mildly amused, until, against my better judgment, I let you pull me in as well.

I could tell how immediately embarrassed Arya was. This man who had once serenaded me with such crudeness—dancing to the same song was all it took now to turn his neck a deep red. I felt self-conscious as well. Perhaps because you were watching, perhaps because it was so unusual to have the formal barrier between a wife and a brother-in-law shed. Or perhaps it was something more dangerous—the way I began to be intoxicated by the memory of Dev's looks, his clothes, his scent. Fortunately, the record was almost over—we retired to different corners of the room the instant it came to an end.

You hated the flip side, "Hawaiian Wedding Song," but put it on today. You tried to draw us back, but soon realized how impossible it was to lure us into dancing to so slow and intimate a tune. Instead, you began making exaggerated sweeps across the floor with arms raised, as if waltzing to Andy Williams' crooning with an imaginary partner. As usual, the song made you sleepy—when the last note faded, you yawned on cue.

But you were unwilling to let the evening end just yet. When Arya kissed you good night, you put up such a fuss that he agreed to sit by your bedside and relate a story to you.

"Once there was a boy named Ashvin," Arya began. "Unlike other boys, Ashvin was special—he had not only Shiva, but also Vishnu living in him."

"Shiva was quiet, and Vishnu was lively," you responded. By now, you could recite all the different attributes for the two from Arya's letters. "One came from the moon, and the other from the sun."

"So you can imagine how much of a problem this caused," Arya said. He began spinning out a variation of the tales in his letters, about how Shiva wanted tranquillity for Ashvin, while Vishnu kept encouraging the boy to shout and laugh. In this one, instead of the two gods battling over Ashvin, Vishnu transformed himself into a beautiful woman to seduce Shiva and keep the peace between them. "Shiva found himself helpless in front of her beauty—the soft skin, which was the color of lotus petals, the silken hands and feet, the sweet, succulent lips." By the time Shiva succumbed to Vishnu's charms to become one with him and restore harmony to the world, you were asleep.

Arya kissed you. "He reminds me so much of Dev when he was the same age." Outside, atom bombs still went off on the street, rocket flashes lit up the sky. Arya covered your sleeping form to the waist with a sheet, then followed me out into the drawing room.

We stood around awkwardly, on opposite sides of the sofa. "I suppose I should be going." The intonation suggested a question more than a statement.

It would have been a simple matter to reply, to agree with him. But I hesitated—seeing Arya put you to sleep like Dev used to had heightened my intoxication. It wasn't arousal I felt but a headiness, a nostalgia, so overwhelming that it was almost physical. How long had I inhaled the scent of Dev's toiletries without being aware of it, brushed against his kurta without thinking about it twice? Over how many years had the contours of his facial features, so similar to Arya's, been impressed into my mind? Whether or not I had been in love with Dev, or attracted to him, or happy, or satisfied, made no difference. His memories had been forever implanted within me, their rootholds tenacious and deep, their shoots ready, at the slightest stimulus, to start rising back into life. I could no more help responding to these memories than I could control a reflex in my knee or the twitching of an eye.

My hesitation must have been plain for Arya to see. He moved closer. "I got your letter," he said. "I can't tell you how depressed it left me. It wasn't just my own disappointment I could taste, but Sandhya's as well. Tell me, what can I do to show you how much I've changed? If not for me, then at least so that Sandhya can be at rest."

I tried to reply, tried to summon up my letter and the points I had enumerated in it. But the reasons I had listed didn't cooperate—they danced around, refusing to be pinned down in my head. All I could think of was Dev's after-shave—why had its scent not dissipated as yet? It had been hours since Arya had bathed.

"You don't know how awful the last four months have been. Hiding in filthy holes, eating rotten food, scurrying from place to place every night. The only thing that separated me from a rat's existence was the hope that I would be able to make it here someday. Everyone told me not to leave the safety of the small towns, but I was ready to risk everything, just to see you and Ashvin."

His face loomed closer now, like some moon trying to ensnare me in its gravity. His eyes were large and absorbing, as I remembered from those days in Nizamuddin. I felt again the sensation of being drawn in by his unwavering stare—was he trying to hypnotize me?

"I don't expect to be able to enjoy my liberty much longer. I can feel them closing in on me—every day I think that this might be the last one I'm free. They've already caught three out of the five HRM people who work at my level. One of them, Madhuram, Indira Gandhi's goons tortured so badly, I heard that he might not survive. If I'm going to languish in some prison cell, I need some hope to cling on to—or if not that, at least a memory."

His fingers brushed the back of my wrist resting on the sofa. Was there a reason I didn't move away, why I allowed him to continue stroking? I could feel his hand sliding over mine now and squeezing it. "It would mean so much to me," Arya whispered. Why were my own fingers so acquiescent, why didn't they protest in any way?

The other hand was on my shoulder now, his lips in my hair, his chin against the nape of my neck. Each contact hushed and dreamlike—could he have succeeded in his attempts to mesmerize me? He stood unmoving behind me for a long time, as if he had bitten me in secret and was waiting for the venom to work its way through my body. Finally, when there was no resistance left, I felt him turn me around and kiss me. The couch seemed to vanish, like a prop whisked off the stage in a play. The floor stretched out all around us, smooth and white and bare.

Hadn't I lived through this once before—another uncushioned floor somewhere long ago in my past? This time, though, a pillow from the sofa waited—I felt it cradle my head as I reclined in the center of my drawing room. Arya stared down at me, as if poised at the edge of an exclusive pool, whose waters he could finally explore. I imagined Sandhya hovering somewhere behind him, her eyes starry with approval, her lips spread in a grateful smile.

And now Arya kneeled shirtless between my legs, and I could see how the hairs flecking his chest had begun to whiten like the ones on his head. He cradled my neck in the crook of an arm to get to the buttons of my blouse. As I felt the cloth lift from my body, I wondered if such a momentous occasion in my life shouldn't be marked once more by something melodramatic like the lights going off. Perhaps Nehru or Gandhiji could emerge from the darkness and stand next to Sandhya to watch, maybe even applaud. At the very least, the ceiling should open up above us to reveal a sky ablaze with fireworks.

But the night outside was not visible from where I lay—even the firecracker bursts on the street were muffled by the door to the bedroom in between. The electricity remained on, harsh and glaring, to illuminate Arya as he stripped the rest of his clothes off. The scent of Cinthol and

Godrej vanished abruptly—what took its place was the smell of his desire. The familiar sweet emanation of overripe fruit, which began permeating the air in the room.

The odor jarred me out of my trance. The cells in my brain snapped alert as Arya loosened the drawstring of my petticoat. I felt the material being pulled down over my thighs, the breezy sensation of bareness as my pubic hair was exposed. *Was this what I wanted?*—the question lit up in my mind. Arya gazed down again, as if admiring the waters of his pool one final time before wading into them. Then, with a contented exhalation, he sank into me, and his throat emitted a groan.

At first, he seemed satisfied to simply lie there. His breath smelled of turnips, from the curry I had fed him; his skin was slick, as if oil had seeped from his pores. Even after all the weight he had lost, his body was still heavier than Dev's. "I've dreamt of this since the night you first arrived in Nizamuddin," he whispered boyishly into my ear. I waited under him without breathing, wondering if by some miracle, I might satisfy him with a hug.

He began inching himself into position, and I recognized what he was preparing for. How should I slow him down, explain the spell from which I had just emerged?

"All those years I waited patiently on the sidelines," Arya said. "Never allowing myself to appear too interested in case I scared you away. The letters I wrote so painstakingly—did your response have to be so curt? 'I always want to think of you as Ashvin's uncle.' Why? Am I not good enough to be your husband? Am I not as good enough as my brother? Is he the only one who gets to marry someone as beautiful and perfect and sophisticated as a Sawhney girl?" As if to punctuate his last point, I felt his penis jab against my groin.

So far, I only had an abstract intimation of the danger into which I had thrust myself. Now, with Arya signaling the imminence of his entry, the full seriousness of my situation seized me. I tried to squirm out from under him, but his arms caged me in like bars. His body was everywhere—his chest pressing into my breasts, his crotch rubbing against my pelvis, his thighs smearing me with their sweat. I panicked at the image of the violation to come, at the thought of my own powerless-

ness. The muted explosions outside reminded me that there would be little chance of being heard if I shouted for help. "I don't want to do this.
Let me go, please," I said. Even to me, it sounded as if I was just labor-
ing through the motions, making one last protest for form, after leading
him on.

"Don't worry, I'm not here to hurt you," Arya said, as he slid his
thickness against my thigh. He kissed my neck, then raised himself on
his arms, as if readying himself for the plunge. "I'm just here to change
your mind."

I braced myself. Was there some way of making it less repugnant, by
focusing my attention elsewhere? Then I heard you call out to me.
"Mummy," you said, and I bent back my head to see an upside-down
image of you standing sleepily outside the bedroom door. "The atom
bombs woke me up." Your voice quavered—had you come out because
you sensed something awry?

I began to say your name, but it emerged as a sob. "It's all right,
Ashvin," Arya said. "Go back inside."

But you moved closer. "Did you hurt Mummy? Why is she crying?
What happened to your clothes?"

Arya sat back up on his knees, undaunted by his swinging nakedness.
I reached out towards my sari, to drape it over myself like a sheet. "Go
back to bed. Yara uncle will tell you when you can come out again." He
patted you firmly back towards your room.

"No. I want Mummy to come with me." You took my hand and tried
to pull me up from under Arya.

"Yara uncle's going to get very angry if you don't listen to him. Now
leave your mummy alone and get back inside."

"No."

For a moment, the two of you silently challenged each other with
your stares. Then Arya slapped you. You were stunned for an instant,
then flew back at him, and began raining your fists down on his head.
"Let Mummy go!" you shouted, trying to topple him over with a
wrestling lock around the neck. Arya bore your attempts for a few seconds, then tore your hands off and sent you careering into the gramophone console. The radio teetered in place, but a stack of records and the

gramophone itself slid off and crashed onto the floor. You lay dazed on the ground, surrounded by glossy black fragments of broken record.

"How dare you touch my son!" I shouted, striking my palm against Arya's face. He caught my wrist and hit me back—I tasted blood in my mouth. We scuffled on the floor, and I tried to pull away, but Arya grabbed me by the shoulder and dragged me back. "Ashvin," I gasped, trying to twist around to see if you were still lying hurt on the ground.

But you were already standing, throwing pieces of the broken gramophone at Arya. The handle, the microphone, a bracket that had come off—they all missed and clanged harmlessly to the floor. Then you spotted the turntable and took the record off. You hurled it across the room, striking your uncle in the face and shattering the bridge of his nose.

Arya's blood dripped onto my face, speckled the parting of my hair. From the landing outside our flat, Zaida's voice called out, asking if everything was all right. Hearing it, Arya sprang up with a roar. I tried to latch onto his foot, in case he went for you once more. Instead, he lunged to the door and threw it open. Still naked and bleeding and bellowing, Arya charged past Zaida, down the steps towards the street.

THAT NIGHT, AS ZAIDA helped me wash his blood out of my hair, I kept thinking of Arya skulking outside. I wondered if he would come back, and almost asked her to stay. By the time she left, after making sure we had suffered only cuts and bruises, it was so late that even the celebrations outside were dying down. You stood in the balcony, gazing at the sky to catch the last remaining rocket flashes. Below, urchins roamed the pavements, searching through the litter for unexploded firecrackers. You shivered, even though the night was warm with smoke. I put my arm around your waist and led you back inside.

We pushed the beds together for the night, the way they used to be—you were too upset to leave my side. For a while I sat straddling the seam between the two mattresses, rubbing Iodex over your bruises. You neither wanted to play a game nor be told a story. Instead, you worked your head into my lap and stared at me, your eyes doleful, your face full of turmoil. Every once in a while you would begin a sentence, but then not complete it—about Yara uncle, about me, about yourself. A part of me wanted to squeeze your trauma away, wipe from your memory the sight on the floor. I felt a heaviness in my heart, or perhaps it was shame, that you had seen your mother in that condition. Surprisingly, I also felt guilt—wasn't it enough to have lost your father, that for my sake, you had now been forced to drive your uncle away? "Will he come back?" you asked as I rubbed in the Iodex. I heard fear in your voice, mixed with a trace of wistfulness.

"Don't worry about your uncle tonight. What you did was right—we won't be seeing him for a while."

I felt the soreness in my shoulder blade, where Arya's fingers had dug in. I tried to apply some Iodex to myself, but you took the jar from my hand and did it for me. Your fingers felt light on my skin—the astringency of the iodine began to clear the smell of Arya from my memory.

My hair was still damp from its shampooing, so you brought in a towel from the bathroom and spread it over my pillow. You pressed at the strands, then arranged them into different patterns—a stream of ripples, a sunburst of rays. I let you carry on, since you seemed so completely distracted by this play. "If you're going to make your mummy into such a princess, tell me, how is she going to be able to sleep?"

Your fingers curled a lock behind my ear and began to run down towards my chin. They came to a stop where Arya's hand had left its mark on my cheek. "It's swollen," you said, dabbing at it lightly. "Does it still hurt?"

"Don't worry about Mummy. You saved her, remember? Like her very own Prince Charming. All you were missing was a horse, or it would have been a real fairy tale." My words seemed to cheer you, so I continued. "Rajesh Khanna couldn't have done it better if he was rescuing one of his heroines. Whether it was Mumtaz or Zeenat Aman or Hema Malini. Which one do you think Mummy should be? Perhaps if she was a little fatter, she could even be Yogita Bali."

We both remembered the film, with Yogita Bali making a thunderous splash when she had jumped into a pool to escape being molested by the villain. You began to laugh. Then, abruptly, you grew somber. "Yara uncle—was he trying to do the same thing to you as that bad man in the movie?"

I made room for your head beside me on the pillow. "This isn't the time to think of these things." I kissed you several times on your head, as if contact with my lips would conduct away the thoughts inside. "The important thing is that we're both all right."

You looked like you were getting sleepy. Just as I thought your eyelids would close, they opened up. "You can't be Yogita Bali," you said. "You're not big enough, like her. Over here." You ran your hand across your chest to indicate you meant my bosom.

"I saw you." You blushed. "On the floor."

I AWOKE LATER THAT NIGHT. I must have slept for only an hour or so, because it still wasn't light. I had been dreaming—something with you in it—a dream that hovered tantalizingly at the edge of my consciousness, refusing to be enticed back in. I began to sit up, then stopped— you were asleep in the fold of my arm, your face snuggled against my bosom.

I thought about extricating myself, spreading you out more comfortably, climbing over to lie in your bed. But I stayed where I was, and let myself luxuriate in the feeling of your head at my breast. It hardly mattered that my shoulder blade felt stiff, that the Iodex didn't seem to be working. Fears of Arya prowling naked through the Emergency outside, waiting to strike again, faded to a faraway corner of my mind. I lay back and tried to synchronize my breath to yours by following the rhythmic motion of your chest.

The dream called to me again—I willed my mind to empty, my attention to float free, to lure it back. What flitted in, as I watched you sleep, were thoughts of Parvati. The son she created to ward off her loneliness, using bath oil and sandal paste and dabs from her own skin. What would happen if Shiva never returned from his ascetic wanderings? Would Parvati and her boy spend the rest of their years in each other's company? Playing hide-and-seek in the forest, eating when they wanted to, sleeping where and when and how they wished? Leading a life that had need for neither husband nor father, that was fulfilled and immutable and carefree?

Or would time change things? Would she notice his lip sprouting, his voice beginning to crack, his features being altered from the ones she had sculpted so lovingly? Would her own beauty fade, her step begin to waver, the wrinkles start to form over her skin? Would there come a time when she would grow too frail for the romping, too listless for the hide-and-seek, too old to sustain the breezy existence they shared? Or perhaps he would tire of it first, would want to strike out on his own, explore the world beyond, leave the forest and his aged, unattractive mother with it?

Surely, though, if she was lavish enough in her devotion, he would not leave. Her love would be a golden playroom, an enchanted palace, whose comforts he would be loath to surrender. A love so indispensable, like air itself, that a life without it he could not conceive. What choice would he have, in the face of such extravagance, except to love her back with a matching intensity?

But she had to be careful how much she allowed him to love her. Wasn't there another son to give her pause, the one named Andhaka, the blind offspring of Shiva and Parvati? What lust erupted in his heart, how ravaged he was by passion, when his sight was restored and he was confronted by his mother's beauty. It was only after Shiva burnt off his flesh and drained the blood from his body that he eventually became worthy to be a son again.

You press yourself closer against my body in your sleep, as if you are whispering into my breast. Could Andhaka's desire be smoldering in your subconscious as well, waiting for the future to manifest itself? What if I fall into the trap of loving you too much—who will sustain me if you ever left?

I try to rein in the darkness of my thoughts, to concentrate once more on recalling my dream. You murmur in your sleep, and I pull you tighter to myself. I gaze at the hollow of your throat as it rises and falls, and ponder the traversing of each breath. If I had a wish, I think it would be that we stayed like this for decades. Time passing us by, letting you remain by my side, inscribing nothing on your chest.

PART FIVE

chapter
thirty-two

ARYA WAS CAPTURED FIVE DAYS LATER, IN BOMBAY ITSELF. TO THE twenty-odd boons of the Emergency, so widely advertised around the city on billboards, I mentally added another—it kept me safe from my brother-in-law. Perhaps Hema found out he had visited me on Divali, because she sent a long, vituperative missive, in which she reviled me for leading her brother on and then turning him in. Among other rambling insults, she accused me of being selfish and perverted—charging that I had gotten rid of Arya just like I had deposed Dev, since I couldn't bear the thought of sharing your affections with any rivals. ("Even Kali would be less bloodthirsty," she wrote.) Oddly, she also suggested that I had engineered Arya's nose to be broken on purpose, so that I didn't have to worry about anyone else marrying him. The next summer when we were in Delhi, however, with Arya still incarcerated, she was warm and cordial, with no mention made of her charges.

After Arya's visit, I had rejoined the beds. Cuddling up to me soon became a habit with you—there was a sense of safety in being together, of coziness, of protection. I would awaken to find your face pressed against some part of my body—the crook of my arm, the cushion of my abdomen, the curve of my neck. Sometimes I just went back to sleep—

at other times, I arranged my pillow under your head and climbed over to occupy your bed instead.

I'm not sure why I became troubled by the frequency of these entanglements. There were no prying neighbors to cluck their disapproval, no Roopa around to make her nasty insinuations. From where did the unease spring that finally prompted me to push the beds against opposite walls of the room one afternoon?

The last time I had done this, after Roopa's visit, you had barely seemed to notice. This time, you were confused by the new arrangement that greeted you upon your return from school. "Which bed will we use? Aren't they too small for us to fit on just one?"

"We'll each use our own. If they're joined, we always end up on the same side—that's why Mummy has separated them."

"But I like sleeping on your side."

"You're ten already, Ashvin—you're getting too big. You want Mummy to have a good night's rest, don't you, and not be cramped?"

"But they're so far apart. How will I save you if some bad man comes at night?"

"Nobody's going to come. And even if someone did, I'm right there, in the same room."

"Daddy never minded when I slept next to him."

You didn't kiss me that night, retiring instead after brushing your teeth to your newly appointed side of the room. When I went over to tuck you in, you pretended to be asleep. The next day, you were more pensive than usual, as if brooding over some weighty problem. Even my announcement that I had made almond kheer for dessert didn't elicit a nod or smile. As I spooned it out, tears began trickling down your cheeks. "Mummy doesn't love me anymore," you burst out crying, and I felt guilty, mortified.

We made a game of joining up the beds again—I pushed while you sat, pretending to be the captain of a ship, commandeering it across the ocean of the bedroom floor. Twinges of doubt arose in me as I held you asleep in my arms afterwards. Had I yielded too easily? Had I not given it enough time? But I felt my apprehensions dissolve when I gazed at your face, peaceful and guileless in the moonlight.

The beds remained joined. The hardest times to reconcile were when you transgressed too conspicuously on my side. When your face found its way deep into my bosom, or a palm settled flagrantly between my thighs. I would lie in the dark wondering whether to wake you up, or try to pry off your sleeping form. It was not as if you were conscious, as if you were making some crude advance. Where was the shame in any contact that was innocent, no matter how it might appear in anyone's eyes?

What troubled me more was the issue of my own reaction. I lived in a vacuum, untouched by anyone except you. Which meant there was only you to keep my need for physical connection satisfied. What if I enjoyed these accidental caresses more than I should? Could there be some part of me getting aroused, some unspeakable desire deep within being gratified? I could almost feel Roopa sear these questions into my mind.

I kept a vigil for the slightest sign of stimulation in my body. I resolved to disengage myself from any contact the least bit titillating. The pleasure I derived from cuddling with you would remain innocent, beyond reproach. It would strictly be my maternal needs being fulfilled.

To my relief, nothing improper turned up in my scrupulous monitoring. There were no embarrassing flushes, no heat spreading dissolutely up my body. The sexual part of me that I had locked away so long ago remained caged, safely hibernating. I began to relax about our sleeping arrangements. The specter of my sister's disapproval faded from my mind.

THE CHANGES, WHEN THEY OCCURRED, crept up on me. Your face never ended up against my neck or my shoulder anymore—it zeroed in on the cleft of my bosom with unerring regularity. Each time I eased away, you tossed and turned and returned to the same position, often with a hand falling across my breast as a further provocation. Once, I awoke to find you splayed out on my chest, like a conqueror resting atop an edifice he had climbed.

And yet I couldn't muster the will to sunder the beds once again.

Even if you were aware of what you were doing, what, really, was the harm in it? Why should there be any impropriety in physical closeness? It wasn't as if Andhaka could have taken over already, as if lust could possess a heart so young.

Perhaps I let myself get too used to the feel of your body against mine, to the reassurance of its weight, like that of a snuggling pet. Each night transported us to our own private island, cocooned us in the sheets, separated us from everyone else. You turned eleven, then twelve and thirteen, and we continued enjoying our closeness in bed.

I was slow in recognizing the signs of puberty. You had always been private while disrobing or preparing for your bath—now you became painfully shy even while taking off your shirt. Still, I caught a glimpse of you once while handing you a towel through the bathroom door—the nascent wisps of pubic hair shocked me. In bed, you clung on to me sometimes, and were aloof at others—demanding a separate sheet one night, and the next, wanting to nuzzle beneath the covers.

Perhaps it would have been easier had Dev been still around, had I grown up with brothers as siblings. There was nobody to educate me about the changes you were going through—it was not something I could brush up on through an article in *Eve's Weekly*. One night, while you were asleep, I felt your puberty asserting itself against my thigh. I reacted so strongly that you awoke at my recoiling.

In that one moment, my ignorance was dispelled. I would pull the beds apart come morning. Then I saw the confusion on your face, its sleepy innocence. I remembered how distraught you had been the last time I separated the beds. I decided to keep things as they were, not call attention to what had happened.

There came mornings when you tried to cover the evidence of dreams that had played out wetly, and I tried my best to feign unawareness. Sometimes I would find a pillow awkwardly arranged in the center of your bed to hide the stain underneath. On other days, the first thing you would insist on upon waking was to go to the bathroom and wash your pajamas yourself. At times you were responsive, nuzzling at my neck as before, melting into my embrace. But there were also nights when you seemed to resent my very presence, when my endearments only made things worse.

On these occasions, you shut your eyes tightly, and reclined on the edge of your mattress farthest from my bed. Nothing stirred you—not the stickiness of the air, not my exhalations or sighs. I lay awake and tried to distract myself from the rejection I felt. Drops of perspiration dampened my back and I wondered if you were sweating as well. What always surprised me was how physical was my longing, as if someone had taken away a favorite pillow I was addicted to hugging to myself.

But eventually, even if it was after a few days, you always returned to my side. I let you cover my face with kisses on these nights. Did it ever occur to me that these tokens could have been for my benefit, not yours? That you might have been guiltily trying to compensate for my deprivation? The monsoons came and went, the weather grew cool, then warm, then once again wet. For months you maintained your back-and-forth, and I was too wrapped up in my own presumptions to realize what you were going through.

"What a bizarre practice, to sleep together like that." Zaida was not talking about the two of us, but Gandhiji—there had been an article in *Blitz* about his virgin experiments. For years, it seemed, the Mahatma had slept next to women, some of them teenagers—the motive being to hone his abstinence, to put his celibacy to the test. "Who knows what must have gone on under the covers? What he, or the women, must have really felt?"

I felt tempted to counter Zaida, to offer the example of our own nightly practice, in Gandhiji's defense. But something stopped me from making this revelation. Was it because my views on motherhood were too hard to explain, too unconventional? How would I articulate my central idea—that pure intentions always guaranteed the purity of the experiment?

That October, when you were fourteen, your Sharmila auntie came to visit. After Roopa's fall from favor, she had become the most popular aunt, the one with whom you spent the most time on Delhi vacations. You developed your love for science from her—she talked to you about chemistry and physics for hours. On her last Bombay trip, you had campaigned unsuccessfully to sleep between us—this time, to my surprise, you volunteered to take the living room couch without being asked.

For the next few days, you were more animated than I had seen in a while. Sharmila brought you a large box filled with old equipment from her college—diode valves and an ammeter, vials filled with chemical salts, and even a Bunsen burner, which she managed to hook up to the cooking gas. Every evening, after you came back from school, she produced blue and yellow precipitates magically out of colorless solutions in the kitchen. One day, she showed you how to read the current in a circuit, the next, she helped you construct an erupting volcano to take to school. She bought you an expensive illustrated book on space exploration as a parting gift—"He's the closest I'll ever get to having a child of my own."

The evening Sharmila left, I was changing her sheets on your bed, when you casually mentioned you'd like to continue sleeping in the living room. When I asked why, you hung your head and said, "No reason."

"You know the sofa's too soft. It's not good for your back."

"But Daddy used to sleep on it all the time."

"Only because you were the one occupying his bed." I fluffed up your pillow. "Don't you want to sleep next to Mummy anymore?"

You didn't say anything, so I continued. "That's called the living room, you know—because you're supposed to *live* there, not use it to sleep every night. Besides, what would we do with the empty mattress by Mummy's side?"

Your face crumpled, revealing a flash of despair that made me stop. Suddenly all your ambivalence of the past several months was eloquently explained. You could no longer bear the thought of sleeping by my side—how could I not have seen it before? Was that pity I had glimpsed in your look? "Of course you don't have to worry about Mummy," I assured you. "You can sleep wherever you like."

The sofa *did* turn out to be unsuitable—there was no fan to keep you cool, and the springs were so worn that you almost rolled off some nights. I continued my game of movable beds, pushing them up against the walls again and bidding you to return. "It's much better this way," I said, pointing to the reinstated arrangement with a bright and shiny smile. "You here and Mummy there—everything will be fine."

It was obvious even to me that you weren't quite taken in by my cheeriness. You slunk into the bedroom each night, kissing me apologetically, examining me with concern, as if for signs of breakage, as if I was fragile. Every few days, you pressed your head into my bosom as before, or threw yourself atop me with apparent playfulness while I was in bed. Once you even presented your cheeks, adorned with pearl-perfect tears to kiss away, after you had cried. But it was not the same—I could no longer enjoy these bursts of affection at face value. There was always the nagging notion that this was a show for my benefit. That you were going along guiltily with a role you thought I wanted you to play.

YOU SPOTTED THE ELECTRONICS kit in the window of a shop in Colaba, lying next to the board games of Property and Spell-O-Fun. We had gone there to buy you a new shirt for your fifteenth birthday. The set was obviously imported—on the cover were two boys with freckled cheeks and splendidly blond heads, pointing their screwdrivers in excitement at an incandescent set of electric tubes. "It might be rather expensive," I cautioned, but you said you only wanted to have a look at it, and led me up the steps.

Ever since Sharmila's visit the previous year, your interest in science had increased steadily. The ammeter had been a favorite—once you even tried rigging it up with wires to my arm to measure electric currents through my skin. By now, you had acquired other odds and ends as well—mostly salvaged from Zaida's old radio that no longer worked. You were already well beyond your just-completed ninth standard syllabus—even assembling a microphone, which when you spoke into it, chirped.

The electronics set, at eight hundred and thirty rupees, was quite an extravagance. You nodded when I explained it was too expensive to get. All that evening, though, I felt a gnawing regret. This would be the ninth birthday observed deprived of your father's presence.

When you found the set under the wrapping paper of my present, you let out a gasp. We were having a small party—Zaida, the Dugals, and Mrs. Hussain from upstairs. Hema's son Tony, whom you liked so much, had stopped by on his way to Poona as well. For a moment, you didn't move, just stared incredulously at the box in your hands. The blond children still pink and elated on the cover, the electric components so radioactively aglow, they might melt through the cellophane. "It costs so much," you said, looking up at me in wonder. You leaned your mouth forward to kiss me, and I bent towards you as well.

Something happened, though, in that split second before our lips met. You slowed just inches from my mouth, then turned ever so slightly to miss my face and hug me around the neck instead.

It was not significant, really, the pinprick that I felt. You were fifteen now, so of course I understood you wouldn't want to show too much affection in front of Tony and the rest. I was quite willing, you must realize, to brush it off, to leave it at that. It was only after everyone had left, when you came up to kiss me several times on the mouth, that the guilt on your face made me react. When I found myself chafing at your presumption that I could be languishing for your kisses, that you felt obliged to dole them out as charity. "I'm your mother, you know," I said softly. "You needn't feel as if you have to reward me each time like that."

You looked up, startled, but the words kept issuing from my mouth. "You're much too old anyway to be kissing me anywhere except on the cheek. A boy of fifteen should know enough not to touch his mother's mouth with his lips."

I tried to apologize later, after you rushed out of the room and were lying facedown in your bed. "Sometimes mummy doesn't know what she's saying. What can she do to make up?" You brushed my hand off when I tried to rub your back.

It took an hour of sitting contritely by your side before you allowed yourself to be held. You buried your head deep in my chest like you used to and drew your seat up towards my lap. It had been a long time since I had sensed such genuineness in your affection, such need, free of artifice, in your person. "You can kiss Mummy all you want, just like you used to, now or anytime you'd like. And if there are times when you don't want to, she'll understand that as well."

You raised your head and looked up at me shyly. "Like I used to? You won't mind?"

"No matter how big you become, you'll always be my little darling." I pressed my lips to yours.

There was a shine in your eyes. I tried to scan your face, but you burrowed it again into my blouse. You started rocking against me. I put my arms around you and moved in unison, as if cradling you to sleep. It was nothing like I remembered from even a few years ago—you were taller than I was now, your body gangly, your feet dangling to the floor. But I continued rocking, ignoring the awkwardness, letting the childhood image of you blossom in my mind.

It all happened so fast that I couldn't have stopped it even had I been able to keep track. One moment, I was holding you in my arms, whispering a song in your ear, experiencing those same pleasurable sensations that used to dart through my body. The next instant, I realized your lips had found their way past my blouse to nuzzle against my breast. Before I could raise myself up from the mattress, your arms encircled my body. Your face pressed deeper against my flesh, your motion became more frenetic—so much so that I thought you would roll us right off the edge. I spoke out your name, but you didn't hear me—I grabbed onto a side of the bed to try and steady myself. Moisture spilled from your mouth and smeared over my skin, you surprised me with your strength. You arched your head back and opened your mouth to draw in a deep and wrenching breath. A sob gurgled up from your throat, you loosened your grip and stopped rocking. Your eyes blinked open—unfocused, full of confusion, and then horrified realization.

You sprang off me, sprang off the bed. There was a smear of wetness on your pajamas. Before I could say anything, you fled out of the room. The sound of the bathroom door slamming shut reverberated through the walls and the floor.

THAT NIGHT I AGED more than on the evening I left my father's house in a doli. The guilt spread through my body and solidified around the crystal of pleasure I had allowed myself to feel while rocking you—it formed a permanent lump of self-accusation in my being. I saw in horror all the precautions I should have taken, all the lapses I had allowed, all my foolish arrogance in thinking I could aspire to the example set by Parvati.

What tormented me the most was the effect my lapse had on you. Whenever I tried to explain, a tremor appeared in your face. I didn't dare broach the idea of altering our sleeping arrangements—your strategy for coping seemed to be that every routine be kept the same. Even the practice of our good-night kiss had to be continued, though on the cheek instead of the lips.

The days went by and you remained remote—cut off, it seemed, from everything but your books and snails. One afternoon, near the beginning of the new school term, I showed up as the four o'clock bell rang. I caught you as you filed out of the building with the rest of the boys. "I came to pay the electricity bill, so I thought I'd ride the bus back with you," I explained. You regarded me without emotion.

We walked across the compound towards the path leading to the bus stop, and I pointed out the tree. "I know it's past the season, but let's go look if there are any keris left." You vacillated for a moment, then followed silently.

The few keris that hadn't fallen had been gouged by parrots or shriveled to the pit. "Perhaps," I offered, "we should go and get some mango ice cream instead."

"You know, all this is not necessary."

"I don't understand. You like ice cream."

You looked down at the ground, and picked up a stone. Then you turned your gaze back at me. It was not quite withering, but carried an intensity that made me shift uncomfortably. You swung around and hurled the stone towards the tree.

Had you been aiming at a keri, you couldn't possibly have been so wide of the mark. The stone sailed clear past the nearest branch and crashed perfectly into one of the windows on the third floor of the rectory behind. "Run," I said, and grabbed your hand instinctively to follow the children who were fleeing.

But you didn't budge. You looked at the ground, as if searching for another stone to throw. You stood there nonchalantly, even as Father Bernard came out of the building, his cane swinging. "Stay where you are!" he yelled. He huffed up and caught you by the collar. "It was you, wasn't it?"

The cane was making alarming sounds as Father Bernard swished it excitedly through the air. "He's not the one," I said. "I'm Mrs. Arora— he's my son, he's with me."

The vice principal turned as if noticing me for the first time. "You've been here before, haven't you?—I've seen you next to the mango tree. You know that this is a serious offense, breaking school property? If he didn't do it, who was it?—there's nobody else here I can see."

"It must have been one of the children who ran away. Now can we go, please?"

Father Bernard released you and patted your head. He looked into your eyes as if about to share a confidence, and addressed you in his most avuncular tone. "Did you do it?"

I felt a small surge of anger. "I already told you he didn't. Don't you believe me?"

Father Bernard ignored my words. "Did you?"

"Yes." You looked at me as you spoke.

Father Bernard smiled understandingly. He smoothed out your collar and patted you again. "You're a bit old for this sort of thing, so come, we'll settle this in my office."

I stepped forward. "He's not going anywhere. I'm his mother, I told you. I take full responsibility."

"Perhaps Mrs.—Arora, was it?—perhaps you don't realize what a serious offense this is. And what an example you're setting for your son, lying like this. If you can't teach him the proper way, then the school will. You can take him away if you want, but then don't bother bringing him back."

"This is hardly the way—"

"Mummy, please." You turned to Father Bernard. "We don't have to go to your office. If you could punish me here, we could be done with it."

"Ashvin, come with me at once. I'll complain to the principal himself."

But you were already bending forward and putting your hands on the mango tree. Father Bernard raised his cane and swung it through the air a few times to limber it, then stepped forward and took aim. I tried to look away as he raised it again, but couldn't. There was black paint on the tip, I noticed, which had begun to wear, revealing the beige wood underneath. Then Father Bernard's arm came down, his robe fluttering with the effort, his left foot moving forward as if it were a step in a dance he was performing. I heard the thwack of wood against cloth—cloth covering something it couldn't quite protect. You gasped as if you had been expecting to remain silent, as if the sound had been forced out of you involuntarily. On the third stroke, you straightened up and turned around, as if you had had enough, as if you had changed your mind. But Father Bernard forced your head down and spread your hands on the tree again. "Not yet, son," he said, and took aim once more with the cane.

He hit you ten times in all, then left wordlessly. The children who had gathered to watch looked eagerly at your face, to see if you were crying. Your cheeks were flushed, but there were no tears. You pushed aside the hand I offered to help you up, and looked at me defiantly. "I'm fine," you said. "You don't have to say anything."

June turned to July, July to August. Time, space, emotion all seemed to freeze between us—we were like two figures embedded a fixed distance apart in a paperweight. Each morning, I looked anxiously towards you for any signs of change in your demeanor, any traces of thaw in your remoteness. Just as I was beginning to wonder if this suspended state would continue forever, your uncle moved to Bombay.

chapter
thirty-three

THE FIRST LETTER FROM ARYA HAD ARRIVED IN JANUARY 1977, WHEN Indira Gandhi experienced her mysterious change of heart about the Emergency. She suddenly declared elections and released all her political prisoners, including Arya, from jail. I recognized the writing when the letter came, and almost tore it up; but it was addressed to you, and propriety held me back. "I miss you and hope we can be friends once more. Not a day has gone by during these last fifteen months in prison that I haven't felt remorse for what I did." At the bottom of the page was a P.S. "By the way, don't worry about my nose—it's mended in a way to give me an aristocratic air."

You did not reply to that letter, or the one that followed immediately after. Perhaps you, like me, still mistrusted your uncle. I saw you pore over the text of each letter, agonizing about whether to respond. Once, you even asked if I would be willing to compose an appropriate reply. But you were proficient enough in Hindi now, I reminded you—I would not assist in writing back.

Hema sent me a newspaper interview in which Arya related how he had been beaten and tortured with electric shocks while incarcerated. Her letter arrived the same week that the chief of police went on television to accuse former detainees of making up such stories to aggrandize their political standing. Indeed, Arya did get an offer to stand for office from a plum seat in Punjab. He handily won in the election that March, like most of the candidates in the Janta coalition which routed Indira and her Congress Party.

After the elections, the letters stopped. Hema sent us the occasional clipping about Arya's tenure in the government, but he did not personally write until almost three years later, in 1980. The Janta coalition had recently collapsed under the weight of its own bickering and Indira had been swept back to power. "It's just as well," Arya wrote about the seat he had lost. "I'm glad to be out of the government, out of an institution that's so corrupt." He announced his intention to move to Bombay. "With both Babuji and Mataji gone, there's only Hema auntie left to keep me company here. We'll meet as soon as I get there—maybe I can even make it by May, in time to celebrate your fifteenth birthday."

I found his words unsettling—the casualness with which they rolled across the page, as if the past had been squared. What if he was returning to renew his designs on me? What if I ran into him on the street or found him standing in front of our doorway? Would he apologize, as he had to you in his letters, or go on the offensive, forcing himself in to try to play out that Divali night again? But your fifteenth birthday came and went, and we did not receive any further intimation from him. The crisis with you demanded my full attention, leaving no room to entertain abstract fears about your uncle.

I soon discovered that there might not be any need to worry about Arya's motives after all. It seemed he was returning to stoke the flame of a romance more long-standing than me: the HRM. Indira had followed up her victory in the national elections by trouncing the opposition even more decisively in the recent state assembly elections. *India Today* described the Janta coalition as thoroughly demoralized and in complete disarray. Member groups such as the HRM were searching deep within their souls for ways to reinvent themselves and reconnect with the public. A line near the end of the article said Arya had moved to Bombay to lead the rejuvenation efforts there.

It surprised me that your uncle had not tried to look you up—there had been no mention of another letter from him. In recent weeks, all you seemed to do was study—returning home hours late from school some evenings, even going there to read in the library on Saturdays. I supposed it was necessary, this distance you so scrupulously maintained, this time you were presumably using to heal the rift between us. I tried to distract myself from my sense of forlornness, tried not to dwell on all the extra hours of solitude I faced. Reserve was an improvement over stoniness, I consoled myself.

For a while, I looked for a job. In the years since my stint at the nursery school, I had conducted brief experiments with various kinds of employment—as a transcriber for a law firm, a proofreader for the Bombay University press, even an aide at the Prince of Wales Museum. Although the income provided a welcome bonus to the insurance money interest on which we subsisted, none of the jobs ever really engrossed me. I especially hated the way I could not be at home when you returned from school, and quit each time over the inflexibility of the schedule.

This time, I simply didn't find anything—the job market in Bombay had dried up, and I refused to ask Paji for help. I resumed my excursions to Chowpatty—the same pilgrimages on which I had whiled away my time in the city all those years ago when I first arrived. By now, a small park had sprung up on the upper beach, with trees to offer protection from the sun and rain. My favorite was the large spreading pipal in the middle—I sat under it with a cone of peanuts and read one of the afternoon papers like *Midday*.

One Saturday, I noticed a front-page article on the inauguration of a pilot program by the HRM, to teach Bombayites self-defense. It quoted the noted HRM leader, Mr. Arya Arora, as saying that for centuries, invaders had successfully overrun India because of the weakness of its citizens. "In this day and age, with enemies at our border, with antisocial elements infesting our communities, it is even more important that we train our youth for a strong defense." There would be free classes in activities ranging from calisthenics to wrestling, offered by seven participating gyms and akharas in the city. "I encourage all Hindus between twelve and forty years of age to participate." Arya himself appeared in a picture on the inner page where the article continued, smiling at the camera as he cut a ribbon.

I was about to move on to the *Busybee* column, when I found my gaze pulled back to the photograph. There was something about the group of youths just behind Arya, all of them wearing identical caps. I could make out only a few of their faces—one in particular looked over Arya's shoulder, straight at the camera. I stared at that face for a full minute, until the warmth left my fingers and the last hopeful ray of doubt faded from my mind. There was no mistaking it, even through the poor resolution of the photo—that it was you standing behind your uncle.

I began walking towards Opera House, the newspaper open and fluttering in my hand, as if your picture were that of a missing person with which I intended to stop and question pedestrians. Halfway over the bridge, I started running. A taxi pulled up, and I clambered in, telling the driver to take me to St. Xavier's School. A few boys in blue cadet uniforms stood in formation under the mango tree, but otherwise the school grounds were deserted. The entrance to the main building was open, but the library door, when I tried it, was locked. "It's closed today," the school watchman told me when I found him rubbing tobacco in his palm at the gate.

"There must be people inside—my son has been coming here to study every Saturday."

The watchman popped the tobacco into his mouth and chewed on it thoughtfully. "I've worked here for six years, memsahib, and I can't remember a single time the library has been open on a weekend."

The photo caption said that the inauguration had taken place at the Shivaji Gymkhana in Bandra. I took a taxi to Churchgate to catch a train. There was a class on lathi wielding in progress at the club—I scanned the participating boys, but didn't see your face. The office was closed, but an attendant pointed me towards a room at the back. Two men sitting on wicker chairs sipped tea inside—they told me to come back on Monday afternoon if I wanted to meet Arya sahib.

"Do you know where he lives?" I asked, and the men exchanged knowing glances. "I'm his sister-in-law, you see," I lamely added, trying to correct my mistake.

"He has a flat somewhere in Worli," one of the men replied with a leer. "Surely as his *sister-in-law* you must have a phone number for him?"

You returned late that evening. I was sitting in the balcony, waiting, and recognized the blue of the shirt you had on when you were just a speck up the street. I meant to be calm, perhaps not even confront you directly, but as soon as I saw you, all those intentions evaporated. I ripped out the page with the photo from the newspaper and thrust it in your face. "Is this what you've been doing at your school library on Saturdays?"

I had been tiptoeing around our estrangement so long that my anger took you completely by surprise. You made no attempt at evasion or stonewalling, just let the words tumble out freely. You had been visiting Yara uncle for over a month now—not only on Saturdays, but also on the evenings late from school. You told me how he took you along on his rounds of the HRM network, and enrolled you in yoga classes at their gymkhana at Byculla. How his flat was furnished with little more than some chairs and a bed, though there was a pooja alcove with a complete set of miniature idols (including incarnations of Vishnu you'd never seen). "Usually I just go there and sit around with him—he reads out Hindi poetry, or teaches me to meditate."

I felt numbed at first by your ready confession, but then the emotion returned to fill me. "How could you not have told me?" I finally asked. "All the stories about your studies—you've never lied to me before."

"I thought you'd have been angry. I didn't think you'd let us meet."

I managed to suppress the feeling of betrayal that welled up inside, managed to keep my hurt contained. I saw no use forbidding you from seeing Arya—it would only give you something to rebel against. Perhaps these trysts were needed to coax you out of your reclusiveness, the price to be paid for what I had allowed to take place. I stifled the urge to ask why you felt it necessary to punish me like this. "I can never forget what he tried with me, Ashvin. But he's your uncle—had you asked, I wouldn't have stopped you from seeing him."

I wonder how things would have played out had I been able to squelch this fraternization right there and then. In the months to come,

I watched helplessly as Arya insinuated himself deeper and deeper into our existence. Not a day passed without the name of your beloved Yara uncle issuing from your lips. "Yara uncle feels I should exercise more often." "Yara uncle thinks the Congress government is going to fail." "Yara uncle says film actors are all Communists." You were always accompanying him to events—a special pooja for Dassera, a temple drive for flood victims, a blessing ceremony by some dignitary of the HRM. The religious slant to these activities worried me—I started having the same paranoid fears against which Paji railed.

Perhaps most ominous were the tilaks you flaunted, just like your father before you, when he had discovered religion overnight. You came back from the small shrine at Tardeo with the holy marks smeared prominently on your forehead every weekend morning (you were still shy about displaying them at school). For a few weeks you tried observing the fast for Hanuman on Tuesdays, but had to stop after you almost fainted in gym class one afternoon. You resumed the search for Dev's lost guruji, making a fortnightly trek to Dadar by train.

There were benefits as well to having a father figure in your life again—for instance, an increase in your self-confidence. I noticed it in all the little ways you asserted yourself—demanding money back from the fruit seller for mangoes rotten inside, insisting the barber retrim your hair until he got the curve above your ears just right. You tried to make yourself look more imposing—doing push-ups in the morning and drinking extra glasses of milk. When that failed to bulk you up, you developed aggressive opinions on politics to compensate. You had particularly harsh words for Indira Gandhi, even though her beloved Sanjay, the son whom she had picked to be her successor, had just been killed. "Do something," you exhorted, each time she appeared on the television, her expression numb, her face creased. "Now that you're no longer being dominated by that scoundrel son of yours, save the country from its decline."

You were obviously parroting Arya's lines, but I tried not to let my recognition show. Past the swagger and the posturing, I could still see the unsureness you tried to conceal. I found it almost painful to watch—this desperation to come off as world-wise. (Did everyone go through such a phase? Had I? Had Roopa?) I tried to appear encouraging, to nod intelligently at your bluster with a smile.

But then your precociousness took on a chauvinistic edge. You stopped watching movies on television, declaring them too racy, finding fault with the costumes worn because of the way they emphasized the actresses' breasts. "Look at those girls!" you exclaimed, walking along the street with me. "Don't they know how un-Indian are the jeans they have on?" You made bombastic pronouncements about the loss of ancient Hindu values, invoking the epics and the Vedas as if intimately familiar with these texts. "All the centuries of foreigners we've been forced to absorb—this is the result—what else can you expect?" You complained one day about the admission policy of your school, about the disproportionate number of Catholics accepted by the Jesuits in charge. "It's a plot to take over the country, all these Christian schools run by them." Another day, you turned on your history teacher, Mr. Nawaz, after a test in which you didn't do so well. "What does he know? He's a Muslim," you said.

"How does Mr. Nawaz being Muslim have to do with anything?"

"Yara uncle says they twist everything around to suit their own purpose. History, especially. They've managed to infect all our textbooks with their lies."

"Zaida auntie is a Muslim too. Do you want to go and tell her Yara uncle says she's a liar?"

"He wasn't talking about Zaida auntie. In any case, I don't take history lessons from her."

Even more disturbing was the attitude of intolerance you brought back each time you visited the HRM gymkhana at Byculla. A ramshackle colony bordered the north edge of the field where the club stood, whose residents were all Muslims. Sometimes you complained about the loud religious music they played, supposedly to ruin the concentration of club members trying to meditate. At other times, it was their lack of cleanliness—how cow blood had been found on the club premises, how hovering over the whole area was the stench of stewing beef one couldn't escape. "They're stealing all our jobs, these Muslims," you came home and declared.

"Since when have you become so knowledgeable about the job market? And what jobs are these you're talking about, anyway?"

"Just go to any factory and you'll see. The Muslims have taken over completely. Even the Hindu owners have been brainwashed into allowing them into their mills all over the city."

I would have laughed at such nonsense issuing from the mouth of a fifteen-year-old, had I not seen the earnestness in your expression. "Have you been to these mills yourself, Ashvin? Or talked to these workers in person? In the future, get some proof before you go repeating such an outrageous accusation."

I wondered what exactly went on at the gymkhana beyond the yoga sessions in which you claimed to participate. Was it just affinity for your uncle that kept you returning? What in the atmosphere there could be so fascinating? Each time I contemplated making a trip to investigate, the thought of encountering Arya kept me away.

I remembered the shakha where Arya had worked in Nizamuddin, with its bare-walled rooms, its scraggly field, its rickety benches. It had been a club clearly aimed at the lower classes, offering such earthy activities as kabaddi and mud-pit wrestling. How had you made the jump from your school to such a place? St. Xavier's boasted of a proper basketball court, a manicured cricket pitch, a set of running tracks marked off neatly in chalk every day. "We turn boys into gentlemen," the slogan in the catalog for last year's Republic Day parade had read. Wasn't this the world to which you more comfortably belonged? A world with smart ironed uniforms and blue-striped ties, and a school badge inscribed with the inscrutable Latin motto *Duc in Altum*. A world of class picnics at Juhu Beach and lemon pastries during lunch break, and a dramatics club that two years ago had given you a part in *Oliver Twist*. You had had your run-in with Father Bernard, it was true, and were never too friendly with your classmates, but could you really have become so alienated? "Yara uncle says that the gymkhana is where one finds the real India. The boys in my school have all been spoiled by the West on their brain."

I tried to imagine you smearing your thin body with mud from this real India, locking chests with streetwise youths in the wrestling pit. Your groin wrapped in the same kind of langot they wore, made with cloth so coarse it could have been woven on a village spinning wheel. Every muscle straining to find the slightest advantage over your opponents, the sweat from your skin mingling with theirs. (What did it smell like, this sweat of theirs? Cheap groundnut oil, rude curry mix?) And afterwards, the pats on your back, the tousling of hair, the communal shower to wash the dirt away. Were these the rugged games you felt you had to play to prove your manliness, the kind of rough camaraderie you craved? And what about the other wrestlers who were being so welcoming—how could they not notice your gentility, not recognize you were an outsider in their midst?

Even more baffling was how you could have been swayed so easily by the crude propaganda of the HRM. The fabrications you swallowed, then spouted back at me with such conviction. Couldn't you see they were aimed at the poor and disaffected, meant for their consumption? "Just take a walk through the Muslim colony—even the most run-down hut will have a fridge and a television set," I'd hear you insist. What dissatisfaction in your life could such notions possibly prey upon—you, who were so educated, who had grown up amidst so many Muslim neighbors? "They'll take over the whole city, the whole country, before we know it. We have to go into their colonies and have it out face to face."

"Is that what your Yara uncle is teaching you? That you have to go fight Muslims? I don't care what that man thinks or does, but I'll not have my own son joining in. You're not returning to Byculla—I'll see how he fills your head with such hate."

For an instant, your eyes lit up, as if you were going to challenge me. What would I do if you walked out, declared you were old enough to make your own decisions? But your defiance subsided into sullenness. "Yara uncle doesn't hate Muslims," you mumbled. "I must have overheard someone else. Next time I go to the gymkhana, I won't listen."

Perhaps your rants were for my ears—a repudiation to distance yourself from me, a rebuke to remind me of your lingering resentment. Or perhaps it was more straightforward than that—you were simply trying to impress your uncle, in an effort to create a more comfortable fit for yourself in his HRM. I knew I had to sweep away this pretense, penetrate the façade you had built around yourself. But how would I compete with the vast machinery of the HRM? I had no virile activities to entice you with, no battle cries with which to divert your attention. The lone arrow in my quiver, trite and unsharpened, was my affection.

Spring was approaching, its arrival soon to be celebrated with Holi. I would use the festival to put my affection to the test.

YOU HAD NOT EVEN turned four when Dev initiated you into your first Holi celebration. He pulled out a squeeze bottle and sprayed you with colored water as you sat at the breakfast table. For a moment, you simply looked down at your shirt, shocked by the red soaking into the cloth—the streams running down your arms, bleeding into your eggs. Before you could cry (and before I could stop him), Dev wrapped your hands around the bottle and showed you how to pump—the squirts landed all over his front. It took mere moments for you to learn the rest—smearing yellow and blue and green powders on Daddy, reloading the bottles from the buckets of red and purple water in the bathroom. I ran around the room trying desperately to cover the furniture with newspaper, but mayhem erupted before I could finish. At some point, the two of you decided you had chased each other enough, and turned your attention on me. Instead of trying to dodge the streams of color, I spread my body protectively in front of the walls and allowed myself to be sprayed.

Despite my efforts to save them, neither the walls nor the furniture came through unscathed. The purple dye turned out to be particularly stubborn, tinting our nails and the edges of our scalps for several days (you were delighted to go to your nursery school thus marked). The next year and the year after that, I had us all wear the ruined clothes from the first Holi, and laid down strict rules on taking the celebration to the corridor outside. You discovered in Pinky a perfect victim—she ran screaming lustily up and down the steps as you attacked her, without ever being able (or willing) to escape.

But then Dev died, and even though Pinky sauntered hopefully past our door each Holi, there seemed little motivation on your part to play. Some years, I did buy a half rupee's worth of red powder on the day of the festival—we would brush it perfunctorily on each other's cheeks and leave it at that. Even when we started observing Divali and all the other holidays, Holi remained uncelebrated, perhaps because of its close association with Dev.

I decided, this year, to end the period of mourning. This year, I would lure you out of your aloofness and lead you back to the playfulness we had shared. On the eve of the festival, I went to the bania's and bought the same Butterfly brand of red and purple crystals Dev used to get. I also asked for a scoop from every bin of colored powder they had in the shop, with a double scoop of the red. Dev would dissolve the crystals the night before—he said the water turned darker that way. Not wanting to tip you off, I filled the buckets but left them uncolored, and hid my purchases in the cupboard.

In bed, I suddenly realized that the clothes from that first Holi would no longer fit you—we'd have to sacrifice a new outfit. It would have to be whatever you chose to wear that morning—I could hardly steer you to something old if I wanted the surprise to remain. Perhaps I'd squirt you at breakfast, just like Dev had that first year (this time leaving the eggs unstained). Then, before you could recover, I would rub you with handfuls of color.

This was what I looked forward to the most—simply being able to touch you again. Everything had become so fraught between us that even the most innocent forms of physical contact had waned. The goodnight pecks on the cheek had stopped—we no longer exchanged the slightest pat or caress. What I longed for was to hug you, and be hugged in return—to experience again the feel of your hair, your face, your skin under my palms.

Tomorrow would be the day for it—Holi was the one time each year when the rules about who could touch whom were suspended. Longings given release and tensions spent, when even someone's wife or husband could be daubed in play. Back in Rawalpindi, it was the only occasion on which we saw our parents engage in contact. Paji stiffly held out his face so that no powder spilled on his clothes when he was dabbed. But Biji lost all inhibition, dousing us with colored water, then running laughing up and down the steps. She allowed herself to be cornered in the verandah when all her mischief was spent, to receive the rubbing down and drenching she craved from us.

I looked across the room now at the back I wanted to rub so much myself. Perhaps, as with Biji, the festival would make you forget your reserve—perhaps tomorrow we would reconnect.

WHEN I AWOKE the next morning, the reflection from a vehicle on the street stained the ceiling red. Surely a promising sign, I thought to myself, an endorsement that I had been right to embark on this venture. Then I noticed your unoccupied bed. I looked for you in the living room and the kitchen, but did not find you there. On the floor of the empty bathroom stood the buckets of water, patiently waiting to be colored.

You could have left for only one place, of course—to play Holi with your gymkhana friends. The thought left me deflated—you had defeated my plan without even giving me the chance to launch it. All morning, I wallowed in my gloom, taking out the colors twice from their hiding place to feel them slip through my fingers. I made several trips to the balcony, watching the revelers below get rowdier, their clothes acquiring a uniform reddish purple tint. A boy squirted color on them from a window in the facing building—he turned his gun on me, but I was out of range.

"What are you waiting for?—go play Holi with your son," Zaida ordered, when she stopped by to put the red on my cheek as she did every year. "And if there are others around him, why should you care?"

I took a taxi to Byculla. The gymkhana, when I reached it, looked deserted. I found a lone youth, his undershirt dyed a violent purple-green, snoozing in the wrestling pit. In the distance, two boys chased each other with water guns around the field. I wondered where everyone had gone.

A troubling thought occurred to me. Holi was the easiest time of the year to ignite smoldering tensions—there were few more surefire ways to enrage people than by spraying color at them. What if Arya had led you all into the Muslim colony—hadn't you mentioned something about a face-to-face confrontation? I remembered the riot at Mahim last year incited by a pack of youths who splashed worshippers emerging from a mosque with paint. A few well-chosen insults at the colony, a few provocative spurts of color, and it would be easy to send the whole place up in flames.

The clubhouse, when I scanned it, yielded no clues to where its members were. It was smaller than I had expected—a freestanding structure with a shingled roof, and a decorative floral molding above the doorway. Could this be a storehouse for lathis and knives, one of the HRM repositories for swords and guns? I looked at the cream-colored walls, the wooden window shutters, the geranium plant near the doorway. They lent an atmosphere of quaintness, like that of a hill station bungalow—there seemed nothing sinister about the place.

I walked around the perimeter, trying to peer in through the windows, but it was too dark to see anything inside. I thought about trying the door, but something made me hesitate. You had always been secretive of this part of your life—simply walking in unannounced seemed too brash an intrusion to make.

I turned around, and was about to leave, when behind me, I heard the door open. "I saw you walking around outside," the familiar voice called out.

"It's been much too long, Meera, since we met," Arya said.

chapter
thirty-four

THE FIRST THING I NOTICED WAS THAT ARYA'S NOSE LOOKED CLEARLY broken, not aristocratic as he had claimed in his letter. As he spoke, I realized he could no longer enunciate sounds like *n* and *m* properly. "Ashvin's in the annex across the field," he said, and it took me a few seconds to decipher his new pronunciation of your name. "Come, I'll take you there."

I was surprised how unfazed he was upon seeing me, how naturally he seemed to behave. No hint of what had passed between us, or the way in which our last meeting had ended, troubled his face. "I've been asking Ashvin to call you here for weeks—I didn't realize today was going to be the day. Had I known, I'd have arranged for a proper lunch and display."

"It wasn't planned. I thought I'd come play Holi with Ashvin."

"Yes, he's been here with the other boys, at it since morning. Look what they did to me." He gestured at the extravagant splashes of green and purple on his kurta, then ran a hand through his hair to show me the cloud of color that arose from his head. I suddenly felt self-conscious about my unblemished sari, and wished I hadn't washed off the red Zaida had rubbed on my cheeks. But Arya didn't seem to notice, or at least didn't try to use to his advantage the fact that I wasn't the one you had stayed with to celebrate. "I had some papers to fill out, so I managed to sneak away here."

About to close the door, he stopped. "Would you like me to show you, inside?" Then, before awkwardness could set in at the thought of me accompanying him alone into the darkened interior, he laughed. "It's mostly an office—there's nothing really to it. Much more interesting is what we're going to do here." He swept a hand across the field. "The city had almost signed this over to us when the Muslims in that colony you see there objected."

A surreal feeling took hold of me as we made our way across the grass. Why was I out walking so nonchalantly with this man, the one by whom I had barely escaped being molested? I half expected us to be holding hands, like long-standing friends out on a stroll. "That's where we hope to build a proper gym in the future," Arya indicated, and I noticed again the meaty power of his palms. Surprisingly, they were not stained with color—perhaps he had used the ends of his sleeves to keep them tucked in.

"We have to plan for the next decade or two," Arya said. "The days of the old-style akharas with the guru and his wrestling disciples are numbered." He began pointing out spots earmarked for various planned recreational facilities, as he might to impress a trustee on a site visit. I felt I should stop him, try to steer the conversation to something more substantial. Didn't accounts have to be settled, apologies made?

But I wasn't able to cut in—so intent was Arya on his articulation that to interrupt felt somehow churlish. "Today's boys get impatient when we ask them to build their bodies with stone joris and dumbbells," he lamented. "They've peered through the windows of Tawalkar's and the other private gyms sprouting all over the city, seen the sleek and dazzling machines inside—they want the same. Except they don't realize how much all that shiny steel costs—we invest what we can, but that's a lot of money to raise." He looked earnestly at my face, and for an instant, I wondered if he was going to ask me for a donation. "Do you know, some of them even balk at entering the sandpit? They noticed wrestling mats at the Olympics on TV last year and want to know when we'll start using the same."

Arya shook his head. "Do you remember that shakha I used to run at Nizamuddin? So simple, so basic, and yet so . . ." He left the thought uncompleted, as if it was a joint reminiscence we were sharing, as if I was aboard with him on magic memories floating us back to the same halcyon days. Again, I felt overcome by a sense of unreality. What would be the next step? Ice cream espresso at the Oberoi café? Sandhya's letter pulled out to impress me with his sincerity again?

We reached the annex to which Arya had referred—it turned out to be little more than a compound walled in on three sides, with a shrine to Hanuman in one corner. "It's still not quite constructed yet," Arya apologized. "All those Muslim objections. . . ."

The color-throwing phase of the day seemed spent—empty buckets lay strewn all over the place. A few youths, clad in wet scraps of cloth wrapped around their groins, took turns washing color off under a tap protruding from one of the walls. Several others, already scrubbed and clothed, lounged around on the benches at the far end.

I spotted you instantly among them. "Look, Ashvin," Arya announced, "look at whom I met." You glanced up. Maybe it was my imagination, but your expression turned sullen. "Your mother's come to play a bit of Holi. Do we have some color left?"

You shook your head. "All the buckets are empty. We used the last of the powder to decorate Hanuman himself."

"Actually, I brought some with me." I opened my purse and took out the newspaper packets in which the colors were wrapped. "There might even be some crystals for tinting water in there."

You stared at the packets without touching them. "But I'm done playing already. I've taken my shower."

"So what?" Arya said. "Every day is not Holi. You can take another bath for your mother, can't you?"

"But my clothes. These are the extra ones I brought—the clean set."

I felt foolish for coming. Even had you not washed as yet, you'd be embarrassed to play with me, surrounded by all your friends. "It's fine, there's no need to get dirty again," I said.

But Arya took you by the hand and led you aside. He cupped his palm around the back of your neck, and talked to you in a calm, patient way. I tried to ignore the stares from the youths on the bench. Even the ones under the tap had forgotten their showering and stood gawking unabashedly in their underwear.

You returned from your conversation with your uncle, your expression no longer hostile. To my surprise, you opened the packets one by one, and examined their contents with interest. Someone brought buckets filled with water and you dissolved both the purple and the red crystals in them. Then, with perfect amicability, you asked me which powder I wanted to start with.

In an instant, the decade of Holis we'd missed since Dev died came to an end. Color flew, streams of dyed water spurted through the air, clothes turned green and blue, skin was tinted red. I squeezed my eyes shut as you launched your attack, but forgot to close my mouth—the powder tasted dry and chalky on my tongue. Although I could barely see, your shirt was suddenly in my grip—I held on to it as you struggled to escape, and managed to give you a good smearing around the head. Some of the other boys, seeing the engagement, forgot about their clean clothes and joined in as well. At one point, while trying to escape a spray of purple, I tripped and fell. You were astride me at once, rubbing the color over my clothes, on my body, into my hair. You looked a little maniacal, face painted like some warrior, laughing with your teeth streaked orange. Someone splashed us with the remaining colored water—first the purple, then the red.

I could have remained there a long time. Your knees straddled against my sides, the weight of your body snug around my waist, drops of red-purple dripping onto my face from the wet locks of your hair. The color had an earthy scent to it, but surprisingly, I could still delve beneath it to detect the familiar fragrance of your sweat. You looked down upon me, your laughter subsiding to a half smile, then flickering behind something else—shyness or uncertainty, I couldn't tell. We stayed there for a moment, enthralled in each other's gravity—the moon and the earth, the earth and the sun. Then the spell broke, the grass around us began to reappear, and with it, the buckets and the benches and the people. You looked around, then rose and took a step back. I expected you to help me up, but it was your uncle who extended his hand.

Arya beamed. "I'm glad you were able to do this with Ashvin. Next year, you'll have to come earlier, so you can play with the rest of us as well." He gestured for you to come stand next to him. "For now, though, since the color's all gone—" He turned back your collar and ran his fingers through the patch of red powder on your neck. "May I?" he asked me, his fingers color-laden and outstretched.

I imagined everyone around us looking on, holding their breath. There seemed nothing to do but nod my head. A shiver ran down from my ear through my shoulder as his fingers smeared the red onto my cheek. But I girded myself and managed not to flinch.

On the ride back home, I sat in the back seat of the taxi with you, our clothes wet. I wondered what Arya could have said to convince you to play Holi with me. How had you allowed your uncle to get so close, to control you with such sure influence?

You turned to me from the window. "Yara uncle must have been quite hurt when you didn't reciprocate. The least you could have done was to rub some color on his face as well."

I NEVER DID FIND out Arya's secret words to change your attitude towards me that day. (A religious imperative to honor your parents? A threat?) I did, however, see, quite starkly, the error in the strategy I had adopted ever since your uncle reappeared. All the times I avoided him, all the pains taken to ensure our paths never overlapped. By cutting myself off from him, I had encouraged you to cut yourself off from me as well. So when Arya sent an invitation for the annual HRM martial arts showcase the next week, I went.

The function was eerily reminiscent of the HRM event I had attended more than a quarter of a century ago in Nizamuddin. This time, Arya was the main speaker, and his talk had the same blustery feel to it. The fact that some of his consonants didn't come out correctly through his nose only augmented the effect of menace in his words.

"People accuse us of being hatemongers. But they're wrong—all we hate is injustice. We might not want to break bread with Muslims, but we have nothing personal against them. They're all descended from Hindu blood anyway—it's their ancestors who converted, who came under the influence of foreigners and were led astray. We're ready to welcome them back into the fold at any time—just let them acknowledge their Hindu roots and learn to coexist."

He recited the usual litany of grievances—how Muslims were plundering jobs and usurping Hindu rights, how the government was squeezing out tax money to send them free to Mecca. "Coexistence is simply not in their vocabulary—look how they've even stopped us from building our gym."

He had a new name for the enemy—they were the "limbus"—the lemons—in our midst. "Instead of mixing with us to make sweet lemonade, they go around curdling everything, like limbu juice dropped in milk. And our leaders just keep encouraging them—this she-devil we're cursed with now and her imbecile father who gave away half our country in the first place. Mark my words—father and daughter will be rooting side by side in the same filth soon, when both are reborn as pigs."

Lest anyone didn't get the violent thrust of his message, Arya was more explicit in his final exhortation. "India is the land of milk and honey, not lemons and milk. Tell the limbus they better go back to Pakistan if they can't mix. Tell them to stop taking our jobs, to remove their bigoted objections to our gym. Because if they don't, we've all drunk the milk of Kali Ma here, and all they can expect is this." With that, Arya sliced a lemon in half with a knife, then squeezed its juice into the dirt and ground his foot in. "Now on with the celebrations."

One after another, the familiar martial arts exercises were performed on stage—the wrestling, the lathi twirling, the marching with rifles represented by sticks. Except with one dismaying difference. Right after the wrestlers, but before the recruits wielding lathis, came a group of young men carrying swords. Two of them did most of the fighting in the center, while the rest performed some minor maneuvers on the side. You were among the latter—when you saw me, you gave your sword an extra wave in the air.

—

AFTER THE END OF THE FUNCTION, Arya came up with you to where I sat, still dazed, in my chair. "I was so glad to hear from Ashvin that you were coming. We weren't able to do it on Holi, but finally a chance to drink coffee with you again." He filled two glasses from a thermos and handed one to me. "I made it myself, so it's not going to be as good as the one at the Coffee House in Delhi, I'm afraid. Perhaps next time I can take you to the restaurant at the Oberoi."

You lunged around, slicing through the air with your arms. "My part today was only for ceremony. But if I practice, perhaps by next year, I can be one of the fighters in the display."

Arya mussed up your hair. "Now, now, Ashvin, we'll have to see about that."

I barely heard the rest of what he said—the talk of yoga practice, of the upcoming rally at Juhu, of the HRM summer retreat in Nasik to which he'd invited you. All I could concentrate on was Arya rubbing the back of your neck and squeezing you to himself, as if you were his own son. And the ease with which you responded, your eyes all sparkle and scintillation, in a way I had not seen for months. "It's a beautiful setting, the campgrounds we own in Nasik—only for the most promising from our ranks, I'll have you know. Right next to a lake—Ashvin's going to love bathing in it after the exercises we perform in the fresh morning air, aren't you, Ashvin? Maybe you can visit too while we're there. I could show you around—have you ever been to where the Godavari River begins?"

Could this then be what Arya had truly returned for—to stake his claim on you? Was he trying to impress upon me even now, as he wrapped his arm around your shoulders with such propriety, such sureness, just how effortlessly he could pluck your affections away? You broke forward to feint through the air again, stabbing at the back of a chair in a mock thrust. I imagined a real sword in your hand, imagined you slicing through lemons with its blade—squeezing each lemon half between your fingers to void their juice into the earth. My Ashvin, my child. Paji's grandson. Learning to carve open limbus as you breathed in the fresh Nasik air. I would not allow it to happen, could not allow it to happen—my son growing up a fanatic, a member of the HRM.

Perhaps Arya read my mind, because he stopped his talk about the retreat in Nasik. "I hope I didn't upset you with my address today. It's all politics, you know—these speeches have to be fiery, I have to energize the crowds a little through what I say. We're not trying to foment anything—we're just trying to get people motivated enough to stand up and fight for their fair share."

"By killing the limbus, as you call them? Is that what you plan on teaching in Nasik? Are you going to lead Ashvin into that colony so he can chop off a few heads if they don't agree to your gym?"

Arya smiled reproachfully. "Do you really think I'd let any harm come to Ashvin? That I'd try to corrupt his brain, try to make a killer out of him? No, Meera, I'm setting my sights on much higher things—he's going to be a leader, not a follower, our Ashvin. It's good that he comes to the gymkhana, it gives him a sense of identity, a sense of connection with ordinary people, not just the pampered brats from that school of his. What you're probably misunderstanding is today's display—believe me, that's only for camaraderie—the yoga is what really gives one discipline. Ashvin had to beg me to be allowed on stage—he's supposed to be only learning yoga, not even taking lessons in swordplay."

He shook his head, as if I had been deeply unfair to him. "I'll say it again, Meera—I would never let Ashvin get in harm's way."

Down the row, you were still thrusting at the chairs—it didn't seem like yoga you were interested in. I watched Arya take a sip from his glass, the wronged expression still playing nobly on his face. A line of coffee remained on his mustache, dyeing it a milky brown.

"Do you remember what I told you at the Coffee House in Delhi? About the movement taking over the country? About how the bankrupt legacy left by Nehru is finally going to be replaced?"

I was surprised he had brought it up. "Yes, but as I recall, the HRM wasn't able to fix anything. With Indira gone, things only got worse. JP died, and your movement died with him."

"True, but the question is why? Why did the movement not succeed? Because what came wasn't pure enough, that's why. A government that simply unites the opposition, the Hindus with the Communists, is bound to fail. No wonder we couldn't even hold on to our seats for three years before that churail was swept in again.

"The key factor is purity, Meera. We've learnt our lesson, I'm prepared to say. No more mongrel governments. No more kowtowing to Muslim interests just to be in the majority. We're going to do it successfully this time—do it only with the right parties, the right way. Just think of it for yourself. The country is eighty-five percent Hindu. *Eighty-five percent*. The number can't be denied. All we have to do is build a fire. Find the right spark to ignite their minds. Once they know where their interests lie, their voice will carry the day. It's only a matter of time before we teach them to unite and assert their political will.

"This is what I'm grooming Ashvin for, Meera. To lead us all into the coming order. A new age, a new yuga, not of Nehrus or Gandhis, but of Ram and Shiva. Where the population itself will insist on Hindu values being returned to their rightful place, where the teachings of the Vedas will once more hold sway. Where the law will be straightened to treat everyone alike, where minorities won't be coddled with special rights. An age where our ancient civilization will peak once more, where neighbors will respect our might as we set an example on the world stage."

I had meant to let him carry on, but his words were so preposterous that I broke my silence. "It all sounds very grand when you say it, but you'd be bringing back a past that never existed. This age of Shiva you're talking about is the age of the bullock cart, not the atomic age. Without Nehru's vison we'd have no science—without Indira, no nuclear bomb. We'd still be happily prancing around with our lathis on the world stage."

"Actually, Meera, it's just the opposite," Arya calmly replied. "Read the Vedas, and you'll find out what a wealth of scientific knowledge they contain. Remember, we Hindus gave the world the number zero, without which science wouldn't have even been invented. Indira can take all the credit for our bomb—even claim she discovered zero herself, for all

I care. But really, it's Hindu widsom that's responsible, it's the Hindu way of life, it's Hindu scientists, carrying us through age after age."

"I didn't realize the scientists in India were all Hindu. That the Vedas are what they turned to for nuclear know-how."

Arya ignored my comment. "In a way, it's good that Indira won the elections. It forces us to come up with new ideas to counteract this propaganda she has everyone enchanted with. To reach out to people with our message, to beat the HRM drum in every town and village. Already one can see she's not as strong as before—she'll never be able to ban the HRM or force our movement back into the bottle again." He glanced towards you, then fixed me again in his gaze.

"A decade from now, a few years more or less, we'll have this country in our grasp once again. That's when you'll see how high Ashvin will rise, realize how his uncle's molding helped him seize the day."

I COULD HAVE KEPT arguing with Arya that day, flung all sorts of cutting rejoinders in his face. That underneath the veneer of his words, I had recognized the usual message of intolerance and hate. That the backward-looking philosophy of the HRM was bankrupt, and I would do everything in my power to repudiate it. That I would rather see you remain tethered to the ground than climb the rungs of the future he envisaged.

But I restrained myself. There was no point in showing my hand or revealing my intentions—it was better to leave Arya with the hope that he might be able to sway me. Clearly he was not going to give you up so easily—my idea of negotiation had been laughably naïve.

Or had it? Suppose I were to extend the most unvarnished bargain possible—your freedom in exchange for my acquiescence—surely he would be inclined to accept? I spent a whole night mulling this possibility, examining the practicalities of how I would ensure Arya actually kept his end of the agreement. Then I imagined myself enfolded in his arms; my sheets, my skin, my lips smelling of him, and realized it was a price I couldn't bring myself to pay.

My idea spawned variations. In one version, I lured Arya home some evening, then arranged for it to look as if he was forcing himself on me when you walked in. (The timing would be too difficult to get right, I reluctantly concluded.) In another scheme, considerably less feverish, I simply planted doubts against Arya in your mind—questions about his motives, qualms about his good intentions. This was the strategy I decided to go with. "I wish your uncle wouldn't look at me like that," I said each time I picked you up at his house. "He keeps brushing against me for some reason," I complained, after I accompanied you to a function of the HRM.

One day, I pressed in deeper after an argument over the summer retreat he wanted you to attend. "I know you love your Yara uncle, but don't you realize he's being so friendly just to get to me again?"

"That's not true. He's not even come to our house once—you're the one always going there. It's me he likes, not you."

"Then tell me this, Ashvin—all those years back, when he was writing those letters to you. Whom did he come after in the end?"

The next week, I deployed my first outright lie, after you brushed off my concerns about neglecting your studies to cavort around with your uncle. "He's touched me already, you know. The evening we accompanied him to the wrestling match, and again when we saw him at the pooja the other day."

"You're lying. Yara uncle would never do that."

"No, of course not, your Yara uncle is a saint. Isn't that the reason you had to break his nose for him?"

"That was so long ago."

"And now he's changed? Suddenly he's so virtuous that he's become your hero? Someone to defend against the word of your own mother? Should I tell you all the other things he was whispering in my ear, acts he promised we would perform together?"

You ran out of the room. No matter how much I persisted (with allegations that sometimes seemed so compelling, I almost believed them myself), your trysts with Arya continued.

And then, one evening, I decided to use the vein of guilt that I knew ran through your consciousness. You had returned three hours late from school, so I asked you where you had been. "Each time you go and see him, it only gives him more encouragement, makes him bolder. It's like telling him that whatever he wants to do with your mother is fine—is that the message you want to give?"

"No."

"You have to decide, Ashvin—you're almost sixteen now, so you know what I'm talking about. It's nice that you can go do all these things with your uncle, but is it worth the risk?"

"You always twist things around. I wish you'd stop thinking like this."

"No, *you* think, Ashvin—if you were to come back and find me the same way as before. Do you still remember that Divali—have you forgotten what he was doing to me on that floor?"

"It's not true. You're just being jealous. I'm not listening to anything you're saying anymore."

"Maybe you don't think there's anything to it," I said, unable to stop myself. "Why not Yara uncle, too, if I can let you, my son, get away with it?"

"What do you mean?"

"You know what I'm talking about, Ashvin. The night of your fifteenth birthday. Just because I didn't say anything at the time, doesn't mean I approved, that I'm open to everyone else. You should be ashamed of yourself for harboring such a thought—I'm not some family bicycle, on which you can offer your uncle a ride as well."

SO IT COMES DOWN to this, Ashvin—the issue on which your mother must be judged. Was it too destructive, what I did to sunder you from your uncle, even though I used only words? Could it really have been in your best interests, or was it my jealousy taking control? The thought of being displaced in your affections, which I could not endure.

What I can say in my defense is that in the heat of the moment, I didn't see any other way to go. My correction had to be quick and effective—else wouldn't Arya have appropriated your soul? This much you must believe—I had no desire to cause you injury with the cauterizing words I spoke. Though I suppose I could have accepted defeat, surrendered you to his hands, left your future for him to mold. Surely happiness must take root in the cadres of the HRM as well.

The day after our exchange, you came home so early that I asked if there had been a problem at school. Over the months you had been staying out late I had forgotten this was the regular time you were supposed to return. "There's nothing wrong," you replied, and took your books into the bedroom. In the evening, you filled your plate with rice and lentils and sat in the balcony to eat your dinner alone. That night, and every night after that, you took care to sleep with your back turned towards my bed.

On Saturday, when I asked if you were going to the HRM gymkhana for your yoga session, you replied you didn't need the class anymore. "I know the exercises well enough now to do them myself at home." You didn't mention Arya's name all weekend, in fact you barely spoke.

Two weeks later, Arya came to our flat. I had just emerged from my bath—I opened the door with my hair wet. I felt an acute embarrassment as he greeted me—I realized I didn't even have my dupatta on. But my immodesty barely seemed to register on him. "Could I speak to Ashvin?" he said, and looked past me into the room beyond.

I withdrew into the kitchen to allow you to converse. It was about the summer camp—there had been a preparatory meeting at which you had failed to show up the night before. "I already told you I can't go this year," I heard you say.

"Do you realize what an honor this is, what strings I pulled to get you asked? Besides, you'll be sixteen in a few weeks—if not this year, you're never going to go."

I didn't trust myself not to intrude again, so I went into the bedroom and shut the door. I could still hear you arguing, so I stood in the balcony and watched the cars below. When I came back to the living room, you were alone.

"Did Arya uncle leave?"

You turned, and on your cheek I saw the angry outline of Arya's fingers imprinted in red. "He did. I hope you're happy. I hope you're finally satisfied." Before I could say anything, you stalked away.

chapter
thirty-five

A FEW SUNDAYS LATER, THE PHONE RANG. SCHOOL WAS ALREADY IN vacation, and you had squatted on your bed all week, it seemed, constructing some sort of audio amplifier with your electronics kit. Even though it was the hottest part of the summer, you insisted on keeping the door shut so you weren't disturbed.

"Hello, Meera." It was Paji on the other end of the line.

Although one could dial between cities directly now without a trunk-call booking, it was still very unusual to receive a phone call from Delhi. My heart began to thump in my ears, as I braced myself for some horrible emergency. "Has something happened to Biji?"

"Your mother is fine, as surly and impossible as ever. I was calling to respond to Ace's—I mean Ashvin's—request. Could I talk to him?"

It was such a relief to learn no calamity had befallen anyone that I didn't ask Paji what he meant by your request. "Give my love to Biji and Sharmila," I said, and called you to the phone.

Your conversation with your grandfather lasted for barely a minute or two. After thanking him profusely, you turned around with face flushed. "I'm leaving in June. I'm going away to Sanawar."

"What?"

"The boarding school there. I asked Nanaji for help. Remember when he made the promise long ago that he'd pay for it if we ever wanted? Thankfully, he hadn't forgotten. They usually don't accept anyone in the eleventh standard, but he's on their board and says there will be no problem with admission."

"I don't understand. When . . . ?"

"I know I should have asked you first. But there was so little time left, with classes beginning next month. It really won't cost anything. Nanaji's even sending money for the uniforms. It's amazing how he agreed to everything without asking any questions. I think it was what I wrote in my letter about the gymkhana and Arya uncle that must have done it. He said on the phone that he was proud of me for breaking away, that it was the best thing for my future."

Your expression softened. "I'm sorry I didn't tell you first. I know how much you're going to miss me. It'll pass by quick, don't worry. It's only two years until I graduate."

I felt unsteady. "That's very nice of Nanaji," I forced myself to say. I thought you were going to hug me, but you didn't.

THE DAYS THAT FOLLOWED were filled with activity. We had to buy cloth and visit the tailor for your uniforms. Sanawar was at a high altitude, so I contacted Sharmila to send sweaters from Delhi. The school stocked a special material of wool, together with an embossed pocket emblem, which one ordered from them to have a blazer stitched. There were textbooks needed—not only for the eleventh standard, but also (since there were differences in the syllabus) the tenth. One day, a three-page medical questionnaire arrived in the mail—we went to Dr. Kagalwalla's dispensary to have it completed. He heard "something fluttery" while examining your chest through his stethoscope, and it took an X-ray and EKG to satisfy him that everything was fine.

Although I tried to lose myself in these preparations, I was periodically overcome by the enormity of the change I faced ahead. Most cruel seemed the sheer suddenness of it. I knew you wouldn't be away just two years, as you had tried to reassure me. You already talked about going to one of the technology institutes spread far and wide over the country after you finished school. Even beyond, once you got your degree, who knew to which city your job would take you?

In the back of my mind I always realized I would have to give you up—but only at some abstract time in the future, far away as yet. To whom should I protest about being cheated out of the last few remaining years I had left?

Despite any anger you still harbored, you granted me more of your company than usual. I was thankful for this extra time we spent together. We went several times to Chowpatty in that last month—ordering extravagant ice cream sundaes and enormous plates of channa bhatura almost every day at the Cream Centre (the generous check that arrived from Paji helped). We visited all your favorite childhood haunts—right down to the zoo and the fountains at Hanging Gardens. You even sat next to me on the sofa and endured old movies on the VCR.

It was during the time we were watching *Aradhana* again that it struck me. Sharmila Tagore had just been sentenced to prison after taking the blame for the murder committed by her son. As she grew old behind bars, I realized that my wish for an opportunity for sacrifice was being answered at last. The chance to smile as I bid you off, the years of loneliness stretching ahead. Finally I was being given the chance to attain the stature of a proper tragedienne.

On the night before your departure, I kept glancing over to catch another glimpse of you lying across the room. How often I had seen you like that in the light from the balcony, your nose and chin illuminated in silvery silhouette. How much more would I have cherished each such sighting, had I known their number was coming to an end. How much more would I have savored every mundane action of yours, every shared moment we spent.

I remembered the night Hema slept at home before her wedding—Mataji next to her one last time, cradling her head. Couldn't I, too, pull my bed softly to yours? Ease your head from its pillow and cradle it as well? I looked at your sleeping form and wondered if this longing still held you in its sway as well. Wasn't it not so far back, that day of Holi, when you sat astride me on the ground? How right it felt, how natural it seemed, your weight pressing against my waist. I know you thought it too—I could see it in your face.

Were there still some confused impulses darting around in your head that hadn't been damped out yet? Beneath the desire to punish me for separating you from your Yara, did you still have some need for closeness left? Or had the craving transferred itself completely, striking up its lone encampment in my chest? The fear of losing you that made me want to hug you so tight that if only for an instant it was quenched?

I imagined going over to your bed. Standing over you, like you once did over me—our positions reversed from the dream I used to have. What would you do when you opened your eyes—reach for my hand, pull me down next to yourself? A filigree of moonlight to adorn our nestling bodies, the shadows tucking in everything else?

For a while, I would just lie there, awash in your essence, replenishing myself in your touch, in the field of your presence. Would your scent be stronger now, more distinct, more mature? As we embraced, would I feel muscles running across your arms and back that I hadn't noticed before? Would your teardrops taste the same if my lips encountered any on your cheek? And your chest—would there be light enough to trace the serpentine patterns in which the strands of hair had grown?

Afterwards, once the ache in my chest was quelled, and all the expressions of affection we knew were spent, where would we go? Would we let sleep come claim the night, or would we look for new landscapes across which to rove? Would we huddle gratefully through the hours that remained, or cast around for an expanded vocabulary to explore?

I tried to imagine what forms these explorations would take. Your nose nuzzling for scent behind my ear, your tongue skimming a taste off my throat. Your head seeking out the breast it remembers, your mouth closing around the aureole still familiar from before. Perhaps your fingers caress my navel, the portal to which you were beholden so long ago. They meander down from my belly and pet shyly at the curls they have not touched before.

Your thigh feels hot upon my own, your foot curls and strains against my toes. You lick your lips and I feel you are going to say something, but instead, a swallow rides down your throat. I want to assure you that it will be fine this time, that you don't have to be nervous, that you can let your curiosity roam. This is my gift to you, to help you make this journey, to follow wherever you go.

But you close your eyes and rest your cheek on my chest—either you are content, or uncertain where to proceed. The tips of your fingers, so tentative in their contact, have withdrawn entirely now. I taste the disappointment in my mouth—am I not entitled to curiosity, to a reciprocal chance to explore? The flush of anticipation still flows through my body—my thigh is the one burning, I realize, not yours.

For a moment, I wonder whether to help you along, whether it is for me to take the initiative now. But each time I alight on a possibility, your restfulness makes me shy away from completing the thought. All I can think of is pressing your head to my breast—it seems too sordid to envision anything more. Even this is not for real, I remind myself—you are in your own bed, on the other side of the room.

Perhaps somewhere out there is a world where this distance between us could be dissolved. A parallel universe in which we would no longer be mother and son. Perhaps we are like gods and goddesses, living through successive incarnations, exploring each other's different forms. Waiting for the birth when our roles match up, when we can be one.

I think I will spend the night looking at you. But sleep steals me away before dawn can approach.

THE SUN WAS STREAMING across your empty bed when I awoke, making the white sheets incandescent. The dread rose in my chest as soon as I sat up in bed—I knew what the morning meant. From the bathroom came the sound of you brushing your teeth; a clock struck eight somewhere outside. Your train was at eleven forty-three, which meant there were less than four hours left.

The breakfast I prepared for you that morning felt like a last meal, except the condemned person was myself. The eggs scrambled with onions and seasoned just so, the bread toasted twice to make it more crisp. The glass of Ovaltine with milk poured in from a height to give it a frothy head. I sat across you as you ate—you were subdued and stared at your plate. It occurred to me that perhaps you too could taste regret.

I heated the water for your bath and mixed it into a half-full bucket—another routine coming to an end. The minutes accelerated and I heard the same portentous clock strike—first nine, then ten. We scrambled to pack overlooked items—a flashlight, a lunch box, even your new blazer, still hanging in its plastic sheath in the cupboard. One of the locks proved too big to fit through the suitcase latch, so you went downstairs to the bania to buy another.

We sat together in the back of the taxicab, with Zaida tactfully taking the front. The seat was wide, but somehow your arm remained positioned in reassuring contact with my side. By now, last night's reveries on touch, on longing, were distant blurs in my mind. All I could think of was the scene to come, of you vanishing on your train as I watched in dry-eyed disbelief.

On the platform, you insisted on carrying your luggage yourself rather than hiring a coolie. The Sikh husband and wife sharing your row were very friendly, even though the woman made no move to relinquish your window seat, which she had occupied. We stood outside after stowing your bags, and I tried to pass off my numbness as nonchalance. You were covering up as well, I could tell, hiding your misgivings with an excess of heartiness.

Just before the end, you dropped all camouflage and became completely silent. A glimmer of optimism sparked up inside me—perhaps you were having a change of heart, perhaps you wouldn't go, perhaps I would get a reprieve. I looked at your face and saw the longing I had wondered about—was it something you were revealing on purpose? Before I could get too encouraged, you let a stronger emotion surface—the guilt that you felt, at leaving me.

I thought we might barely hug, but you pressed and squeezed and covered my face with a flurry of kisses. The whistle blew, and I imagined holding on to you as the train departed—let the Sikh lady keep both your luggage and your window seat. But then you had slipped out of my arms and clambered onto the train, and were waving to me. Behind you stood the conductor with a half smile, as if this was a rite of passage, sad but hackneyed, that he had witnessed so many times before. You gave one final wave from the receding doorway, and then I was alone, adrift in the vastness of time.

I'm not sure how I got home—I suppose Zaida must have taken me back. The first thing I noticed was the stack of handkerchiefs I had ironed and folded neatly—I had forgotten to pack them into your bag. I lay awake well into the night, worrying about them. How would you deal with a cold? With what would you wipe your sweat? Did you have enough money to buy new ones? What if in Sanawar, handkerchiefs were something they didn't even sell?

The next evening, I sat by the phone, waiting for the call to tell me you had safely arrived. When it came, the handkerchiefs were all I could babble about. I cursed my forgetfulness as you told me about your dorm, jabbered about mailing you a parcel as you tried to describe your trip. I didn't even get to say how much I missed you—the line went dead as soon as your three minutes were up.

Afterwards, I realized I didn't have a phone number to call you back. It took six days for your first letter to make it to me, six days without any contact. I stared at childhood pictures, pulled out your baby clothes from the trunk, leafed through your notebooks from school. One morning I even ironed each handkerchief again and arranged them in a fresh stack. That each minute could be so long, each second stretch so elastically, I never knew.

It didn't get much better in the weeks that followed. Your letters, when they came, took only so many moments to race through. I tried to teach myself to live in these concentrated bursts of reading them. They never revealed all I hungered for—to whom you spoke, what foods you ate, the pictures on your wall, the books on your desk. I had been spoiled for sixteen years, knowing everything about you, down to the color of the socks you wore each day. I couldn't call you and ask, either—the telephone number you sent was only for emergencies, you had warned.

I watched my favorite old movies every night—*Mamta* and *Aurat* and *Mother India*. Nargis appeared on my screen repeatedly, to shoot her son over and over again. A part of every woman was Kali, just like a part was Parvati—that's what the reviews had explained. Did Kali reside in me as well—would I have consumed you too, had you stayed?

Sometimes the evenings progressed, the streetlamps came on, and still the cassettes played on the VCR. I knew what awaited me in the other room—the sight that made each night so difficult to bear. Your bed all neatly made up, with the sheets and the pillowcases I still changed. And right next to it my own, as stark as the cot from *Aradhana* on which Sharmila slept in jail. We had kept them apart ever since the year you turned fifteen, when everything changed. Was it so wrong of me to join them again?

ONE EMOTION BURNED brightly through the haze of my grief—anger towards Paji. After the movies ran their course, I lay in bed—sometimes yours, sometimes my own. The sheets crinkled in the heat of my fury, the walls glowed orange and red. I played out imaginary dialogues with him—how this was the final straw, how I was fed up of his meddling, how I would no longer allow him to run my life. Sometimes I found myself spouting my lines aloud. "Did you forget I'm his mother? How dare you make such enormous changes in his life without even talking to me?" At other times, I scrambled into the living room and furiously started scribbling out a letter to him, listing all the ways he had derailed my attempts at happiness. "Isn't it enough that you made my mother's life a living hell? Did I have so much left that you had to take away my son as well?"

By daylight, my ire subsided somewhat, though it never completely abated. I made more reasoned plans on how to convey my resentment. Calling him was no use—I always became too tongue-tied when he was on the phone. Sending a letter would not work either—he was much too articulate, much too adept at finding arguments to snake around the written word. I could see him finding elegant ways to counter my accusations, to assert that he had acted selflessly, only to neutralize Arya's influence.

The only option was to confront him in person. To stand in the same library room, refusing to be cowed by the cold blast of the air-conditioning, and pummel him one by one with my grievances. I decided to go to Delhi and have a final showdown with him. Even if it did nothing to change his behavior, the satisfaction of telling him off to his face was something I needed deep inside.

But it was not so easy to get the better of Paji. Before I could get my ticket, he died.

I HARDLY BELIEVED the news when the call came. Surely Paji couldn't have been felled by something as ordinary as a heart attack? It happened on his morning walk, near the intersection of Ansari and Tilak roads. There was a temple at the corner, and for years Paji had been climbing the steps to the shrine at the top. He never went inside, just walked past the entrance, "to show God that His adversary was still in good health." Most of the pilgrims took their footwear off at the bottom of the steps and climbed barefoot, but Paji tromped up in his leather shoes, and made it a point to scrape the dirt off his soles on the top step. He would relish the shocked looks and outraged shouts he encountered—a few times, he had been involved in confrontations with the priest himself. "If your God made everything, then surely He made cow dung as well—why should you object?"

Perhaps if Paji had sat down on the steps when the pain started, or even asked his friend Bansi, who was accompanying him, for help, he might have survived. But he soldiered on, refusing to give anyone in the temple (including the idols themselves, Bansi noted) the satisfaction of seeing him falter. He made it to the top, scraped his shoes on the steps for the last time, and managed to make it all the way around the corner, so that he was completely out of sight of the temple before he collapsed. Bansi said that he had tried several times that morning to get Paji to stop to take a rest, but was dismissed. "It's just gas," Paji said. "That's the most God has ever managed to conjure up to scare me."

For quite some time now, the only interaction remaining between Biji and him had, quite literally, been a battle to the death. A staring contest to see who would outlive the other—nobody expected Paji to be the first to blink. Certainly nobody expected him to be a victim of divine retribution, as everyone now said.

But Paji proved to be iron-willed even in death. After the Emergency was rescinded and Indira Gandhi defeated, it had been Biji's political connections that protected them from reprisals by the new government. Paji never lived down the humiliation, never forgave her for this. He was foresighted enough to plan for the eventuality of his dying first, organized enough to arrange his revenge against Biji in advance. I got off the train in Delhi to find my mother beside herself—the funeral had not taken place as yet. Paji had stipulated something he knew would be a slap across her face—something to repudiate not only Biji, but the religion they both had been born into as well. He left written instructions specifying that there was to be no funeral pyre, not even an electric cremation—he wanted to be placed in a plain wooden box like a Muslim or a Christian and be buried instead.

It took a while to find a graveyard willing to accept a coffin with a Hindu body in it. Sharmila's husband Munshi, the only Muslim in the family, led us in throwing handfuls of dirt into the grave. A reporter from the *Times of India* attended, and wrote an article playing up the unusualness of the funeral arrangement the next day. *"In death as in life, even in these days of communal strife, Rajinder Sawhney has shown the country that the secular ideals of Jawaharlal Nehru have not been forgotten yet."* The Congress Party then felt shamed into issuing a statement, lauding Paji as someone who single-handedly built the entire Indian publishing industry from scratch. (The statement was later retracted when other publishers, who were bigger donors to the party coffers, objected.)

Biji boycotted the ceremony, which she regarded as blasphemous. Upon hearing that the news of this ignominy, which she had hoped would pass unnoticed, was now in the newspaper for everyone to see, she became somewhat unhinged. She stormed through the house, collecting all of Paji's paraphernalia—his souvenirs, his clothes, his books, even the ancient pair of his slippers she used to secretly touch long ago to start her day. "If he wants his body eaten by worms, that's fine with me. Since he refused to be cremated, the least I can do is give a proper end to his things." Sharmila made a plea to have at least the books spared, but Biji seemed particularly determined to ensure that none of them escaped the "purification," as she put it. "All those years he flaunted his learning in my face—look, how foolish of him to have forgotten his library behind." She tore down the plaque with Nehru's disavowal of religion from the wall and added it to her pile.

She had the ceremony performed with real sandalwood, even paying for a Brahmin priest to recite the prayers at the cremation ghats at Nigam Bodh. Roopa's son Dilip, as the eldest male heir, was taken along to light the pyre. Afterwards, Biji insisted that we all sort through the ashes, collecting bits of charred knickknacks and the spines of books that had not burnt. She had them placed in a traditional earthenware pot covered with a red cloth—we drove to Hardwar that very afternoon to deposit them in the Ganges.

Biji hired a boat to take us to the middle of the river, guarding the pot zealously in her lap as the boatman rowed us over. She didn't offer to share the task with any of us, but shook out all the contents herself—reaching in to scour out the last stubborn bits with her bare hands before consigning the pot as well. Unlike the box with Dev's remains, the mix contained little actual ash—mostly heavier remnants that plopped into the water, plus a few unburned leathery bits that floated for a while. I imagined the spines of books from Paji's entire library released into the river, from Shakespeare to Austen, Kipling to Tagore. A giant school of fish liberated from their confines, streaming through the water to turn the Ganges green and gold and red.

Perhaps I could swim away as unfettered as well, now that Paji no longer had his hold on me. I looked at Sharmila weeping as she murmured her farewells—why couldn't I share her grief? Roopa, beside her, was alternating between heartrending wails and long, luxurious sobs—she threw out a hand towards the water now as if trying to latch onto Paji before he swirled away in the Ganges. I tried once more to ignite regret in my heart, but all I could summon was relief.

Then I thought of the red and green and gold fish again. I imagined them swimming through valleys and gorges, past towns and villages, across the vast Gangetic plains. Spreading their knowledge through the water, the learning so consistently championed by Paji over the years, until they reached the open sea.

At home, we opened the letters Paji had left with his lawyer for each of his three daughters. Although he had willed me a generous sum of money for your education, he put the flat in Bombay in your name, Ace, not mine. Rather than being stung by this omission, the idea struck me as almost quaint—Paji worrying about the danger I might pose to the property's ownership by remarrying. *To be a parent is to be guilty*, he wrote. *Remember that, if you feel tempted to judge me. Perhaps you'll understand one day, and forgive me if you think I played too strong a role in shaping your destiny.*

His writing had lost none of its beauty with age. I remembered his hand enfolding mine as he helped me practice my penmanship. "You have to think of the pen as part of yourself—only then will the ink flow smoothly through the nib." I folded Paji's letter back into its envelope and tucked it into my suitcase.

"Would it have killed you to cry a little?" Roopa demanded at dinner. "Even if you didn't love Paji as much, did you forget you were still his daughter?"

I looked at her face. Her eyes were ferociously red—on her cheeks, she proudly wore a palimpsest of grief where streams of tears had dried successively.

"Or do you still hold Paji to blame?—poor Meera, always going around complaining he never loved her enough, that she was never his favorite. I suppose you must feel better now, with all the evidence he's given you today."

She was referring to Paji's will. Roopa's face had crumpled upon learning that the amount mentioned in her letter was only a little more than what Paji had left to Sharmila or myself. She rose out of her chair, visibly agitated, when the lawyer announced that the bulk had gone to an obscure scientific organization based in Madras, whose purpose was to debunk claims of religious miracles. "They're the ones who capture sleight of hand on film, who arrange for a swimming pool when some holy man declares he can walk on water. Your father wants them to use his money to go after the Satya Sai Baba himself."

To her credit, Roopa quickly regained her composure, even managing to hide her disappointment when the lawyer, in response to her delicate questioning, said it would be pointless to contest the will. "It just shows you what a great man he was," she forced herself to say.

Now, however, she had freed herself from any restraints. The desire to draw blood was radiant on her face. "It must be tempting to count what Paji left and be comforted by it. But I know you're not that foolish, Meera, to mistake fairness for love. We all know whom he really cared for inside—it would be difficult, even for you, to delude yourself on that count. As for the money, what choice did you leave him with, anyway? All those years of guilt that you piled up on him, all those times you shamed him into believing he didn't love you enough. I can only imagine how beleaguered he must have felt, how tortured you must have left him. It's a wonder he wasn't driven to leave you his entire estate."

Sharmila, sitting white-faced at the table, began to say something, but I put my hand over hers. "This might come as a shock to you, Roopa, but not all of us have had designs on Paji's money. That's what all these nasty words are about, isn't it? Perhaps we should leave this talk till tomorrow, before you say something you'll regret."

But Roopa was too enkindled to stop midway. "It wasn't just him, Meera, was it? You've forged an entire career of making people feel guilty for not loving you enough. Even I haven't been immune from it. When I think back to the days we first met Dev—how, after all, did you maneuver him into marrying you in the first place? He certainly paid for it, the sweet man—and not just him—we're all paying the price, with Paji's will. I just shudder to think what havoc you must be wreaking now on poor Ashvin."

Hearing your name made me rise to Roopa's bait again. "You know Ashvin has nothing to do with this, so don't bring his name to your lips. As for the will, I've already told you I don't care about it. If anyone's the greedy one, it's you, Roopa—greedy about Paji, greedy about Biji, greedy about Dev. Whenever you've seen me get the slightest bit of love or attention or happiness, you've always tried to snatch it away. I used to wonder how anyone could be so jealous, what I could have possibly done to deserve such treatment, whether you were just insecure. But now I realize that you can't really help your meanness, you were just born filled with it."

Roopa made a sound in her throat between a laugh and a growl. "See? This is just what I was talking about. I'm mean, I'm against Meera, I've wronged her, like everyone else has. Go ahead, fault me, tell me all your problems are because of my hate. You've killed Dev and banished poor Ashvin to a hostel—with Paji gone too, whom else can you blame? I don't mind—from now on, I can be your whipping boy. Every time something goes wrong in your life, I'll be standing by to accept the blame. The truth is that there's only one person who's responsible, and that's you, Meera. It's been you all along, nobody else. All the times you've blundered, all the people you've driven away."

"Yes, say what you like, Roopa—I know you too well to care. You're mean, and you're selfish since birth, and there's no deeper reason for it—what's more, you'll never be able to change. Paji must have seen this ugliness too—did you think you could keep it hidden from him? Perhaps that's what made him stop loving you as much as before—why else would he write the will the way he did?"

Roopa gave a cry and stood up. This time, the tears in her eyes were from fury, not sorrow. "My Paji is dead. You've got your freedom from him. Go now, and don't repeat his name. Don't pretend to speak for him ever again. Go and make some brilliant changes in your life. The money you've managed to squeeze out—spend it as you wish. And once you've transformed yourself, once you've emerged as carefree as a butterfly, be sure to write us about your wonderful happiness."

chapter
thirty-six

ALTHOUGH I HAD NEVER CONSCIOUSLY FANTASIZED ABOUT PAJI DYING, I always harbored a feeling in the back of my mind that it would be a deliverance of sorts when it happened, an escape from his control, a liberation from the existence he had constrained me to live. Now that I was back in Bombay, it was not clear to me how my life was going to change. How would I enjoy my freedom? What brilliant steps would I take, as Roopa had challenged, to make myself happy again?

Could she have been correct about Paji just being an excuse? Someone convenient to fault for all the things that didn't go right in my life? Was I, as she had contended, the only one really to blame? I tried to comfort myself with a list of all the times Paji had subverted the course of my life, but Roopa's troubling accusation remained.

What disoriented me more was the wrenching loss I already felt from your absence. Paji's passing made me feel doubly unmoored, as if my last remaining anchor had been hoisted away. I had never thought of him in this way before, never imagined that his could have been a stabilizing presence over the years, a dependable force to react against. The realization that I now had to navigate life truly alone made me sink into a despondent state.

I began roaming the city streets aimlessly. Sometimes, as I wandered,

I tried to imagine Paji following me. Glancing at his watch from time to time to add up the minutes and the hours I wasted. Perhaps he would shake his head, remind me of the books I could have read instead, the goals I could have accomplished, the degrees I could have earned. *Meera, Meera, Meera. Have you ever thought of how much of your life you've frittered away?*

But nobody followed me—Paji was gone, I reminded myself. It had a strange effect on me, this double bereavement—I felt more widowed than when Dev had passed away. Sometimes I imagined myself to be an ant in a cosmic experiment, designed to test my ability to make sense of things.

It was on one of my rambling walks that I first started thinking of the idea of completion. I had just crossed over the bridge from Chowpatty to take a look at the small garden behind the tracks at Charni Road station. It was never crowded, since it lay hidden from the main path and people hurrying to and from the station barely noticed its existence. A grove of palm trees of a frizzy kind I had not seen elsewhere stood in the center, surrounded by several plantings of hibiscus and mogra which seemed to be in bloom year-round. I especially liked the corner with the ferns—the way the babies nestled amidst their parents, their heads curled in close to their stems like sleeping birds.

Today, though, my attention was drawn to the edge of the garden, where the ornamental banana tree stood. Instead of the healthy specimen so flamboyantly in bloom the last time, I was surprised to now see something barely alive—yellowing fronds blowing weakly around the shriveling trunk. It seemed impossible that such a change could have taken place over the course of a few weeks—had the tree just decided to die, once the show for which it had been planted was done?

By itself, perhaps I would not have made too much of it. But then I started noticing other things. The spent orange flowers from the gulmohar tree strewn all across the path. The outer layer of fern stalks, all droopy and brown, in contrast with the sprightly inner stalks, preparing to unfurl into the air. Drifting leaves and fallen fruits and seeds, all slowly turning into dust. Most poignant of all, a small white bird—not a dove or a sparrow, but a species I didn't remember having ever seen, resting in a bed of canna lilies. At first I thought it was asleep, but then I noticed an ant crawling over its tiny yellow beak. The feathers were plush and unsoiled, their sheen intact—the bird, I could see, was neither aged nor decrepit. I turned it over with the stem of a leaf—there was no indication to show what had felled it, no mark or injury. It was as if it had alighted from the sky one final time and decided there was no reason to fly again.

I thought about the bird all the way home—imagined how it could have orchestrated such a perfect death. Had it spent the summer tending to a nest full of speckled eggs, and once they were hatched, to the fledgling chicks that needed its help? Is this where it had come after seeing them fly away all grown—had it felt so fulfilled that it seemed like a natural time to end its earthly sojourn? Wasn't that what animals did in the forest—find a quiet corner to curl up and die in once they had come to the end of their usefulness? And the fish that I had once read to you about—salmon, were they?—that came back to spawn and expire where they were born?

For the next few days, I was enthralled by this idea of completion. Every time I saw a flower that had drooped in its vase or spotted a beetle lying curled up on the windowsill, I was reminded of it. Shouldn't I be as smart as these organisms? Know not to challenge the order of the universe? Wouldn't it be foolish to persist once my work on this planet was done?

And what could have been that work, Ashvin, but to bring you forth, to nurture you until grown? You were what had given sense to my life, what had made its pieces fit together. The reason I had met Dev and come to Bombay, the years I had lived to bring you up after he was gone. Perhaps everything that had transpired had a purpose behind it—even what happened to tear us apart. Weren't you settling in well enough now in your boarding school—away from me, away from Arya, out of the reach of harm? And now that Paji had left more than enough money to see you through, weren't you assured a smooth passage into life as an adult?

The more I thought about it, the more clear it became that your need for me was done. The evidence was apparent every time I looked at your photographs. Here you were as a toddler between Dev and myself, holding on to each of our hands as you tried to remain standing. There you sat in your navy blue long pants the year after Dev passed away, with a pale smile coaxed out only for Mummy. Even in the photo that Zaida took of the two of us the April before last, there was a vulnerability in your look, a tenderness in the way your head turned towards me. But then came the two pictures sent from Sanawar. In the first you posed with three other boys—what drew my attention most was that your smile was as carefree as theirs. The other, an identity card portrait, startled me even more—dressed in your new school blazer with the fiery pocket emblem, I could see, for the first time, the defiant confidence in your face.

Could there be something else awaiting me in this life beside you, another purpose I had not explored as yet? Paji, of course, would have exploded at such a question—he would have raged about a long list of goals I still had left. But he was gone now, his letters no longer arriving to exhort me on—what was the significance of the timing of his death? Wasn't this the final validation that I needed, the ultimate reminder that my task was complete? The image of his library ashes came to my mind—I pictured myself floating together with them down the Ganges.

The morning after the immersion trip to Hardwar, I had gone to stand in Paji's library one last time. It was disorienting to see the emptiness gaping from the bookshelves all around, the walls denuded of plaques, the desk swept clean. I rummaged around in the drawers, but they had been emptied as well. Then, against the back of the lowermost drawer, I found something missed by Biji—a small volume of the Urdu poetry Paji loved so much. I quickly hid it in my purse—it would be my last souvenir from my father, not to be shared with my siblings.

Now, I pulled out this volume, to see if in it I could find some guidance from Paji. The way I had discovered the book, the verses Paji had underlined, convinced me some communication lay hidden inside. Most of the poems were about ardor and longing, by poets like Ghalib and Dard and Mir. Roses bloomed, then turned to dust, nightingales wept tears of blood, rivers of wine were poured to wash away the violence of love. I paused over each of the marked couplets, studying some for a very long time, wondering if I had discovered what Paji had selected to speak to me. But I found them all inscrutable. I was about to give up on the book, when my gaze fell on a poem in the last section, by Sauda.

> *How long, how long within this world will you remain,*
> *And wander like a vagabond from lane to lane?*
> *You wish today to live until the end of days;*
> *But even so, how long, how long will you remain?*

I felt instantly electrified. Wasn't this exactly the confirmation I was seeking? A reminder that my fate was irresistibly coupled with Paji's, a beckoning that harked back to our biological link? The fact that the lines were unmarked, that Paji had been unable to bring himself to underscore them, made them even more compelling. He had chosen this cryptic way to convey the message, one that he knew was the precise one for me, but didn't have it in his heart to endorse with his pen. I had his blessing, the lines were assuring me, I had correctly interpreted the meaning of his death.

Suddenly, with this piece in place, the jigsaw of my life was complete, the map of my future set. My feeling of aimlessness began to lift, the disorientation I suffered from was relieved. I did not as yet dwell on where this line of thinking was taking me, articulate to myself the resolution to which it would lead. I was like an artist setting aside a half-finished painting or a writer waiting for a plot to jell—this would be a last grand work into which I would not rush impulsively.

Zaida noticed my change of mood. "What's the matter?" she asked. "You keep smiling to yourself these days as if you have some secret to hide." I knew I couldn't let her have the slightest hint of what I was contemplating, so I pretended there was no explanation for my newfound buoyancy.

The only person with whom I knew I could be free was Sandhya. She arrived one night during my gestation period, as I lay thinking in bed. *"How long, how long, will you remain?"* she sang, *"And wander like a vagabond from lane to lane?*" She told me that Sauda had been quite well-known in Lahore. "It took me years to understand I had no purpose left, Didi. You're lucky, you won't linger around uselessly."

She started coming regularly, holding my hand or caressing my cheek, curling up next to me and covering our bodies with the sheet. "It's as simple as getting off from a bus when you reach your stop—I'll be there to help you with your bags when you arrive." I smelled the sweet herbal fragrance of her skin, looked into her clear, unblemished face, the empathy in her eyes. "The things you're worrying about don't really matter in the end—once it happens, all those feelings pass quite quickly."

Sometimes her voice took on a beguiling tone. "You know who else is here, don't you, even if you haven't thought about him for a while, about your Dev? He hasn't forgotten you, Didi, he asks about you each morning—what you're feeling, how long will be his wait. He says he's changed, not to worry about what he was like—when people come here, they don't remain the same."

She was especially soothing each time I thought of you, Ashvin. When I wondered what effect the news would have on you, how you would be able to continue without me. "He's like the son I didn't have, Didi, so I know how you must feel. But you have to remember he'll find his own happiness in the end. Don't confuse his need with your own—he's already stronger than you think."

It was Sandhya who came to my rescue when I got bogged down in my planned goodbyes. I had been wondering whether to wait until after the Divali holidays to get a chance to see you again, perhaps even make a special trip to Delhi to visit everyone there. Sandhya assured me there was no reason to linger just to bid farewell in person. "They all know the love in your heart for them, Ashvin most of all. You'll be surprised how little it will matter, Didi—the important thing now is not to lose your momentum."

One night, Sandhya kissed me just as I was falling asleep. "You're ready now, Didi," she whispered. "I can see it in your face, feel it in my heart. I'll pray for you tonight while you sleep—we'll meet next on the other side." I tried to protest, but she covered my lips with her fingers. "Just do it quickly, remember not to wait too long."

In the morning, when I awoke, the sheet under which we had slept lay folded at my feet. Light streamed in from the balcony, and only the faintest trace of fragrance lingered in the air. I got up from the bed and tiptoed into the other room, as if I might discover Sandhya there, asleep. The sofa was empty, the cushions reclining neatly against the armrests in their pink pillowcases. On the floor near the entrance lay the newspaper, still folded in thirds after being pushed through the slot in the door.

I picked it up. The front page reported that floods had ravaged both Bihar and U.P. India had protested the latest American announcement to sell seven F-16 fighter planes to Pakistan. There had been a stabbing attack by unknown assailants on three more residents of the Muslim colony at Byculla. Indira Gandhi was scheduled to address a conference of women scientists on Saturday morning, followed by a political rally at Chowpatty that evening.

My brain barely registered these headlines—there was something else for which I was searching. Suddenly I knew what it was. I turned to page three, where the more lurid items of local news were located, where the ad for Gulani Clinic ("abortion—safe, affordable, legal") appeared every day. I was not disappointed—there, in the second column, was the report of a young woman who had drowned herself in Mahim Creek. And right next to it, an account of a spurned suitor who had perished by flinging himself, with melodramatic aptness, into a garbage pit from the terrace of his building.

Only later, while scanning through the afternoon *Midday* for similar news items, did I realize what Sandhya meant. I had accepted what I was going to do, I had taken the next step. These articles that I would have squeamishly avoided before—wasn't I already trying to find the best way to do away with myself? I got the nail scissors from the cupboard to cut out a piece on a poisoning death, then sat down in front of the stack of old newspapers to scan through them as well.

By the end of the day, I had a small sheaf of clippings about suicides and suicide attempts. Most people used a handful of popular methods, each one strongly linked with a particular circumstance. Students who failed their exams made a statement by hanging themselves. Burning seemed to be the method of choice for brides harassed by their mothers-in-law, though swallowing Tik-20 was a popular alternative. Financial problems were solved by throwing oneself under cars or trains, while both jumping from heights and drowning generally indicated an unsuccessful love affair.

None of these methods seemed appropriate for me—not so much because of the mechanics of the death itself, but due to the danger of being branded by the associated motive. Although I felt bad for the people in the accounts I had clipped, their reasons were a lot more transparent than mine, their problems more mundane. It would not be a simple case of hurt or disappointment or despondency in my case—I planned to relinquish my life simply because it was something I'd outlived. I wanted this to be understood after I left, for people to realize the integrity of my reasons, their visionary aspect.

For a while, I wondered if I could simply will myself to die. Go to bed one night under a directive to pass away in my sleep. But my brain never obeyed. No matter how strong my resolve, no matter how forceful my command, I always woke up again.

I pondered other methods, ones not as heavily subscribed. Taking sleeping pills seemed very peaceful, but I didn't know how many I would need and where to find a chemist who would oblige. A bullet through the head was instantaneous, but guns in Bombay were even harder to procure than sleeping pills. I had heard of more exotic techniques, like standing with one's feet in water and electrocuting oneself, but I was unfamiliar with the exact modus operandi.

It was an old black-and-white Hollywood movie I had watched once on TV that came to my aid. I remembered a scene of the heroine (who had it been? not Garbo, not Bette Davis . . .) stepping into the bathtub and slitting her wrists. She had lain back and closed her eyes, the water had turned dark and turbid, there seemed nothing to it. True, I didn't own a bathtub—perhaps I could use a pail to improvise. The fact that almost nobody else in Bombay had a tub either ensured that this method would indeed be unique.

In the bathroom stood the same plastic pails between which you had enjoyed being sealed in your childhood bucket games. The yellow one had lost its handle and the red one had a cracked rim. It seemed terribly improper to use them now for the purpose I had in mind, so I went to Grant Road and bought a shiny new pail. Blue, I guessed, would be the most appropriate color for suicide, but they only had the size I wanted in green.

I decided to do it in a week and a half. Then, recalling Sandhya's exhortation to hurry, I moved it to the coming Sunday instead. I told the newspaperwalla to suspend delivery after the weekend, and stopped the ganga from coming for a few days as well. I went to Nana Chowk to pay my phone bill and made out instructions for you on how to cash the signed checks I left.

It was already Thursday, so I began composing my farewells. I wrote a long letter to Sharmila, in which I explained the fine points of my decision and asked her to treat you as her own son after I was gone. I glued shut the envelope, then unsealed it to use the good parts in the letter for Zaida as well. I tried to put down something comforting for Biji, but gave up after several wrenching attempts. There was a short note for Hema, and something for Roopa that I wrote but tore up, listing all the ways in which I had been wronged at her hands.

To be a parent is to be guilty. For you, I started with this line from Paji's farewell.

I AWOKE AT 7 A.M. on Sunday. I had debated whether to try and do something special with Zaida the night before, or make one of my rare calls to your hostel. But I decided not to, in keeping with Sandhya's advice about slipping quietly away. I tried to take interest in the headlines about Indira's rally at Chowpatty the evening before, about the HRM demonstration against her which had been broken up with lathis and tear gas. But I felt too detached to read. It occurred to me that I should have had the paper stopped on Saturday itself.

As I ate my omelet with toast, I realized that this would be my last egg. The thought did not distress me. Food, I realized, had never played so important a part in my life—unlike with my father, for instance, who had always considered himself a gourmet. Dev had been very interested in cuisine as well—how curious to find an interest shared by him and Paji.

I soaped my pubic area thoroughly while bathing—I didn't want there to be any odor if the morgue people examined me. I trimmed the nails both on my fingers and toes, and plucked some stray hairs on my chin. I thought about dressing in a sari, but decided it was too formal, settling on my blue salwar kameez instead. On an impulse, I put on a full set of jewelry as well—the diamond earrings and necklace and gold bangles Mataji had given me just before we'd come to Bombay. Then I took all the pieces off and laid them aside—I didn't want my blood to smudge them.

I had imagined I would perform the act in the drawing room, but the oversized bucket I had bought proved to be too heavy to move when full. So I spread a towel on the floor of the bathroom and set the kitchen stool on top. I unlocked the front door—I had told Zaida I would need some help emptying my cupboards, that she should come in without knocking, around noon. I felt guilty about choosing her to be the one to discover me, but I hadn't been able to think of anyone else. Before returning to the bathroom, I fanned out all the farewells I had written on the floor, with the one addressed to her on top.

I sat down on the stool and stared into the bucket. Tiny ripples lapped at the sides. In the center, I could see my wavering reflection, and behind my head, the bulb in the ceiling fixture. I was surprised at how calm I felt, as if my mind had been drained clean of emotion. I had entered this state at least a day ago, going through all the preparations for my death with single-minded automation. Perhaps all suicides felt this detachment, one spontaneously initiated by the brain to complete the task. It would not be wise to tarry—there could be a hidden reservoir of misgivings somewhere, waiting to be breached. I bared my wrist over the bucket and picked up the kitchen knife.

How exactly had it been done in the movie? Did one hold the wrist underwater, as if trimming the stems of a bouquet of flowers? And what about the blood—should I empty out the bucket halfway to make room for the liquid to come? I didn't quite understand the purpose of the water anyway. Did it serve only an aesthetic function—the clouds of blood billowing into it like in the film? Or was it something necessary— the body sucking it in through the cuts to replace the fluid lost from the veins?

The knife turned out to be a bigger stumbling block. I had sliced meat and skinned fish with this blade—it seemed profane now to perform such a momentous task with it. The paring knife was just as defiled, and the other implements rattling around in the counter drawer were much too blunt. I could, of course, use a razor blade—didn't they recommend that for wrists, in any case? I got up to retrieve the box of Dev's shaving things, the one that you had squirreled away. Only a single blade remained in the box, the one in the razor itself. I realized I couldn't use it either—this was the same blade with which, all those Divalis ago, Arya had shaved.

Then I remembered you had taken the extra blades and put them with your electronics kit, to splice wires with. The kit was now with you in Sanawar, but in your cupboard, I found the packet of the remaining unused blades. I slid the top one out. *Wilkinson* the name read in silver against the black paper wrapping, with the logo of two crossed swords underneath.

About to put back the things I had taken out of the cupboard, I saw the handkerchiefs lying in a neat stack at the rear of the shelf. I had never managed to get them to you. Folded right next to them were more of your clothes—two T-shirts you had left behind, the blue trousers you didn't like, a pajama top that had never fit. I was tempted to put them to my face and take a deep inhalation to see if I could detect your scent. But I restrained myself—I had a bucket waiting for me, a task to fulfill.

I closed the doors of the cupboard, but it was too late. I felt suddenly overcome by a deep sense of misgiving—not about what I was doing, but *where* I was doing it. Killing myself in the home where you grew up, in the same flat that Paji had just willed to you. How would you ever be able to spend a night here again? Would you ever overcome the image of me lying dead on the floor, would buckets of blood spatter the bathroom walls in your nightmares?

I started feeling very claustrophobic. I couldn't do it, at least not here—what I needed at this instant was fresh air. Putting the blade back in the cupboard and leaving the bucket unbloodied in the bathroom, I went down the stairs.

As always, my wanderings took me to Chowpatty. It was early, so there were no crowds yet, even though it was a weekend. The fruit and kulfi stalls were all shuttered, the chaat stands neatly bundled in canvas and rope. I walked across the beach between the cages protecting the tender new tree saplings planted in the sand.

An aerial platform made of planks and bamboo poles was being dismantled at the end near Wilson College. Indira Gandhi must have spoken here the previous evening—a giant wooden cutout of her image from the shoulders up rose from the stage. I noticed that she had resized since the Emergency, when she would appear in versions two and three times as large. But she hadn't aged in the painting—she still had the same spirited smile, the same youthful determination in her eyes. Above her forehead was the trademark shock of white, running like a lightning bolt through her hair.

I walked closer to the stage, expecting to be stopped, but nobody took any notice of me. The workers all clustered around Indira, busy attaching ropes to her periphery. I noticed they had already lowered some of the smaller images to the sand. Standing against the bamboo poles was a life-sized figure of Sanjay, the son she had been grooming to be her successor, the one who had perished a year ago in a daredevil aeroplane stunt. I remembered people heaving a sigh of relief at his death, whispering about how lucky the country had been to escape a rule under his tyranny. There had been years of rumors about how he had dominated his mother, how unnaturally intense was their relationship, how she was so mesmerized by him that she acceded, even before the Emergency, to the most reckless of his whims. I imagined the sight of his body, all mangled and lifeless when she got to the scene of the plane crash. What had gone through her mind during the desperate ambulance ride to the hospital—mustn't she have known he was already dead? They had televised the funeral procession as it had wound the next day through the blazing Delhi streets. She had sat in the open truck next to her son's sewn-up body, with only sunglasses to distance the nation from her grief.

How had she gone on? How had she managed to reassemble all the shards of her soul and continue with the prime ministership—the cycle of interviews and meaningless speeches, the touring of hospitals and factories that mattered even less than before? It wasn't as if her son had simply gone away like you—she had watched a burning pyre consume his body. I could imagine Paji holding up her example once more—an unachievable standard even in the management of adversity.

The workers began lowering their charge from the stage. Slowly Indira came down, like a goddess descending to earth—the white edge of her sari, the neck unadorned by jewelry, the green flecking her pupils to give her a visionary's gaze. A shudder rippled across her as her base came to rest on the ground—she tilted slightly against the poles behind. I gazed up at her—the top of my head only came up to her chin. She seemed less vulnerable now—she had transformed herself from bereaved mother into invincible leader on the journey down.

Now that Indira was earthborne, I wondered which leader would be the next to descend. Perhaps Nehru, swinging to and fro, his face nodding towards the water, his feet treading air. Or my old friend Gandhiji, twirling around to reveal the plywood on which he was painted, alighting on the sand before me as nimbly as a cat. But the workers were already lowering the cloth banners—there was nobody else hovering on the stage. *I will show you the way*, Indira seemed to say. *There's no reason to deal with anyone but me.* Her gaze was steady, both her chin and her nose pointing towards the sea.

What difference did it make if she had subsumed everyone else? What difference did it make, who came to power and who went? For an instant I imagined all the leaders of the past, together with the ones yet to come from the decades stretching ahead. They could replace Indira's image, any one of them, and I wouldn't care. History had ceased to count, as had the future—my bond with you was all that mattered in the minutes I had left.

I made my way over the sand, until it started turning damp between my toes. It was still too early for the hordes of children that would swarm along the shore in the evening. There was a group of pilgrims offering coconuts to the sea towards the Walkeshwar side, but otherwise the beach was almost deserted.

I didn't wait for the waves to advance to lure me in, for an invitation to come from the goddess of the sea. The reason I was here was clear—to worry about what drowning signified (had it been unrequited love? financial ruin?) seemed silly. I took off my chappals and arranged them carefully on the dry part of the beach. Perhaps they would be discovered by some destitute who could use them after me.

For a while, all I felt was the packing of the wet sand under my feet. Then the first wave encircled my ankles. The water felt warmer on my skin than I had expected. A small dollop of foam churned up and clung to my kameez.

The wave withdrew and I was back to leaving my prints on the sand. Another one came in, all the way to my shins. I felt this one give a friendly tug as it went out, trying to encourage me in. I refused to be rushed, however, and stood where I was, staring at the horizon.

To be a parent is to be guilty. They're Paji's words, the last ones he wrote to me. I could see the note I had left for you, my thoughts inscribed in blue on the plain lined paper torn from a notebook. The page carefully folded, the envelope smoothed out and sealed, and as I addressed it to you, the realization that this might be the last time I inked the letters in your name.

I've always tried to focus on your happiness, Ashvin, and been grateful for the drops that fell my way. I'm sure I could have done even better—forgive me for the times I might have strayed. Would Zaida keep the letter to deliver to you in person? Would she sit you down on the dining room table and leave you to read it in private? How would you react, to the memories of your mother as they came flooding in?

You can't imagine what I went through before you were conceived. How much my life changed once you came. How fully I treasured every minute I spent with you, what fulfillment I achieved through loving you. I will always be in your debt for all the years of joy you bestowed on me.

A volley of waves came in to pull at me again. They were polite, genteel, oblique in the invitation they made, rising no higher than my knees.

They left behind sand in the folds of my salwar, and rolled smooth, sea-worn pebbles playfully over my feet.

I turned around to look back. Indira was less imposing now, but her gaze still seemed to follow me. Behind her, the city rose like a divine entity, its buildings a panoply of heads trained in my direction. They regarded me steadily, as if pondering my chosen fate, trying to decide whether to intervene.

To be a parent is to be guilty. The part Paji missed is that to be a child is to be also plagued by guilt. Forgive yourself as well, Ashvin, for anything you think you did. Remember my only wish is for you to be happy—think of it as my last testament and will.

I waded in deeper, until the water was up to my waist. The waves were still respectful, there were no swells surging in, but I felt their pressure on the middle of my body now, each time they swept out or rolled in. I could imagine them trolling me along, playfully at first, and then with brisk dispassion, once their grip was secure.

I don't think I'll ever be able to fully explain why this is the best way to end things. I've tried, I've redrafted this letter so many times, but you're too young as yet to understand. How should I convey the feeling in my heart of having outlived my usefulness? The notion that I've overshot the goals staked out for my life?

I gazed behind me once more. Now, I could no longer make out Indira's expression—she suddenly looked further away than she really could be. The buildings behind her seemed to have lost interest in me as well, their sternness fading, their faces becoming hazy. It was as if the city had decided I was no longer its responsibility, that I had crossed over into the domain of the sea.

I want you never to forget that whatever happened was only my fault. I want you to prove to me that I didn't cause you harm, didn't ruin things after all. I know you'll be brilliant in your studies, that you'll rise really high in whatever you decide to do. I want you to have a happy marriage, to find someone who loves you and you love in return. Promise me this, Ashvin, and you will have given me your blessing to leave peacefully.

Only the sea was relevant now. Soon, it would rise even higher in its embrace. The land would fall away, until my feet would not be able to touch the bottom when I tried. Not that I would have any reason to try—I would have outgrown that need. There would only be the white-capped crests gliding serenely around me. The bay would stretch as far as I could see with no boats anywhere in sight. I would pick a point on the horizon and allow myself to be carried towards it.

I stood there, waiting for the wave that would lift me off the sand. Trying to stop the thoughts of you that kept washing over me.

chapter
thirty-seven

I WASN'T ABLE TO DO IT. I WASN'T ABLE TO SURRENDER MYSELF TO THE SEA goddess. Rather than being soothed by the vastness of the bay before me, with each wave, the doubts in my mind only multiplied. How would you react to my death? What trauma would it inflict? Would you judge me to be selfish? Self-obsessed? Unfeeling?

When the sea finally swelled up to bear me away, it was not the relinquishing experience I had imagined. What swept over me as my feet lost contact with the ground was panic. I gasped as the water abruptly seemed to turn icy, and thrashed to stay afloat. I fought against the foam, trying to claw my way to safety. The sight of my dupatta swirling out of reach further impelled me. Sandhya appeared at my side, trying to calm me down like a mother whispering into the ear of a child enduring a filling. "It will only take a few minutes, you'll be content for all eternity." But I was too crazed to listen to her, too occupied battling the sea.

I did manage to drag myself out. For a long time, I just lay on the sand, letting the water drip from my body. Two boys passing by tried to ignore me. A man in jogging shorts ran by so close that I felt the spray of sand on my face. The sea before me settled right down, like some calculating animal presence trying to appear unthreatening.

By the time I passed the stage again, all the portraits had been carted off—there was no sign of Indira or Sanjay. Nearby, the sand sculptor was packing a mound for a fresh deity, on the site of the one obliterated by the crowds the previous evening. I walked home since I was still too wet to sit in a cab—in any case, I had not brought along any money. The door to the flat was ajar—Zaida paced inside. She had read my letter to her and was awaiting me anxiously, furiously.

I HAD NEVER SEEN Zaida so enraged. She seemed to be using all her self-control not to slap me. She had managed to drag the bucket I had left in the bathroom to the living room—in her hand was the kitchen knife. "Is this why I've been your friend?" she shouted, kicking the bucket hard enough to overturn it, its contents surging across the floor. "And this? Are you mad? Are you crazy?" She brandished the knife in front of my face, as if to teach me a lesson, she was going to disfigure me.

She did, in fact, manage to leave her mark on me that afternoon, though the change didn't take root overnight. It was several days before I could look past the glare of her audacity to discern any sense in her words. "Think about this, Meera," she said, after she'd put down the knife, after she'd helped me mop up the floor, after we'd hugged and cried and had tea. "For the first time in your life, you're truly free."

She was particularly harsh on Paji. "What has that man given you, except birth? Why should you be so respectful to his memory? He scribbles some words to you in his will to try and free himself from blame, and you're clinging onto them as if they're proof he cared? Let him go, Meera, it's not so important to be loved by him. He's dead now, and there's no reason to feel guilt."

Encouraged by my silence, she continued. "And Ashvin, too. Forgive me for saying this, but perhaps you shouldn't be mourning his departure so much, either. The way you've brought him up alone, the way you've built your life around him, the way you've dissolved your existence in his—where has Meera's spirit been hiding in all of this? Why not try to view his leaving as an opportunity, not a denial, tell yourself to be exhilarated, not depressed? Isn't it time, finally, to go out into the world and fulfill yourself?"

Her transparency almost made me laugh out aloud. "I know you want to make me feel better, but do you know how absurd it sounds to claim that being left alone is a desirable thing? That's not why I went to the water in any case. It's because I'm so fulfilled, so complete—there's nothing left that I need."

But Zaida shook her head. "Just mull it over awhile, think what I might be trying to say. I've known you since Ashvin was born, I've seen you together every day. It's true you're his mother, just like I'm my husband's wife, but there must be something beyond that. If I were free, had some money and a college degree, I'd be out there trying to find the answer, rather than sitting around for Anwar to return from his visits to Sewri. Don't you understand, Meera? You've just received that chance. You could work, you could travel, you could do anything you wanted for yourself. Once you accept that Ashvin's gone, then you have nobody on whom to keep falling back. Everything doesn't have to be the tragedy you like to make it out to be."

"I'm not making anything into a tragedy. If you had a son, you'd know how it feels."

"If I had a son, I'd be happy he was striking out, that he was so independent. Forgive me again, Meera, but sometimes you get too absorbed in yourself. You focus too much on one thing and forget all the other opportunities you have. It's too easy, when you're so close to someone, to get confused about what you each need."

"Is that really what you think of me? How nice of you to explain. Perhaps now you should just leave."

Such patronizing airs, such nerve, such complete lack of empathy for my loss, I fumed—not what could be expected from a friend! All week, I kept Zaida at arm's length. Let her dispense her advice to herself, if she felt the need to pontificate rather than trying to understand what I was going through. I headed her off at the door each time she came up to check on me. "You needn't keep worrying. I would've succeeded by now if I still intended to kill myself."

And then one morning, I woke up feeling more charitable towards her. Even though her words had rankled, hadn't she spoken them with my best interests in mind? Certainly, concentrating all my anger at her had calmed the turmoil that led me to the sea. Zaida's mistake had been to believe she could wean me away from my absorption in you—didn't she see this was a part of me, as essential to my existence as breathing? The point she'd made was irrefutable—if I intended to continue living, I had to find some other focus for myself. That Sunday afternoon, I took some oranges down to her flat. She opened the door even before I rang the bell. "I was going to give you one more hour, Meera, then come and drag you down here myself."

Zaida must have been preparing for my visit all week. She launched into an animated discussion of what I should do with the rest of my life—I half expected her to pull out charts and diagrams. "What's crucial is that you make a career for yourself. Not like in the past, under pressure from your father, or just to fill the gaps around the time you spent with Ashvin. This time, you'd be working because you enjoyed the actual work itself."

She started presenting occupations one by one for my consideration. "What do you think of social work?" she asked, and I saw from her expression how much she might enjoy doing that herself. "Journalism might be a good option—all the translations you've done—couldn't you claim them as qualifying experience?" She listed the pros and cons of opening a small store ("I could come each day and help") and even dredged up the stints I'd put in at the museum and the law firm. With each profession I rejected, Zaida grew more determined to find something I'd accept—I realized she might not let me go without extracting some sort of commitment. Surprisingly, it was teaching which she managed to sell to me. "Not the tots who nearly drove you to madness before, but students from the higher standards, who'd be more mature. You'll need a B.Ed., for which you'll have to study, of course. But it'll be completely different this time—you'll be going to college under your own choice, not your paji's."

She pestered me all week. "They say we'll need thirty thousand more women teachers each year to keep up with our growth—didn't you see Indira Gandhi last night on TV?" On Friday, when I still hadn't followed through, she dragged me personally to Bombay University to get the admission form. "My friend's heeding the prime minister's call," she announced to people in line, "becoming a teacher for the future of the country." Even the clerk was moved to set aside the rudeness expected of him and smile. "One day soon, she'll be teaching your own children in her class, I promise you" Zaida said.

We stood outside afterwards, the form folded into a zippered compartment of Zaida's purse, and watched the boys playing cricket on the Oval Maidan. I couldn't tell from their uniforms to which school they belonged—perhaps one of the more expensive ones like Cathedral or Campion. They looked the same age as you, in the eleventh standard or the tenth. Could these be the classes for which I should aim myself?

There was a loud crack as one of the boys hit the ball with his bat— sending it soaring towards the palm trees at the edge of the maidan. I watched him run across the pitch towards the opposite wicket, as his partner made the same dash in reverse. His skin was dark, his legs not particularly muscular—other than the leanness of his frame, he didn't resemble you very much. Even so, I could see in him the same energy, the same confidence, that I had detected in the identity card photo you sent. It suddenly felt fantastic that I might have anything to teach someone so grown and self-assured. What great storehouse of learning would I tap, what reservoir of wisdom would I draw from? I worried again about what I was getting myself into, if my attempts to humor Zaida along had gone too far.

A fielder blew the bails off the stumps in a direct hit, but the boy had already made it back in time for a double run. It occurred to me that if I did end up teaching students this old, then year after year, they would be the same age as you when you left. Would it be clever—this curious way of preserving your image, or would it be too unhealthy a link to the past?

I could, of course, aim for an earlier class. Perhaps the fifth or the sixth, when you were so attached to me—why not preserve the memories I had of you from then? Or the seventh, when students had to switch from shorts to long pants and, paradoxically, you looked so much younger in your new full-length uniform. Maybe the fourth, the year of rainbows, when we shared all those lunches on the school terrace. Or even the first, when Dev and I would each grab an arm and carry you laughing up the school steps.

Suddenly all your classes sprang up simultaneously in my consciousness, clamoring to be chosen. I felt myself engulfed by the waves again, of nostalgia this time, pulling me once more into their ocean. I tried to resist, to fight being swept away, but a part of me wanted to surrender, to be willingly submerged. There was another thwack, and I looked back at the boy in his padded long pants, execute an effortless stroke through the air. The ball rose over the field and climbed into the sky, so high that it was captured in the sun's flare.

At home, Zaida took the form from her purse and smoothed it out on the table. "Here. I want you to fill it out before you change your mind." She held out a pen. "In fact, sign it first, right now, in front of me. I want to be a witness to see you seal your pledge."

I looked at the form. The print was uneven, with several questions about background and education, all crowded into a single page. The spaces left blank for the answers seemed insufficient for all the information asked. There was a rectangular outline in the right corner for a photograph—at the bottom, the box for the signature looked too small.

I remembered a time when the future was like the unmarked sky, open, edgeless, just as vast. How had it been reduced to the size of these ungenerous blanks, how had it shrunk so much?

Perhaps Zaida saw me waver. "Sign," she commanded, before I could bring up my doubts, before I could expound on any of my misgivings. She thrust her pen at me again, this time removing its plastic cap. I took it from her, careful not to touch the ink near the tip, leaking out to form a clot. It was just a form, I told myself, just to indulge Zaida, and yet I felt a gravity to the moment. Starting at the edge and being careful to control each flourish, I squeezed my name into the signature box.

Zaida burst into applause. She watched over me as I filled in the rest of the form. While I heated the rice for lunch afterwards, she launched into a proposal to send me on a tour of the country. "You'll have several months before your classes start, so why not take advantage of it? Jaipur, Simla, Calcutta, Kulu—all the places I've always wanted to visit."

I tried to follow the journey on which she was sending me, to behold the new future for me she envisaged. The exuberance to her cheeks, the optimism in her eyes—perhaps one day I would learn her secret.

I DREAMT OF LUSH VALLEYS cradled between snow-covered ranges. Waterfalls descended down the slopes in fine white streaks. The forests rising up the hillsides were mostly pine. Meadows of purple flowers spread out from their bases. Clouds moved across the sun, or perhaps it was mist. Shadow and light undulated over the landscape.

I wondered if I was on Zaida's sightseeing journey. Did the mountains mean I was near your school in Sanawar? The purpose of my travels had been to find myself. Surely seeing you wasn't supposed to be a part of the trip?

The light was shimmering in a curious way over the forests when I awoke. I saw the reflections of cars on my ceiling, heard the sounds of their horns from the street. On my lap was an open book. I had been studying when I fell asleep.

Perhaps what awoke me was the postman dropping in the afternoon mail. I found your letter nestling between a magazine's pages. I looked at my name, inscribed so neatly it could have been inked by Paji. Inside, you wrote about the chemistry test in which the teacher asked about boron, the one element you had skipped in your studies. "The potatoes were undercooked as usual last night, and they served cabbage for the third time in a week." The school barber cut off too much when you'd gone for a haircut on Thursday. "My roommate Rohil has started snoring."

Tucked in towards the end were a few lines, saying you were not coming home for Divali. "The holidays are only two weeks long, and I don't feel yet as if I've settled in. So I'm thinking of joining some boys on a trek in the Himachal hills. Sorry for the change in plans on such short notice. I hope you don't mind."

It took a few seconds for the words to sink in. Since you had left, almost four months had elapsed. I had been waiting for Divali to see you again, I had been counting on it. I wanted to surprise you in person with my plan to pursue a B.Ed. I stared at your letter. Had you felt any hesitation at setting down the sentences? Could you have imagined how disheartening they would be?

I felt tempted to go roam around the city to clear my mind. Instead, I folded your letter away into the drawer where I had been saving the rest. At the very bottom of the pile, I knew, lay an envelope that didn't belong—the one I had left for you when I had decided to kill myself. I had made Zaida vow that she would not disclose what I had attempted—to you, or to anyone else. *To be a parent is to be guilty.* Each time I had taken the sealed envelope out to tear it up, I had always put it back. Perhaps as a reminder of what I had felt. Perhaps because for once I had recorded these thoughts to you that keep streaming through my head.

I closed the drawer and turned the key in the lock. I picked up the textbook again, the one I was trying to digest. *Principles of Secondary Education* by Mishra and Singh. They had told me that admission to the B.Ed. class was by no means assured, that it would help to have read the book as background before the interview. Zaida would be by soon to check how far I had advanced—she had set up a grueling schedule for me of three chapters a week. Of course, I could have gone to the interview and pointed out that the book was published by none other than my father's Freedom Press. But I had no intention of invoking Paji's name—this time, it had to be my own merit that got me in.

The material was very challenging, and I was surprised at how far I had managed to progress. Now, however, I found it impossible to concentrate. I tried taking the book to the balcony, tried reading it in bed. I made myself some tea and sipped it while flipping through the pages. Finally, I gave up. I unlocked the drawer to read your letter again.

It wasn't so bad, I told myself—the winter holidays would be here soon after the Divali break. It would give me the time to study some more, let you bond with the new friends you had made. Wasn't this exactly the kind of independence Zaida had said I should encourage? The disengagement that would allow me to build my world again? Something flickered in the thought (a hint of anticipation, of resolve?) but escaped before I could capture it. I replaced the letter in its envelope and returned to Mishra and Singh.

But I still wasn't able to concentrate. My gaze kept returning to the envelope. My thoughts to the words within. I sat with the book open in my lap and allowed my mind to drift.

Snow-covered peaks emerge again from my dream. The pine trees are tall and majestic. A river winds slowly through a valley. The sun hides behind a cloud somewhere.

This time, I imagine you in the scene. You are hiking alone up a trail. I wonder about your friends. Perhaps you have left them behind somewhere.

You reach an outcrop that looks over a valley. A path leads down from the ridge. The sun suddenly bathes you in light. You raise your face as if to swallow its rays.

Then the clouds shift again. The sun begins to fade on your face. It lights the panorama spread out below now. You turn towards the gleaming valley that awaits.

ACKNOWLEDGMENTS

Although the stories and personal histories in this novel are entirely fictional, I would not have been able to bring them to life without the crucial firsthand knowledge of India before, during, and since the Partition, shared with me by members of my family. In particular, I am indebted to my parents, my uncles Krishan Lal and Ushab Lal Suri, my aunts Pushap Lall and Kusum Bhardwaj, as well as Virender uncle and especially Satinder Mody. A special thank-you to Gulshan uncle for his memories of the Delhi refugee camps and of the railway colony near Nizamuddin station. Another special thanks to Baby auntie, for her wealth of knowledge about Karva Chauth customs, and for the wonderful tidbit of people making clothes out of parachutes in Lahore.

While I consulted several different sources for historical material, a broader understanding of the prevailing atmosphere of the times came from reading through old newspapers. In this regard, the microfilm archives of the *Times of India* in Mumbai were particularly helpful. For the record, although several right-wing organizations may be found in the political landscape of India (both past and present), the HRM is a fictional group, which I have created here for narrative exigency.

The central myth of Parvati's creation of a son to keep her company in Shiva's absence is standard in Hindu mythology texts, as is the one of how Ganesh gets his elephant head. The Andhaka myth has somewhat different versions—the one used here, of Andhaka coveting his mother Parvati, comes from the *Mahabhagavata Purana*. Shiva's amorous pursuit of consorts other than Parvati (interpreted in a divine, not mortal, sense) is detailed in several of the Puranas (e.g., *Skanda* and *Matsya*), while Parvati's uneasiness about his engagement with Ganga (so subtly conveyed in the actual Elephanta Caves sculpture in Mumbai) is mentioned, for instance, in the *Skanda Purana*.

I have taken the liberty of making up the lyrics to "Light the Fire of Your Heart." However, the title is reminiscent of an actual song, "Diya Jalao," by the great singer and tragi-hero K. L. Saigal, and the reference to audiences greeting the climax with lit lamps is authentic. The glimpses of student life at Wilson College in the late 1950s come from Vispi Balaporia—I am grateful to her for generously sharing her memories.

I wish to thank the friends who have taken the time to read drafts of the manuscript and offer such valuable comments—in particular Nancy and Frank Pfenning, Karen Kumm, Rick Morris, and Deborah Tannen. A special thanks to my UK editor Alexandra Pringle for her passionate interest in this book, and to Shashi Tharoor for sharing his perceptions on the historical and political content. Rosemary Zurlo-Cuva's reading was thorough and painstaking, her suggestions instrumental in making the exposition more compelling. My editor Jill Bialosky brought enormous energy and a spirited new perspective to bear on the novel, honing the characters and broadening their appeal with her insightful efforts. My agent Nicole Aragi mothered this work all the way from inception, critiquing successive drafts with minute and loving attention. My partner Larry Cole kept me going, not only by acting as a sounding board for various incarnations of the book, but also by being such a constant source of vitality in my life.

I am enormously grateful for the support I have received from a PEN/Bingham fellowship and a Guggenheim fellowship, and from residencies at Yaddo, the Virginia Center for the Creative Arts, and the MacDowell Colony. I especially wish to thank the Ucross Foundation for two magical sojourns there—in August 2003, when I experienced a true breakthrough in the writing, and in August 2006, when I completed a definitive second draft.

Finally, I wish to thank the University of Maryland Baltimore County, for the unwavering encouragement, flexibility, and supportiveness extended to me through the years it took to write this novel.

B L O O M S B U R Y

Also available by Manil Suri

The Death of Vishnu

The international bestseller

Vishnu, the odd-job man in a Bombay apartment block, lies dying on the staircase landing. Around him the lives of the apartment dwellers unfold – the warring housewives on the first floor, the lovesick teenagers on the second, and the widower, alone and quietly grieving at the top of the building. In a fevered state Vishnu looks back on his love affair with the seductive Padmini and comedy becomes tragedy as his life draws to a close.

'A wonder of a book. Astonishing'
Amy Tan

'Manil Suri has been likened to Narayan, Coetzee, Naipaul, Chekhov and Flaubert. But Suri has developed a voice all his own … his eye for a story, his wit and astute observations of human folly indicate that, one day, he may himself be someone to be compared to'
Independent

'All the elements of great storytelling are here, the mystic transports of Ben Okri with the intimate charm of Arundhati Roy … enchanting'
Sunday Tribune

ISBN: 978 0 7475 9381 2 / Paperback / £7.99

Order your copy:

By phone: 01256 302 699
By email: direct@macmillan.co.uk
Delivery is usually 3–5 working days.
Free postage and packaging for orders over £15.
Online: www.bloomsbury.com/bookshop
Prices and availability subject to change without notice.

www.bloomsbury.com/manilsuri